BIRTH OF A MONSTER

My mother was lying dead in her bathtub. Her gashed arms were flopped over the sides, and the tub was full to the top with water and blood. A half-dozen phenobarbital bottles were strewn across the floor, floating in inch-deep red water.

I skipped down the hall and called Emergency, telling them in an appropriately choked-up voice my address and that I had a suicide to report. While I waited for the ambulance, I gulped down big handfuls of my mother's blood.

"ELLROY CAN'T WRITE A DULL LINE!"
Publishers Weekly

"THE FIRST ORIGINAL TO APPEAR
IN AMERICAN DETECTIVE FICTION SINCE
THE LATE ROSS MacDONALD"
California Magazine

KILLER ON THE ROAD

James Ellroy

Originally published as *Silent Terror*

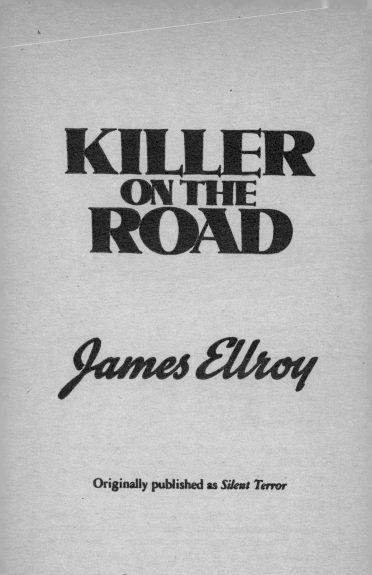AVON BOOKS · NEW YORK

Originally published as *Silent Terror*

AVON BOOKS
A division of
The Hearst Corporation
105 Madison Avenue
New York, New York 10016

Copyright © 1986 by James Ellroy
Published by arrangement with the author
Library of Congress Catalog Card Number: 86-90798
ISBN: 0-380-89934-5

First Avon Books Printing: October 1986

AVON TRADEMARK REG. U.S. PAT. OFF. AND IN OTHER COUNTRIES, MARCA REGISTRADA, HECHO EN U.S.A.

Printed in the U.S.A.

RA 10 9 8 7 6 5 4 3 2

TO
DUANE TUCKER

KILLER
ON THE
ROAD

FROM THE BIG APPLE TATTLER, *SEPTEMBER 13, 1983:*

"SEXECUTIONER" CAPTURED!!! WESTCHESTER BOARDING HOUSE RAID NETS BEHRENS/LIGGETT— DE NUNZIO/CAFFERTY KILLER!!!

At 3:00 A.M. this morning, the sleepy town of New Rochelle was the sight of life-and-death drama as federal agents and local police zeroed in on a tidy little boardinghouse on the edge of the downtown area.

Inside, in a tidy little third-floor room, slept Martin Michael Plunkett, age 35, the suspected sex slayer of two sets of Westchester County lovebirds—Madeleine Behrens, 23, and her boyfriend Richard Liggett, 24, and Dominic De Nunzio, 18, and his fiancée Rosemary Cafferty, 17. Dubbed the "Sexecutioner" by local authorities, Plunkett is suspected of several other similarly brutal killings— murders that span the entire United States and go back a decade.

But the tall, intense-looking killer wasn't in a killing mood when G-men, led by F.B.I. Serial Killer Task Force agent Thomas Dusenberry evacuated the boardinghouse and gave him a bull-horn ultimatum: "We have you surrounded, Plunkett! Surrender, or we'll come in and get you!"

The 800 block of South Lockwood was deathly still in the bull-horn's echo, then the "Sexecutioner's" voice rang out: "I'm unarmed. I want to talk to the head man before you take me in."

Amidst stunned protests from both the New Rochelle SWAT Team and his fellow F.B.I. men, Inspector Dusenberry walked into the killer's room; then, five minutes later, led Plunkett out, handcuffed. When asked what transpired during those five minutes, Dusenberry said, "The man and I talked. He wanted to make sure that when he confessed, his statement would be printed verbatim. He was quite clear about that. It seemed very important to him."

1

Both legal scholars and forensic psychologists continue to take a keen interest in the case of Martin Michael Plunkett, convicted in February on four counts of First Degree Murder in Westchester County, New York.

Sentenced to four consecutive life sentences and currently held in protective custody at Sing Sing Prison, Plunkett, 36, offered no defense at his trial. Acting as his own attorney, he submitted a notarized written statement to the judge and, before a packed courtroom, repeated that statement verbatim:

"On September 9, 1983, I murdered Madeleine Behrens and Richard Liggett. The knife I used to kill them is wrapped in a plastic bag and buried near the southwest corner of the lake in Huguenot Park, near the corner of North Avenue and Eastchester Road in New Rochelle, New York. On September 10, 1983, I murdered Dominic De Nunzio and Rosemary Cafferty. The saw I used to dismember them is wrapped in a plastic bag and buried at the base of a sycamore tree immediately in front of the public library in Bronxville, New York. This is my first, final and only statement regarding the crimes for which I stand accused, and for any others I may be suspected as having perpetrated."

Investigators found the murder weapons Plunkett described, with his fingerprints on them. Forensic technicians ran batteries of tests, and said that the knife's cutting edge matched perfectly to "SS" carvings on the legs of the four victims. Plunkett, who had maintained complete silence since his September 13 arrest, was convicted on the basis of the physical evidence and his statement.

That silence has created a furor among law-enforcement officials who are convinced that Plunkett's number of victims may run as high as fifty. Thomas Dusenberry, the F.B.I. agent who headed the investigation that led to Plunkett's arrest, said, "Based on psychological workups on the Behrens/Liggett and De Nunzio/Cafferty killings and on unsolved murders and disappearances that correspond in time sequence to our knowledge of Martin Plunkett's movements, I suspect him of at *least* thirty additional murders and non-sequitur disappearances. A confession, voluntary or drug-induced, would save law-enforcement agencies untold investigatory hours—many of the cases we 'make' Plunkett for are still open."

But Plunkett, whose school records indicate genius-level intelligence, will not even speak, much less confess, and, legally, he cannot be coerced into doing so. Thus, two disparate sources are petitioning New York State prison officials in an effort to gain access to his criminal memory: law enforcement agencies anxious to "clear" unsolved homicides within their jurisdictions, and forensic psychologists anxious to probe the mind of a brilliant serial murderer. All petitions have thus far been rejected by prison officials, and representatives of the American Civil Liberties Union have said they would legally intervene should mind-altering chemicals be forced on Plunkett in an effort to make him confess.

Perhaps the last word on the Plunkett case was spoken by Sing Sing Warden Richard Wardlow: "The legal and psychological ramifications of this deal are beyond me, but I can tell you one thing: Martin Plunkett will *never* see daylight again. As sympathetic as I am to the cops with open homicides on their hands, they should give it up and be grateful the _____ is in custody. You can't squeeze blood out of a stone."

FROM PUBLISHERS WEEKLY, JUNE 6, 1984: "SILENT KILLER TO 'SPEAK' IN CRIME AUTOBIOGRAPHY"

Literary agent Milton Alpert of M. Alpert & Associates has announced that he will be representing Martin Michael Plunkett, a convicted murderer known as the "Sexecutioner," in the sale of his autobiographical memoir, an account that Alpert says, "pulls no punches, and is destined to be regarded as a classic text on the criminal psyche."

Alpert, summoned to Sing Sing by a phone call from Plunkett, who had maintained absolute silence since reading a declaration of guilt at his trial in February, said that the 36-year-old killer "feels deep remorse over his actions, and wishes to expiate his guilt with the writing of this 'cautionary' memoir."

Since New York law prohibits criminals from reaping financial reward from published accounts of their crimes, all monies earned from Plunkett's "memoir" will go to the families of his victims. "Martin actually *wants* it that way," Alpert stressed.

Law Enforcement agencies throughout America have already expressed great interest in reading Plunkett's in-progress manuscript, purely from a "legal" standpoint—they think it may help them to shed light on unsolved homicides that Plunkett himself (suspected by several F.B.I. officials of being a long-term serial murderer) may have committed. As part of a "mutually beneficial reciprocal agreement," Alpert has agreed to pass along "salient information pertaining to unsolved killings" in exchange for "official police documents to help Martin carry the narration of his book."

The as yet untitled work will be auctioned upon its completion.

I

LOS ANGELES

1.

Dusenberry's estimated body count was low, and Warden Wardlow's stone metaphor only partly accurate. Inanimate objects *can* yield blood, but if the transfusion is to take, the letting must be sanctioned by the object's deepest and most logical volition. Even Milt Alpert, that eminently decent expediter of literature, had to cloak the announcement of our collaboration with justification-heavy sloganeering and words I never said. He cannot accept the fact that he will be earning 10 percent of a valediction in blood. That I feel no remorse and seek no absolution is incomprehensible to him.

A more farsighted person in my situation would seize this narrative opportunity and bend it toward the manipulation of the mental-health profession and liberal legal establishment—people susceptible to cheap visions of redemption. Since I have no expectations of ever leaving this prison, I will not do that—it is simply dishonest. Nor will I cop a psychological plea by juxtaposing my acts against the alleged absurdity of twentieth-century American life. By passing through conscious gauntlets of silence and will, by creating my own vacuum-packed reality, I was able to exist outside standard environmental influences to an exceptional degree—the prosaic pain of growing up and being American did not take hold; I transmogrified it into something *more* very early. Thus I stand by my deeds. They are indigenous solely to me.

Here in my cell, I have everything I need to bring my valediction to life: world-class typewriter, blank paper, police documents procured by my agent. Along the back wall there is a Rand-McNally map of America, and beside my bunk a box of plastic-topped pins. As this manuscript grows, I will use those pins to mark the places where I murdered people.

But above all, I have my mind; my silence. There is a dynamic to the marketing of horror: serve it up with a hyperbolic flourish that distances even as it terrifies, then turn on the literal or figurative lights, inducing gratitude for the cessation of a nightmare that was too awful to be true in the first place. I will not observe that dynamic. I will not let you pity me. Charles Manson, babbling in *his* cell, deserves pity; Ted Bundy, protesting his innocence in order to attract correspondence from lonely women, deserves contempt. I deserve awe for standing inviolate at the end of the journey I am about to describe, and since the force of my nightmare prohibits surcease, you will give it to me.

2.

Guidebooks misrepresent Los Angeles as a sun-kissed amalgam of beaches, palm trees and the movies. The literary establishment fatuously attempts to penetrate that exterior and serves up the L.A. basin as a melting pot of desperate kitsch, violent illusion and variegated religious lunacy. Both designations hold elements of truth based on convenience. It is easy to love the place at first glance and even easier to hate it when you get to sense the people who live there. But to *know* it, you have to come from the *neighborhoods*, the inner-city enclaves that the guidebooks never mention and artists dismiss in their haste to paint with broad, satiric strokes.

These places require resourcefulness; they will not give up their secrets to observers—only to inspired residents. I gave my youthful stomping ground such implacable attention that it reciprocated in full. There was nothing about that quiet area on the edge of Hollywood that I didn't know.

Beverly Boulevard on the south; Melrose Avenue on the north. Rossmore and Wilshire Country Club marking the west border, a demarcation line between money and only the dream of it. Western Avenue and its profusion of bars and liquor stores standing sentry at the east gate—keeping undesirable school districts, Mexicans and homosexuals at bay. Six blocks from north to south; seventeen from east to west. Small wood-frame and Spanish-style houses; tree-lined streets without stoplights. A courtyard apartment building rumored to be filled with prostitutes and illegal aliens; an elementary school; the debatable presence of a "fuck pad" where U.S.C. football players brought girls to watch '50's-vintage porno films. A small universe of secrets.

I lived with my father and mother in a salmon-colored miniature of the Santa Barbara Mission, two stories with a tar-paper roof and a mock mission bell. My father worked as a draftsman at an airplane plant and gambled cautiously—he usually won. My mother clerked at an insurance company and spent her leisure hours staring at traffic on Beverly Boulevard.

I realize now that both my parents had furious, and furiously separate, mental lives. They were together for the first seven years of my life, and early on I remember designating them as my custodians and nothing else. Their lack of affection, to me and to each other, registered inchoately as freedom—dimly I perceived their elliptical approach to parenthood as a neglect that I could capitalize on. They did not possess the passion to abuse me or to love me. I know today that they armed me with the equivalant of enough childhood brutality to fuel an army.

Early in 1953, the air-raid sirens stationed throughout the neighborhood went off accidentally, and my father, convinced that a Russian A-bomb attack was imminent, led my mother and me up to the roof to await the arrival of the Big One. He brought a fifth of bourbon with him, because he wanted to toast the mushroom cloud he expected to rise over downtown L.A., and when the Big One never appeared, he was drunk and disappointed. My mother made one of her rare verbal offerings, this one to allay her husband's depression over the world not being blown to hell. He raised his hand to hit her, then hesitated and slugged down the rest of the bottle. Mother went downstairs to her traffic-watching chair, and I started checking science books out of the library. I wanted to see what mushroom clouds looked like.

That night signaled the beginning of the end of my parents' marriage. The air-raid scare created a bomb-shelter boom in the neighborhood, and my father, disgusted by the backyard construction, took to spending his weekends on the roof, drinking and observing the spectacle. I watched him get angrier and angrier, and I wanted to ease his pain, make him less of a pent-up observer. Somehow I got the notion to give him the "Wham-O" stainless steel slingshot I had found on a bus bench at Oakwood and Western.

My father loved the gift, and took to shooting ball bearings at the above-ground sections of the shelters. Soon his aim became excellent, and seeking more challenging targets, he started assassinating the crows who perched on the telephone wires that ran along the alley in back of our house. Once he even caught a scurrying rat from forty-six feet and eight inches away. I recall the distance because my father, proud of the feat, paced it off in yards, then calibrated the remainder with a metal drafting rule.

Early in '54, I learned that my parents were going to get divorced. My father took me up to the roof to tell me. I had seen it coming, and knew from the "Paul Coates Confidential" T.V. program that many "Post war marriages" were headed for Splitsville.

"Why?" I asked.

My father toed the gravel on the roof; it looked like he was tracing A-bomb clouds. "Well...I'm thirty-four years old, and your mother and I don't get along; and if I give her much more time I'll have shot my good years; and if I do that I might as well pack it in. We can't let that happen, can we?"

"No."

"That's my Marty. I'll be moving to Michigan, but you and your mother will keep the house, and I'll be writing to you, and I'll be sending money."

I knew from the Coates show that divorce was an expensive proposition, and sensed that my father must have had a big stash of gambling money put away to facilitate his move to Splitsville. He seemed to pick up my thoughts and added, "You'll be well looked after, don't you worry about that."

"I won't worry."

"Good." My father took a finger sight on a fat bluejay sitting atop our next-door neighbor's garage. "You know your mother is, well...you know."

I wanted to scream "nutty," "crazy," "fruitcake" and "couch case," but didn't want him to know I knew. "She's sensitive?" I ventured.

My father shook his head slowly; I knew *he* knew I knew. "Yeah, sensitive. Just try to take her with a grain of salt. Get a good education and try to be your own man, and you'll make yourself heard from."

On that prophetic note, my father stuck out his hand. We shook, and five minutes later he walked out the door. I never saw him again.

3.

All my mother required was that I maintain a reasonable degree of silence and not burden her with questions about what she was thinking. Implicit in that was her desire for me to remain moderate in school, at play and at home. If she considered the dictate to be punishment, she was wrong: I could go anywhere I wanted in my head.

Like the rest of the neighborhood kids, I went to Van Ness Avenue Elementary, obeyed, and laughed and hurt at silly things. But other children found their hurt/joy in outside stimuli, while I found mine reflected off a movie screen that *fed* from what surrounded me, edited for my own inside-the-brain viewing by a steel-sharp mental device that always knew exactly what I needed to keep from being bored.

The screenings ran this way:

Miss Conlan or Miss Gladstone would be standing by the blackboard, unctuously proclaiming. They would start to fade visually commensurate with my growing boredom, and involuntarily, my eyes would start to trawl for something to keep me mentally awake.

The taller children were seated at the back of the room, and from my far left-hand corner desk I had a perfect forward/diagonal viewing path, one that allowed me profile shots of all my classmates. With teacher sight/noise reduced to a minimum, the faces of the other children blurred together, forming new ones; snatches of whispered conversations came together until all manner of boy/girl hybrids were declaring their devotion to me.

13

Being loved in a vacuum was like a reverie; street noise sounded like music. But abrupt movement from within the room, or the clatter of books on the hallway outside would turn it all bad. Pieter, the tall blond boy who sat next to me grades three to six, would go from adoring confidant to monster, the noise level determining the grotesqueness of his features.

After long frightened moments, I would seize the front of the room, zero in on either the blackboard writing or the teacher's monologue, and if I thought I could get away with it, interject some sort of comment. This calmed me and elicited full-face looks from the other children, sparking a part of my brain that thrived on producing swift, cruel caricature. Soon pretty Judy Rosen had Claire Curtis's big buck teeth; booger-eating Bobby Greenfield was feeding snot balls to Roberta Roberts, dropping them over the cashmere sweaters she wore to school every day, regardless of the weather. I would laugh to myself, only occasionally out loud. And I kept wondering how far I could take it—if I could refine the device to the point where even bad noise couldn't hurt me.

As for hurt: only other children were then capable of making me feel vulnerable, and even as early as eight or nine that queasy sense of being captive to irrational needs for union was physical—a prescient jolt of the terror and despair that sexual pursuits result in. I fought the need by denial, by sticking to myself and affecting a truculent mien that brooked no nonsense from other kids. In a recent *People* magazine article, a half-dozen of my old neighborhood contemporaries offered comments on me as a child. "Weird," "strange" and "withdrawn" were the adjectives used most frequently. Kenny Rudd, who lived across the street from me, and who now designs computer basketball games, came closest to the truth: "The word was: Don't ___ with Marty, he's psycho. I don't know, but I think maybe he was more scared than anything else."

Bravo, Kenny, although I'm glad you and your cretinous comrades didn't know that simple fact when we were children. My strangeness revulsed you and gave you someone

to loathe from a safe distance—but had you sensed what
it was hiding, you would have exploited my fear and tortured me for it. Instead, you left me alone and eased my
discovery of my physical surroundings.

From 1955 to 1959, I charted my immediate topography,
coming away with an extraordinary collection of facts: the
red brick apartment house on Beachwood between Clinton
and Melrose had a pet burial ground in back; the strip of
recently constructed "bachelor hideaways" on Beverly and
Norton were built out of rotted lumber, cut-rate stucco mix
and "beaverboard"; the apocryphal "fuck pad" was in reality
a bungalow court on Raleigh Drive, where a U.S.C. prof
took college boys for homosexual liaisons. On trash-
collection days, Mr. Eklund up the street switched his gin
bottles with the sherry bottles from Mrs. Nulty's trash two
doors down. The reason for the switch eluded me, although
I knew they were having an affair. The Bergstroms, Sel-
tenrights and Monroes had a nude pool party at the Seltenright house on Ridgewood in July of '58, and it sparked
an affair between Laura Seltenright and Bill Bergstrom—
Laura rolling her eyes to heaven at her first glance of Bill's
outsize bratwurst.

And the projectionist at the Clinton Theatre sold "pep
pills" to members of the Hollywood High swim team; and
the "Phantom Homo" who had cruised the neighborhood
for young boys for over a decade was one Timothy J. Cos-
tigan of Saticoy Street in Van Nuys. The Burgerville stand
on Western served ground horse in its chili—I heard the
owner talking to the man who delivered it one night when
they thought no one was listening. I knew all these things—
and for a long time just knowing them was enough.

Years came and went. My mother and I continued. Her
silence went from stunning to mundane; mine from strained
to easy as my mental resourcefulness grew. Then, in my
last year of junior high, school officials finally noticed that
I spoke only when spoken to. This led them to force me to
see a child psychiatrist.

He impressed me as a condescending man with an un-
natural attraction to children. His office was filled with a

not-too-subtle arrangement of toys—stuffed animals and dolls interspersed with plastic machine guns and soldier sets. I knew immediately that I was smarter than he.

He pointed to the toys as I sat down on the couch. "I didn't realize what a big fella you are. Fourteen. Those playthings are for little kids, not big fellas like you."

"I'm tall, I'm not big."

"Same difference. I'm a short fella. Short fellas got different problems than tall fellas. Don't you agree?"

His questioning was easy to follow. If I said "yes," it would be an admission that *I* had problems; if I said "no," he would launch a spiel about everyone having problems, then share a few of his own in a cheap empathy ploy. "I don't know and I don't care," I said.

"Fellas who don't care about their own problems usually don't care about themselves. That's a heck of a way to be, don't you agree?"

I shrugged, and gave him one of the blank-eyed stares I used to keep other kids at bay, and soon he was fading to a pinpoint as my mind zeroed in on a teddy bear off to my right. Within a split second the bear was aiming a plastic bazooka at the shrink's head, and I started to giggle.

"Daydreaming, big fella? Want to tell me what's so funny?"

I did a perfect segue from my brain-movie to the doctor, smiling as I accomplished it. I could tell he was disconcerted. My eyes caught a stuffed Bugs Bunny toy, and I said, "What's up, Doc?"

"Martin, young people who are very quiet usually have lots of things on their minds. You've got a swell mind, and the grades in school to prove it. Don't you think it's time to tell me what's bothering you?"

Bugs Bunny started waggling his eyebrows and taking playful nips at the headshrinker's neck. "The price of carrots," I said.

"What?" The shrink took off his horn-rims and cleaned the lenses with his necktie.

"Have you ever seen a rabbit with glasses?"

"Martin, you're not following me, you're not being logical."

"Isn't good eye care logical?"

"You're talking in non-sequiturs."

"No, I'm not. A non-sequitur is a conclusion that doesn't follow its known inferences. Good eye care follows eating carrots."

"Martin, I—" The doctor was getting flushed and sweaty; Bugs Bunny was hurling carrots at his desk.

"Don't call me 'Martin,' call me 'Big Fella.' It sends me."

Straightening his glasses, the doctor said, "Let's change the subject. Tell me about your parents."

"They're carrot-juice addicts."

"I see. And what is that supposed to mean?"

"That they have good eyes."

"I see. Anything else?"

"Long ears and fluffy tails."

"I see. You think you're a funny man, don't you?"

"No, I think you are."

"You nasty little shit, I'll bet you don't have a friend in the world."

The room became four walls of hideous noise, and Bugs Bunny turned on me, forcing an awful kaleidoscope of half-buried memories to flash across my brain-screen: a tall blond boy telling a group of kids "Farty Marty asked me to watch traffic with him"; Pieter and his sister Katrin rebuffing my attempt to get them to sit next to me in sixth grade.

The shrink was staring at me, smirking because I had shown myself vulnerable; and Bugs Bunny, his secret pal, was laughing along, spraying me with orange pulp. I looked around for something stainless steel, like my father's slingshot. Seeing a brushed-steel curtain rod leaning against the back wall, I grabbed it and hacked off the stuffed rabbit's head. The shrink was looking at me with amazement. "I'll never talk to you again," I said. "And no one can make me."

4.

The incident at the shrink's office had no external repercussions—I was passed into high school without further psychiatric/scholastic abuse. The doctor knew an immovable object when he saw one.

But I felt like a malfunctioning machine; as if there were a stripped gear inside me, one that could roam my body at will, troubleshooting for ways to make me look small under stress. When I played brain-movies in class, substituting faces and bodies, boy to boy, girl to girl and cross-gender, it was like an obstacle course, sex images assailing me without rhyme or reason. The randomness, the indiscriminate power of what I was making myself see was staggering; the need that I sensed behind it felt like an oncoming tidal wave of self-loathing. I know now that I was going insane.

I was saved by a comic-book villain.

His name was the "Shroud Shifter," and he was a recurring bad guy in "Cougarman Comix." He was a super-criminal, a jewel-thief hit man who drove a souped-up amphibious car and snarled a retarded version of Nietzsche in oversize speech balloons. Cougarman, a moralistic wimp who drove a '59 Cadillac called the "Catmobile," always managed to throw Shroud Shifter in jail, but he always escaped a couple of issues later.

I loved him for his car and for a supernatural ability that he possessed—one that I sensed I could realistically emulate. The car was a gleaming angularity—all brushed steel, all mean business. It had headlights that flashed a

18

nuclear death ray that turned people to stone; instead of gas, the engine ran on human blood. The upholstery was made of tawny cat hides—the flesh of arch-enemy Cougarman's martyred family. It had a steel hangman's pole sticking out of the trunk. Every time Shroud Shifter claimed a victim, his vampire girl friend, Lucretia, a tall blonde with long fangs, would bite a notch in the wood.

Ridiculous trash? Admittedly. But the artwork was superb, and Shroud Shifter and Lucretia breathed a stylish, sensual evil. S.S. had a cylindrical bulge that extended almost down to the knee of his left pants leg; Lucretia's nipples were always erect. They were a high-tech god and goddess twenty years before high tech, and they were *mine*.

Shroud Shifter had the ability to disguise himself without changing costume. He got it from drinking radioactive blood and from concentrating on the person he wanted to rob or kill, so that he soaked up so much of that person's aura that he psychically resembled him and could ape his every move, anticipate his every thought.

S.S.'s ultimate goal was to achieve invisibility. That goal drove him, pushed him beyond his existing gift of *psychic* invisibility—being able to fit in anyplace, anywhere, anytime. Being *physically* invisible would give him a carte blanche ticket to take over the world.

Of course Shroud Shifter would never achieve that end—it would destroy his potential confrontations with Cougarman, and he was the comic book's hero. But S.S. was fiction, and I was flesh, blood and brushed-steel reality. I decided to make myself invisible.

My transits of silence and brain-movies had been a good training ground. I knew my mental resources were superb, and I had cut my human needs down to the bare minimum provided by my cipher mother: room, board and a few dollars a week for incidentals. But the quiet-outsider image I had carried as a shield for so long worked against me—I had no social graces, no sense of other people as anything but objects of derision, and if I was to successfully imitate Shroud Shifter's *psychic* invisibility, I would first have to learn to be ingratiating and conversant on the teenage topics that bored me: sports, dating, rock and roll. I would have to learn to *talk*.

And that terrified me.

I spent long hours in class, my brain-movies quashed as my ears trawled for information; in the boy's locker room I listened to lengthy, and lengthily embellished, conversations on penis size. Once I climbed a tree outside the girls' gym and listened to the giggles that rose above the hiss of showers. I picked up a lot of information, but was afraid to *act*.

So, admittedly out of cowardice, I retreated. I convinced myself that, although Shroud Shifter could get away without disguises, I couldn't. That limited the problem to the procuring of suitable body armor.

In 1965 there were three sartorial styles favored by middle-class L.A. teenagers: surfer, greaser and collegiate. The surfers, whether they actually surfed or not, wore white Levi cords, Jack Purcell "Smiley" tennis shoes and Pendelton's; the greasers, both gang members and pseudo "rebel" types, wore slit-bottomed khakis, Sir Guy shirts and honor farm watch caps. The collegiates favored the button-down/sweater/penny-loafer style that is still "in." I figured that three outfits in each style would be sufficient protective coloration.

Then a fresh wave of fear hit me. I had no money for purchasing the clothes. My mother never left any cash lying around and was stingy to an extreme fault, and I was still too afraid to do what my heart most desired: break, enter and steal. Disgusted by my cautiousness, but still determined to put together a wardrobe, I seized on my mother's three walk-in closets full of girlhood clothes she never wore.

In retrospect, I know that the scheme I concocted was undertaken out of desperate fear—a delaying tactic to put off my inevitable crash course in social dealings; but at the time it seemed the epitome of good sense. One day I ditched school and took an assortment of sharp kitchen knives into my mother's bedroom closet. I was hacking a cape out of one of her old tweed overcoats when she came home from work early, caught me and started screaming.

I put up my hands in a placating gesture, still holding a serrated-edge steak knife. My mother screamed so loud that it seemed that her vocal cords would snap, then she managed to get out the word "animal" and pointed to my midsection. I saw that I had an erection, and dropped the knife; my mother slapped at me with clumsy open hands until the sight of blood trickling from my nose forced her to stop and run downstairs. In the course of ten seconds the woman who bore me went from cipher to arch-enemy. It felt like a homecoming.

Three days later, she gave me my formal reprimand: six months of silence. I smiled as my sentence was passed; it was a reprieve from my awful fears regarding the invisibility mission, and the opportunity to screen unlimited brain-movies.

Although my mother only intended for me to remain silent at home, I took her edict literally and took my silence everywhere I went. At school I would not speak, *even* when spoken to—I wrote out notes when teachers needed answers from me. This created a stir, and much speculation on my motives, the most common interpretation being that somehow I was protesting the war in Vietnam or expressing my solidarity with the Civil Rights movement. Since I was getting excellent grades on exams and written reports, my lack of speech was tolerated, although I was subjected to a battery of psychological tests. I rigged each test to show a completely different personality, flabbergasting school officials, who, after many failed attempts to get my mother to intervene, decided to let me graduate in June.

So now my classroom brain-movies were accompanied by the outright stares of my classmates, a number of whom thought I was "cool," "trippy" and "avant-garde." Breaking through seemingly impenetrable objects was the main theme, and the awed looks I was getting made me feel I could do *anything*.

Along with that feeling grew a bitter hatred for my mother. I took to prowling through her belongings, looking for ways to hurt her. One day I got an impulse to check out her medicine cabinet, and I found several prescription bot-

tles of Phenobarbital. A light snapped on in my head, and
I tore through the rest of her bedroom and bathroom. Underneath the bed, in a cardboard box, I got the confirmation
I was seeking: empty prescription bottles of the sedative,
scores of them, the dates on the labels going back to 1951.
Inside the bottles were stuffed small pieces of paper covered
with a tiny, indecipherable pencil scrawl.

Since I could not read my zombie-mother's words, I had
to make her speak them out loud. The following day, at
school, I passed a note to Eddie Sheflo, a surfer who was
rumored to "think Marty's act was bitchen'." The note read:

"Eddie—

Can you cop me a dollar roll of #4 Bennies?"

The big blond surfer refused the dollar bill I was holding
out and said, "You got it, strong silent type."

That afternoon, I substituted Benzedrine for Phenobarbital, and replaced the light bulb over my mother's medicine
cabinet with a dud. Both types of pills were small and white,
and I hoped the dim light would add to the confusion.

I sat downstairs to await the result of my experiment.
My mother came home from work at her usual time of 5:40,
nodded hello, then ate her usual chicken-salad sandwich
and went upstairs. I waited in my father's favorite left-
behind chair, absently perusing a stack of "Cougarman Comix."

At 9:10, there was a thumping on the stairs, and then
my mother was standing in front of me, sweaty, bug-eyed
and trembling in her slip. I said, "Hitting the carrot juice,
Mom?" and she grabbed at her heart, hyperventilating. I
said, "Funny, it never affects Bugs Bunny this way," and
she started jabbering about sin and this awful boy she slept
with on her birthday in 1939, and how she hated my father
because he drank and was a quarter Jewish, and how we
have to turn the lights off at night or the Communists will
know what we're thinking. I smiled, said, "Take two aspirin
with a carrot-juice chaser," and about-faced out of the house.

I prowled the neighborhood all night; then, at dawn,
returned home. When I flicked on the living-room light, I

saw red liquid dripping from a crack in the ceiling. I went upstairs to investigate.

My mother was lying dead in her bathtub. Her gashed arms were flopped over the sides, and the tub was full to the top with water and blood. A half-dozen empty Pheno-barbital bottles were strewn across the floor, floating in inch-deep red water.

I skipped down the hall and called Emergency, telling them in an appropriately choked-up voice my address and that I had a suicide to report. While I waited for the ambulance, I gulped down big handfuls of my mother's blood.

5.

The Rosicrucians got the house, the car and all my mother's money; I got a custodianship hearing. Since I was within six months of high-school graduation and my eighteenth birthday, a formal foster home was deemed a waste of time, and my twelfth-grade guidance counselor told the juvenile authorities that I was "too inward and disturbed" to be cut loose as an "emancipated minor." My refusal to attend the funeral or contact my father in Michigan convinced him that I "needed discipline and guidance—preferably a male figure." So the Juvenile Housing Board sent me to live with Walt Borchard.

Walt Borchard was an L.A. cop, a big, fat, good-natured man in his early fifties. He had spent most of his twenty-three years with the L.A.P.D. on the elementary-school lecture circuit, delivering cautionary tales on dope, perverts and the evils of the criminal life, showing little kids his .38, chucking them under the chin and admonishing them to be "straight shooters." He was a widower with no children, and he lived in the largest apartment in a twelve-unit building that he owned. A one-room "bachelor" was always kept available for the homeless juveniles the housing board referred to him, and that twelve-by-eighteen crawl space a block from Hollywood Boulevard became my new home.

The previous tenant had been a hippie, and he left behind a deep-pile chartreuse rug, Beatles posters on the walls and a closetful of bell-bottoms, fringed vests and Day-Glo tennis shoes. "Acid head," said "Uncle" Walt when I moved in.

"Got the notion he could fly. Flapped his arms and jumped off the Taft Building, and you know what? He was wrong. Went out stoned, though. Coroner said he was on a snootful of shit. You ain't got any crazy notions, have you?"

"I have vampire tendencies," I said.

Uncle Walt laughed. "So do I. Matter of fact, last night I bit the girl downstairs in number four. Listen, Marty, just lay off the dope and be nice to the other tenants, go to school and keep your pad clean and we'll get along great. The board's paying me to have you here, and I ain't looking to get rich, so I'll kick back thirty scoots a week for you to mess around with, and I'll keep you in groceries. You gotta observe curfew until your birthday, though, off the streets by eleven. Lots of nice necks to bite on the Boulevard, but wrap your biting up by 10:59. And if you need anything, you know where I am. I love to talk, and I ain't bad at listening."

The arrangement jelled. I now had a new neighborhood to learn, my very own safe harbor to return to and a new, glamorous aura at school: I was the guy who never shed a tear when he found his mother dead, the guy with his own "crib," the guy who bent the administration to his will with his extended silence and who now teased people with occasional one-liners like: "Blood reigns, come stains," and "Shroud Shifter will prevail." I felt like I was coming of age.

My life consisted of school and brain-movies, nighttime walks along the side streets bordering Hollywood Boulevard and captive hours spent listening to Uncle Walt Borchard's homespun philosophy. His one-liners were less terse than mine, and he was considering publishing them in book form when he retired from the L.A.P.D. Among his most-repeated nuggets of wisdom were:

"God bless the queers—more women for the rest of us";

"I wouldn't want the niggers moving into the neighborhood, but I'll be damned if I'll do anything to keep 'em out; and if they *do* move in, I'll be the first one to welcome 'em with a bucket of ribs and a big bottle of T-bird";

"We've got no business being in Vietnam unless we're

willing to *win*—and *that* means dropping the hydrogen bomb";

"If God didn't want man to eat pussy, then why'd he make it look like a taco?"

And on and on. He was lonely and filled with guileless goodwill. His lack of mental resourcefulness and need for a constant audience disgusted me, and I dreaded his knocks on my door. But I kept still. Above all else, I knew the value of silence.

The new neighborhood was distressing because of its *lack* of silence. There was the constant nighttime roar of cars headed for the Boulevard, and heavy foot traffic, shoppers returning from the all-night markets on Sunset, and furtive hippies making dope buys in side-street shadows. Even the visual quality was noisy. The neon haze that blanketed the sky seemed to crackle and hiss with intimations of the sleaze it was heralding.

After five months in Hollywood, I gave up on neighborhood prowls and spent all my nights in my room, screening brain-movies. Sometimes Walt Borchard came over and insisted on talking; I tuned him right out and continued the show. More and more, the scenario revolved around the triad of Shroud Shifter, Lucretia and me, plundering in our brushed-steel car, seeking invisibility. The scenes became almost multidimensional—the *feel* of myself pressed between the super-criminals, the *scent* of motor oil and blood, the gurgling *sounds* our victims made when we attacked their jugulars. As an internal cinematographer I had improved greatly over the years, and now my prowess had grown to incorporate all the latest technical developments. My brain was equipped with deluxe color, wide screen, stereophonic sound and Smell-o-Vision. Had I been able to charge tickets for admission, I would have become a millionaire.

In April of '66 I turned eighteen; in June, I graduated high school. I was now technically an adult, and could leave Walt Borchard's care. Having no money and no job, I pondered my options. Then Uncle Walt told me I could stay for a nominal rent payment, and he would even help me find a job. The pathetic motive behind the offer was obvious. No one had ever listened to him so attentively as I had, and he couldn't stand the thought of losing such an excellent audience. The symbiotic aspect of it all appealed to me, and I agreed to stay.

Borchard got me a job at the Hollywood Public Library, on Ivar just south of the Boulevard. My duties were to shelve books and walk into the Men's Room and clear my throat loudly every half-hour—a strategy aimed at disturbing homosexual assignations. The pay was a dollar sixty-five an hour, and the work was tailor-made for me—I screened brain-movies all day.

One evening in June I came home from the library and found Uncle Walt cleaning out the garage in back of the building. Late sunlight was glinting off a collection of brushed-steel implements that he was wrapping in an oil-cloth. The tools looked mean—like something Shroud Shifter would own. "What are they?" I asked.

Borchard held up an instrument that looked like a scalpel. "Burglar's tools. This baby's a lock pick and a gouger. You use the flat edge to slip the lock, and the sharp edge to whittle doorjambs. These other babies are a window snap, a push-drill and a chisel pry. Big daddy at the end is a suction-cup glass-cutter. What's the matter, Marty? You look jittery."

I took a deep breath and feigned indifference by shrugging. "Just a headache. Why do the handles have those deep brush marks? For a grip?"

Borchard hefted the chisel pry. "Partly, but mostly the ridges are there to prevent fingerprints. See, possession of burglar's tools is a felony, and if a burglar gets caught with them it's a bust; and if he gets caught with them inside a pad he's burglarizing, it's an extra charge. But these heavy brush marks won't sustain fingerprints. So if he's inside a pad and we nail him, he can stash the tools and say 'Those things ain't mine,' even though it's patently obvious they are. The ridges also make a good backscratcher."

I smiled while Uncle Walt poked at his back with the

handle of the chisel pry; then I said, "If they're illegal, how
come you have them?"

Borchard draped a fatherly arm around my shoulders.
"Marty baby, you're a smart kid, but a trifle naive. I was
a burglary detective for three years before I joined the
Speaker's Bureau, and you might say I managed to acquire
a few things at a five-finger discount, if you catch my drift.
Tools are a good thing for a man to have, and I use the
gouger-pick to play darts with. Tack a picture of L.B.J. or
one of them other liberal chumps to my wall and let fly.
Thwack! Thwack! Thwack! Come on, let's go up to my pad.
I've got a couple of frozen pizzas yelling 'Eat me!'"

That night I kept Borchard's monologues pinned to one
subject: *burglary.* I did not have to feign rapt attention: this
time it came of itself, as if the projector I used for brain-
movies were on strike and I had found something better. I
learned the practical uses of the beautiful brushed-steel
tools; I picked up the rudiments of nullifying burglar-alarm
wiring. I learned that dope addiction and a propensity for
bragging about their exploits were the most common burglar downfalls, and that if a thief wasn't too greedy and
rotated his target areas, he could elude capture indefinitely.
Criminal types imprinted themselves in that part of my
mind where only the logical lived: pad crawlers who stole
cash and loose jewelry they could swallow if the cops showed
up; credit-card thieves who ran up a string of purchases
and sold the stuff to fences. Watchdog poisoners, rape-o
burglars and brazen smash-and-grabbers joined Shroud
Shifter in my mental entourage.

Around midnight, Borchard, groggy from pizza and beer,
yawned and steered me toward the door. On my way out,
he handed me the chisel pry. "Knock yourself out, kid. Tack
up old L.B.J. and nail him a few times for Uncle Walt. But
try not to hit the wall, that beaverboard's expensive."

The steel ridges seemed to burn themselves into my hand.
I walked back to my room knowing that I now had the
courage to *do it.*

6.

The following night, I struck.

My day had been nothing but furious brain-movies and external shaking, and the head librarian twice asked me if I felt "under the weather"; but when dusk hit, a long-buried professionalism took me over, and my mind honed in on the exigencies of the job at hand.

I had already decided that the dwellings of solitary women would be my "meat," and that I would only steal what I could reasonably carry on my person. I knew from previous Walt Borchard monologues that the area just south of the east Griffith Park Road was relatively cop-free—it was a low-crime middle-class neighborhood that required only cursory patrolling. Holding that inside information in front of my brain's viewfinder, I walked there after work.

The streets off Los Feliz and Hillhurst were a mixture of stucco four-flats and small houses, narrow and broad front lawns. I circled the blocks from Franklin northward in a figure-eight pattern, checking for cars or the absence of them in driveways and for flimsy doors that looked ripe for prying and whittling. The pick-gouger rested in my back pocket, wrapped in a pair of rubber gloves I had purchased during my lunch hour. I was ready.

The sun started setting around seven-thirty, and I got the feeling that the driveways that were still empty would stay empty—there had been a big crush of people returning home for work between six and seven, but now incoming traffic was dwindling and I was seeing more and more dark

houses bereft of cars. I decided to wait until full darkness
hit, then *move*.

Twenty-five minutes later I was on New Hampshire Avenue, approaching Los Feliz. I hit a stretch of dark one-
story houses and started walking across the front lawns,
perusing mailboxes for the names of single women. The
first four designated the inhabitants as "Mr. & Mrs."; but
the fifth house was *meat*—Miss Francis Gillis. I walked up
to the door and rang the bell before fear could take hold.

Silence.

One ring; two rings; three. The darkness behind the front
window seemed to deepen with the echo of each ringing,
and I slipped on my gloves, got out my instrument and stuck
it into the narrow space where the door met the doorjamb.
My hands were shaking, and I was prepared to push, gouge
and whittle. But then my tremors accelerated, and the flat
edge of the pick nipped the lock slide just right. The door
clicked open on a perfect fluke.

I stepped inside and eased the door shut, then stood perfectly still in the interior darkness, waiting for the shape
of the front room to make itself known. My body from knees
to pelvis tingled, and as I stood there thinking of Shroud
Shifter, the feeling localized itself in my groin.

Then there was a scrabbling sound, and a powerful blunt
force knocked me onto my back. Teeth snapped at my face,
and I could feel a section of my cheek being ripped loose.
Two yellowish eyes glowed immediately in front of me, huge
and weirdly translucent. When I saw cataracts near the
black pinpoints in the middle, I knew it was a dog and that
Shroud Shifter wanted me to kill it.

The teeth snapped again; this time they grazed my left
ear. I felt legs digging into my stomach, and I swung the
gouging edge of my tool in and up, just where I thought the
animal's lower tract would be. It was a perfect imitation of
S.S.'s gutting motion; and when the blade pierced skin, and
entrails slid out warm and wet, I felt myself approaching
orgasm. I rolled out from under the dog just as he began a
series of reflex death snaps, pressing myself into the floor
as I came. My eyes were now accustomed to the darkness,

and I could see a pillow-strewn couch a few feet away. I dragged myself to it, grabbed a large tufted cushion and flung myself on the dog and smothered him.

My head was reeling as I got to my feet, found a floor lamp and turned it on, casting light on a Danish Modern living room with a Plunkett Modern still life square in the middle of it—bloodsoaked carpet, dead German shepherd with a crocheted pillow for a head. My hands were shaking, but a blank-framed brain-movie kept me calm inside. I set out to perform my first burglary.

In the bathroom I cleansed my cheek wound with witch hazel, then pressed a styptic pencil deep into the cut. Soon a crust formed, and I crisscrossed the area with tiny adhesive bandages and walked into the bedroom.

Slowly, methodically, I went to work. First I stripped off my bloodstained shirt, rolled it into a ball and rummaged in the closet until I found a blue button-down shirt that would not arouse suspicion on a man. I put it on and checked out the result in a wall mirror. Tight, but I did not look incongruous in it. My pants were soaked with blood and entrail residue, but they were dark, and the stains were not that noticeable. I could safely wear them home.

Thinking *loot*, I dug through drawers, cupboards and cabinets, coming away with a small cedar box full of twenty-dollar bills and a velvet box of sparkling stones and pearl strands that looked genuine. I thought about making a search for credit cards, but decided it was inadvisable. The dead dog might mean that this burglary would receive more police attention than usual, and I did not want to risk fencing cards that would be the object of special cop scrutiny. For a first-time "caper," I had stolen enough.

With the gouger, cash and jewelry stuck in my pants pockets, I took a last walk through the house, turning off lights. When I picked up my bloodied shirt, Shroud Shifter sent me a little commemorative embellishment, and on my way to the door I dumped a box of dog biscuits by the Shepherd's pillowed head.

7.

The night on New Hampshire Avenue was the beginning of my criminal apprenticeship and the start of a terrible series of conflicts—internal battles waged by the jigsaw pieces of my emerging drives. Over the next eleven months, I wondered if the different parts of me would ever reconcile themselves to the point where all the pieces would dovetail perfectly, allowing me to become the man of mean business I aspired to be.

I continued my burglary career two nights later, hitting three dark apartments on the same East Hollywood block, using only my pick-gouger to break and enter. I stole $400 in cash, a box of costume jewelry, sterling silverware and a half-dozen credit cards; and it wasn't until I was home safely that I realized I was disappointed—my triple success felt like an anticlimax. A window punch job the following night forced the reason consciously into my brain: my first B & E had been blood and grit and viscera and courage, my subsequent ones a refining of skills, and not nearly so exciting. The realization sank in as the need for circum-spection and super-caution; I must never, *ever*, get caught. Intellectually, that realization held me—for a while.

But other truths came hard on its heels.

For one, I could not bring myself to sell or fence the jewelry and credit cards I stole. I was afraid of establishing criminal connections that might make me vulnerable to blackmail, and I needed to *touch* the concrete rewards of my deeds. The hard plastic embossed with anonymous wom-en's names made their *lives* feed into my brain-movies, so

32

that each card was good for hours and hours of escape from boredom. The jewelry gave added tactile weight to my screenings, and I never even bothered to learn whether it was real or fake.

So, as my burglary forays progressed, my only practical "take" was money, usually accrued in tiny amounts. I retained my library job, and kept my stolen cash in a savings account. Walt Borchard taught me how to drive, and early in '68, six months into my apprenticeship, I got a driver's license and bought a car, an innocuous '60 Valiant. It was while charting wider territory in it that my most dangerous conflict came into focus.

A dreary Valley neighborhood of tract houses was unfolding in my windshield, and from the number of children playing in cement front yards I could tell that single women were at a minimum. I decided to head west toward Encino, but *something* kept me pressed to the edge of the right lane, with my *eyes* pressed to the identically laid-out driveways I was passing. Then a stray dog ambled down the sidewalk, and the picture within the picture hit me.

I had been staring at circular pet doors inset in the regular side doors that were stationed in the same place on every house I had passed for a half-dozen blocks. Suddenly I could *smell* the house on New Hampshire Avenue ten months before—a metallic scent that filled my nostrils and made my hands quiver on the steering wheel. I pulled to the curb, and the memory came back full. Along with it there was a bombardment of flashbacks from my other senses—the *taste* of my mother's blood mixed with water; Beware of the Dog signs I had seen while choosing previous burglary sites; how it *felt* to climax. The dog on the sidewalk started to look like Shroud Shifter's hated foe, Cougarman. Then the *acquired* sense of reason took hold, and I got out of that dreary and dangerous neighborhood before it could hurt me.

At home that night, I fondled my pick-gouger and shut down the movie theatre that was there to entertain me twenty-four hours a day. When a blank screen was in front of my eyes, I filled it up with what I knew and what I should

do about it, in plain typeface that left me no room for embellishment.

You have been unconsciously trying to relive killing the
dog;

You have been doing that because the excitement made
you come;

You have been taking needless risks in order to achieve
sexual gratification;

If you continue taking those risks, you will be caught,
tried and convicted of burglary;

You must stop.

My brain-typewriter flashed a series of huge question
marks in response to the last statement, and as they struck
blank paper they felt like blows to the heart. I gripped my
gouger harder and harder, and my mind flailed for the answer to the most self-destructive dilemma known to man.
Then another set of statements hit:

Cut it off—don't let it be the death of you;

Hold it in like Shroud Shifter;

But he has Lucretia;

Make yourself have dreams that will give you release;

But that is betraying myself;

Do what *everyone* does to *them*self;

No;

No;

No

Touch yourself, maim yourself or kill yourself; but do it
now.

I stripped, and walked to the full-length mirror on my
bathroom door. Staring at my image, I saw a tall, bony boy-
man with pasty skin and fierce brown eyes. I recalled the
sleep-time explosions that had come not from dreams but
from an accumulation of hateful images from my brain-
movies, and I thought of how shameful it felt when I awoke
to proof of what I secretly desired. My heart pounded, and
shortness of breath made my whole body flutter. I held the
sharp edge of the gouger to the underside of my genitals,
then to my throat. I drew thin trickles of blood at both
places, then gasped at what I was doing and hurled myself

away from the mirror and onto my bed. There, with the handle of the burglar's tool making brushed-steel indentations in my groin, I wept and gave myself release—the bitter price of being able to continue.

8.

My brush with self-annihilation filled me with a resolve to fantasize less and steal more. The diminished mental life hurt, but the boldness I gained in its backlash staunched the festering of the wound. In a week I pulled five jobs, each in the jurisdiction of a different police department, each with a different form of entry, netting a total of seven hundred dollars and change, two Rolex watches and a Smith & Wesson .38 that I planned to file down until it was completely ridge-surfaced—the ultimate burglar's weapon. Then fate bonded me to history, and my ascent and descent began at the same time.

It was June 5, 1968, the night after Robert Kennedy was shot in L.A. He was lying close to death at Good Samaritan Hospital, the place where I was born. The T.V. news showed huge crowds holding a vigil outside the hospital, and huge crowds meant empty dwellings. Walt Borchard had told me that residental areas surrounding medical facilities were loaded with nurses—good places to "patrol for pussy." The combination of factors spelled "burglar's heaven," and I drove downtown with visions of big empty houses dancing in my head.

Wilshire Boulevard was a constant stream of horn-blasting cars, a premature funeral procession. The sidewalk in front of the hospital was packed with gawkers and premature mourners weeping and waving placards, and hippies were selling "Pray for Bobby" bumper stickers. There were a number of women wearing nurse's uniforms in the crowd, and a nice solid feeling started to grow in the pit of my stomach. I parked in a lot on Union Avenue, several blocks east of Good Samaritan, and went walking.

My initial fantasies about the neighborhood had been inaccurate. There were no big houses, only ten- and twelve-story tenement-type buildings. I lost my solid feeling when I tried the outside doors of the first three red brick monoliths I came to and found them locked. Then, at the corner of Sixth and Union, I looked back on the block I had passed and saw floor after floor of dark windows, in building after building with identical side-access fire escapes. I retraced my steps and began squinting upward for *open* windows.

The third building on the east side of the street caught my eye; it had a half-open window on the fifth floor, within an arm's length of the fire-escape landing. I looked around for possible witnesses, saw none, and dragged an empty garbage can over to just below the fire escape's drop rungs. Swallowing a teeth-chattering burst of fear, I stepped on top of it and hoisted myself up.

The night was clear but moonless, and I pulled on my gloves and forced myself to tiptoe like Shroud Shifter did when he approached a victim. At the fifth-floor landing, I looked out and down, again saw no one watching me, and tried the fire-escape door. It was unlocked, and beyond it there was a long, threadbare hallway. It was the safer access route—if my target door could be easily snapped. But the window, with three feet and a sixty-foot drop between me and it, somehow seemed more powerful and sinister.

With my right leg stuck out to full extension, I tried to lift the window. It stuck, but as my foot gained purchase, I was able to push it open all the way. Squatting down, I flung my leg into the dark space beyond it, anchoring myself. Then, before I could panic, I pushed off the landing with my other foot, grabbed the wooden window frame with both hands and executed a perfect silent entry.

I was now standing in a modest living room. As my eyes became accustomed to the dark, I saw mismatching sofa and chairs; brick and board bookshelves stuffed with paperbacks; a hallway off at a right angle directly in front of me. A strange sound was coming from the far end of it, and

I went tingly with the thought of a possible watchdog. Pulling out my gouger, I treaded down the hallway until I saw an open door spilling candlelight and what I knew immediately to be the sounds of lovemaking.

A man and woman were on the bed, entwined. They were covered with sweat, and were moving snakelike, in counterpoint movements: him relentlessly forward, up and down, in and out; her sideways with her hips, jabbing outward with crossed legs wrapped around her partner's back. A candle sitting atop a bookshelf acted in concert with a light breeze blowing from an open window, sending long flutters of light through the darkness—a flame dance that ended at the point where the lovers were joined.

Their moans rose, subsided, became half-verbal gasps. I watched the candlelight illuminate him inside of her. Each flicker made the point of bonding both more beautiful and more gutter-explicit. I stared, transfixed, oblivious to the risk I was taking. I don't know how long I was standing there, but after a while I began to anticipate the lovers' movements, and then I started moving with them, silently, from a distance that seemed vast but intimate. Their hips rose and fell; mine did also, in perfect synchronization, brushing an empty space that felt alive with growing things. Soon their moans escalated in unison, reaching toward a point where they would never subside. I caught myself about to cry out with them, then bit down on my tongue as Shroud Shifter sent me professional caution. At that point my whole being rocketed into my groin, and the two lovers and I came together.

They lay gasping, clutching each other fiercely; I pressed my back into the wall to hold down the residual shock waves of my explosion. I pressed harder and harder, until I thought my spine would crack; then I heard whispers, and a radio voice filled the bedroom. A somber-voiced announcer was saying that Robert Kennedy was dead. The woman started to sob, and the man whispered, "Sssh. Ssssh. We knew it was going to happen."

The last three words startled me, and I moved back down the hall to the living room. I saw a pair of cord trousers draped across an armchair and a purse on the floor next to it. With one eye on the candlelight glow emanating from the bedroom, I pulled a billfold from the back pocket of the cords and a wallet from the open purse. Then I eased myself out the door before the beautiful candle magnet could draw me back to the lovers.

At the car, before I could even bring myself to examine my loot, I had an eerie moment of clarity. I knew I had to do it again and again, and unless my criminal profits made the risk worthwhile, I would die from submission to that desire. I thought of the jewelry and credit cards hidden in my closet at home, and of the names and hangouts of fences Walt Borchard had mentioned in his many beery monologues. I drove home, picked up my stash and went out to carve another notch on my professionalism. En route I felt sated; gently calm but determined. *Loving.*

My calmness turned to apprehension as I parked on Cahuenga and Franklin, a half block from the Omnibus—infamous "O.B.'s," the place Walt Borchard called "a pus pocket even by Hollywood standards, a real carnival of low-life; fences, bikers, hookers, dope dealers, junkies and fruits." Even before I walked in the door I could see his appraisal validated. There were a half-dozen motorcycles parked on the sidewalk in front of the low cement building, and a group of rough-looking men in leather jackets were passing around a bottle of whiskey. Pushing through the swinging doors, I saw that the inside was a grand tour of things I had never seen.

There was a bandstand at the front of the large, smoky room. Shirtless Negro men were pounding conga drums on top of it, and a white man in back of them was swinging a colored arc light in the direction of the horseshoe-shaped dance floor. There was a line of youths, both male and female, standing at the periphery of the gyrating throng of dancers, and every few seconds one of them would move toward a door I could glimpse in back of the bandstand.

Walking into the lowlife maelstrom, I fingered the loot in my windbreaker pockets for luck and courage. Joining the line of hippies, I got a clear look at the dance floor. Men were dancing with men, and women with women. I caught the scent of a ripe, musky substance and knew it had to be marijuana. Then I felt an elbow in my side, and a marijuana stick was in my face. "Toke," a girl with stringy red hair said. "It's Acapulco Gold. You'll fly."

I thought of Shroud Shifter and psychic invisibility, then said, "No thanks. Not my scene."

The girl narrowed her eyes at me and took a "toke" herself. Exhaling, she said, "Are you a nark?"

"No, I came here to do business."

"Buying or selling?"

"Selling."

"Groovy. Grass? Speed? Acid?"

S.S. was whispering "when in Rome" in my ear. Impulsively I said "toke," and grabbed the joint. I put it between my lips and dragged deeply. The smoke burned, but I held it in until it felt like a hot poker was singeing my lungs. Then I belched the smoke out and gasped, "Jewelry, watches, credit cards."

The girl toked and said, "I'm Lovechild. Are you a criminal or something?" She handed me back the joint, and as I sucked in the smoke I could see Shroud Shifter and Lucretia doing a slow grind together on the dance floor. Other dancers bumped into them, and Lucretia snapped at their necks until they backed off. Within seconds the dancers were on their *knees*, and S.S. and Lucretia were *naked* and coiled together in a serpentlike mass of arms and legs. I toked again, and heard music oozing from the bandstand: "I gotta get high, and fry on the sky! geez some china white in a purple haze thigh! Don't ask why!"

Lovechild shoved herself against me and pouted, "Don't Bogart! Don't Bogart! It's expensive!" With my eyes still on Shroud Shifter and Lucretia, I reached into my right windbreaker pocket for a lady's Rolex to keep her calmed down. My hand closed on metal, and I pulled what I was grasping out. Then someone shouted, "He's got a gun!"

The line of hippies parted, and Shroud Shifter and Lucretia vanished. I heard the jabbered syllables "fuzz," "heat" and "pig" over and over. Reality clicked in, and I forced my marijuana-addled brain to come up with the name of the "boss fence" that Walt Borchard said worked out of O.B.'s. I trained my unloaded .38 at Lovechild and hissed, "Cosmo Veitch. Get him."

The crowd was getting itchy; I could feel them sizing me up. I had my height and square clothes going for me, but aside from that I was bone-skinny and only twenty years old. If someone decided to turn on normal indoor lights, I would be exposed as a non-cop imposter.

Old brain-movies and memories came to my aid; I felt my features congeal into my "don't fuck with me, I'm psycho" stare. Shroud Shifter was whispering words of encouragement and pointing at his diaphragm; I knew he wanted me to speak in a deep, tough guy's voice. "Ease back, citizens," I said. "This isn't a bust, this is just between me and Cosmo."

The remark seemed to nullify the crowd. I could see tense faces unclench in relief, and the dancers immediately in front of me backed off onto the floor and resumed gyrating. I saw that I was still holding my .38 at waist level, and that the line of hippies had dispersed. I was concentrating on keeping my face in darkness when I heard a male voice in back of me. "Yes, Officer?"

I swiveled slowly and smiled at the voice. It belonged to a boy-man with hard eyes, a hard, short body, granny glasses and a ponytail hairdo. I said, "Someplace quiet," and pointed my gun toward the back of the bandstand. Cosmo walked ahead, and led me to a small room filled with bar stools and disconnected jukeboxes. The light was bright and harsh, and I kept my whole being concentrated on looking and sounding older than my years. "I'm Shifter," I said. "I've been working Daywatch Burglary out in the Valley and I've heard good things about you." With my gun pointed to the floor, I emptied the contents of both my windbreaker pockets onto a bar stool. Cosmo whistled at the accumulation of jewelry, watches and credit cards. S.S. was making "be cool" gestures, and I sighed and said, "Name a figure, I haven't got all night."

Cosmo fondled the two Rolexes, then poked through the jewelry, holding several red stones up to the light. "Five hundred," he said.

I felt another jolt of the marijuana. "Cash, not trash." Shroud Shifter's "be cool" motions got more emphatic, and I added, "Six hundred."

Cosmo took a roll from his pocket. He peeled off six hundred-dollar bills and handed them to me, then pointed to a back door. I stuck my gun in my pocket, bowed and exited like a great actor leaving the stage after curtain calls for a bravura performance. I had conquered sex and achieved psychic invisibility on the same day. I was inviolate; I was golden.

9.

Watching.

Stealing.

Watching *and* stealing.

I spent a feverish twenty-four hours trying to reconcile the dual logistics. The homes of young married couples? No, too risky.

Surveillance of attractive young women with sleep-over boyfriends? No, too hit-or-miss. Finally an idea dawned, and I walked down the hall and knocked on Uncle Walt Borchard's door.

"Friend or foe?" Uncle Walt called out.

"Foe!" I called back.

"Enter, foe!"

I opened the door. Uncle Walt was sitting on the living-room couch, wolfing his usual dinner of pizza and beer, a newspaper spread on the floor to catch cheese drip. "I...I need to talk," I said in a mock-sheepish voice.

"Sounds serious. Sit down and have a slice."

I took a chair across from Borchard and declined the pizza he pointed to. "Have you ever worked Vice?" I asked.

Borchard chewed and laughed at the same time—as complex a feat as he was capable of. Swallowing, he said, "That *does* sound serious. You okay, Marty?"

"S—s—sure. Have you?"

"No, I haven't. Are you in trouble, kid?"

"No. The vice squad arrests prostitutes, right?"

"Right."

"And call girls? You know, like really good-looking prostitutes? Not the cheap hooker type, but, you know, *beautiful* girls, girls who have their own apartments to take guys to so it's not cheesy, like in a motel?"

Borchard laughed so hard that an anchovy popped out of his mouth and landed on the coffee table in front of him. He popped it back in, rechewed it and said, "Marty, are you looking to get laid?"

I lowered my eyes. "Yes."

"Kid, it's 1968. Girls are giving it away like never before."

"I know, but—"

"Have you tried Patty downstairs? She's spread her legs so many times they'll have to bury her in a Y-shaped coffin."

"She's ugly, and she's got pimples."

"Then put a paper bag over her head and buy her a tube of Clearasil."

I forced out a trickle of crocodile tears, and Uncle Walt said, "Aw shit, kid, I'm sorry. You're cherry, right? You're a late starter, and you want a nice-looking cooze for your premiere fuck?"

I wiped my nose and said, "Yes."

Uncle Walt got up and ruffled my hair, then went into his bedroom. He returned a moment later and handed me a hundred-dollar bill. "Don't say I never gave you anything, and don't say I never bent the rules for a buddy."

I put the money in my shirt pocket. "Gee, thanks, Uncle Walt."

"My pleasure. Now listen real close, and in an hour or so you will be de-virginized. *Are* you listening?"

"Yes."

"Good. Here's some astonishing information: the L.A.P.D., of which I am a member, *does* allow a certain amount of high-line prostitution to go on in the Hollywood area. Isn't that *shocking*? Well, there's a part of the Boulevard, just West of La Brea, loaded with call-girl cribs. The girls hang out at the better hotel bars—like the Cine-Grill at the Roosevelt, the Yamashiro Skyroom, the Gin Mill at Knickerbocker and so forth. The girls sit at the bar and sip cocktails and eye the single men, and it doesn't take a genius to figure out what they do for a living. The standard operating procedure is that they mention a figure and suggest that you adjourn to their pad. The standard pop for an all-nighter is a C-note, which I just happened to press into your horny paw. Now, you're under the drinking age, so act frosty when the bartender asks what you're having. Act gentlemanly with the lady of your choice, tell her a C-note is tops, and pour her the pork till the hogs holler for hell."

I stood up. Uncle Walt chucked me under the chin and laughed. "Some young lady's gonna burn more rubber than the San Berdoo Freeway. Now get out of here, my pizza's getting cold."

An hour later I was not getting "de-virginized." I was sitting at the bar of the Hollywood Roosevelt Cine-Grill, watching a woman in a tight black sequined dress make small talk with a bluff-hearty man wearing a summer suit dotted with conventioner's buttons. The woman was a bleached redhead, but pretty; the man had a solid, muscular look. I sipped a Scotch and soda and kept my nervousness at bay by imagining them as Shroud Shifter and Lucretia, unwinding from a long day of stalking victims. I could almost *feel* the two together in bed.

They left the bar abruptly. As they got up to leave, I realized I was screening brain-movies, and that I had lost sight of them in physical reality. I counted to ten and pursued.

I saw them get into a cab in front of the hotel, and I ran for my car. The cab was easy to follow; traffic on the Boulevard was heavy, and they got stuck at the back of a line of cars at La Brea. I was right behind, reaching under the seat for my gloves and gouger. When the light turned green, I smiled: the cab was already pulling to the curb; Uncle Walt's "call-girl block" had been gospel.

The couple got out of the cab. I parked hastily two car-lengths in back and watched them enter a large pink apartment building shaped like a southern plantation house. The woman did not use a key to open the front door, so I had my initial access. I waited ten seconds, then sprinted full-out, slowing as I opened the door on a long, pink-carpeted hallway. The two were just entering an apartment at the far left end of the hall.

I scanned mailboxes and willed the aura of a cool young man who belonged in an outré pink plantation on Hollywood Boulevard. It was easy, and affecting such supreme nonchalance made me feel brazen. There were no people in the hallway, but a variety of T.V. and stereo noise was booming from inside individual apartments, so that there was a general high noise level. I walked toward my target, checking out the doors on my way. The opener knobs were not reinforced, and there was at least a sixteenth of an inch's play at the door-doorjamb junctures. If the hooker hadn't set an inside chain, I could enter.

At my target door I listened for the sound of pre-sex amenities; all I could hear and *sense* on the other side was silence. Giving the hall a quick eye circuit, I slipped on my gloves, inserted the pick side of my tool and jiggled at the lock. I could feel individual spring-slides give one at a time, and when the third one clicked softly, I pushed the door open a fraction of an inch—just enough to glimpse a dark living room–dinette. Shaking my head to keep brain-movies away, I entered, twisting the doorknob out and then closing the door soundlessly.

Voices, not sounds of passion, drew me in the direction of the bedroom, and glimpses of flawed bodies were what I saw through the crack in the door. My heart crashed as I held an eye up to my inch-wide viewfinder. He was flabby; she had tattoos on her shoulders and thighs. Her pubic hair was obviously dyed to match the shade of her head; he kept his socks on. I tried to make them into Shroud Shifter and Lucretia, but my brain camera wouldn't focus, and their voices were so grating that I knew their lovemaking would be hideous—and I could never join them.

"...I been in this building before," the man was saying. "When I was in L.A. with the Moose convention in '64."

"Lots of working girls work out of here," the hooker answered. "Some of them I run myself. You wanta get started?"

"Not so fast. You're a *madam*?"

The hooker sighed. "More like a big-sister confidante, like a therapist, really. I *do* fix up dates and take a cut, but I like to be a pal, like a big sister who knows the ropes."

"Whaddaya mean?"

"Well, once a week I get together with the working girls I know, and we shmooze and talk tricks, and *you know*."

The man giggled. "You ever make it with another chick?"

The woman groaned. "Oh, Jesus. Look, I think I'm gonna need a drink for this. You want one too? Maybe it'll quiet—"

I saw what was about to happen, and padded for the door. When my hand was on the knob, I saw a purse lying on a chair a few feet away. I grabbed it, and managed to extricate myself from the apartment just as the bedroom door started to open. Then I ran.

The purse yielded $9.43 and sexual information that kept me watching, hoping, stalking and sometimes stealing for over a year. The money, of course, was negligible. It was the hooker's notebook that kept me busy.

It was a makeshift ledger of customers, their phone numbers and the dates of their prescheduled assignations, and a list of the other girls that Carol Ginzburg, the "Therapist-Confidante" "ran," along with the names and phone numbers of the "tricks," and notations as to whether the "date" would be held at a motel, the "trick pad" or the girl's apartment itself. It boiled down to a wealth of possible watching-stealing sites, and in the case of the preset "dates," it allowed me the time to perform reconnaissance forays before the assignation.

With Shroud Shifter determination, I set out to write my own ledger. First, using the normal L.A. "white pages" and Walt Borchard's police "reverse" directory, I compiled a list of addresses to go with the phone numbers; then, one weekend when Uncle Walt was out of town on a fishing trip, I staged a break-in of the back garage and stole the remainder of his set of burglar's tools, his power lawn mower and an allegedly valuable stack of *National Geographics*.

The mower and magazines I dumped in the Silverlake Reservoir; the tools I wrapped in a nylon tarpaulin and stashed in a hollowed-out tree trunk two blocks away.

Next came a series of "recon" missions.

Carol Ginzburg and her "girls" met each Sunday for brunch at the Carolina Pines coffee shop on Sunset and La Brea—it was designated in her ledger as "girltalk." I eavesdropped at three of their sessions, and studied the "girls" themselves, eliminating "Rita," "Suzette" and "Starr" as stupid floozies; sizing up "Danielle," "Lauri" and "Barb" as acceptable for one-third of a triad melding. Lauri was particularly lovely—a tall, stately honey blonde with a Scandinavian accent. I decided that I would hit her "trick pad" dates first, and set out to chart the territory and hone my breaking-and-entering skills.

I did it all very methodically. Lauri had a date in Coldwater Canyon every third Wednesday; I checked out the house, found it impregnable, with home-to-police-station wiring, and crossed it off my list. She had a once-a-month Monday tryst in one of the less plush sections of Beverly Hills; the windows were child's play and there was plenty of hedge cover adjoining the bedrooms. That was to be "hit" number one, on August 7, 1968.

And so on down the list, with Lauri's dates first, Barb's second and Danielle's third. The three girls all lived in Carol Ginzburg's pink plantation house, so actual "at-home" tricks would have to be bypassed—I could not risk repeated burglaries in the same building. Also, some of the trick pads were too well exposed and too burglar-proof, and had to be eliminated. But when all was said and done, I had a list of nineteen "probables," all cased and calendar-marked—tryst burglaries that, if all went well, would last me until January 1970. And I had a built-in fail-safe: the girltalk coffee klatches. If the police had been alerted to the rash of hooker-connected burglaries, I would be among the first to know.

In the daytime, my life continued as usual as I waited for the seventh of August—I worked at the library, ran brain-movies, willed psychic invisibility. But at night, I *worked* at my hideaway—an abandoned maintenance shed

I had discovered deep in the Griffith Park woods. In the glow of a battery-powered arc light I learned the *feel* of all six keyhole picks in my tool set, the imperceptible little *give* they activated when inserted and jiggled. I bought dozens of brand-new brushed-steel door locks at hardware stores, and got to know how to nullify the various brand names. I practiced windows with my suction-cup glass tool; I ran the dark hills of the park to build up my wind in case I ever had to flee a trick pad on foot. I came to believe that my first burglary year was an incredible mélange of chance, heedless bravado and beginner's luck. I had been a child voyager then. Now I was a consummate craftsman.

August 7, 1968.

The notation in Carol Ginzburg's trick book said 9:00 P.M., so I left for Beverly Hills at 7:30 to facilitate the means to a last-minute brainstorm. The night was stifling hot, cloying. I parked in a meter space on Wilshire three blocks from my target and walked over, assuming the easy gait of someone with plenty of time and nothing to fear. At Charleville and Le Doux I saw the home of Mr. Murray Stanton, lit up like a Christmas tree in anticipation of a hot night with Lauri. Passing the driveway on the sidewalk, I could hear the window-mounted air conditioner humming at full power. I walked casually over and cut the cord, nipping it just at the point where it stuck out of the window and into the machine. Squatting down, I admired my work. The cord was frayed on its own, and the break looked natural. I walked into the backyard and squatted behind a line of rosebushes to wait.

At 8:20 I could hear a male voice muttering "Shit"; seconds later I heard windows being opened on both sides of the house. I caught a glimpse of Murray Stanton in silhouette. From a distance he looked as if he could pass for Shroud Shifter.

At 9:00 exactly, the front door chimes sounded. I slipped on my gloves, shut my eyes, ran brain-movies and counted to five hundred simultaneously. Then I walked to the window farthest from the bedroom and elbowed myself up and into the dark house.

Squeals of ecstasy directed me to the bedroom door. I could see that it was pressed shut—not locked, and there was a light coming from beneath it. Taking a chance on the lovers having their eyes shut, I toed the door open an inch.

Murray Stanton was lying on top of Lauri, pumping, and the plague of acne cysts on his back made him an insult to Shroud Shifter. Lauri, tall, blond and regal from what I could see of her body, was examining a framed photograph which had been resting on a nightstand beside the bed, with her other hand resting on Stanton's pimpled shoulder, her fingers pushed out as if she was afraid the pustules might be contagious. *She* was the moaner, and she was a bad actress; the peak of her performance was when she put down the picture to scratch her nose. She was beautiful enough to be Lucretia, but she reminded me of someone else, someone strong and Nordic buried in a deep compartment in my memory vault.

I continued to watch, unaroused. After a while, Lauri stopped squealing and bit at the fingernails of each hand. Stanton's movements became more frenzied, and he blurted breathlessly, "I'm gonna come! Say 'It's so big!' Say 'It's so big it hurts!'"

Lauri mouthed the words, trying to hold back giggles. The satirical note in her voice would have been obvious to anyone but a piggish acne case approaching orgasm. I walked back to the living room, Shroud Shifter at my side, whispering, *"Steal, steal, steal."*

In the living room, I started to obey. I was reaching for a billfold atop a coffee table when I got an astonishing typed-out brain message: *Don't steal, because the acne pig will blame Lauri, and then you won't know who she is.*

The message was so powerful that by reflex I complied. But on my way to the window I pocketed a tiny framed photograph of a trio of smiling children.

Watching.
Stealing.

Watching *and* stealing.

Those twin pursuits ruled my waking hours over the next year, and nightmares ruled my sleep. I had hoped that man-woman-me would be my trinity, but it wasn't. It was a triad of: watch perfunctory sex motivated by greed and desperation; steal for emotional survival and the rationale for watching; dream to figure out the mystery of Lauri. That my dreams inevitably became nightmares was the worst part.

Laurel Hahnerdahl was Lauri's real name, and from impersonating a police officer over the telephone I learned that she was born in Copenhagen, Denmark, in 1943, and that she came to America in 1966. Her occupation was listed as "model," she had no relatives in the United States, and she possessed no criminal record. That was all the Department of Motor Vehicles and the L.A.P.D. Records Bureau could give me.

We could not possibly have ever met, but she seemed almost symbiotically familiar to me. I prowled her apartment twice and found nothing to jog my memory; I observed four of her dates, without stealing, and still could not decipher the mystery. I dreamt of her constantly, and it was always the same: I was watching her make love to a man who looked like Shroud Shifter, and my vision got blurry, so I moved closer, only to turn into a sightless, armless, legless, voiceless inanimate object. All I could do was hear—and then I heard thunder—crashing thunder hiding thousands of unintelligible voices trying to tell me what Lauri meant. My nightmare would invariably end at that point, and I would wake up erect and drenched in sweat.

Lauri returned to Denmark in April of '69, and Carol Ginzburg threw a brunch in her honor to celebrate her return to her homeland. I was distressed to see her go—and angry at myself for not having solved who she was—but with her departure came a diminuendoing of my nightmares, and I was able to put the riddle she represented out of my mind.

So I continued to watch and steal, until the hope of ever again feeling what I did on June 5, 1968, died from too many turgid bed performances, too many pathetic expressions of loneliness. With my disillusionment in watching came a concurrent new joy in stealing, and I ran up eleven straight scores, pawning the loot to Cosmo Veitch, reveling in the fact that although he finally figured out I wasn't a policeman, he at least was heartily afraid of me. From the late summer of '68 to the midsummer of '69 he paid me a total of seven thousand two hundred dollars for the goods I stole. I kept the cash in a steel safe-deposit box at a bank on La Brea, holding it for the time when I would quit my library job and move out of Walt Borchard's lowlife building.

But in August of '69 a series of events coincided to temporarily halt my criminal career. Sharon Tate and four others were butchered at her Benedict Canyon house, and when coupled with the similar La Bianca slayings on the other side of town in the Los Feliz district, the murder spelled panic and created a boom in all manner of security devices and services. Angelenos were buying guns and watchdogs, and were buttressing themselves against the still-uncaptured killers in specific, and the 1960's in general. Burglary was getting to be a riskier business.

And Carol Ginzburg finally put two and two together and connected the trick-pad robberies to her stolen "John" book. I listened at the Sunday restaurant brunch as she told her girls "coincidence, shmoincidence, something strange is going on." She described her theory of a very cool robber who only hit intermittently out of caution, and how she was hiring a private detective to look into things. I paid my check and left the coffee shop as she spoke.

With watching and stealing gone, all that was left of my trinity were the nightmares. Even with Lauri gone, they came back, whispers taunting me between peals of thunder. I did not know what they were saying, but when I woke up, I could taste blood.

10.

Without limbs to propel me and sight to guide me, my dreams became excursions into weightlessness. I was the prey of noises that tossed me about like a rag doll; I was at the mercy of thunder that singed my body. Only an undercurrent of consciousness kept the lid on my nightmares and saved me from the ruination of terror-induced insomnia. I knew, during the worst of the buffeting, that feeling the thunder-heat meant I could not possibly be disembodied. When I awoke each morning both refreshed and filled with a residue of fear, I knew that I possessed an automatic-pilot device that would always keep me short of the edge.

Yet, still I dreaded sleep, and sought to postpone it through the pursuit of utter exhaustion.

With my bank account as a cushion, I quit the library job and spent my days expending physical energy. I joined a gym in West L.A. and lifted weights for two hours daily; in the course of a month my lean frame started to cord over with muscle. I ran the Griffith Park hills until lightheadedness made me collapse and hot showers at home felt like benevolent heat. Then, at night, I disembodied others.

It was a ritual spurred by awareness of my own body and driven by a desire to quash the nightmares. I became a trawler after human beings in their most prosaic poses, a brain-movie director adept at improvising drama out of street passersby and their throwaway gestures. Night after night I cruised the slow lanes, watching. I saw hands pluck at trouser legs and hemlines and *knew* how those people took their sex; neon lights shimmying across gang boys in

tank tops told me why they did the things they did. My
brain camera had an automatic slow-motion lens, and when
beautiful bodies demanded an extra-close scrutiny to yield
the truth of their poetry, that device clicked in and let me
linger on all the lovely swells and junctures of flesh.

After a few weeks of mobile watching, my nightmares
de-escalated, and I went from movie director to surgeon in
an effort to kill them off altogether. My experimental surgery involved cross-gender limb transplants—men's legs to
women's torsos, women's faces to men's bodies, with special
attention paid to the mental incisions that made the grafts
possible. Driving close to the curb, I would take a bead on
a hand-holding couple, then slow down until we were moving at the same speed. When streetlights illuminated their
faces, I amputated limbs and heads and rearranged the
parts; effortlessly, bloodlessly. And although unable to express the meaning of the act in words, I knew I was evolving
three-way symbiotic unions that transcended sex.

The combination of daytime exertion and nighttime
brain-movies finally brought my dreams to the point where
they were no more than an occasional nuisance. As a precaution against their recurring in force, I slept with the
light on, and if I happened to awake during the night I
would walk to the full-length mirror on my bathroom door
and stare at my own body. I was strong now, and getting
stronger, and when I touched probing fingers to my muscles
I felt an almost electric charge. The charge would run down
to my groin and end at a verbal terminus: the word *burglary*.

I succeeded in pushing the word and its giddy connotations aside for weeks, until, in early October, a series of
bodies stirred the old embers, and fate supplied the wind
that forced me into a brushfire.

I was driving north on Pacific Coast Highway at dusk,
wending my way toward the Topanga Canyon turn-in, the
Valley, and watching. It was unseasonably warm, and groups
of surfers crowded the blacktop that paralleled the beach.
Male and female, they were all young and lithe, and my
foot eased off the gas involuntarily. A foursome caught my
eye: two boys, two girls, all sleek brunettes. My mind went

into a pre-surgery "prep," then went blank. I could not improvise with their bodies, and I knew it was because they were too perfect.

Although I made every effort, my mental scalpel would not descend, and the quartet grew more and more lissome. Car horns honked behind me; I saw that I had stopped dead and was holding up traffic. I started to get scared, and checked my brain arsenal for brushed-steel cutlery to maim the four with. Then, *against my will,* the brunettes turned to blonds, and the boys were kissing the boys and the girls the girls, and a car brushed my rear fender, the driver yelling, "Get a license, you faggot!"

I punched the gas reflexively, and my old Valiant tore across a busy intersection against the light, narrowly missing an old woman pushing a baby carriage. I took my eyes from the road and glued them to the rearview; the four perfect ones had vanished. I drove slowly out to the Valley, knowing it was only a matter of time until I would break, enter, watch, steal and come—regardless of the risk.

Full darkness brought an awful boredom. The only people out were flaccid and homely, unworthy of my machinations, and the beautiful brunette/blondes wafted inside me like a mental musk. I switched from commercial streets to residential, knowing full well my ultimate intent, and the houses I passed were uniformly brightly lit—bastions of cheap, incomprehensible happiness. My only alternative was to eat, go home and hope for a dreamless sleep.

I stopped at a Bob's Big Boy on Ventura Boulevard. There was an attractive couple in a booth near the door, and I took a counter seat that gave me visual access to both of them. I was in the conscious process of turning them blond when they got up and walked over to the cashier. A pair of burly young men in denims took their place, the taller of the two pocketing the tip. As his hand scooped the coins, I turned it into a reptile's claw; soon both youths were fixed in my mind as buffoonish lizards. Then their loud voices made me stop brain-gaming and listen:

"...yeah, for-real hippie hookers. I'm talking chicks who love their work, who groove on ballin' more than money.

Cheap, too. The one chick, Season, hit me up for a ten-spot in the morning; the other, Flower—can you dig it?—goes for even less. You gotta listen to their rap about this guru guy they groove on, but who cares?"

"And you're tellin' me they hang out at the Whiskey every night? That they've got a pad off the Strip, and they spread all night for a tensky?"

"I don't blame you for not thinkin' it's for real, but listen: they got an altered motive, or whatever you call it—they're recruiters for this guru guy Charlie, and they tell you the fuck bread is for 'The Family,' and you should come out to this ranch where they live. It's a hype, but who cares?"

"And these chicks are boss foxes?"

"Primo."

"And all I gotta do is hit the Whiskey and ask around for them?"

"No, just go there and look cool, and they'll find you."

"Then why the fuck am I sittin' here lookin' at your ugly face?"

Not knowing I had just crossed paths with history, I left a dollar on the counter and drove to the Strip and the Whiskey Au Go Go. A neon sign announced "The Battle of the Bands"—"Marmalade" vs "Electric Rabbit"; "Perko-Dan & his Magik Band" vs "The Loveseekers." Parking spaces were scarce, but I found a spot in a gas-station lot across the street. Knowing this was a criminal mission—not an exercise in mental surgery—I walked over to the door, paid my cover charge and entered into a dark cavern of high-decibel noise.

The amplified electrical twanging was hideous, and had nothing to do with music; the darkness that enveloped everything but the stage was soothing and an unwitting ally—I could not see the people who were jammed together at matchbook-size tables; there would be no fetching bodies to distract me from my mission. The six gyrators who banged guitars in the glow of strobe lights would force me to search for "Flower" and "Season"—their "stage presence" was a frenzy of long matted hair, Day-Glo "threads" and sprayed body fluids.

Turning away from them, I found an empty table and sat down. A waitress materialized, placed a napkin in front of me and said, "Three-drink minimum, three-fifty a drink. If you want liquor, I have to see some ID. If you want to leave and come back, I'll have to stamp your hand."

I said, "ginger ale," handed her a five-dollar bill and squinted into the darkness. After a few seconds, the shapes of sitting people came into view. I decided to keep my eyes fixed on a midpoint among the rear tables, hoping to catch Season and Flower moving between them in their "recruiting" efforts. I was moving into my own world of pure concentration when I felt a hand on my arm and heard a breathy female voice. I was caught off guard, and my knees jerked up and hit the table, knocking it over. The girl who had spoken to me scuttled out of the way, and I saw that she was lovely, with waist-length black hair. Smiling, I willed an aura of psychic invisibility and spoke in a tone of pure nonchalance, pure savoir faire. "I just got back from the Continent, and the cafe accommodations there are more accommodating. Won't you sit down and join me for a drink?"

Her mouth dropped, and her loveliness turned fatuous. "What? You mean you're clumsy?"

"Just captivated," I said. "Won't you sit down?"

The girl said, "Captivated?" and gave me a look that was half-contempt, half-befuddlement. An errant strobe flash magnified her mouth; she was both slack-jawed and sneering. The sneer crept over me, and I mentally hacked off her limbs and tossed them in the direction of "Electric Rabbit" and their off-key wailing. The girl muttered "Weirdo" under her breath, then waved to someone in back of me and called, "Season! Wait!"

My targets.

The girl threaded her way toward an Exit sign by the back tables. I hesitated, then followed. When she got to the door she huddled with two others; from ten yards away I saw that both of them were long-haired and wearing buckskin pants and vests. I was not close enough to determine their genders, and I had to keep my brain scalpel from hacking through their britches so I could tell. Suddenly

what the two had between their legs was the most important thing in the world. I was moving to the door when the
black-haired girl skipped back into the nightclub melee,
and the buckskin pair pushed through the door to the street.
I followed.

The two crossed Sunset in an androgynous swirl, fixed
by a steel tracking device that kept me oblivious to everything else around me. Dimly, I realized that I was jay-
walking straight through a stream of traffic, and that horns
were honking and tires squealing. Still I pursued; still I
kept my tunnel vision activated. When the street was behind me, with residential darkness looming ahead, a turning car illuminated my prey. I saw that they were male and
female, both slightly built, a mustache on the young man
the only distinguishing feature. My tracking device snapped
off, a "caution" switch snapping *on* in its place.

I held back and took deep breaths; the buckskin pair
rounded the corner and walked up the side stairs of a pink
stucco apartment building with exposed doorways. "Season" opened the third door from the end and flicked on an
inside light, then pointed the young man in. When she
closed the door behind them, the light went off immediately.
She had not used a key to enter; the door was most likely
unlocked.

I waited for twenty excruciatingly long minutes, then
walked over and up to the door. "Caution" burned behind
my eyes in red neon, and I put my ear against the plywood
surface and listened. Hearing nothing but the crackle of
electricity coursing through my body, I entered.

The apartment was completely dark, and the spongy
carpeting seemed to seduce me into it, slowly. The walls
felt like an embrace; the stale air was warm. When my eyes
were able to pick out details, the cheap wrought-iron and
Formica fixtures did not register as sterile—they came alive
as objects belonging to people I wanted to know. The heat
of the four-walled vacuum settled near my physical center,
smothering the Caution sign. I saw a short hallway and a
doorway strung with beads immediately in front of me.
Darkness reposed behind it, but I knew that would not stop

me from seeing. I tiptoed to the last barrier separating me from the lovers.

Grunts, giggles and squeals of pleasure sounded behind it. Parting the beads and squinting until my eyes ached allowed me to see shadow-light on ankles locked together; breathing in gave me the taste of marijuana. The love noises grew more intense, and the words I was able to discern— "yeah," "give it," and "come"—issued from vulgar voices. It rattled me, and cold air started to seep into my sensual womb. To staunch the freeze, I turned myself dumb and stared *through* the beads until I saw two women writhing, friction producing sparks where their nipples rubbed together; two men joined groin to groin, their straining limbs keeping the juncture point hidden. Then all four became one, and I got lost trying to see who was where. I came then, my hands tightly grasping the beads.

Astonishingly, I wasn't heard. I stood rock-still, enclosed by heat and bombarded by a series of Caution signs with missing and rearranged letters. It was as if a full-body dyslexia were trying to push me one way or the other, toward some hellish, irrevocable act. I stood very, very still, then heard Season's voice for the first time. "It's just the wind and the beads. Isn't it pretty?"

The male lover answered, "It's spooky."

Season sighed. "It's nature. Charlie says that after Helter Skelter, when the big corporations are all gone and the land reverts to the people, man-made things and nature will work together in perfect harmony. It's in the Bible, and the Beatles and the Beach Boys, and Charlie and Dennis Wilson are doing an album about it."

"You've got this Charlie dude on the brain."

"He's a wise man. He's a shaman and a healer, and a metaphysician and a guitarist."

The male lover snorted, and Season sang, "'You say you want a revolution, we-el-el, you know, we all want to change the world.' Charlie calls that the gospel according to Saint Paul and Saint John."

"Ha! You want to hear the gospel according to Saint *Me*?"

"Well...okay, sure."

"Then dig: good food, good dope, good vibes and good fuckin', and if someone gets in your way, lock, load and fire between their eyes."

"And death to the pigs."

"Not my scene, my dad's a cop. What's Charlie say about instant replays?"

"What do you mean?"

"Come here, I'll show you."

Season giggled. I could feel the air heating up behind the bead curtain, and I got out of the womb before the warmth could claim me.

That night my dreams were a compendium.

I was armless and legless. A phantom named Charlie chased me, and I wanted to see why pretty young girls talked about him after they had made love with someone else, so I let myself be caught, screaming when I saw that Charlie's face was a mirror that reflected not my face, but a collage of butchered sex organs. Walt Borchard taunted me for screaming, then shoved hundred-dollar bills in my mouth to shut me up. My mother grabbed at the money and tried to tourniquet her gashed arms with it; my father toasted a mushroom cloud rising over downtown L.A. Knowing that total silence would save me, I fastened brushed-steel clamps over my lips and turned a series of external gears that would keep my brain's synapses from sparking. I started to feel impregnable, and tried to laugh. No sound came out, and a new array of mirror-faced enemies approached me, holding big metal keys that would unlock my voice, my brain, my memory.

I woke up at dawn, choking and gasping for breath. I had bitten through my pillow, and my mouth was filled with cotton and foam rubber. I spat it out and breathed deeply, then went into a coughing attack. I tried to bring my right arm over to wipe my eyes, but there was no feeling at all on the right side of my body.

I whimpered, "No, please," then sent a "kick" signal to my right leg. It hit the floor, so I knew that part of me had not been amputated. Gritting my teeth, I signaled my arm:

"Grab, tear, rip, gouge, live." There was a stirring under the sheet, then my hand extricated itself from the wall by the bedstead. Blood and mortar covered my fingers, and I looked at the hole my nightmare had dug. The perfectly outlined apertures held my attention like cave hieroglyphics. I stared at them until feeling returned to my hand and I passed out from the pain.

I spent the day in a zombie state—sleeping, walking to the bathroom sink to soak my hand, returning to sleep. The ache in my fingers was dream proof that I existed as a functioning machine, and when I woke up to stay at dusk, I knew what I had to do. After removing the remaining plaster fragments from under my fingernails, I drove back to the womb to wait for the most perfect bodies it could give me.

Parked at the curb by the pink stucco building, I waited. At 7:00, Flower and Season left the apartment and hiked up to the Strip; at 8:19 Flower returned with a rodentlike hippie boy. The combination of the girl's fatuousness and the rodent's body flab spelled "no." I continued my surveillance.

Flower and her weasel consort left at 10:03, parting company at the corner. Season and a rail-thin man of about thirty passed Flower on her trek back up to the Whiskey, exchanging words. Season was the one I wanted in my triumvirate, but her skinny partner looked mean-spirited and consumptive. Impatient, and itchy from the long transit of no brain-movies, I stayed put.

Shortly after midnight, Season and her lover exited the apartment and walked south, away from the Strip. I realized then that the girls probably synchronized their arrivals and departures, and laid odds that Flower would be returning within ten minutes. My hand ached, and I willed the throbs to a low ebb by concentrating on the question that had plagued my dreams: Who was "Charlie"?

True to form, Flower rounded the corner a few minutes later. A large man in army fatigues was with her, and he carried himself with an authority that was anti-hippie, anti-counterculture, and purely masculine. Approaching the building, he took off his cap and smoothed his hair. It was a lustrous blond, and I knew he had to be Charlie.

Now my waiting was all shivers and tremors and tingles through the groin. Knowing Charlie would find a quick, violent coupling vulgar, I allowed for pre-sex mood-setting, then walked up to the door. With my heart thundering, I opened it and walked in.

The front room was pitch-dark, and I left the door ajar a few inches for light, then moved straight to the beaded curtain. I peered through, and candlelight framed him on top of her. I touched myself, but that part of me felt cold. My heart was going "ka-thud, ka-thud, ka-thud," and I knew that soon the lovers would hear it. Touching myself again, I felt not coldness, but *nothing*. I whispered, "Charlie," parted the curtains and walked to the bed. A breeze sent the light over entwined legs. I gasped and bent over and touched them.

"Oh God!"

"What the fu—"

I heard the words and moved backward; a light flashed on, and the legs I had been caressing kicked out at me. Then Charlie was pulling a sheet around himself, and all I could do was run.

I dived for the curtain, and a blow caught me in the back of the neck. Flower squealed, "Helter Skelter coming down!" and I fell to my knees. Then the front-room light went on, and a force around my neck uprooted me. I caught a topsy-turvy view of Tahiti and Japan via Pan American Airways, and billboards for the Jook Savages and Marmalade. I tried to run a defensive brain-movie, but my brains felt as though they were shooting out the top of my head. Charlie was screaming, "Fuck Fuck Fuck!"; then we were on the walk-way outside, and people from the adjoining apartments were staring out their windows at *me*.

With my neck being twisted off its axis, I kicked sidelong at the gargoyles; glass flew into a succession of stunned fáces. Screams and approaching sirens were ringing in my ears as Charlie dragged me downstairs, and the last thing I heard before blacking out was Flower singing an impromptu Beatles medley.

11.

The caress cost me close to a year of my life.

I was arrested and charged with one count of Breaking and Entering, and the pick gouger in my pocket earned me a second charge of Possession of Burglar's Tools. A voyeurism "beef" was pending, but my public defender told me that Uncle Walt Borchard talked the D.A. out of filing the charge—he did not want me to get a sex offender "jacket." On attorney's advice, I pleaded guilty at arraignment. My sentence: a year in the Los Angeles County Jail and three years formal probation. When the judge handed down the decree and asked me what I had to say for myself, I broke the pattern of silence/monosyllabic replies that I had maintained since the moment of my arrest. "I have nothing to say—yet," I said.

My "practical silence" had snapped on automatically, the moment the sheriffs snapped the handcuffs on my wrists and I learned that my assailant was not the phantom Charlie, but a man named Roger Dexter. The cops, prisoners and legal officers I dealt with between arrest and sentencing expected terseness and faraway stares, and my behavior at the West Hollywood substation did not ring as incongruous. I was also 6'3", 185, rawboned and strange, and the bullies in the tank had plenty of frailer "fish" to toy with. No one knew that I was terrified to within an inch of my life, and that my jailhouse protector was a comic-book villain.

Shroud Shifter's counsel blunted my nightmares, eased my memory of the moment when I touched flesh, and let me concentrate on surviving my sentence. Our dialogue was so constant that even while holding sustained physical silence, I felt hyper-verbal inwardly, with typefaced warnings imprinting themselves across my field of vision whenever I felt especially frightened:

Counting the "good time" and "work time" you will receive for working as a trusty, you have 9½ months in jail to endure. Your confreres will be stupid men and violent men prone to victimizing those weaker than they.

Therefore, you must utilize your outsize physicality without affecting a macho demeanor that will attract violence;

Therefore, you must never let your fellow inmates know that you are much more intelligent than they are, or that your own criminal tendencies derive from deeper needs and curiosities;

Therefore, you must utilize practical silence, and psychic invisibility, *and* a new, finely honed "protective invisibility"—assuming the personas of those you are with, *blending in until you are indistinguishable from your fellow inmates.*

Thus, mentally armed, I arrived at the L.A. "New" County Jail to serve my sentence. The structure itself, only recently completed, was a massive angularity of steel and glossy concrete, all painted blue-gray and orange, with long corridors inset with holding tanks and inmate "modules"—four-tiered cellhouses fronted by narrow catwalks. Escalators connected the six floors, each of them equivalent in height to a three-story building; the corridors ran the length of three football fields. The mess halls were the size of movie theatres, and the string of administrative offices was an eighth of a mile of steel-reinforced doorways. After a ten-hour stint of holding-tank waiting, skin-searching, lice-control spraying, blood-testing and more waiting, I was assigned with five others to a four-man cell to await trusty classification and my work assignment. With miles of trudging blue-gray/orange concrete behind me, and an accumulation of obscene conversations ringing in my ears, I stretched out on the bunk I had snatched from a pudgy Mexican youth and let overall impressions overtake me.

Containment was the word most summarily accurate, and I knew it would come from the concrete and steel that held me in, and from the impoverished minds of my keepers and fellow prisoners, and from the noise level of the air I breathed. And with Shroud Shifter beside me, I knew that my self-containment within that containment would be impenetrable.

I waited four days for trusty classification, learning jail nomenclature and sharpening my skill as a dissembler. Aside from "chow calls," I spent all my time in the cell, sleeping and listening to hyperbolized accounts of criminal and sexual exploits, participating in conversations only when asked direct questions. I began to get the impression that boredom overruled violence as the salient fact of jailhouse life, and that my greatest personal danger would come from laughing out loud at ridiculous tales told with straight faces.

So, when Gonzalez, the fat Mexican kid whose bunk I grabbed, opened a line of talk with his standard, "You talk about bonaroo pussy, man," I bit at my gums until chuckles were forestalled; when Willie Grover, aka Willie Muhammed 3X, came in with his standard, "Sheeeit! You talkin' pussy, you talkin' my language! I poked my ten-incher in more Brillo pads than you fuckin' seen!" I poked my fingers against the cell wall to stifle belly laughs. The other inmates—two white men named Ruley and Stinson and a Mexican named Martinez—played off Gonzalez and Grover conversationally, and I was soon able to determine the sex and crime sub-themes that would induce them to talk.

Thus, the first days of my formal sentence became a crash course in socializing under duress. When queried about my "beef," I said, "B and E. I was rippin' off pads in West Hollywood." When asked about my hand, still swollen from trying to dig a way out of my nightmares, I said, "I wasted this dude when he caught me in his crib." The nods I got when I spoke the words encouraged me; the appraising eyes that roamed my newly muscled body told me that none of my "cellies" could risk voicing disbelief. My criminal verisimilitude was holding.

And, while lying on my bunk pretending to read back issues of *Ebony* and *Jet*, I listened, picking up colloquialisms and etiquette information to inform my jailhouse pose with even greater authenticity.

My year sentence was called a "bullet"; the mess-hall slang for Salisbury steak, hot dogs and breakfast jelly was, respectively, "Gainesburgers," "donkey dicks" and "red death." Inmates awaiting sentencing and classification were called "blues," a reference to the denim uniform I was now wearing; an informant was a "snitch"; a homosexual was a "punk"; the deputy sheriffs who served as jailers were "bulls."

If an inmate offered you candy or cigarettes, refuse him immediately, because he wanted to "turn you out."

If a "fruit jockey" made a sexual advance toward you, "wail on his head," even if the "bulls" were right there, because if you didn't "put him straight," you would acquire a "fruit jacket" and be "hit on" by all the "boodie bandits" looking to travel up the "Hershey Highway";

Address the "bulls" as Mr._____ or Deputy _____, but never initiate conversations with them on matters not germane to your "khaki gig" or "righteous business";

Do not seek the friendship of blacks, or you would be considered a "nigger rigger" or "spook juke" and be subject to attack from the "Paddys" (whites), "Beaners" (Mexicans) and the "War Council" (whites and Mexicans who banded in emergencies to form a united front against blacks);

And always, always, "be frosty" and "hang tough."

On my third day in the cell I got a letter from Uncle Walt Borchard. My hands shook as I read it.

10/16/69

Dear Marty—

Your bust tears it, I guess. I didn't come to see you at the West L.A. Substation because the officer who called to tell me where you were also told me about

the burglar tool he found on you, and I'm no dummy—
I can put two and two together. I was the one who got
your sex beef cooled, because no 21-year-old kid should
have to go through life as a registered sex offender—
unless he hurt somebody, which apparently you
didn't—except me.

You could have talked to me, you know. Most kids
steal a few things, it's like a phase. But you pumped
me for burglary info and stole from me, and that cuts
it.

I cleaned out your pad, and I stored your stuff. I found
your bankbooks and your safe-deposit box slips and
keys, and I'll hold them until you get out. I don't know
where you got the money, and I don't care what's in
the boxes. The West L.A. Sheriffs impounded your car,
and it's not worth trying to reclaim—let them auction
it. When you come by to get your stuff, go to Mrs.
Lewis in #6—I don't want to see you, and she's got
everything in her closet.—Walt Borchard.

Finishing, I felt a brushed-steel door close on a long part
of my life. Another door opened, this one embossed with
dollar signs I had thought would be lost. Willie Muhammed
3X said, "You look happy, homeboy. Your bitch get some
sex shit past the censor?"

"My uncle died," I said.

"And you happy about that?"

"He left me six grand and some other goodies."

"Righteous, but he was your kin, and you happy?"

I threw the letter in the toilet and flushed it, then screwed
my face into my newly patented white-trash glare. "He was
a punk, and he got what he deserved."

After morning chow on my fourth day in the "blocks,"
the module jailer's voice came over the PA system: "Lopez,
Johnson, Plunkett, Willkie and Flores, roll it up for classification." The electrically operated cell door slid open, and
I joined the other men on the catwalk. A deputy appeared

moments later, and led us down a series of corridors to a small room with blue-gray cement walls. A photograph of Sheriff Peter J. Pitchess, encased in a plastic sheath, was the only wall adornment, and the room held no furnishings of any kind.

When the deputy locked the door on us and departed, my colleagues descended on the photo with crayons, and soon the sheriff of Los Angeles County had swastikas on his collar points, Frankenstein bolts on his neck and a giant phallus in his mouth. The four hooted at their artwork, then an electrically amplified voice called out, "Good morning, gentlemen. Classification time. You've got sixty seconds to wipe off Sheriff Pitchess, then we want Plunkett, Flores, Johnson, Willkie and Lopez at the inside door in that order."

Catcalls answered the ultimatum:

"I got sixty minutes with yo mama, punk!"

"Sheriff Pete too busy playin' with my pee-pee!"

"Power to the pee-pee!"

I laughed at the two-sided ritualism, then ambled over and stood by the inside door. Two inmates were rubbing at the picture with saliva-soaked handkerchiefs. Just when the sheriff was chaste again, the door opened and a uniformed deputy pointed me toward a row of cubicles, muttering, "The one on the end." I walked there, down a drab hallway with chin-up bars bolted to the wall.

A deputy was sitting behind a desk in the last cubicle. He pointed to a chair in front of him. When I sat down, he said, "Your full name is Martin Michael Plunkett?"

I wondered what kind of voice to assume. Seconds passed, and I decided to sound educated, in hope of getting a desk job. "Yes, sir," I said in my normal voice.

The deputy sighed. "Your first time in jail?"

"Yes, sir."

"Your first mistake, Plunkett. Don't call deputies whose names you don't know 'sir.' Other inmates consider that brownnosing."

"Right."

"That's better. Let me run down your vitals. We've got

you as 6'3", 185, D.O.B. 4/11/48, L.A. One count B and E, one count Possession of Burglar's Tools, even bullet, three years' formal probation, release date 7/14/70. Sound about right?"

"Yes."

"Okay, now the personal stuff. What's your occupation?"

"Librarian."

"How far did you go in school?"

I glanced at the papers the deputy was holding; instinct told me his information was scant. "I have a masters degree in library science."

The deputy drummed the tabletop with his fingers. "You've got a fucking masters degree at twenty-one?"

I chuckled self-effacingly. "From a small college in Oklahoma. They've got a special, accelerated masters program."

"Jesus, librarian-burglar. Only in L.A. Okay, Plunkett. Are you a homosexual?"

"No."

"Diabetic?"

"No."

"Epileptic?"

"No."

"Addicted to any mind-altering chemicals?"

"No."

"Are you taking any prescription medicines?"

"No."

"Are you an alcoholic?"

"No."

"Good. I am, and it's no fucking picnic." The deputy laughed, then said, "Now the twilight-zone stuff. Do you think there are conspiracies out to get you?"

"No."

"Do you think people laugh at you behind your back?"

"No."

"Do you hear voices when you're alone?"

"No."

"Do you ever see things that aren't really there?"

I bit my tongue to keep from laughing. "No."

Stretching his arms, the deputy said, "You're a paragon

of fucking sanity, but let's test your brain. What's ninety-seven and forty-one?"

Without hesitation, I said, "One thirty-eight."

"Go, Bookworm. One-eighteen and seventy-four?"

"One ninety-two."

"Two eighty-four and one sixty-six?"

"Four hundred fifty even."

"You musta been burglarizing adding machines. What's—"

Falsetto giggles erupted from somewhere in the row of cubicles. A high voice cooed, "I can play this guessing game just as good over in the Swish Tank at the Old County. I got sent there—"

The deputy rapped the table. "Pay attention, Brainboy. That's Lopez trying for the Queen's Tank; he thinks it's safer over there. Here's my change-up pitch. What's four and four?"

"I don't know," I said, smiling.

Smiling back, the deputy looked over his papers, then said, "One psych question I forgot. Are you prone to night sweats or nightmares?"

For what seemed like an eternity of split seconds, I was without limbs, the captive of nightmare flashbacks that I thought jail had contained. Finally Shroud Shifter was there, whispering, "*Slow and easy.*" "No," I said hoarsely.

The deputy said, "You're sweating now, but I'll chalk that up to first-timer's nerves. Last test. Go over to the bars and chin yourself as many times as you can."

I obeyed, attacking the bars, hoisting myself up-down, up-down, up-down, until I was drenched in day sweats that could only terminate in benevolent, dreamless exhaustion. When my muscles finally gave in and I fell to the floor, the deputy said, "Thirty-six. Anything over twenty is automatic Trash & Freight, so I gotta say you outsmarted yourself. Go to the holding room and wait; someone'll take you to the T.F. dock."

I got up and walked into the holding tank. The other inmates were there, embellishing Sheriff Pitchess with glasses and a Hitler mustache. The high-pitched voice I had heard in the cubicles trilled, "You sweaty hunk, aren't you cute!" and I felt a hand on my shoulder. I pivoted, and saw that Lopez was giving me a vamp look, while the others were sizing me up for my reaction.

I held back, feeling something sickly sweet and mawkish. Then I got a jolt of terror that felt like someone was sticking a live wire into my brain. I looked at the three appraising and accusing inmates, and they turned into mirror-faced Charlie before my eyes. Lopez cooed, "I really groove on sweat," and I hit him with my bad hand, then my good one, then bad-good, bad-good, bad-good until he was on the floor and spitting out teeth. I was zeroing in on his throat when the three inmates pulled me off and the classification deputy walked out, shook his head and said, "Lopez, you dumb shit, look what you've done now. Willkie, you take Plunkett to the Freight Dock; Johnson, you take Lopez to the Infirmary. You got a first-timer freebie, Plunkett. Don't do it again."

The inmates let me go, and Willkie gave me a gentle push out into the corridor. My vision was rimmed with red and black, and the throbbing in my hand felt like the restraining thread that kept me from exploding like a shrapnel bomb. Willkie smiled and said, "You're good."

Trash and Freight;
Listening;
Protective Invisibility.
The next six weeks of my sentence were spent juggling those pursuits. Assigned as a khaki trusty to the T&F detail, I worked the hardest job in the L.A. County jail system and received the rewards that came with it: a private cell, three meals a day from the officers' dining room, and weekends off, with the free run of the honor trusty's module—four tiers with ultrawide catwalks suitable for crap shooting, T.V. and card room, and a library filled with paperback Westerns and picture histories of Nazi Germany. The rewards were dubious, but, strangely, I came to love the work.

At 2:00 each morning, the module jailer awakened us individually, racking our cells one by one, then flashing a pen-

light in our eyes. I always snapped awake with a sense of relief.
Since beating up Lopez, my sleep had been 100% dreamless,
but the fear of nightmares was always just a half-step away,
and a quarter-step beyond that was the certainty that the
jail/nightmare combination would be horrific.

After head count on the bottom catwalk, we were fed
breakfast in the officers' dining room. A dietitian employed
by the county theorized that large men doing twelve-hour
shifts of heavy labor required a commensurate fuel intake,
and we were loaded up with huge trays of bacon, eggs,
overcooked steaks and potatoes drenched in a nauseating
gravy made up of flour, water and salt pork. My fellow
trusties reveled in their special menu, devouring the food
with the what-the-fuck panache of men determined to die
young; and, not wanting to seem different, I greedily "scarfed
up" along with them. And when we broke for lunch at 11:00,
I was hungry.

Because the work was nonstop lifting, hauling, stooping
and shoving. The jail was the distribution point for all cor-
rectional facilities within the county system, and every stitch
of its institutional linen hit the T&F dock before being
loaded into the trucks that would take it to its final destination. We did both the loading and unloading, and every
laundry bag we moved weighed at least a hundred pounds.
That part of the job was relatively easy and clean. Then,
after lunch, with our muscles burning and aching, and stu-
porous from thousands of more calories, the slaughterhouse
trucks pulled in.

Here I both worked and listened, and used my protective
invisibility to its greatest advantage.

The other inmates found the meat transfers revolting,
and mitigated their disgust by talking themselves through
it. It was understood among them to save their best stories
and crime schemes for the two hours or so we spent wres-
tling sides of beef and pork out of the trucks and into the
storage freezers some hundred and fifty yards from the dock.
With blood soaking my khakis, and fat and gristle sliding
beneath my hands, I took in tales of good sex and hilarious
sexual misadventures; I learned how to hot-wire cars and

procure a variety of fake ID's. I nodded and laughed along
as the stories were told, and since I always strained with
the heaviest pieces, no one seemed to notice that I had no
tales to tell.

Women, beds and fast cars;

Shoplifting techniques;

The going prices for dope;

Pornographic details on women once loved, but later de-
spised;

Wistful sighs over women still loved;

How to successfully exploit homosexuals for favors.

All this came to me while my body was pushed to its
limit, with the blood of dead animals trickling down my
pants. I knew that the stories I heard were now *my* stories,
a part of my memory, and that the ritual of strain/ache/
lift/blood/learn that gave them to me made them belong to
me more than to the men who had actually lived them. And
when the last slaughterhouse truck was unloaded, I always
lingered on the dock, letting the autumn Santa Anas warm
the crimson sheen on my body.

In a sense, Trash & Freight gave me my body.

My gym workouts had been the start, changing me from
skinny to rangy, but my first six weeks of T&F added bulk
and muscle definition, giving me a big man's symmetry. Constant flinging of thirty-pound laundry bags made my wrist
muscles bulge to twice their old size; stooping to lift the
hundred-fifty-pounders built a wedge of hard ripples along
my lower back. Hauling beef sides resulted in a thickening
of the chest and a cording at my shoulders, and my arms, continually pulling, tossing and lifting, hardened to the point
where a pin could not easily penetrate the muscle. During
laundry hauls, I surreptitiously scrutinized the other bodies
working beside me. All of them were strong, but beer bellies
and ugly barrel chests predominated. Mine was the most
nearly perfect, and by the time I was released it would be that
much closer to perfection.

After work and a long solitary shower, I would listen to
the men playing cards on the catwalk, then retire to my

cell and read the texts of the Nazi picture books. The subject matter did not interest me, but the juxtaposition of printed horror stories and shouts from the catwalk felt somehow reassuring. Then, after evening chow and lockup, I segued from observation and invisibility to rituals of affirmation.

When the cell doors were racked shut, I stripped nude and imagined a full-length mirror in front of the bars. I felt my body for signs of new muscle, and mentally collated both the day's practical criminal information and the sexual anecdotes I had heard. After a few minutes, other rituals made themselves heard—the creaking of bunk springs on either side of my cell told me that fantasies and touching were happening. Here I moved straight into the meat-hauling stories, assuming both gender roles alternately, using the name "Charlie" when I played the man. The process felt like usurping the memories of others, loading myself up with experiences I had never had in order to make myself more inviolate for not having had them. As the mattress squeaks surrounding me escalated, so did my recreations. Without touching myself, I always came in the role of "Charlie," staring through blackness at my own mirror image.

On December 2, I found out who "Charlie" really was, and my self-containment exploded into pieces.

Banner headlines of the *Times* and *Examiner* delivered the news: Charles Manson and four members of his "family" had been arrested and charged with the Tate-LaBianca murders. Manson—known to his followers as "Charlie"— ruled a "hippie commune" at the near-deserted Spahn Movie Ranch in the Valley, and presided over nightly dope and sex orgies. Statements made by the three female members of Manson's "death cadre" pointed to the killings having been perpetrated out of a desire to create social upheaval— an unrest that would ultimately lead to the Armageddon that Charlie called "Helter Skelter."

I was taking a break on the laundry dock when I read those first accounts, and I shook from head to toe as memories of my own recent past blipped across the newsprint. I *saw* the two buffoons in the restaurant, and *heard* one of them say, "They're recruiters for this guru guy Charlie, and they tell you the fuck bread is for 'The Family,' and you should come out to this ranch where they live"; Flower squealed, "Helter Skelter is coming down fast"; and Season described the man the *Examiner* labeled "an ex-con Svengali with mesmeric brown eyes" as "a wise man, a shaman, a healer and a metaphysician."

The T&F jailer called out, "Back to work, Plunkett." After reading a concluding paragraph that promised pictures of the "satanic cult savior" in the next edition, I obeyed. On the slaughterhouse dock that afternoon, I was incapable of assimilating anecdotes, and my body churned with only one thought: Charlie Manson had brown eyes, and so did I. Given that one identical point, would the resemblance grow or crumble?

The evening edition of the Los Angeles *Times* gave me my answer. Charles Manson was a thirty-four-year-old, flaccid, sunken-chested wimp barely over five feet tall, with long, greasy-looking hair and a scraggly beard. I felt relieved and disappointed as I studied the photographs of him, and I could not place the reason for my ambivalence. The feature article on Manson's background clarified my feelings only slightly—he was an ex-convict with previous convictions for pimping, forgery, narcotics possession and car theft, and he had spent over half his life in various prisons. This made me feel only contempt—one jail tour, exploited for outside-of-society learning skills, could be considered acceptable; a series of them pointed to self-destructive institutionalization. I began to wonder where this man would take me.

For a week he took me on a roller-coaster ride of frustration and self-analysis.

Manson became the talk of the jail, and the T&F trusties were divided in their opinions, some considering him a "stone psycho," others admiring his hold over women and his dope-and-violence life-style. I stayed out of the discussions, listening to them for what they said about the participants, but trying to limit my Manson intake only to the facts I could glean from the media. Putting aside the expressions

of outrage that bracketed everything written about Charlie
and his family, I composed a treatise that seemed factually
sound:

Charlie was a street-smart manipulator of directionless
young people, a good dope scrounger, well-versed in rock
and roll, science-fiction, religious thought and the plethora
of social movements impressionable youths were susceptible to, and, obviously, he had evolved his own ethos from
them—one that was seductive to rootless kids. That was
impressive.

Yet, as a criminal he was a complete bungler, trusting
people who ultimately informed on him;

Yet, when interviewed, he came across as a mindlessly
sloganeering psychotic;

But, he had created a fiefdom that revolved around his
most extreme sexual fantasies; *but* people had murdered
at his command; *but* he had the power to usurp my late-
night mirror rituals, transmogrifying them into agonizing
question-and-answer sessions.

Was there some dark cosmic reason why you crossed this
man's path?

His sexual power resulted in *your* one aborted coupling
and thence a year in jail. Does that mean something hideous?

Intellectually and physically, you are capable of snapping him like a twig, but he was on the cover of *Life*
magazine while you haul laundry bags as a criminal nonentity. What does that fact bode for your future?

I knew those questions were unanswerable, rendered as
such by my bottom-line sense of powerlessness. I bludgeoned the line as best I could, shutting down all thoughts
featuring Charlie and me as the symbiotic twins of celebrity
and failure by hauling heavier and heavier loads on the
dock, then doing hours of calisthenics in my cell, creating
my own world of physical primacy and exhaustion. But that
stratagem was always undercut by Manson headlines, Manson stories, Manson gossip and speculation. Trusties talked
about Charlie on the dock, and I almost jumped out of my
skin; a T.V. documentary on "The Family" featured inter-

viows with Season and Flower, and I felt like ripping the
set off the catwalk wall. Then, his grand jury and arraignment proceedings completed, the "Hippie Satan" was transferred to the High Power Tank at New County, and we were
living under the same roof.

I knew we were converging; that fate was planning a
rendezvous, and that all I had to do was continue my present
course and my questions would be answered by the mirror
man himself. So I wrestled super loads on the dock, knowing
it was fear and doubt driving me; I lay on my bunk after
work, worried that the body I was achieving would ruin my
psychic invisibility, that I would be singled out for the rest
of my life as a brick shithouse for other men to test themselves on. I began to perceive my dilemma as visibility or
invisibility/screaming selfhood or the subtle power of an-
onymity. The pluses and minuses equaled out on both sides,
made all the more cogent by knowing that my destiny was
uniquely different and bold. Although I had never avowed
a belief in God, I began to pray every night for him to get
me to Charlie, so I could confront his brown eyes and see
what they boded for mine.

The road to Manson started on a rainy Wednesday morning a week after he transferred into High Power. I was
lugging cartons of canned goods from the dock over to a
protective overhang when I heard, "Catch, showboat!" and
caught a crate of lettuce square in the back. The blow
stunned me and dropped me to my knees; I heard shouts of
"Grandstanding motherfucker!" and "Come on, muscle-
man!" Then, getting to my feet, I picked up a distant echo
from Flower and Season's fuck pad: "Lock, load and fire
between their eyes."

From my knees I assumed a sprinter's crouch, then
pushed forward and ran head-on into my accusers. Startled,
the men made no move to separate. I hit them like a
pile driver, and when I saw a flabby bicep directly in front
of my eyes, I bit it, swallowing the small piece of flesh I
was able to tear off.

Now the group dispersed, and my own momentum carried me back to the ground. I got up again and whirled

around, seeing a group of outsize men standing shock-stilled, with amazement on their faces. Holding my ground, I listened, picking out whispers: "He bit me," "...fucking Dracula," "Not me, man!" Then the T&F jailer walked over. My point made, I let myself be handcuffed and led back to my cell.

I was given five days' solitary confinement in the Adjustment Module—a row of one-man cells with no bunks and only a bucket to urinate and defecate in. No reading material was allowed, and nourishment was six slices of bread and three cups of water per day. If the jailers considered the Spartan accommodations to be a hardship, they were wrong; the decreased caloric intake purged my body, and the dark eight-by-five crawl space was the perfect habitat for the perfectly blank mind I willed for the length of my stay. When my cell was unlocked and I was walked out to my new "home"—the custodial trusties module—I felt relaxed and calm. Assigned to a cell with three other men, I was told my job: push a broom up and down the cellhouse catwalks ten hours a day, six days a week. I had only one question: "Do I ever sweep out High Power?"

"Sooner or later," the module jailer said.

It was somewhere between the two; indeterminate hundreds of hours and thousands of catwalks and corridors down the line, with what felt like millions of miles of pushing my broom behind me—always blank-minded, with the mirror man's questions sealed off, but ready to be hurled at a second's notice. I don't even remember what day it was, but when the custodial detail jailer said, "Plunkett to High Power," I grabbed my broom and dustpan and walked there on automatic pilot, stopping only to read the inmate roster at the front of the module.

And there it was in black and white: Manson, Charles, cell A-11, and the California Penal Code number for First-Degree Murder—187 P.C.—next to his name in red.

The jailer racked the gate, and I entered the A-tier catwalk and looked down it, seeing the narrow-barred enclosures of one-man security cells. No noise was coming from within them, and I counted eleven over and marked the point in my mind. Then, as if I had all the time in the world, I pushed my broom down the catwalk, pivoted and said to the bars of A-11, "Hello, Charlie."

Darkness seemed to throb inside the cell; I thought briefly that the mirror man was gone. I was about to grab the bars and strain my eyes to see in when a soft tenor voice sang, "You tell me it's the in-stit-tu-tion, we-el-el, you know, you better free your mind instead." There was a pause, then the voice said, "I can see you, but you can't see me. You believe that song's message, trusty?"

I laid my broom against the bars and squinted into the cell; all I could see was a shape on the bunk. "Yes, and I figured it out a long time before the Beatles did."

Charles Manson snorted. "You just think you did. Saint John and Saint Paul got it from me, you got it from them. Cause and effect, karma coming back to roost. Now we're both here. You groove the energy?"

I snorted back. "It's a convenient interpretation. Tell me about Helter Skelter."

Manson said, "Listen to the White Album and read your Bible. It's all there."

The shape on the bunk took form; Charlie looked frail and old. *"Tell me about Helter Skelter."*

Manson laughed. It was a liquid sound, as if the hippie Satan were expelling drool. "You, me, God's outcasts, on Harleys and dune buggies. The niggers rising up. The land reverting to me."

"In your padded cell?"

A dry chuckle this time. "Ye men of little faith. If you knew the Beatles' message, you wouldn't be here."

"You're here."

"My karma, trusty. My energy directing me to the people who need to hear my message most."

From a deep part of my Q. & A. vault a question took hold, and before I could revert to verbal sparring, I asked it. "What's it like to kill somebody?"

Manson got up and walked over to the bars. I saw that he came up to just below my shoulders, and that his "mesmeric" brown eyes had the sheen of the far-gone psychotic.

It would be easy to pluck them out and squash them into goo on the catwalk floor. "I never killed nobody," Charlie said. "I was framed by the Establishment."

"By the Institution?"

"That's right."

"Then use your free mind to break out of here."

Manson laughed. "Jail's my karma. Teaching know-nothing jailhouse cynics is my energy. Tell me, unbeliever, what do you know?"

I squatted so that my eyes and the eyes of the sawed-off Satan were at the same level. Shroud Shifter jumped into my mind, making pantomime motions that spelled out *SEIZE THIS MOMENT*. With the most quintessentially cool voice I had ever willed, I said, "I know that people kill and take what they want and don't get caught; and if they do get caught, they don't rationalize their failure with mystical jive talk to make themselves look big; and they don't blame society, because they had free will from the gate. And I know that there are people who kill by themselves, who don't send doped-out hippie girls to do what they're afraid of. I know that real freedom is when you do it all yourself and it's so good that you never have to tell anyone about it."

Charlie hissed, "Pig," and spat in my face. I let the spittle settle, astounded by my eloquence, which had seemed to spring from deep nowhere of its own volition—as if that statement, not Manson's answers to my questions, was what I had been waiting for with my blank mind these past weeks.

When I remained immobile, saliva dripping off my chin, Charlie began singing: "Hey Jude, don't make it bad, let Helter Skelter make it be-et-ter. Remember, make the pigs get out of your mind—"

Shroud Shifter interrupted the music by superimposing *CASTRATE HIM* across Charlie's forehead. I reached for a deep draft of cool and said, "I fucked Flower and Season at your place by the Strip. They were lousy fucks and even worse recruiters, and they used to laugh about your little one-inch cricket dick."

Manson hurled himself at the bars and started screaming; I picked up my broom and began sweeping my way

down the catwalk. Hearing clapping on the tier above
me, I looked up. A group of deputies were applauding my
performance.

A pleasant weight embraced me in the following weeks.
I knew it came from my confrontations with the loading-
dock trusties and the cut-rate Satan, and it felt like a reprise
of the old invisibility. My bodybuilding obsession started to
feel callow; running brain-movies palled before the simple
scrutiny of what was going on around me. My dreamless
sleep continued, and as my release date approached I started
looking forward to gaming probation officers, employers
and my daily parade of workaday acquaintances. A potent
notion simmered on the back burner of my brain: I could
live anonymously and on the cheap, without nightmares
and dangerous drives, and possess my own mesmeric power.

Charles Manson's power over me diminished and fizzled
out, until his jailhouse celebrity was nothing worse than a
nuisance, like the swirl of a mosquito who deftly avoids
squashing. The eloquence of my attack on him faded also—
until, three weeks before kick-out, my fictitious masters
degree was noted, and I was assigned to the library, with
one specific task: chronologically file forty large cartons of
news magazines recently donated to the L.A. County jail
system.

The cartons contained issues of *Time, Life* and *Newsweek*
going back to the forties. I was left alone in a storage cellar
with them for eight hours a day, with a bag of sandwiches,
a Thermos of coffee and a Swiss Army knife for cutting
cardboard and twine. The job was peacefully methodical
until I hit a spate of recent issues featuring articles on
Satanic Charlie, and read non-hyperbolic prose that sum-
marized him as awesome.

I put those issues aside, enraged that high-paid writers
could be duped by a pseudo-mystic drool case. With the
Manson prose stuffed into a mildewed corner of the cellar,
I abandoned my collating job for five days running, spending my work time reading through the old magazines for
accounts of stupid killers who were ultimately caught, con-

victed and squashed like bugs. I read only the stories on
L.A.–area killers; and as I recognized street names and
locations, I felt the murderers' self-destructive pathology
enter me and become utter disdain for the limelight. Then,
when my history of fatuous violence extended back to 1941,
I got out my knife.

Juanita "Duchess" Spinelli, the murderous leader of a
robbery gang, hanged at San Quentin, 11/21/41—slash,
slash. Otto Stephen Wilson, triple–woman slayer, gassed at
Quentin, 10/18/46—slash, slash, slash—one for each victim.
Jack Santo, Emmett Perkins and Barbara Graham, immor-
talized in the movie "I Want to Live," but fried for their bungled robbery-murders on 6/3/55—multiple slashes. Donald
Keith Bashor, burglar–bludgeon killer who plied his trade
just east of my old neighborhood, executed 10/14/57—stab,
gouge, and rip for being so stupid so close to me. Harvey Murray Glatman, the sadistic T.V. repairman who "offed" three
women after photographing them bound and gagged in ag-
ony—"snuffed" by the state on 8/18/59—slashes of contempt
for his whimpering on the way to the gas chamber. Stephen
Nash, the toothless drifter and self-described "King of Killers," terminated a week after Glatman on 8/25/59—gentle
knife thrusts for spitting at the chaplain and sucking in the
cyanide gas with a grin. Elizabeth Duncan, who hired winos
Augustine Baldonado and Luis Moya to kill her son's wife,
earning all three of them trips to San Quentin's green room
on 5/11/62—numerous page-rippings for the drunken, par-
simonious unprofessionalism of the job.

And on and on up to Charlie Manson, fate as yet un-
decided, but limited to two choices: the gas chamber or the
rubber room at Atascadero—stab, slash, gash, rip, and
urinate on his face beaming up from *Newsweek*.

When the mound of paper was reduced to confetti, I buried it behind some abandoned milk cartons and thought of
how sweet and peaceful my anonymous life would be.

12.

Over the next four years I metamorphosed into an object.

I became a depository for images; a memory bank. In essence, 1970–74 were my years of interpreting the human scene around me, but not fantasizing it into sexually gratifying variations. I know today that that hellishly stringent restraint is what finally caused me to burst.

I was released from jail on July 14, 1970, and went immediately to Uncle Walt Borchard's apartment building and picked up my bankbook and safe-deposit box keys. The woman Borchard left my belongings with tried to hand me a big bundle of old clothes, but I smelled defeat clinging to them and said, "No."

With interest, my savings account held a balance of $6,318.59, and my safety-box swag was still intact. I withdrew three thousand dollars in cash and the contents of all three boxes. From there it was only a hop, skip and jump to Cosmo Veitch's pad off the Boulevard. I sold Cosmo my entire stash of watches, jewelry and credit cards for $1,500, and from there it was just a simple hop to a Ford dealership on Cahuenga and a "Summer Clearance Sale" on used vans. I purchased a '68 Econoline, steel gray in color, paid $3,200 cash for it, and drove to West L.A. to look for a safe, innocuous place to live.

I found an apartment on a quiet side street south of Westwood Village, and paid six months' rent in advance. The building was mostly inhabited by older people, and my three-room dwelling was cool and painted a restful gray similar in shade to my van. All that remained to be accom-

84

plished in my return to society was to report to my probation
officer and get a job.

My P.O. was a woman named Elizabeth Trent. She was
stylishly liberal, and gushed instant empathy as she laid
down the terms of my probation: don't steal, don't fraternize
with criminals, don't use drugs, hold down steady employment and report to her in person once a month. Aside from
that, she told me to "party hearty," "reap good karma" and
"call if you need anything." Leaving her office after our
initial conference, I pegged the woman as a post-hippie with
man trouble, someone who meddled good-naturedly in the
affairs of others to alleviate her own personal turmoil. Probation would be easy.

Employment was even easier than my one hour a month
making nice with Liz Trent. From '70 to '74 I held down a
series of menial jobs undertaken from one criterion: their
potential to keep me mentally aroused without fantasy
adornments. I was, by turns:

A deliveryman for "Pizza Soopreem," my territory a West
Hollywood area rife with unemployed artists, writers and
actors who sent out for pizza and beer 24 hours a day; night
manager of a pornographic bookstore across the street from
the notorious open-all-night Hollywood Ranch Market;
dishwasher at a singles bar/restaurant in Manhattan Beach;
shipping clerk at a mail-order house specializing in bondage
attire.

All the jobs allowed me to observe lives caught off guard
in small moments of flux. While working Pizza Soopreem,
pizza orderers of both genders came to the door nude; and,
occasionally, impoverished ones offered themselves to me
for the tab. My gig at Porno Villa was a doctoral degree in
the machinations of sexual guilt and self-loathing—the men
who purchased beaver and fuck-and-suck books were pitiful
negative exemplars of the strength to be gained from total
abstinence.

Big Daddy's Disco was "Candid Camera" gone x-rated
and tragicomic. The kitchen boss had bored a hole through
the dish-room wall into the ladies powder room, and when
the *Playboy* calendar that covered it was lifted, you had a

squint oyed view of the makeup mirror and one toilet stall.
The whole kitchen crew would take turns watching and
giggling, but I always waited until they went home at 1:00
A.M. and I was left alone to clean up. Then I watched and
listened; then I saw an array of young women tingle at the
thought of coming assignations or cry at the mirror after
a long night of barside rejections. Women discussed men in
explicit terms, and I picked up their stylized lexicon; they
snorted cocaine to give themselves courage, then smoothed
the facial hollows it caused with powder. With one eye
through the wall I became the mental chronicler of small-
scale desperation, and it felt like tamping down my self-
containment with a velvet hammer.

I was an object of assimilation and interpretation, and
I coveted the touch of other sleek objects. Hearkening back
to Shroud Shifter and my youth, I filled my apartment with
brushed steel—pencil sharpeners and siding samples and
cookery and Swiss Army knives with sharp blades that I
brushed myself with industrial steel wool. As the years
passed, my collection of knives grew, until I possessed the
entire Swiss Army catalog, mounted on my living-room
wall at angles that I changed on whim. Then I became
interested in guns.

But *hand*guns were what I desired, and as a convicted
felon I was forbidden by law to own them. They were also
expensive—more so if illegally procured—and the thought
of violating my precious invisibility to obtain one was
frightening, a potential apostasy that I knew would lead
me back to all my old dangerous drives.

I had just begun work at Leather N' Lace, the bondage
mail-order house, when the gun infatuation hit me. My job
entailed opening the incoming envelopes containing checks
and orders for whips, chains, dog collars, dildoes, dungeon
equipment and the like, logging the orders while the checks
cleared, then shipping them out when the front office gave
the word. The mail room was packed to the rafters with perverse goodies made in Tijuana, most of the devices constructed out of cheap black leather and low-grade alloy metal.
The ugly objects glared at me all day, and to keep fantasies

at bay I put my mind to the task of turning them into something useful. No ideas took hold, and I used up my spare time
reading handgun catalogs. The longing I felt perusing glossy
pictures of Colts and Smith & Wessons and Rugers was awful,
compounded by how the sex fools were constantly sending
cash in their envelopes, the heft of coins a dead giveaway. I
could steal the money, and the thefts would be attributed to
the post office; I could obtain fake ID from criminal sources
and use the stolen money to buy a big magnum or .45 auto;
or I could steal more money and buy a street weapon. The
more I thought about it, the more it moved me—and the more
frightened I got.

So I did nothing, and nothing did me back.

Everywhere I went, ugly objects stared me down. When
I took long walks at night, corrugated metal trash cans
screamed, "Coward!"; neon signs blipped the penal code
numbers of enticing offenses. It was as if my most sup-
pressed brain area had suddenly developed the ability to
run movies without my consent.

So I continued to do nothing, and nothing continued to
do me back.

I kept my job at Leather N' Lace, and resisted the desire
to fantasize and steal incoming cash. In March of '74 my
probationary term ended, and Liz Trent cut me loose with
the admonishment, "Find something you really like, and
do it really well." Those words gave me a temporary "something" that quickly backfired.

I was shipping orders the following day when I noticed
the tubing on Leather N' Lace catalog item #114—"Anal
Annie's Love Bench." I saw that the circumference was
slightly larger than the muzzle specification of an S&W
magnum I was particularly fond of, and remembered a jail
rap on the construction of homemade silencers. Knowing it
was a quasi-legal antidote to *nothing,* I bought the necessary tools and did it "really well."

A hacksaw, a mound of metal fiber used for air-
conditioning insulation, a metal pipe threader and a short
length of iron tubing joined seven inches of "Anal Annie"
in my living room, and with my Swiss Army knives I went

to work. First, I sawed and cut and assembled the pieces;
then, with an "exact replica" toy magnum as my guideline,
I cut thread for the muzzle. When I saw that I had a snug
fit, I crimped large wads of fiber into the length of tubing,
then rammed the smaller iron "bullet passage" straight
through the middle of it. The passage would, I judged, carry
a .357 hollow point with 1/32 of an inch to spare, causing
it to "tumble" toward its target. With the basic assembly
completed, I held the silencer to the floor and hammered
the front of the tubing around the end of the bullet passage
until only a little hole protruded.

It was the most beautiful object I had ever seen.

But with that "something" behind me, "nothing" hit
harder and harder, reminding me that without the magnum
my silencer was no more than a paperweight. I carried it
with me as a talisman on late-night walks; and now if trash
cans glared at me I kicked them over; and if parked cars
offended me with their garish colors I used the silencer to
cut S.S. on their sides. It was callow rebelliousness and
hollow rage, but holding that hand-fashioned piece of cheap
metal was the only thing that kept the hallucinogenic 187
P.C.'s from devouring me.

I came to believe that a change of locale would make
things better. L.A.'s very familiarity was dangerous, and if
I could escape its web of nostalgia and self-destructive temp-
tation, then I would be safe. Living in a different city would
infuse me with caution and quash the criminal fantasies
that were attempting to destroy me. I made up my mind to
get out, setting a strict departure deadline three weeks in
the future—April 12—the day after my twenty-sixth birthday.

The time passed quickly. I quit my job, liquidated my
bank account and loaded my van with my clothes, toilet
articles, and talisman/silencer, leaving my other steel objects behind to symbolize old ties being broken. The loss of
my knives hurt and warmed at the same time—I knew it
was a conscious sacrifice aimed at avoiding catastrophe.

On my birthday night I took a farewell walk through
my neighborhood. No objects glared at me, and no weird

numbers flashed before my eyes. Only thunder and rain hit, drenching me to the bone. Looking for a place to keep dry, I noticed the neon sign in front of the Nuart Theatre: "Save the Seals."

I ran over. The lobby was deserted, so I headed for the men's room to get some paper towels. I had my hand on the door when I heard a high keening sound issue from the theatre proper. I forgot about drying myself and walked straight toward it.

Seals were being beaten to death on the screen. Their yelps were what I had heard, and now they were joined with sobs from the audience. The sound was thrilling, but the sight was ugly and pathetic, so I closed my eyes. The absence of sight brought the taste of blood—the blood of every body I had ever desired. Soon I was sobbing, and the taste deepened until the yelps were replaced by music. I opened my eyes, and people were filing past me, giving out looks of sympathy and commiseration. My shoulders were patted and my hands were touched—as if I were one of them. None of the people knew that the origin of my tears was in joy.

II

SAN FRANCISCO

13.

The city I chose was San Francisco, and my only reason for doing so was that its topography was antithetical to L.A.'s. Terraced hillsides and Victorian houses would not pulse with hidden messages from my past, and the city's relative lack of neon would mean diminished penal-code hallucinations. Los Angeles had formed me and owned me and driven me out; San Francisco was the opportunity to nullify my personal history and forge new drives in memory-free surroundings.

So, with the simple traversing of 430 miles, I went from increasingly lucid indicators of my destiny to an amnesia made easy by San Francisco's newness. I rented an apartment on 26th and Geary in the Richmond District, wiping out the bulk of my savings furnishing it with innocuous non-steel furniture and pastoral framed prints. The exigencies of behaving like so-called normal people were softly satisfying, and I began to think I could play the role for a long, long time.

Deciding to give myself a week before looking for work, I explored the city. Quaintness, oldness and prettiness were manifest, and a sense of grace seemed to imbue the people I saw on the street—they were, on the average, far more attractive than L.A. inhabitants, with a greater ethnic diversity, and a fairly large number of them were traffic-stopping blonds.

I didn't stop for them, though; an unseen weight pushed my foot onto the accelerator when those comely reminders of my past appeared. It was solid evidence that my benign amnesia was holding. Other signs—dreams filled with pastel colors, quiet nighttime walks, the loss of my gun obsession—added up to the magically simple word *happiness*.

And continued happiness required money. My week of tranquility had eaten up all but two hundred dollars of my funds, and I needed the quick replenishment of a weekly paycheck. On my eighth morning in San Francisco I got out the Yellow Pages and looked for employment agencies with casual labor pools. I found a half-dozen of them listed, all on the same block of South Mission. I drove there, anxious to carve another notch on my serenity.

It was a skid-row block, the kind that in Los Angeles had always depressed me. But here the seediness seemed almost charming, and as I locked my van and consulted my agency list, I got a feeling of belonging. Propelled by it, I pushed through a door marked "Mighty-Man Job Shop" and walked up to a paper-littered front counter.

A young woman with shoulder-length black hair looked up from her desk and smiled at me, then said, "You're the man from Orinda who wanted three slaves—oops—I mean Mighty-Men to do yard work, right?" She consulted some forms in front of her and added, "Eddington, right? You said you'd send your chauffeur to pick the winos—I mean workers—up?"

Caught off guard by her directness, I blurted, "What?"

She smiled at my befuddlement. "You mean you're not Eddington, but you need slaves?"

I looked into her eyes and saw that she was probably high. "No, I—"

"Then you came to ask me for a date?"

I realized I was being flirted with. I got a hollow "nothing" feeling, and reflexively grasped for Shroud Shifter's counsel, then snapped to the fact that this was San Francisco, not L.A., and S.S. was supposed to be obsolescent. "I'm new in town," I said. "I need work, and I saw your ad in the Yellow Pages."

The woman said, "God, I'm sorry, it's just that you're so neatly dressed, and...well...mostly the guys we get are boozehounds and dopers, you know, looking for a few bucks to get bombed on. Are you crashing here on the Row?"

"I've got an apartment," I said.

She looked surprised. "Where?"

"Twenty-sixth and Geary."

Now she looked astonished. "God, my boyfriend lives on that block. Listen, you look sort of middle-class, so I'll hip you to something. We pay our guys minimum wage for menial stuff like passing out handbills, unloading non-union trucks, that kind of thing. Our basic scam is that we pay in cash at the end of the day. That way, the slaves blow their money on wine and dope every night and come back the next morning. If you can afford to live in the Richmond, you *can't* afford to work out of here."

Now I was astonished—I was starting to like the woman. "I spent my savings moving in; now I need to find work so I can keep the place."

"Wow, a real working man in a bind." The woman took a cigarette from the pack on her desk, lit it and smoked in silence for long moments. Finally she snapped her fingers and walked to the counter. Leaning forward conspiratorially so that her hair brushed my face, she said, "Go over to the S.F. State campus and check out the bulletin board outside the student employment office. They've got lots of jobs listed for decent bucks. Just rip off the cards for the jobs you're interested in, call the numbers and tell them you're a grad student who goes to school at night so you can work full-time. You're big and you look smart, so you should get hired. Got it?"

I said, "Got it," and drew away from the cascade of hair. The woman straightened up and smiled, and I knew that she had relished our contact. Holding out her hand, she said, "I'm Jill, by the way."

Intending a perfunctory shake, but taking the hand gently, I said, "I'm Martin."

"Good luck, Martin."

"Th-thank you for your help."

* * *

Consciously shutting down the delicacies of the exchange, I followed the woman's advice and drove to the San Francisco State campus. The bulletin board she had mentioned was covered with cards offering work, and I deviated from her plan only by memorizing the jobs and phone numbers rather than stealing the information. From a pay phone I called the advertisers, getting three no-answers for the clerical openings, and a brusque male "Yes" for the manual labor card.

"I'm calling about the job you posted at S.F. State," I said.

"Are you a full-time student?" the voice asked.

"I'm a night grad student."

"Are you husky? Pardon my French, but this is no job for a candy-ass."

"I'm six-three, two hundred and strong. What exactly do I have to do?"

"Have you got transportation?"

"Yes. What—"

"I'm a real-estate developer in Sausalito. I need a husky kid to clear tree stumps out of my new site. It's tough work, but the pay is a five-spot an hour, off the books, with no deductions. What's your name?"

"Martin Plunkett."

"Okay, Marty, I'm Sol Slotnick. You want the job?"

"Yes."

"Can you meet my foreman tomorrow? In Sausalito?"

"Yes."

"Okay, then write this down: Over the Golden Gate, off the highway at exit four, right turn, left turn at Wolverton Road. You'll see a big field with signs posted—Sherlock Homes, a logo with the detective guy. Tomorrow at eight. Got it?"

"Yes."

"A-okay. You're gonna need tools, an ax and a scythe, but I'll supp—"

I interrupted my new employer. "I'll supply my own tools, Mr. Slotnick."

"Do your own thing, huh? Okay, kid, good luck."

That night I devastated my remaining money. At an army surplus store I bought khaki work pants and shirt, a pair of waterproof hiking boots, a webbed cartridge belt and my first instruments of brushed-steel utility since my burglar's tools years before: one short-handled ax, one long-handled ax and one heavy-duty gardener's scythe. The ax heads were coated with transparent Teflon, and guaranteed to be "self-sharpening"—the more you used them, the sharper they were supposed to get. It sounded too good to be true, so I bought a sharpening stone to back up the claim.

The next day I drove across the Golden Gate Bridge to the "Sherlock Homes" site. It was a huge clearing overgrown with brush and dotted with tree stumps, surrounded on all sides by thick pine forest—months of work for one man. The foreman told me that Mr. Slotnick wanted the job completed by September 10, when the construction crew was scheduled to begin laying the foundations, and if I was lucky and the environmentalists didn't fuck things up, I could get an additional job chopping down trees across the highway at the proposed site of Slotnick's "Singles Paradise" tract. After explaining that all I had to do was uproot every tree stump on the property and chop down all the brush and let it lie for the bulldozers, the man pointed to the tools affixed to my belt and said, "You look like a pro, so I won't be coming around to check on you. Payday is every Friday at five, here." Shaking my hand, he left me alone with nature.

And nature, even though I was conspiring against her, gave me four and a half uninterrupted months of exhilarating beauty and blessedly mindless work.

I swung and hacked with my axes and scythe from April through August, eight hours a day, seven days a week, oblivious to heat waves and torrential rain. Shock waves pulsed through my body as I worked, and I felt myself getting stronger and stronger, but I never worried about developing attention-attracting muscles as I had in jail, because the scent of hay and ripped wood protected me, the pines enveloped me, and when I chopped with my eyes closed I saw pretty soft colors, shades that got darker the harder

I swung, but still remained kind and gentle in my mind. Completely exhausted at the end of each day, the colors held at the corner of my vision as I drove home, ate dinner and fell immediately into deep sleep.

I was parking my van outside my apartment one night in early September when I heard, "Martin! Hi!" The words didn't fully register at first—no one had addressed me by name in months, and I was exhausted from an especially long day's work and hungry for food and sleep. Then the voice repeated itself—"Hi, Martin!"—and I looked across the street and saw a pretty woman with long black hair. The hair, backlighted by a streetlamp, drew me like a magnet, and I walked over to her.

She was standing on the sidewalk with a man, and they were weaving very slightly, as if tipsy. It took me a few seconds, but finally an image of hair brushing my face gave me the woman's name. Shroud Shifter, appearing out of nowhere, hissed, *BE NICE*. "Hello, Jill," I said. "Nice to see you."

Jill giggled and reached for her companion's arm. "We're really zonked. Did you get a job? You must have, you've still got the place."

Shroud Shifter was waving a conductor's baton, whispering something I couldn't hear. "Yes, I followed your advice. It worked, and I've been working ever since."

Jill said, "Great. Steve, this is Martin; Martin, this is Steve."

I turned my attention to the boyfriend, a surly type with ridiculous muttonchop sideburns. S.S. was saying *BE NICE BE NICE BE NICE*. I said, "Hey, Steve, what's happenin'," and stuck out my hand hippie-style. Steve said, "What's happenin', man," and gave me a counterculture bonecrusher. I winced in mock pain, and Jill laughed. "Steve's an airline mechanic, and he's really strong. You want to come up for a drink or something?"

At the "or something," S.S. waggled his eyebrows. I said, "Right on," and Jill got between her boyfriend and me and took our arms, saying in a stage whisper, "I am so stoned." Her hand on my elbow felt alternately hot and cold and soft and hard, but the touching wasn't the least scary. We walked three abreast halfway down the block and up the steps of a Victorian four flat, and Steve unlocked the door and flipped on a light switch. Jill dropped my arm and said, "There's something Stevie's been after me to do for a long time, and now I'm just stoned enough to do it." She skipped through the living room, and my eyes automatically circled the four walls.

Airline posters were crookedly Scotch-Taped along them, and of all the countries represented, Tahiti and Japan jumped out at me, as if I had once visited them. Shutting the door, Steve said, "I been all these places at least twice. You work for Pan-Am, you get two free trips a year, bring your chick if you want." He pointed to the ax clipped to my belt. "You a carpenter?"

I said, "I'm a tree surgeon," and surveyed the room again, wondering why places I had never seen seemed so familiar. Steve was giving me a strange look, so to put him at ease I added, "Jill got me my job. I was broke when I first landed in town, and I hit Mighty-Man looking for a gig. Jill sent me down to the S.F. State employment office."

Steve said, "Jill's the friendly type," and S.S. sent me a series of snapshots: Jill flirting and sleeping with other men, but always returning to Steve, who was grateful to have her back and would take her on long reconciliation trips to exotic places, courtesy of his employer; Steve brooding over being treated like a doormat, getting drunk with his mechanic buddies and railing against Jill, but always calling her from the bar to tell her he'd be late.

"What are you drinkin', man?"

Steve's voice snapped me out of the movie he had been co-starring in. "You got a beer?" I said.

"Does a bear shit in the woods? Come on, let's hit the fridge."

I followed Steve into a small kitchen. More airline posters were taped to the walls, but the grease-coated pictures of Paris and the Bavarian Alps did not dig at my memory. Steve caught my look again, and said, "You're scopin' them posters like a man who needs a vacation." He opened the refrigerator and pulled out two cans of beer. When he handed me one, I said, "Yeah, Tahiti or Japan, maybe."

Popping his can, Steve said, "Those places suck. The food sucks, and the Japs look like the slopes in 'Nam." He guzzled beer and belched, then laughed. "Coors, breakfast of champions. We had the Coors Olympics at work last year. Guy who won drank four six-packs, held it in for two hours, then filled a gallon gas can with piss. That was the triathalon. Get it? Three events, like in the real Olympics. You been to 'Nam?"

I leaned against a grease-spattered wall and pretended to sip my beer. Shroud Shifter teletyped *BE SMART BE SMART BE SMART* across Steve's face, and I said, "I was Four-F. An old football injury."

Steve belched. "You didn't miss much. You play End?"

"What?"

"What do you mean, what? You're tall, you musta at least tried out for End."

"Third-string quarterback," I said self-effacingly.

Steve smiled at my calculated commiseration. "Third string, the story of my life. I wonder what Jill's doing. She usually loves to bullshit with visitors."

"Did somebody mention my name?"

I turned my head in the direction of the words. Jill was standing in the kitchen doorway wearing a robe, with a towel wrapped around her head like a turban. She said, "Remember those old Clairol ads? 'If I've got only one life, let me live it as a blonde'? Well, watch."

With a flourish she pulled off the towel and shook her head. Her lovely black hair was now peroxide yellow, and Shroud Shifter flashed *DON'T LET HER DON'T LET HER DON'T LET HER DON'T LET—*

I unclipped my self-sharpening, Teflon-coated, brushed-steel ax and swung it at her neck. Her head was sheared cleanly off; blood burst from the cavity; her arms and legs twitched spastically; then her whole body crumpled to the floor. The force of my swing spun me around, and for one second my vision eclipsed the entire scene—blood-spattered walls; the body shooting an arterial geyser out the neck, the heart still pumping in reflex; Steve, frozen on his feet, turning a catatonic blue.

I reversed my stance, flipped the handle so that I had the blade side out, and roundhoused my return shot left-handed. The blow caught Steve in the side of the head, and there was a sound like cracking eggs amplified ten million times. The blade stuck, and for long seconds I was holding the already dead man up on his feet. Then I yanked, and the body pitched forward while my ax flew in the opposite direction, brains and blood lubricating its flight.

Then Steve fell and began making gurgling sounds;

Then *his* limbs did *their* death dance;

Then a jet of blood burst from his skull into my eyes.

Then I came, and all the colors I had seen on the job combined, and hurled me to the floor to form a triad.

I awakened hours later. A telephone was ringing, and I could taste linoleum and blood. Opening my eyes, I saw a section of floor and two beer cans lying on their sides. I began to sense what had happened and held back sobs, then sent brain messages to my arms and legs to see if I had been given amputation as punishment for my crimes. My fingers scratched a cold surface and my legs jerked, and I felt grateful. The phone stopped ringing, and I wondered whom to be grateful for. Then the piece of floor and the beer cans were gone, replaced by red print on blank paper: *ME ME ME ME ME ME ME.*

On blank brain film, I typed *YES YES YES YES YES. TELL ME WHAT TO DO.*

Shroud Shifter said, Open your eyes. I obeyed, and he and Lucretia were there nude. I was memorizing their bodies when S.S. rebuked me in the harshest voice he had ever used: We are fantasy parents you have utilized since childhood. We give you what you need so that you may do what you have to do. You have experienced what some people would call a psychotic episode. In point of fact, sooner or later, premeditatedly, you would have done what you did.

Pausing, Shroud Shifter allowed me a moment to respond. I typed *why?*

He said, you are a murderer, Martin.

It was the first time he had ever addressed me by name.

I begged him to say it again, so that I would know what to do. He consented.

You are a murderer, Martin.

You are a murderer, Martin.

You are a murderer, Martin.

With my destiny ringing in my ears and my self-admitted fantasy father leading me step by step, I earned the title. First I thoroughly wiped every surface I might have touched, then I negated the forensic evidence of my ax blows by desecrating the two corpses at the places where I cut them down, using a kitchen knife and meat mallet to subterfuge blade marks and impact points. The work was messy, but I willed my brain to consider it tedious. When I was finished, I washed my hands, took off my bloodsoaked khakis, put on a jump suit from Steve's closet and wrapped up my clothes and boots in seven layers of trash-bag plastic. With my bare feet free of foreign matter, I picked up my ax and webbed belt and checked my watch. It was 3:16 A.M. Turning off the lights, I left the apartment. There was no one on the street. I walked home and fell asleep seeing colors.

From the front page of the San Francisco Examiner, *September 4, 1974:*

COUPLE BUTCHERED IN RICHMOND DISTRICT APARTMENT

The hideously butchered bodies of a young man and woman were discovered last night at the man's apartment. Police were called to the scene when neighbors reported "strange odors" coming from a downstairs unit at 911 26th St.

"I knew there was something dead in there," Thomas Frischer of 914 26th St. said to paramedics. "This heat we've been having made the stink stand out real good." Breaking down the door, the officers found the bodies of the apartment's tenant, Steven Sifakis,

31, a mechanic at the Pan-American Airways terminal at San Francisco International Airport, and his girl friend, Jill Eversall, 29, an employment counselor at the "Mighty-Man" employment agency. In a statement made exclusively to *Examiner* reporters, S.F.P.D. Sergeant W. D. Sternthall, senior officer of the unit that responded to the "unknown trouble" call, said, "I knew there were dead people in there, so I held a handkerchief over my nose coming in. When I saw the bodies, the first thing I thought about was the Sharon Tate killings from four or five years ago. The scene was unbelievable. The kitchen was covered with dried blood, and there was a dead man on the floor with his skull crushed in. That wasn't the worst. There was a dead woman in the kitchen doorway. She'd been decapitated, and her head was lying on the living-room carpet. I saw the murder weapon—a kitchen knife—on the kitchen floor near the man's body, and sent my partner back to our prowler to radio for detectives and the medical examiner."

Soon the quiet Richmond District was ablaze with the flashing lights of police vehicles. Eight teams of patrolmen began house-to-house canvassing, and Deputy Coroner Willard Willarsohn examined the bodies and attributed the cause of death to "massive trauma caused by repeated knife thrusts and loss of blood," adding that the couple had been dead for "at least 48 hours, maybe up to 52."

While comprehensive questioning of neighbors was being conducted, friends, relatives and the employers of the deceased were contacted. When expressions of shock, outrage and grief were set aside, the investigating officers knew this:

One—Sifakis and Miss Eversall were longtime lovers, and were last seen together dining at the Molinari Delicatessen in North Beach on Monday night, September 2, at 7:30, fifty-one hours before their bodies were discovered; and, two—both victims were known for frequent unexplained work absences. Thus, no one at their places of employment thought to report them missing. An anonymous acquaintance of the couple told our reporters: "Stevie and Jill were party people. They liked to get high and boogie, and they were careless about the company they kept. They picked up hitchhikers, and, well, Jill liked to swing. Stevie liked to drink with the bikers over in Oakland, and I think this is going to be tough to solve because they both knew so many transient-type people."

Meanwhile, with no clues, police are broadening their efforts, and an S.F.P.D. spokesman has announced: "This is a major crime, and it will get major attention. We are appealing to the citizens of San Francisco for information to aid us in our investigation, and we will not cease in our efforts until the killer or killers is caught."

From the front page of the San Francisco Chronicle, *September 6, 1974:*

NO LEADS IN RICHMOND SLAYINGS— VICTIMS' ASSOCIATES BEING QUESTIONED

Despite a massive investigation, the police have made little headway in their efforts to solve the brutal murders of Jill Eversall and Steven Safakis, found stabbed to death in Safakis's 26th Street apartment Wednesday night. According to S.F.P.D. Chief of Detectives Douglas Lindsay, the 50-hour hiatus between the crime and the discovery of the bodies has given the killer or killers an edge, and the lifestyle of the victims poses frustrating investigatory problems. In a formal statement made to the media this morning at City Hall, Lindsay said:

"With the basics covered, I can tell you this. Mr. Sifakis and Miss Eversall were last seen dining alone Monday evening in North Beach, and they met up with the person or persons who killed them somewhere between the restaurant and Mr. Sifakis's apartment. Despite widely broadcast public appeals and the questioning of virtually every resident in an eight-block radius surrounding the apartment building, no eyewitnesses can be found—no one saw the victims in the company of another person or persons. The only fingerprints found in the apartment belonged to the victims themselves, or to known associates of theirs who have since been cleared as suspects. The murder weapon—a saw-bladed steak knife—was found on the scene, and we believe it was what the killer or killers used to decapitate Miss Eversall. Mr. Sifakis, who died from blows to the head, was mutilated in the cranial area after death with the knife, but we believe a steel meat mallet from his kitchen was the actual instrument of murder. Forensic technicians have painstak-

ingly examined the apartment and have gained no salient information, and we have ruled out robbery as a motive, having
inventoried the apartment with friends of Mr. Sifakis. Nothing appears to be stolen, and no one heard the actual murders—which
had to have happened abruptly for the carnage to have gone unheard.

"Circumstantially, we believe the killer or killers to have left in
the early morning hours, wearing Mr. Sifakis's clothes, carrying
their own bloodstained clothing in plastic trash bags taken from
under the sink. The killer or killers' departure was not observed,
and we are currently collating data on suspicious vehicles seen in
the area that night.

"Our investigation is now centering on the victims' life-style.
Jill Eversall worked at a skid-row day labor pool that hired transients
with criminal records, and during her three years with the agency
she befriended a number of men with dubious backgrounds. She
was plagued by obscene phone calls throughout that time, and
repeatedly told friends that some of the men she associated with on
the job frightened her. We are now extensively checking out laborers
associated with the Mighty-Man Agency, along with other skid-
row habitués.

"Steven Sifakis possessed two convictions for marijuana sales,
and was tenuously connected to a number of Oakland motorcycle
gangs. At the moment, we believe that the murders may be drug-
related. Narcotics officers are involved in that aspect of the investigation, and officers attached to the Sex Crimes Squad are checking
on the whereabouts of registered sex offenders known to use violence. Although the victims were not sexually abused, forensic
psychiatrists involved in the investigation have concluded that the
killer or killers were acting out of sexually motivated rage. Both
Miss Eversall and Mr. Sifakis were involved with other partners in
the recent past, and jealousy remains near the top of our list of
probable motives. Those former partners are now being checked
out.

"In conclusion, we are doing all we can to find the killer or
killers, and we are convinced that the victims' loose life-style holds
the answer. Existing evidence and psychological mockups point to
this as a one-time-only crime—not the work of a repeating psychopath."

From the Berkeley Barb, *September 11, 1974:*

HEAT HUGE IN WAKE OF SENSATIONALIZED SNUFFS

Last month Tricky Dicky resigned, and you thought things were looking up. You were right, but now the other shoe—or should we say hobnailed boot—has fallen. On September 2, Jill Eversall and her main man Steve Sifakis were brutally offed at Steve's Richmond District crib. The killer hasn't been caught yet, unfortunately, although the fuzz is trying. In some respects—too hard.

You see, Steve and Jill had an open thing, and they grooved on getting mellow with grass, and they weren't uptight about who they hung out with. Jill had a gig at a slave market on South Mission, and—are you ready?—she liked helping the down-and-out guys on skid row find work. So...

So the San Francisco cops have concluded that Steve and Jill's "loose life-style" was the cause of their deaths, and although deploring that life-style, they have set out to find the snuff artist/artists with bulldog determination. (Steve and Jill lived in the nice, safe Richmond, after all—why, it could have been someone ... decent!) In the course of their investigation they have violated the civil rights of scores of peaceful "loose life-stylers."

Item: In an early-morning raid, the fuzz rousted a half-dozen long-haired young people sleeping in Golden Gate Park, and when they found a pocketknife on one young man, they put a gun to his head and screamed, "Tell us why you sliced those people in the Richmond!"

Item: Workers drinking wine outside the Mighty-Man slave office were loaded into a van and hauled to the City Prison, where they were skin-searched, then harassed by homicide detectives. One plainclothes pig demanded that an old man admit to being hot for Jill Eversall. When the old man refused, the cop broke a wine bottle over his head.

Item: A number of innocent men with sex-offense records have been hassled by cops threatening to expose their records to employers and friends.

Item: Cops interrupted a chanting service at the Hare Krishna

Temple on Delores Street, shaking down the chanters for dope and weapons. When the Temple's head dojo demanded an explanation, one officer exclaimed, "I think the Richmond killings are cult-connected. My mom lives on Twenty-ninth Street! Don't gimme no shit! I'm here to enforce the law!"

We at the Berkeley *Barb* wish to protest the above cited lawlessness and point out another law that may soon take precedence— the law of equal and opposite reaction. Breaking the law to enforce the law is never justified, even if the crime is murder.

14.

While the events described in the preceding accounts were taking place, I was invisible in the storm center, lucid and gracefully careful, as apprentices should be when they finally achieve the status of Professional.

You are a murderer, Martin.

Awakening from my post-killing color sleep at 7:30, I automatically shaved and showered and prepared myself for work. I knew exactly what I had done and what I had to do, and went about it free of waking colors and brain-movies. First I dressed in my spare set of work clothes; then, knowing it was unlikely that the bodies had yet been discovered, I tossed Steve's jump suit in with my bloodied khakis, web belt and ax, wrapped the plastic bundle up tightly and carried it out to my van. I drove to the clearing site as if my day portended business as usual, and I buried the death kit in a marsh area outside downtown Sausalito. Getaway step one completed, I sat on a rock and charted the remaining steps in mental typeface, "Business As Usual" my basic escape theme.

Neighbors may have seen you with the ax, so you need to obtain an identical ax illegally, then wear down the blade so that it will appear blood-free and well used if subjected to forensic scrutiny.

Your alibi is that you were home asleep at the time of the murders. The other tenants will corroborate you as an early riser, early returner and quiet tenant, and no one saw you on the street talking to Steve and Jill. No witnesses were present at the Mighty-Man office when you met Jill, and if she told people about meeting you and the police question you about it—you must deny it, because that line of questioning will, logically, follow their first *routine* questioning of all neighborhood residents. And if you change your story after first claiming not to have known her, you will become a major suspect.

The police will be taking down license numbers of every vehicle in the surrounding area, cross-checking the registration against the California Criminal Records Bureau's files. Your burglary conviction and the fact that you recently completed your probationary term and moved here from Los Angeles will be noted, and you will be subjected to intense questioning and possible physical abuse. You must never waver in your denials of guilt, even under extreme duress, and you must refuse to take a polygraph test.

You are a murderer, Martin.

In the end, my scenario translated into reality with almost perfect fidelity. I shoplifted an ax identical to my old one at a hardware store in Sausalito and devastated the cutting edge on the site's few remaining tree trunks. I continued my mop-up work for Mr. Slotnick, and the foreman came by and told me that on September 10 I was out of a job, because the site was going to be plowed, and the "Eco-freaks" had put the kibosh on Big Sol's "Singles Paradise" tract. I maintained my business-as-usual plan, and the delay in discovering the bodies made my confidence grow in quantum leaps.

Then, fifty hours and ten minutes after *the* moment, I heard the sirens, and I looked out my front window and saw red twirling lights proclaim my name. I watched as the red was intensified by more and more police cars, then I went to bed and slept, and dream lights spelled out "You are a murderer, Martin."

Loud knocks on my door awakened me at dawn. I put on a robe, walked over and yawned into the peephole. "Yeah? What do you want?"

A perfunctory voice answered, "Police, open up."

In an instant I knew they had already run their vehicle cross-checks and had knowledge of my record. The thrust of my performance came to me, boldly embellished. I rubbed sleep from my eyes, opened the door and reverted to my old jailhouse persona. "Yeah, what is it?"

Three hard cases were on my doorstep. They were all as big as me, and they were all wearing crewcuts, cheap summer suits and scowls. The one in the middle, distinguishable only by a badly stained necktie, said, "Don't *you* know what it is?"

"Fill me in," I said. "It's six-fucking A.M., and I'm dying to hear what you have to say."

The cop on the left muttered, "Comedian," and motioned for me to step aside. I complied with feigned reluctance, and the three filed into my living room, the necktie man immediately pointing to my ax and scythe propped up against the wall by the door. "What are those?" he asked.

I looked him straight in the eye. "An ax and a scythe."

"I can see that, Plunkett. What do you use them for?"

I acted surprised at his mention of my name, and made myself hesitate three seconds, watching the other two fan out to search my apartment. "To trim my nails," I said.

"Don't fuck with me," he said, easing the door shut.

"Then tell me what this is all about."

"I'll get to it. How long have you lived in San Francisco?"

"Since April."

"Why do you possess those tools?"

"I've been working at a building site in Marin, and I use the tools to dig out tree stumps and brush."

"I see. Who got you the job?"

"I got it off the bulletin board at S.F. State."

"Are you a student there?"

"No."

"Then what gave you the right to the job?"

"Being broke gave me the right. What's—"

"Shut up. Are you sure you didn't get the job at the Mighty-Man Agency?"

"I'm positive."

"How many burglaries have you pulled in San Francisco?"

"Three trillion at last count. I—"

"I said don't fuck with me!"

I flinched backward and looked scared. Shifting performance gears, I said, "I pulled one B and E in L.A. five years
ago, and I did a year, and I stayed clean and topped out my
probation and moved here. I was a fucking kid when I pulled
that B and E, and I haven't done it since. Now what do you
want?"

The necktie cop hooked his thumbs in his belt. The pose
allowed me a view of his holstered .38, and staring straight
into his eyes gave me glimpses of the low-voltage brain
behind them. "You know this is serious," he said.

I cinched the belt of my robe. "I know this is more than
a burglary roust."

"Smart lad. Did you see the police cars on this block last
night?"

"Yes."

"Wonder what was happening?"

"Yes."

"Make any attempt to find out?"

"No."

"Why not?"

"I've had enough of cops to last me a lifetime. What—"

"I'll tell you in due time. You like pussy?"

"Yeah, do you?"

"Had any lately?"

"In my dreams last night."

"Cute. You like blondes or brunettes?"

"Both."

"Ever get a woman to dye her hair for you?"

I laughed to cover my shock at the unanticipated question. "Snatch hair, you mean?"

The necktie cop snickered, then looked over my shoulder.
I turned and saw his partners going through my kitchen
drawers. When one of them gave a negative head shake,
Necktie said, "Let's change the subject."

"How about baseball?"

"How about boys? You bisexual?"

"No."

"Into three ways?"

"No."

"You take it up the ass?"

"No."

"Oh, you eat it then?"

I started to get angry for real, and my hands twitched at my sides. Necktie noticed my change of expression, and said, "Strike a nerve, cool cat? Maybe you got reamed doing your bullet in L.A.? Maybe your switch gets flipped by boys now, and you hate yourself for liking it. Maybe your switch flipped Monday night about nine o'clock when Steve and Jill suggested a party? Maybe you misinterpreted the whole scene, and when Jill wouldn't put out you took it out on Steve with a meat mallet, and you chopped off Jill's head because you didn't like the way she was looking at you. How many people you killed, Plunkett?"

In the course of a microsecond, an astonishing thing happened. As I felt the color drain from my face I became my performance, my real anger became perfect real shock, and I was the innocent man falsely accused. Stammering, "Y-y-yyou mmean pppeople wwere mmurdered," I knew that the necktie cop bought it straight down the line. When he said, "That's right," I saw his disappointment that I wasn't guilty; when he said, "Where were *you* Monday night?" I knew the rest of the interrogation was just a formality. The revelation passed, and as I assumed a normal, sane sense of culpability, it took every ounce of my will not to gloat. "I-I w-was here," I stuttered.

"Alone?"

"Y-y-yes."

"What were you doing?"

"I-I got home from my job around eight-thirty. I ate dinner, then I read for an hour or so and went to bed."

"A swinging evening. That what you usually do?"

"Yes."

"Don't you hang out with friends?"

"I haven't really made any friends here."

"Don't you get lonely?"

"Sure. Who do you think—"

"I'll ask the questions. Do you know a woman named Jill Eversall or a man named Steven Sifakis?"

"Are they the ones...?"

"That's right."

"What do—did they look like?"

"She was a foxy brunette, about five-six, nice tits. You like tits?"

"Come on, Officer."

"Okay, what about Steve Sifakis? Five-eleven, one-ninety, reddish brown hair with muttonchop sideburns. He was supposed to be hung like a mule. You dig big cocks?"

"Just my own." I heard the two cops in the kitchen laugh, and turned around to look at them. One man was shaking his head and drawing a finger across his throat, the gesture obviously intended for Necktie. Turning back, I said, "Can we wrap this up? I have to go to work."

"We may damn well wrap you up, Plunkett," Necktie said slowly.

I went in for the kill, knowing I could outgame any machine in captivity. "This is getting old, so why don't I wrap this up? Since I didn't kill anybody, why don't we all hotfoot it down to the station. You hit me with a lie-detector test, I pass it, you cut me loose. What do you say?"

Necktie looked past me to the leader cop. I resisted the urge to watch their signals, and concentrated on the stain that gave the cop his impromptu name. I had just decided it was chili when Necktie said, "Did you see anybody on the street when you came home Monday night?"

I considered my "victory" question for a moment, then said, "No."

"Hear any strange noises?"

"No."

"See any unfamiliar vehicles?"

"No."

"Ever fuck Jill Eversall or score grass from Steve Sifakis?"

I gave Necktie a look of contempt that would have wilted the Pope. "Come on, man."

"No, you come on. Answer my question."

"All right. No, I never fucked Jill Eversall or scored grass from Steve Sifakis."

One of the cops behind me cleared his throat; Necktie squared his shoulders and said, "We may be back." The leader cop said "Stay clean" as he walked past me to the door, and the other one winked.

Of course they never came back, and I spent the next several weeks enjoying my anonymous fame as the "Richmond Ripper," an appelation bestowed on me by an *Examiner* reporter. "Business as usual" were my watchwords, and I imagined myself under twenty-four-hour surveillance, my every move being scrutinized by equally anonymous forces anxious to bring me down. The conscious cultivation of paranoia kept me coming home at night when I wanted to be on the street listening to people talk about me; it kept me going to university job boards, searching out work, when I wanted to be spending the money I had hoarded on guns. It would not let me collect newspaper clippings on my crime, nor would it let me do what I most wanted to do—move on to other cities and see how they affected me. The regimen boiled down to asceticism in place of celebration, and the only thing emotionally satisfying about it was that I knew it was making me stronger.

Ten days after the killings, I found another "Heavy Labor" job—weeding an entire hillside on the edge of the U.C.-Berkeley campus. The work was tedious—exacerbated by the fact that I didn't need the money—and eavesdropping on students' conversations made me angry: Watergate and Nixon's recent resignation were their favorite topics, and when they deigned to talk about me, I was dismissed as a "psycho" or "sick puppy." I decided that on October 2, a month to the day from the murders, I would celebrate.

The time passed slowly.

I worked on the hillside, listened to students talk and read newspapers on my lunch hour. Reading the papers was like being dangled on an ego string. Articles comparing me to the Manson Family, "only smarter," felt like yanks into the clouds; paragraphs attributing my murders to the "Zodiac" killer—a mystic psychopath who sent lurid communiqués to the police—felt like being flung to the dirt. Eight straight days of no print space was the complete abandonment of a mother hurling an unwanted child into a garbage heap.

Nights were the slowest to pass.

On my way home, I would sometimes see cops rousting long-haired youths, and I would know, somehow, that I had been the catalyst of that minor chaos. Cutting a street-swath through people in my van was satisfying, because I knew they knew of my actions. But at home, in my cocoon of caution, there was only me. And though "you are a murderer, Martin," was now my identity, I had not yet decided to stay yanked in the clouds through continuous killing.

By October 2, the Richmond Ripper case was stale media bread, and my instincts told me that the police had gone on to matters of more urgent priority. Logic joined my heart in telling me to celebrate, and I did.

It took me an entire day and night to find what I wanted, and the four-hundred-dollar price tag was infinitesimal compared to the effort of talking out of the side of my mouth to a long succession of South San Francisco hoodlums, exchanging "pedigrees" and criminal amenities, then going on a half-dozen wild-goose chases before connecting with a retired pawnshop broker looking to liquidate "hot stock." The ultimate transaction was quick and effortless, and I was the unlawful owner of a brand-new, never-registered, untraceable Colt .357 magnum "Python" model revolver.

Now I had two talismans—one handcrafted, the other earned. At home I brought them together, threaded cylinder to muzzle. They fit perfectly, adding a tactile weight to my new identity. On my way to work the next morning I bought a box of hollow-point ammunition, and with the loaded and silencered hand cannon under my shirt, I dug weeds out of the soft dirt until dusk. Then, framed by dormitory lights and a starry night, I practiced.

Muzzle flash, recoil, the dull thuds of the silencer; slapping sounds as the bullets tore into the spade-furrowed dirt.

Cordite and soil in my nostrils, and headlights from passing
cars on the road above me momentarily illuminating the
craters made by individual shots. My right wrist aching
from the magnum's internal combustion; emptying the spent
shells into my pocket after every sixth explosion; reloading
in the dark and firing, firing, firing until my box of hollow
points was empty and the hillside smelled like a battlefield
sans blood. Then the drive home, trembling inside, anxious
to hit the open highway and just go.

But going was, at that point, inimical to business as
usual, which meant "stay." So I did stay, finishing my weeding job, but continuing at U.C.-Berkeley as a backup cus-
todian, sweeping and mopping on the regular crew members'
staggered days off. I set my go day as Thanksgiving, November 24, and continued to live on the cheap, allowing
myself one luxury: ammunition.

So as not to arouse suspicion by repeated purchases of
single boxes, I drove to San Jose and bought a gross of them,
a total of 7,200 rounds. I secreted the box in a heavily
wooded area near the Berkeley side of the Bay Bridge, and
every night after work I fired at imaginary targets on the
water. Each muzzle burst/recoil/silencer thud/wave kick
brought me closer to go, but I still didn't know what it
meant.

I found out the day before my departure.

My homemade silencer was virtually destroyed from
overuse, so I drove to South San Francisco to find the pawnshop dealer who had sold me the Python, to see if he had
connections who could sell me a professional replacement.
The man smiled as I made my request, took a picture of
sailing ships from his wall and twirled the dial of the safe
behind it. Within moments I was screwing a C.I.A. "Black
Beauty" suppressor to the muzzle of my magnum and handing over five hundred dollars as payment. More than satisfied, I tucked the gun into my waistband, covered it with
my shirttail and walked outside to my van. Seeing a coin-
operated news rack filled with *Chronicles*, I walked over to
buy one, hoping for a back-page mention along the lines of

"still no clues in Richmond Ripper case." I was about to feed the machine my fifteen cents when I noticed a poster tacked to the telephone pole beside the rack.

Banner print exclaimed "The Wages of Sin!!!" and below the words there was a crystal-clear photographic reproduction, with S.F.P.D. 9/4/74 written on the bottom. The words below that had to do with salvation through Jesus, but the picture in the middle caused me to shake so hard that it was impossible to read the exact message.

Jill Eversall's severed head lay in the foreground in living black and white. The rest of her body was sprawled in the kitchen doorway. Beyond it, Steve Sifakis's akimbo legs, blood-streaked walls and floor were visible. Shroud Shifter typed *ugly ugly ugly ug*—across my vision, then erased the line and replaced it with *wrong disarray not ugly amateur disarray not ugly not bad amateurish not ugly not bad.*

I ripped the poster off the pole and wadded it into a ball, then threw it into the gutter and ground the cardboard with both feet until my boots were soaked, seeing the Tahiti and Japan airline posters on Steve Sifakis's walls and the original memory that had eluded me—Season's lover hurling me topsy-turvy, darkness into light, similar posters on the wall as he beat me into humiliation. S.S. took on Country Joe McDonald's voice and sang, "Ashes to ashes and dust to dust, stormy weather cause your pump to rust." His voice faltered in mid-stanza, but I knew he was telling me to go out and buy a beautiful Polaroid camera to go with my magnum. Other instructions followed, not verbally, not typed, but telepathic. Only over the next fourteen hours, as I methodically accomplished each task, did they come to typeface life:

Buy the camera and film.

Go home and load all your property into your van, including the furniture you had originally planned to leave behind.

Drop off your keys with the old lady downstairs.

Buy a holster for your weapon, cut a hole in the bottom to accommodate the silencer, then clip the magnum to the springs underneath the van's driver's seat.

Sleep well, and take U.S. 66 east toward the Nevada line early tomorrow morning.

Dispose of all your furniture except the mattress after you are free and clear of the San Francisco area.

Keep the Polaroid close at hand.

Those duties behind me, professionally rendered and typefaced and check-marked upon completion, I drove east through lush Nevada pine forests, solo, with no Shroud Shifter as co-pilot. Traffic was non-existent, my gas tank was full, and I had three thousand, six hundred dollars in the glove compartment. The camera was an arm's length away on the passenger seat. Mountains loomed behind the tall trees. I felt very peaceful.

Then I saw the hitchhikers.

They were a teenaged boy and girl, both long-haired and wearing Levi's jackets, jeans and backpacks. I pulled to the side of the road and stopped, and seconds later the boy was at the passenger-side door, the girl directly behind him. With one hand I pulled up the locking button, with the other I reached under my seat for the holstered magnum.

"Thanks, mister!"

I fired three times, chest high, and from the way the boy and girl pitched backward I knew my shots had caught them both. Setting the hand brake and hitting the emergency blinker, I slid over the passenger seat and out of the van. The teenagers were lying on the gravel shoulder, dead. I looked past their bodies, saw that the shoulder dropped off in a small slope, and kicked the corpses over the side, then spread loose gravel on the blood from the exit wounds. A stopwatch with a ten-minute timer jumped into my brain, and I got my Polaroid from the van and ran down the hill with it.

The hitchhikers were lying in soft dirt at the bottom, joined in a jigsaw-puzzle posture—her head on the rear crook of his right leg, their fingertips crossed at divergent angles. The bodies reminded me of signal flags sending the word *disarray* in semafore, and I almost forgot caution in my desire to make them perfect.

But I didn't. First I checked his chest and back, then hers, and when I saw a back exit wound on the girl and rips on her pack next to it, with no marks on the outside, I knew the spent slugs were inside. With my stopwatch reading 1:37 elapsed, I pulled down the zipper and tore through panties and blouses until my fingers hit hot steel. I put the rounds in my shirt pocket and let them burn, then furiously kicked a shallow grave out of the dirt surrounding the three of us.

6:04 elapsed.

I wiped the girl's backpack free of fingerprints with my sleeve, then stripped the two corpses and threw their clothes and packs into the grave.

7:46 elapsed.

With the lovers nude, I placed the girl on her back and spread her legs; the boy I positioned on top of her. When the simulated intercourse was perfect, I snapped my first picture, watched the camera expel the blank print paper and waited.

9:14 elapsed.

Photographic perfection imprinted itself, and weirdly, preternaturally, I knew the image was a clue to my fixations with blonds, Lauri the hooker, and things much, much older.

10:00 elapsed, alarms sounding; the realization that Shroud Shifter and I had finally merged as one. I covered the bodies with loose dirt and arranged heavy branches over the plot to hold them down.

Tick tick tick tick tick tick tick tick tick.

Giving myself commemorative bonus seconds, I put the snapshot in my pocket; saw that the blood on my collar was no more than the amount caused by a shaving cut; realized that next time I should steal money and possibly credit cards. When it was time to go, I obliterated my footprints by walking sideways over them on my way up the hill. At the top, the landscape was absolutely still. My van looked new in the fall sunlight, and on impulse I named it the "Deathmobile," then drove away.

III

CRIMES OF OPPORTUNITY; NIGHTMARE ASSAULTS (1974−1978)

From Boss Detective *magazine, December 28, 1974 issue:*

CAMPERS' PET MAKES GRISLY DISCOVERY
SEX SLAYER SOUGHT!

Without the keen nose of Buford, a three-year-old basset hound, the bodies of Karen Roget and Todd Millard, missing since Thanksgiving Day, might never have been found. Buford, who belongs to Mr. and Mrs. J. Bradley Streep of Sacramento, California, was frolicking off his leash near a campground adjacent to U.S. 66 outside Hastings, Nevada, when, according to Mr. Streep, "He started yapping like crazy and started to dig in the dirt. When he came up with that first bone, I almost dropped my cookies!"

The bone was human, and Mr. Streep (who briefly attended chiropractic college some years before) recognized it as such and ran for the campground and his C.B. Meanwhile, while his owner contacted the authorities, Buford continued to dig, and soon unearthed the skeletal remains of two bodies, along with their clothing and backpacks containing ID, spare clothing and a collapsible tent. The keen-snouted hound was happily munching on a footbone when Mr. Streep returned with Lewis County Sheriff's Deputy J. V. McClain, who gasped at the positions of the skeletons.

"The bodies were arranged in a ... uh ... posture suggesting sexual intercourse," Deputy McClain told *Boss Detective* correspondent Robert Rice. "Even though decomposition was complete, you could tell what the killer had done."

Shocked though he was, Deputy McClain radioed for reinforcements and checked the clothing lying underneath the bodies in their grave. After discovering driver's licenses belonging to Sacramento residents Todd Thomas Millard, 17, and Karen Nancy Roget, 16, he recalled a missing-persons bulletin on the two. "They were last seen in Hastings on November 24, Thanksgiving Day," he said. "Almost a month ago, and from the condition of the bodies I knew they were dead that long."

The Lewis County coroner soon arrived and deduced the means of death. "From rips and bloodstains on their clothing and backpacks, it is safe to assume that the two were shot."

A team of late-arriving officers made a search of the area but could not find expended bullets, and the scene was roped off while the remains of the teenagers were removed and technicians looked for other clues. The Streeps and Buford continued on their vacation, with hearty kudos from Lewis County authorities, who immediately launched an investigation. Three days later Sheriff Roger D. Norman told reporters:

"We have few clues in the vicious murders of Todd Millard and Karen Roget. The time that elapsed between the killings and the discovery of the bodies has hindered us severely. We have not been able to turn up any witnesses, and the known associates of the deceased have provided us with no real leads. We have, however, ruled out robbery as a motive, and we are now centering our efforts on combing the files of known sex deviates."

Meanwhile, bereaved family and friends mourn Todd and Karen, and pray for the police to find the fiend who killed them.

From True Life Sleuth, *March 1975 issue:*

FIEND OR FIENDS STALKING NEVADA/UTAH ROADWAYS! CRIMES CONNECTED?

Police continue to be baffled by a rash of fiendishly clever, seemingly random killings throughout Utah and Nevada. Since New Year's, four young men, all runaways from wealthy homes, have been found murdered. The common denominators have been robbery as the presumed sole motive, the affluence of the victims and their "runaway" status. Aside from those factors, the killings differ so markedly that investigating agencies are not sure whether the crimes are connected. The four dead are:

Randall Hosford, 18, discovered in a culvert outside Carson City, Nevada, on January 2. The youth was a "remittance man" living off stipends from his wealthy Northern California family, and was known to roam the western states by thumb, always carrying credit cards and large amounts of cash. His wallet had been picked clean when police discovered his strangled body, and the current disposition of the investigation into his murder is—no clues.

Lee Richard Webb, 20, of Las Vegas. The son of a casino owner, young Webb was last seen hitchhiking outside Las Vegas on January 19. His body was found a week later, in the desert forty miles from the gambling mecca. The youth had been robbed and strangled. Disposition—no clues.

Coleman Loring, 19, and his friend Ralph De Santis, 21, the sons of wealthy Moab, Utah, mining contractors, found bound together, robbed and shot through the hearts in a cave outside Moab on January 26. No expended shells were found, although the large entry and exit wounds point to a large-caliber murder weapon. The boys were hitching to Las Vegas for a weekend of gambling, and were known to be carrying over two thousand dollars in cash. Disposition—no clues.

Postscript: At press time, our Carson City correspondent reports this flash bulletin:

Police have recovered credit cards belonging to the late Randall Hosford. An unidentified man (who has been cleared as a murder suspect) told C.C.P.D. detectives that he met a "tall, nondescript man in his late twenties" named "Shifter" in a bar, and the man sold him the cards for a hundred dollars apiece, promising that they were "stone cold." The C.C.P.D. as yet has no line on "Shifter," and the man he sold the cards to has been charged with receiving stolen goods.

From the Have You Seen These People? *column of* True Life Sleuth *magazine, June 1975 issue:*

Editor's Note—Normally, this feature displays Motor Vehicle Department photographs of people reported missing, but since all of the people listed are either below the minimum age required for a license in their state, or do not possess a license, we are running their physical stats and last-known whereabouts only. We at *True Life Sleuth* wish to alert the proper authorities to the fact that these five people disappeared from two adjoining states within an eight-week period.

Everett Bigelow, white male, of Provo, Utah. Last seen in Provo on 3/4/75. Age—71, height—5' 11", weight—155 lbs. Gray hair, blue eyes, slight build. Known to frequent beer bars, no identifying marks or tattoos.

Hazel Leffler, white female, age 67, of Bostang, Utah. Last seen talking to unidentified white male outside Bostang shopping center on March 11. Dyed black hair, brown eyes, 5' 6", 170 lbs. Build—portly. Wears glasses and uses a cane to walk.

Wendy Grace Sanderson, 14, and her neighbor Carl Sudequist, 16, both of Putnamville, Nevada. Last seen together at a picnic area near Putnamville on 4/9/75. Both Caucasian. The girl is described as 4'6", 88 lbs., blond hair, green eyes; the boy as 5'8", 140, brown hair and eyes. At last sighting, both youths were wearing the navy blue uniforms of Saint Mary's School, Putnamville.

Gregory Hall, 37, of South Las Vegas, Nevada. White male, 6'1", 190 lbs., brown hair, blue eyes. Last seen hitchhiking near Northern Utah/Nevada border on April 30, 1975. Recently paroled from the Nevada State Prison, and now on record as a possible parole absconder. (Prison photos to appear in the next issue of *True Life Sleuth* to feature *Have You Seen These People?*)

Editor's note—any information regarding the current whereabouts of the above-listed people should be directed to the Utah State Police, Nevada State Police and the Missing Persons Hotline of *True Life Sleuth—Toll Free 1-800-MISSING.*

From True Crime Detective, *July 1975 issue:*

DEMONIC DEATH FOR DEAF & DUMB DISHWASHER!

Dateline—Salt Lake City, Utah, June 16, 1975:

The body of a deaf and dumb Salt Lake City youth was discovered on the salt flats surrounding the Great Salt Lake early this morning. The victim, Robert Masskie, 18, worked as a dishwasher at Colonial Joe's Restaurant, Salt Lake City, and had just cashed his two-week paycheck. No money was found on his person, and at this early hour of the investigation police are assuming robbery as the motive. Coworkers of the friendly handicapped lad expressed shock at his death, and fry cook Martin Plunkett, 27, said, "Bobby was an inveterate hitchhiker, and that's dangerous. Please tell your readers to be careful and not hitchhike."

Sound advice. There are no clues as yet, but we will update the investigation's progress in next month's issue of *True Crime Detective*.

From Boss Detective *magazine's "Missing!" feature, December 1975 issue:*

Last seen 10/30/75 on I-95 on the outskirts of Ogden, Utah, "talking to a tall young white male" who may be the owner of a late-model grayish van.

Kenneth Neufeld, 41, white male, 6'0", 175, brown hair and eyes, Marine Corps tattoo on right forearm.

Cynthia Neufeld, 39, white female, 5'4", 130, blond hair, brown eyes, no identifying marks.

Reported missing on 12/1/75 by their teenaged children. Their abandoned vehicle was discovered in woods outside Ogden, 12/4/75. Extensive search of area yielded no clues. Photographs of Mr. & Mrs. Neufeld available from Missing Persons Bureau, Ogden Police Department, and from Utah State Police. Direct all queries and information regarding Mr. & Mrs. Neufeld to those agencies.

From Boss Detective, *April, 1977 issue:*

ZODIAC KILLER PROWLING COLORADO? KILLINGS OF COLLEGE STUDENTS LINKED? RITUAL MARKINGS WORK OF COMIC-BOOK CULT?

Aspen, Colorado, is a year-round mecca for young people seeking good times, and it is the undisputed winter "party capital" of the United States, renowned for its skiing and ski-lodge bonhomie. Young people come to Aspen to cut loose and get away from the grind of college and jobs. You can bargain on a good time in Aspen, but since January 1976, eight college students have gotten more than they bargained for—they disappeared from the face of the earth. The eight are:

Cindy Keneally, 22, of Chicago, Illinois, last seen 1/18/76;

George Keneally, 20, of Chicago, her husband, last seen 1/18/76;

Gustavo Torres, 23, of Sao Paulo, Brazil, last seen 1/26/76;

Mills Jensen, 24, of Aspen, last seen 3/1/76;

Craig Richardson, 17, of Glenwood Springs, Colorado, last seen 4/1/76;

Maria Kaltenborn, 21, of Akron, Ohio, last seen 6/2/76;

John Kaltenborn, 22, Maria's husband, last seen 6/2/76;

Timothy Bay, 16, of Glenwood Springs, last seen 8/18/76.

Police investigating the disappearances were (at first) quick to point out the transient nature of pleasure spas like Aspen, and last year, in the spring of '76, when the number of vanished people stood at five, they pooh-poohed the idea of massive foul play. But then, during the spring of '76 thaw, melted snowbanks yielded the mutilated bodies of Mr. and Mrs. Keneally and Mr. Torres, and they knew a fiend was on the prowl.

The subzero temperatures that had prevailed all winter preserved the bodies to gruesome effect. Mr. & Mrs. Keneally were nude and arranged in an explicitly sexual posture, and Mr. Torres (who disappeared eight days after the Keneallys) was positioned a few feet away. All three victims died from slashed throats and were marked about the torsos with "S.S."

Authorities thought at first that the markings indicated a Nazi killer—"S.S." being the initials of Hitler's secret police. But then that theory was dropped in favor of attributing the murders to the "Zodiac" killer, a mass murderer active in Northern California in the late '60's–early '70's. The "S.S." body markings were aslant, so that they resembled "Z's"; and the Zodiac killer (who sent messages to San Francisco–area police stating that he was "claiming slaves for my afterlife") sometimes marked his victims that way.

An entirely different theory was advanced by Glenwood Springs resident Martin Plunkett, the assistant librarian at the local library. Plunkett, 28, a crime buff and childhood comic-book collector, said that the markings could be a reference to the "Shroud Shifter," a

comic-book villain popular in the 1950's and '60's. The Aspen
police thanked Mr. Plunkett for his phoned-in theory, and local
comic-book collectors were investigated and cleared, bringing the
long, frustrating case of murder/disappearances back to its current
state—no clues.

In a press conference held last month, Aspen Chief of Police
Arthur Whittinghill stated, "The Keneally/Torres murders were certainly the work of one person or persons, and I suspect the sexual
aspects of the crime were subterfuge—the work of a killer or killers
bent on obscuring motive. The other five disappearances may or
may not be related, and since no other bodies have turned up, I
lean to the theory of separate killer-abductors. The Zodiac-Comic
Book speculation I view as nonsense, and the important thing now
is for all Colorado residents and visitors below the age of twenty-
five to be wary of strangers."

From Boss Detective, *November 1978 issue, the "Missing!"*
feature:

The nine people listed below have vanished between April 1977
and our press time of October 15, 1978. All were last seen in various
parts of Kansas and Missouri, all are Caucasians and college students. Photos are available from the Missing Persons Divisions of
the Kansas and Missouri State Police. Direct all inquiries to those
agencies. The missing are:

Janet Cahill, 21, 5'3", 116 lbs., brown, blue. Last seen in Holcomb, Kan., 4/16/77;

Walker Cahill, 17, (Miss Cahill's brother), 5'8", 135 lbs., brown,
blue. Last seen in Holcomb, 4/16/77;

James Brownmuller, 24, 6'3", 205 lbs., blond, blue. Last seen
outside Wichita Falls, Kan., 6/9/77;

Mary Kilpatrick, 20, 5'1", 95 lbs., blond, blue, last seen in
Wichita Falls, 6/11/77;

Thomas Briscoe, 22, 5'11", 175 lbs., brown, brown. Last seen
in Wichita Falls, 7/7/77;

Karsten Hanala, 26, 6'1", 200 lbs., brown, hazel. Last seen
outside Tompkinsville, Kan., "speaking to large white man driving
van," 8/6/77;

Christine Muldowney, 19, 5'9", 135 lbs., blond, blue. Last seen in Joplin, Mo., 3/13/78;

Lawrence Muldowney, 17, 6'2", 185, blond, hazel. Last seen in Joplin, Mo., 3/13/78;

Nancy De Fazio, 20, 5'4", 125, black, brown. Last seen near Blue Lake, Mo., 10/1/78.

Concluding note: Assumptions of death aside, credit cards belonging to several of the above-mentioned people have turned up in "hot" transactions all over America, and the two card-frauders thus far apprehended have airtight alibis for the times of the card-owners' disappearances. Those two men have been cleared as suspects after rigorous polygraph examinations, and one man (during polygraphing) stated that, "I bought my card from a guy who got it from another guy—a guy with a weird name like Stick Shifter."

15.

I killed them all, and the murder/disappearances mentioned in the preceding articles comprised approximately two-thirds of my 1974–78 body count.

Some were crimes of opportunity and convenience; some were assaults against waking and sleeping nightmares and the occasionally recurring urge to live in childhood fantasies. All were perfectly carried out.

My basic tool was the Deathmobile, and my basic means of avoiding capture was the complete eschewing of criminal patterns. I never spoke of my exploits. I never used drugs or alcohol; I never made purchases with the credit cards I stole, and I only sold them to drunken and drug-wasted lowlifes I met in bars—men who later identified me as "big," "tall," "young," and "the Shifter," but who would never be able to pick me out of a police lineup. I never killed when there was the remotest possibility of eyewitnesses, and the few partial witnesses who spotted me talking to roadside acquaintances I would later kill would *never* be able to ID me, because I always kept my back to the highway. "Big," "tall," "white"—certainly. Martin Michael Plunkett—no.

Caution.

Between 1974 and 1978 the gross yield from my robbery-murders was $11,147.00. I did not, of course, carry that amount of cash on my person—I kept it in bank safe-deposit boxes, the banks themselves spread across the western half of America, the rent on them paid for ten years in advance,

131

the keys safely hidden in wooded areas nearby, so that the final key was my memory.

Ultra-caution.

Deathmobile II, purchased in Denver with the proceeds from my Aspen killings, replaced Deathmobile I when I realized the imprudence of driving with an illegal handgun clipped under the seat. The .357, the detective magazines I kept as mementos of my exploits and the marijuana I habitually harbored to seduce hippie types with would, if subjected to police scrutiny, arouse suspicion of the worst sort. I needed to keep them within a few moments' reach, but out of reach of the most heavy-duty cop shakedown. Deathmobile I had no suitable hiding places, but studying the owner's manuals of various make vans revealed that late-model Dodges had an undercarriage made up of metal "pockets," rectangular-shaped, with openings on the side. I surmised that two or three of the pockets would hold all my contraband items. In order to achieve a look of uniformity I would have to cover all the ends with wire or steel, but the peace of mind I would gain would make the effort worthwhile.

So, in March of '77, I bought a '76 Dodge 300 van and performed major surgery on the undercarriage, blocking off all twenty pockets with wire mesh. Inside four of them I kept my .357, my magazines, and my drug supply. Behind the seats, along with my legal belongings, I kept a supply of tools and flares to aid me in my role of Good Samaritan motorist, and my Polaroid was always up front with me, loaded.

Caution.

Ultra-caution.

Preparedness.

Those three watchwords combined to italicize, bracket and underline *methodology*. Within that word, conjugations of the first three combined to form rules:

Wipe all van surfaces victims might have touched.

Kill with the magnum only as a last resort, and try to retrieve the spent rounds.

Bury all victims as deep as the ten-minute stopwatch will allow.

Sex-kill only when the nightmares and fantasies start to hurt, and tear up the snapshots within four hours, after memorizing and mentally cataloguing the most minute details.

During '74–'78, I was only to sex-kill/strip/position/photograph a total of four times. The first time, after leaving San Francisco, I acted out of a need to rectify the disarray of Eversall/Sifakis; the following instances were fueled by nightmares and impacted sexual longing. Still, I knew instinctively that what I was looking for was beyond relief and orgasm, and I had enough presence of mind to carefully choose my victims—their selection based on an instinct as to what their bodies would look like together.

The Keneallys nude in the Colorado snow killed my nightmares and made me come, but did not ease my curiosity, so eight days later I placed Gustavo Torres beside them, and felt an ancient third party knock at the door of my memory. Dimly afraid of what the knocker might say, I retreated until the nightmares got terrible and my groin felt like it was holding back bomb bursts; then I found the Kaltenborns hiking near Glenwood Springs and spent hours arranging them and snapping pictures, myself nude as the third party. Again there was instant release and weeks of comfort, but no penetration of the memory.

Sensing that the memory originated in my childhood and corresponded to my old demon of blondness, I waited for two years, until I found a pair of potential lovers who were perfect beyond perfect—the Muldowney siblings of Joplin, Missouri—blond, blue-eyed and lovely. Promising hashish, I lured them out to a deserted stretch of hills, strangled them and stripped them and took pictures of them and touched them and touched myself and even risked my own safety by staying past dark with their bodies.

The effort did not enlighten me.

The effort did not enlighten me because, at base, I was killing for monetary caprice, biological gratification and to

make the hurt go away. The nine months after the Mul-
downeys went by in a blur, and then even my memory
exploration was rendered capricious, for a nightmare materialized in live human form, and I had to kill for survival.

IV

LIGHTNING STRIKES
TWICE

16.

January 4, 1979.

I was driving north on U.S. 5 in a snowstorm, my destination the all-year resort town of Lake Geneva, Wisconsin. My traveling stake was low, due to winterizing Deathmobile II with top-of-the-line snow tires, goose-down sleeping quilts and expensive insulation paneling, and my nearest bank cache was in central Colorado. Crossing from Illinois into Wisconsin, I looked at the big snowdrifts forming and knew they would be a long, deep freeze for whoever was unlucky enough to cross my path.

The decision made, I brainstormed with *caution* and *preparedness*. I thought of highway patrolmen prowling for stranded motorists to help, and of old Aspen killings and how difficult it was to strangle or bludgeon with legs mired in snow. Massive walls of bare spruce trees flanking both sides of the road caught my peripheral vision, and I imagined them as receptacles for bloody hollow points. The answer of shoot/rob/retrieve/bury came to me, and I pulled over and took my magnum from its undercarriage hiding place.

The snowfall got steadily worse, and toward noon I started wondering whether I should find lodging or park and wait the storm out. I was in the process of deciding when I saw a Cadillac erratically positioned on the left-hand side of the highway, nose out, the car in imminent danger of getting sideswiped.

I pulled over and tucked the .357 into the back of my pants, making sure my down jacket covered the butt. The highway was traffic-free, and I ran across it to the Cadillac.

There was no one inside, and I saw a faint trail of single snow-dusted footprints leading over to the right shoulder and northward. Stalking now, I returned to the Death-mobile and drove slowly ahead, one eye on the space cleared by my left wiper blade, the other on the roadside.

Half an hour later, I saw him, trudging in ankle-deep drifts. He turned around when he heard my motor, and something about the snow on his head made me reach for the Polaroid.

I tooted the horn and braked; the man waved frantically at his presumed rescuer. Setting the hand brake and hitting the blinkers, I squeezed out the passenger door to confront my victim.

He was middle-aged and portly, and his aura of affluence in distress undercut the lovely crown of snow he was wearing. Panting, he said, "My wife's been after me to get a C.B., now I see why." He pointed to my Polaroid. "Shutterbug, huh? I heard you guys would go anywhere for a picture, now I believe it."

I pulled out my .357 and placed the silencered snout on the man's nose. He said, "Hey, what the—" And I smiled and said, "All I want is your money."

Shaking more from fear than from the cold, he said, "Money I got," and I heard his teeth clicking. Motioning him toward the spruce trees some thirty feet away, I let him walk ahead; then, when he was ten feet from a solid bank of wood, I shot him twice in the back.

The silencer went pffft-thud; the fat man flew forward; splintering wood echoed. I set my stopwatch at eight minutes for ultra-caution, then counted to twenty slowly, to give my victim time to die. When I was sure he would not disturb me with reflex jerks or blood sprays, I grabbed him by the heels and dragged him over to the set of trees most likely to have caught the death rounds. Seeing the ends of the hollow points imbedded side by side in a young sapling, I pried them out with my fingers and put them in my jacket pocket, then hauled the man through an open tree space and over to a snowdrift already three feet deep. Covering my gloveless hands with my sleeves, I took his billfold from his inside jacket pocket, extracted a wad of hundreds, twenties and tens and a collection of credit cards. Stuffing them into my rear pants pockets, I stood back, deep-breathed and unhitched the Polaroid from my shoulder.

4:16 elapsed.

I inventoried my person, touching magnum, spent rounds, stolen cash and plastic. The footprints and blood were *fait accomplis;* fresh snow would cover them soon. Looking down at the dead man, I saw that his crown of snow gave him an air of the Romantic era, as if he were a fop in Beethoven's time disguising his ugliness with a powdered wig. That thought jarred me, and I leaned over and snapped a close-up of the back of his head. The camara ejected blank paper, and when the snow-crown image came through, I put the picture in my front pocket, flipped the man over and snapped his eyes-bulging, mouth-bloodied death mask. My memory was blipped again, and with six minutes down I scooped snow over the corpse until it was a pristine white mound. Finishing the job, I studied the face shot on my way back to the Deathmobile.

With the .357 back in its safety compartment, I continued my journey, the photos on the dashboard where I could view them against the powdered-wig snow. I drove on slowly, hugging the right lane, imagining Mother Nature covering my tracks back at the death site. The storm was reaching blizzard proportions, and I knew Lake Geneva before nightfall was impossible—I would have to seek shelter soon. My wiper blades were barely able to dent the powder hitting the windshield; after turning into a long S-shaped bend, I had to get out and clear it by hand.

That was when I saw the roadblock.

It was sixty yards up, and I knew it couldn't be for me— I had killed the fat man clean, an hour and a half earlier, and if I was identified as the killer, the police would have made a moving approach. Drawing myself drum-tight inside, I scrubbed the windshield clean with my sleeve, got back in the cab and tore the death pictures into pieces and dropped them into the snow outside my passenger door. Remembering the spent shells and credit cards in my pocket,

I flung them out, then dropped the Deathmobile into gear and eased up to the barricade.

State troopers holding shotguns were lined up against the strung-together sawhorses, and there were a half-dozen blue-and-white cruisers behind them. As I braked, two cops approached the Deathmobile in a flanking motion, shotgun muzzles pointed straight at me. From behind the roadblock, an electrically amplified voice barked: "Man in the silver van! Open the door of your vehicle, get out with your hands above your head and walk to the middle of the pavement! Do it slow!"

I obeyed, very slowly, snow raining down on me, the two troopers continuing to hold their beads, the eyes of their 12-gauges huge and black against the snowfall. When I reached the middle of the asphalt, a third cop grabbed my arms from behind, drew them behind my back and handcuffed my wrists. Once I was immobilized, a swarm of troopers leaped over the sawhorses and descended on the Deathmobile, and the two shotgun cops lowered their weapons and approached. The handcuff cop frisked me from behind and said, "Clean," and the other two pointed me to my van. Troopers were over, under and in Deathmobile II; it made me angry, and I sensed that indignant was the way to play my first hard interrogation since Eversall/Sifakis four years earlier. "What the fuck is this?" I said.

The shotgun cops pressed me into the side of my van, and leaned into it themselves. It gave all three of us a break from the wind and snow, and the older cop, who had a lieutenant's bar pinned to the front of his Smokey the Bear hat, said, "Your name?"

"Martin Plunkett," I said.

"Address?"

"I don't have an address. I'm going to Lake Geneva to look for work."

"What kind of work?"

I sighed angrily. "Lift operator or bartender in the winter, maybe caddy during the golf season."

The other cop took over. "You a professional transient, Plunkey?"

"Call me by my correct name," I said.

The lieutenant plucked my wallet from my back pocket and handed it to a trooper inside the Deathmobile's cab. "Run him all-points," he said. Turning to face me, he said, "Mr. Plunkett, you have the right to remain silent. You have the right to have legal counsel present during questioning. If you cannot afford counsel, an attorney will be appointed to you free of charge."

I breathed the pitch in. In the background I could hear my name and driver's-license stats being spoken into a radio mike, and the van shakedown looked to be just about over. The wise-guy cop said, "You got a statement to make, Plunkey?"

I sneered à la Bogart. "You suck cock, dick breath?" The trooper balled his fists, and the lieutenant grabbed me and led me a few yards away. I heard a voice yell, "Vehicle looks clean, Skipper!" and the lieutenant said, "Don't affect an attitude, young man. It's not the time or the place."

I affected a hurt look. "I don't like being rousted."

"Rousted, eh? Been 'rousted' before?"

"I was arrested for burglary about ten years ago. I haven't been in trouble since."

The lieutenant smiled and brushed snow from his lips. "That's the kind of story I like to hear, especially if it gets corroborated by the warrant check we're running on you."

"It will be."

"I sincerely hope so, because three young ladies have been raped and murdered around here lately—one this morning back near the Illinois line—which is what this is all about. What type blood you got, Martin?"

I didn't know how to react to the coincidence, and the shocked look on my face must have been convincing, because the lieutenant shook his head and said, "Ain't that the worst possible? What's your blood type, boy?"

"O negative," I said.

"That's mighty fine, and I tell you what we're gonna do. First, assuming you haven't got any outstanding warrants, you're gonna drive your van to the next town, Huyserville, and you're gonna hang out in a nice clean cell at the jail and get a blood test, and if it comes back O negative, you're a free man, because we typed the rape-o sonuvabitch we're looking for from his semen, and he's O positive. Thank mom and dad for their genes, boy, 'cause any O positive stranger in my stretch of Southern Wisconsin is in for some rousting."

A trooper stuck his head out the van's driver's window. "The sleds squeaky, and daddy-o's got no wants or warrants. One burglary conviction back in '69, that's it."

The lieutenant unlocked my handcuffs and removed them, then said, "Greer, you ride shotgun with Mr. Plunkett here to Huyserville, find him a cozy cell and get Doc Hirsh over to administer a blood test. Martin, you drive carefully, and resign yourself to a night in a hick burg, because these roads ain't fit for man or beast. Now get going."

I got in the Deathmobile and nodded at my copilot, who had his service revolver on his lap, his finger inside the trigger guard. The roadblock was pulled apart, and I accelerated into a blinding wall of snow. Concentrating on my driving kept me reasonably calm, but I felt cut down the middle: half of me proud of my performance; half of me frightened that the dead man's Cadillac would be discovered while I was stuck in Huyserville—or that after I left and the corpse was found, my presence would be remembered and I would become a murder suspect. The fears seemed insoluble, futile to speculate on. I cleared my throat and said to the trooper, "Is there a hotel in Huyserville?"

He snickered. "Cockroach palace. If you have to stay overnight, stick to the jail. You're a transient, right? Three hots and a cot's all you guys want, and you get that at the slam—*if* you're innocent and we let you go."

I nodded. The trooper had an unpleasant conversational style, and I remained silent and let him fondle his gun. The storm was raging now, and it took me an hour to drive the ten miles to Huyserville, a town consisting of one business block and the Wisconsin State Police Substation where I was to be held. Pulling into the station lot, the trooper said, "Sure hope you ain't guilty, pal. Two of the dead girls were from here."

The station's interior was spotless and surprisingly modern, and I was placed in a cell by myself. Only moments later, an old man carrying an archetypal black satchel showed up, and the cell door was racked by remote control. I rolled up my sleeve automatically, and the doctor removed swabs and a syringe with a plastic tube at the end from the bag. He said, "Make a fist," and when I did, he swathed the crook of my right arm and inserted the needle. When blood filled the tube, he said, "An hour for the results," and left me alone. When the cell door was racked shut, I got very frightened.

The doctor's hour stretched interminably, as did my fear, which was not fear of being uncovered as a long-term mass murderer—but fear of being contained, not held in custody, but in the captivity of all the small moments of my past four years—the long, small moments not spent stalking, stealing, killing and thinking—but the time spent working at tedious jobs, cultivating invisibility, being cautious when I wanted to act boldly. The fear was that, inexplicably, these hick-town cops knew who I was, and knew further—inexplicably and preternaturally—that the most vicious way to punish me was to turn me loose, never to scheme/stalk/steal/kill again—my sentence a life made up of all the long, small in-between moments that used to allow me my freedom.

The hour stretched, and I knew that the sixty minutes had doubled and tripled, and that if I looked at my watch for corroboration I would lose every bit of my thirty-year cache of control. I thought of reaching for Shroud Shifter as a separate entity, and rejected the idea as naked regression; I began to fear that killing and holding in sex to the explosion point had somehow changed my blood type, and now I was going to be castrated for someone else's crimes. The notion of foreign blood inside my own body brought me close to screaming, and I began cataloguing long, small in-between moments to prove to myself that I wasn't going insane. I thought of every fleabag apartment I had lived in since leaving San Francisco; every stretch of desolate road where I never found anyone; every person I met who was too ugly, too poor, too well-connected and too uninteresting to kill. The litany had a salutary effect, and I looked at my watch and saw that it was 6:14—my brain-tripping had eaten up over four hours. Then a voice outside the cell resounded softly. "Mr. Plunkett, I'm Sergeant Anderson."

Before I could think, I blurted, "Was my blood all right?"

The voice said, "Red and healthy," and the man it belonged to stepped into focus on the other side of the bars. My first impression was of looking at the most immaculate advertisement for authority I had ever seen. The man, clad in the Wisconsin State Police uniform of olive twill trousers, tan gabardine shirt and Sam Browne belt, was a perfect componentry of muscular litheness, bland good looks and something else that I couldn't place. Standing up, I saw that he was just over six feet tall, and that his lank, reddish brown hair and toothbrush mustache gave him a youthful aura that his cold blue eyes played against—and lost. The exquisitely tailored uniform transformed his good looks into another something else I couldn't decipher, and when we were face-to-face, with only the bars between us, it hit me. I was in the presence of an exceptionally powerful will. Regrouping, I said, "Red, healthy and O negative, right, Sergeant?"

The man smiled and patted a paper bag he was holding. "Right, O negative. I'm O positive myself, never made me more than a five-spot when I was broke in college." Taking a key from his belt, he unlocked the door, and when I took a step forward, he blocked my path. For an instant the cold blue eyes fired up, then a lopsided grin nullified them, and Anderson said, "You ever notice how two people just getting acquainted talk about the weather, Martin?"

The softly enunciated "Martin" terrified me. I stepped back and said, "Yes."

Anderson stroked the paper bag. "Well, we've got some real weather to talk about—twenty-six inches of snow expected by morning, tristate storm warning, roads closed within a five-hundred-mile radius. Look, I hope it wasn't presumptuous, but Lieutenant Havermeyer got called up to Eau Claire, which makes me acting watch commander, and I took the liberty of booking you the very last available room in Huyserville." He took a key from his back pocket

and handed it to me, and when our fingers touched, I knew
he knew.

"Martin? You feeling a little queasy?"

The soft, solicitous words went through me like a knife,
and I started to weave on my feet. Anderson himself was
a blur, but his hand on my shoulder was like a tree root
holding me up, and his voice was perfect clarity. "Baaad
weather. I was patrolling south of here this morning, saw
this '79 Caddy Eldo parked on the throughway, didn't look
nice, so I pushed it off the shoulder, probably covered with
snow by now. Wonder what happened to the driver. He'll
probably end up in some timberwolf's lunchbox, nice juicy
humanburger. Don't you want to know what's in the bag?"

Shroud Shifter sent me flash-lines of asterisks, question
marks and numbers, and when the numbers computed to
1948–1979, I tried to bring my hands up to Anderson's
throat. But I couldn't; he was holding all two hundred and
five strong pounds of me still with one firm hand on my
shoulder and the admonishment, "Ssssh, ssssh, ssssh."

Swaying underneath the trooper's hand;

Adjusting to the rhythm and somehow liking it;

The cell about to tilt upside down, but saved at the last
second by a choirboy voice: "I don't think you can handle
seeing it, so I'll tell you. I've got a beeautiful Colt Python
with a pro-model suppressor, and some credit cards, and
some of those *True Detective* magazines, and some ripped-
up Polaroid photos, allll taped up and smeared with fin-
gerprint powder, which reveals—you guessed it—two
viable latents belonging to Martin Michael Plunkett, white
male, D.O.B. 4/11/48, Los Angeles, California. Does it ever
snow in California, Martin?"

The hand and voice let go, and my back hit the metal edge
of the top bunk. The contact jarred me, and Anderson came
into real focus—as an adversary. Straightening up, I began
to sense the vaguest outlines of the game he was playing. I
could still feel his hand and voice, but I was able to shake off
their residual warmth and say, "What do you—"

I stopped when my voice came out an imitation of Anderson's, softness wrapped in menace. Anderson smiled and

said, "The sincerest form of flattery, so thanks. What do I want? I don't know, you're the Hollywood boy, you write the scenario."

I made my voice grating—all hard baritone edges. "Suppose I walk out of here, get my van and just go?"

"Suppose you do? You're free to. You won't get far, though. That is a killer storm out there."

"Do I get my—"

Anderson shook the paper bag. "No, you don't. Don't ask me again."

The game's outlines cleared a little more. It was coming down to a holding action. "What are you going to do with the things in that bag?"

"Keep them."

"Why?"

"Because I like your style."

"And when the storm cl—"

Anderson turned, his voice grating. "Clears, you're free to go."

I fingered the key in my pocket. Anderson said, "The hotel's directly across the street and two doors down, and the Wisconsin State Police is picking up the tab because we inconvenienced an innocent man."

I walked out of the cell and through the station and into the snow. It enveloped me, and crossing to the hotel I saw my van parked at the curb, gone from silver to powdery white. I thought of heading into the storm, the Deathmobile as a vehicle of suicide; I thought of driving flat out, but cautious, *moving*. Panic was coming on, naked and ugly and picayune—and then I remembered how Anderson's hand felt on my shoulder, and I knew that if I ran, he would never know that I was just as dangerous as he was.

Staying was the only way out.

I ran to the hotel, and got to the dilapidated coffee shop just as it was about to close. Ravenous, I ordered roast beef, hot rolls and potatoes, and wolfed them down. Then I went into the lobby and sat in a big chair by the fireplace to get up some guts.

My hours of waiting passed quickly this time; my fear

was not steeped in malaise—it was edgy, masculine—like what bullfighters must feel before entering the ring. At 10:00 I took out my key, saw 311 embossed on it, walked up to the room and unlocked the door.

An overhead light had been left on, and it illuminated a dreary 20's-vintage room—threadbare carpet, big spongy bed, battered desk and dresser. The plainness forced me backward, not in, and I knew that what I had been expecting was a naked man. The wish image vanished after a second, and I stepped into the four-walled time warp and shut and bolted the door.

Wind rattled the ice-rimmed windows, and a nauseating blast of heat came in through the vents. There were no chairs, so I moved to the bed. I was about to position myself on it when I saw that the coverlet was already occupied.

Polaroid prints were spread on the white chenille, three rows of four color snapshots laid out evenly so that they covered the whole bed. I bent to look at them, and saw vivisection progressions: four nude teenage girls—all brunette and pretty—intact in the top photographs, gradually dismembered as the pictures worked toward the footrail.

The vents shook with another heat blast, and I flailed with my eyes for a sink. Seeing one next to a connecting side door, I ran to it and vomited my meal. I was splashing cold water on my face when I heard a click and saw Anderson walk through the door.

Grabbing a towel from the rack beside the sink, I wiped my face. Anderson leaned into the wall sideways, accomplishing the pose with the grace of a gifted male model. It struck me then that every small moment of the man's life was infused with eloquence. "Don't tell me you didn't already know," he said.

I held down an urge to rip the pose to pieces with my hands. "I knew. *Why?*"

Anderson smoothed his mustache and gave me a grin that made him look a guileless seventeen. "Why? Because *I* knew. There's a two-lane that parallels the throughway south to the Illinois line, and back near Beloit it's elevated. I saw you check out the Cadillac, and I saw you cruise for

the driver, and sweetie, I knew you didn't have good deeds
on your mind. I gave you a lead, then I tracked you by
radar. When you stopped, I waited five minutes, then idled
up to about six hundred yards in back of you and parked.
I had my binoculars on your van, and I saw you put the
magnum back in its hidey-hole. That's when I knew I really
liked your style."

Nineteen sixty-nine took over 1979, and I thought, "Lock,
load and fire." I centered in on Anderson's neck, and I almost
had up the guts to do it when he smiled and said, "Bad
idea, Martin." Knowing it was full lips and a crinkling
mustache that stopped me—not the warning—I made a
full-body eye circuit, and something external forced me to
say, "Dye your hair blond."

Anderson snorted and pointed to the bed. "Blonds are
for sissies. Brunettes are my meat."

I saw a gilt-framed picture of my father and a nude
woman, both of them wearing powder-white wigs. Shocked
that I could still recall the man's features, and fearful of
where the picture frame was taking me, I shut down the
image by thinking of my snow-haired victim seventy miles
south. Anderson's perfect stylishness was fixed directly in
front of me, forcing me to keep my eyes open and con-
straining my brain work, and I finally got up the courage
to fire, roundhousing a right hand at his perfect nose.

He slipped the punch perfectly, grabbing my wrist, twisting it behind my back and holding me still with a firm arm
around the chest. Enveloped by perfect strongness, a perfect
voice eased my fear: "Whoa, sweetie, whoa. You're bigger
and stronger than me, but I'm trained. I don't blame you
for being mad, but you've got nothing to worry about. Here,
I'll prove it."

Anderson's grip loosened, and he turned me around so
that I was facing him. The absence of pressure left me
feeling hollow, and I concentrated on the trooper's regrouping movements to cut the edge off the vacuum. His hands
went to his front and back pockets and came out with wads
of cash, and he said, "See? Your money. When I searched
your van I saw that the glove compartment had been pried

open. There was no money in your hidey-holes, and I knew
a bright boy like you wouldn't travel without a nice roll,
so I figured one of Wisconsin State's finest ripped you off.
Since I know my fellow officers, I knew exactly who to look
for. I let him off with a reprimand—more than you're getting, and for a whole lot fucking less."

I took the money and stuffed it into my pockets. "Why?"

Anderson smiled. "Because I like your style."

"Then what do you want?"

"The Python and the suppressor, you know, mementos.
Some conversation, the answers to a few questions."

"Such as?"

"Such as 'How many people have you killed?'"

I looked around the room, knowing there had to be a
catch, that the cracked vase on the dresser had to be a
listening device, or the curtain-covered window a sighting
point for snipers with x-ray scopes on their rifles—hick-
town killers who would fire on me at my first admission of
murder. After a moment I knew I was thinking Shroud
Shifter childishly, and I turned my gaze back to Anderson,
roaming the tight contours of his uniform for concealed
recorders. The trooper laughed at this, and said, "I get the
distinct impression that you're looking for more than a body
wire, but anyway, let me cool out your paranoia, okay? For
starters, I'll state that I am Sergeant Ross Anderson of the
Wisconsin State Police, and also the killer referred to in
the Milwaukee papers as the 'Wisconsin Whipsaw.' There.
That make you feel better?"

It did, for despite his stylishness and aura of danger, I
knew that he was not in my league in what mattered most
to both of us. Getting a bold sense of having achieved parity
with perfection, I said, "About forty. You?"

Anderson's jaw dropped; I had eclipsed his perfection.
"Jesus Christ. Five. You want to tell me about it?"

I remembered his words when I pleaded for my magnum.
"No. Don't ask me again."

"Touché. Why?"

"Because they're mine."

Ross Anderson stretched and said, "Then I guess we've

reached an impasse." He moved to the bed and scooped up his death photos, and when he walked to the connecting door I was blocking his path. "Tell me about yours."

Smiling, Anderson slipped the pictures into his shirt pockets, buttoning the flaps over them. Raising his eyebrows in a parody of a come-hither look, he moved back to the bed and sat on the edge of it. I looked around the room and saw that there were no chairs. Knowing that Ross had designed it that way, I played along and sat down beside him. With our eyes averted from each other but our knees touching, he said, "No pun intended, but I've been dying to tell someone, someone special and safe, so I guess unilateral is better than nothing.

"When I was in my late teens I had a buddy, and we used to go pheasant hunting over near Prairie Du Chien. He was a doper and kind of a sleaze, but he let me call the shots, and he was up for just about anything. We spent a lot of time talking about the Nazis and the concentration camps, and he had a collection of daggers and arm bands. He actually took all that stuff seriously—the master race and the Jews and the commies, the whole shot. I was fascinated by it—but he believed in it.

"We were up near P.D. one day, right after Thanksgiving in '70. Gunning for ringnecks with twelve-gauges, double-aught buck, which if you know wing shooting, is much too big a load for birds. You see, we weren't sportsmen or game-cuisine lovers—we just liked to shoot things.

"It was about zero, and there were no other hunters around. We didn't have a dog to flush the birds, and essentially we were just looking for something to do. We were carrying pumps instead of double-barreleds, so we were glad there was no one around—we were kids, and any real sportsmen would have been able to tell by our weapons that we weren't serious hunters.

"About dusk we start heading back to the car, and this old fart materializes out of nowhere. Big old red-faced guy with a thousand-dollar Browning over and under, and about another grand in L.L. Bean threads on his back. He starts giving us shit about our guns, and didn't we respect hunting traditions and where were our hunting licenses—and then—zap! I look at my buddy, we have this moment of telepathy and blow the old fart to kingdom come, blam blam blam blam blam—five rounds apiece—we vaporize the cocksucker."

I stared at the wall and gripped the mattress with both hands; beside me I felt Ross breathe in short spurts. Finally he took a huge breath, and continued:

"Needless to say, we didn't get made for the snuff, and we were both scared shitless until the job got pinned on these two niggers who held up a gun shop in Milwaukee and ripped off a half-dozen Mossberg pumps—the same model my buddy and I had. The jigs got convicted on circumstantial evidence, and my buddy and I went our separate ways, because we were afraid of what the two of us together meant.

"So five years pass, I put it out of my mind and join the W.S.P. I love being a trooper, I'm a cop now, above suspicion. To make things even better, my buddy moves to Chicago and gets married, out of place and out of mind, we haven't seen each other since the day the splibs got sentenced to Life and we celebrated with two cases of beer and said au revoir. Everything is just peachy and I'm getting ready to ace the sergeant's exam, and then blam blam blam blam blam!

"What happened was that buddy boy was back in Wisconsin, harvesting a weed crop outside of Beloit, living in a cheapo furnished room in Janesville. Friends of friends told me, so I went looking for him. I checked out his flop: pictures of Hitler on the walls, bags of weed all packaged up ready to go, hate literature on the dresser. Totally unacceptable. I found out he was taking I-5 to Lake Geneva every third day or so, to sell smoke to the vacationers there, and I got his vehicle stats from the Illinois D.M.V. That stretch of road was on my beat, I knew I'd see him sooner or later, and sweetie, I was prepared.

"The next day I'm parked, running radar checks, and buddy boy's old junker cruises by. I hit my cherry lights and siren and pull him over, and he goes, 'Hey, Ross!' and I go 'Hey, Billy!' and we shoot the shit through the window for a few minutes, then I tell him I have to go back to the cruiser and check my two-way.

"Back at my blue-and-white I hyperventilate to sound panicky, then I call in a 415—Armed Suspect, Officer Needs Help, I-5 north of exit sixteen. I go back to buddy boy's car and shoot him twice in the face, then I take a Saturday Night Special from my pocket, wipe it and put it in his right hand, stick his arm out the window and pop off a shot with his index finger—blam!—out into the cabbage fields. When the other units arrive, I'm weeping because I had to kill my old buddy Billy Gretzler that I used to go pheasant hunting with. Naturally all the evidence backs me up, and the plainclothes troopers who investigate all officer-involved shootings check out Billy's room and find Der Fuhrer and the weed and conclude that, all things considered, my ret-roactive birth control was justified. I had a rep for coolness before the shooting, but after it I got one for sensitivity. That Ross Anderson, boy. Killed an old buddy in the line of duty, it broke him up, but he kept on truckin' and made sergeant anyway. Ross the Boss, what a guy."

I took my hands from the mattress; they were numb from squeezing my way through Ross's monologue. Wanting to distance myself from him, I moved down the bed so that physical contact was impossible, continuing to stare at the wall. The aftertaste of his story hit me in waves, a one-two-three punch of callowness, bravado and style. I knew something essential was missing, but I pushed thinking about it aside, and when Ross poked my arm and said, "Well?" I launched my own death travelogue.

But I didn't talk about my killings themselves.

It was the long, small in-between moments that I spoke of; the law-abiding time that felt incriminating to my own heart; the self-imposed sentence of constant movement, different cities, renting hotel rooms and apartments to appear normal when sleeping in the Deathmobile would have sufficed; the dubious celebrity of being mentioned in detective magazines written for near-illiterates; tweaking the police with self-incriminating clues, a fifth-class substitute for Martin Plunkett in worldwide neon; being relegated to moronic alliterative titles like the "Richmond Ripper," "Aspen Assassin" and "Vegas Vulture"; feeling the nightmares always there behind the thrills, emblazoned in the neon my name should be written in.

I stopped when the discourse started to feel like a giant genuflection to Ross Anderson's male-model stylishness. Turning to look at him, I got an urge to maim his beauty, carve my name across his body for the world to see. He smiled then, and I realized the thrust of our respective powers—I emasculated with guns, knives and my hands; he was capable of doing it with a wink or a grin. The missing part of his story came to me, and I said, "What about the girls? The brunettes? You didn't tell me about that."

Ross shrugged. "There's nothing to tell. After snuffing Billy I realized how much I loved blood sport. I've always dug foxy young brunettes, and sport's sport."

"But why?"

"I don't know. The die was cast somewhere, and thinking about it bores me. Apples and oranges. You like blonds, I like brunettes; that guy they caught last year, the Pittsburgh Pistolwhipper, he liked redheads. Like they used to say back in the '60's, 'Do your own thing.'"

I moved closer to Ross; my work shoes touched his spit-shined paratrooper's boots. "Could you ch—"

Cutting me off with a wink, he said, "Could I change my M.O.? Sure. You want blonds, I'll give you blonds. I've got a traveling assignment coming up. Check the eastern U.S. papers out, starting about a month from now."

"What?"

Again the wink—a velvet glove that smothered all possible queries. "Enough said. Listen, Martin. This is really my room. I keep it for long shifts and snow-in's. You can stay if you want, but there's only the one bed."

The look in Ross's eyes told me he was talking comradeship and style, not standard meanings. I took off my shoes and lay down, and Ross unhooked his gun belt and wrapped it around the bedpost only inches from my head. He lay down beside me and flicked off the wall light and seemed to fall into sleep concurrent with the abrupt darkness. Exhaustion hit me, and as the most incredible day of my life flickered out, I got frightened and stroked the grips of the .38, drawing comfort from knowing I could murder the murderer lying next to me.

Thus reassured, I slept.

Sunlight and the sound of heavy machinery awakened me dreamless hours later. I immediately felt for Ross, found the other half of the bed empty and jumped up. I was moving toward the sink and a cold-water bracer when he walked through the connecting door, a small revolver in his hand.

I grabbed at the sink edge, thinking of betrayal, and Ross gave me his rakish teenager grin and flipped the gun so that it was butt out. Handing it to me, he said, "Smith and Wesson .38 Detective's Special. Safe, serviceable weapon, very cold. You didn't think I'd let you walk out of here unarmed, did you? Ross the Boss, what a guy."

I flipped the cylinder open, saw that the gun was loaded and stuck it in my back pocket. I couldn't say "Thank you"— it felt acquiescent—so I asked, "Are the roads clear?"

Ross said, "Being plowed now. You should be able to truck by noon."

I stood there, thinking of the taped-together snapshots and my magnum, not knowing what to say or do. Seeming to read my mind, Ross said, "Your stuff is safe with me. I'll never rat you off, but I may need you someday, and the evidence is insurance."

I was reverberating with the implications of "need you" when Ross leaned forward and kissed me on the lips. I leaned into it and tasted wax on his mustache and bitter coffee on his tongue, and when he broke contact and about-faced through the door, I was flushed and hungry for more. I did not yet know that the kiss would push me and haunt me and hurt me and drive me for the next two and a half years of my life.

V

LIGHTNING SCATTERS

From the Milwaukee Tribune, *February 19, 1979:*

'WISCONSIN WHIPSAW' INVESTIGATION ON BACK BURNER; DEAD MAN KILLER?

It is now over six weeks since the "Wisconsin Whipsaw," a rapist/slayer who terrorized the Janesville-Beloit area during December and January, claimed his last victim.

On the snowy morning of January 4, the butchered body of Claire Kozol, 17, of Huyserville, Wisconsin, was discovered in a cabbage field near the Illinois border. She had been raped, beaten to death and dismembered—in a manner identical to Gretchen Weymouth, 16, whose body was discovered a few miles away on December 16, and Mary Coontz, 18, also of Huyserville, who was found in a duck blind on the outskirts of Beloit on Christmas Day. All three young women were attractive, slender brunettes, and forensic psychiatrists attached to Wisconsin State Police Headquarters in Madison were convinced that a highly motivated and exceptionally vicious psychopathic killer was operating in the Southern Wisconsin area. Their psychological profile (based on previous case histories and physical evidence from the three killings) concluded that the murderer would continue to kill the same type of victim in the same manner, until captured or killed himself.

A task force of twenty Wisconsin State Police detectives were assigned to the investigation full-time, and they were assisted by officers from the Janesville and Beloit police departments. Elaborate decoy traps to snare the killer were set up, in anticipation of another murder attempt in the near future. The net was tightening, and police officials were certain the blood-crazed murderer would step into it soon.

But he didn't, and there have been no further killings matching the Wisconsin Whipsaw's M.O. since Miss Kozol's body was found on January 4. Wisconsin State Police Sergeant Ross Anderson, who supervised the decoy deployment, has a theory as to what happened.

"It's a theory based on the Psych. 101 course I took in college and circumstantial evidence," the trooper, 29, told reporters. "But instinctively I credit it.

"On January 5, the day after Miss Kozol's body was found, I was supervising snowplowing on I-5 south of Huyserville when I spotted the rear of a car, partially covered by snow, off the roadside. I dug through the snow and saw that the car was a '79 Cadillac with Illinois plates. There was no driver trapped inside, and I checked the glove compartment and found ID belonging to a man named Saul Malvin, age 51, of Lake Forest. When I saw O+ blood on a donor card, my skin prickled. We typed the rape-killer from his semen—and he was O+.

"I radioed the Lake Forest P.D., and they told me that Malvin's wife had reported him missing that morning—he had left the previous morning to visit friends in Lake Geneva. I took a vest I found in the backseat, drove to Huyserville for a K-9 team, drove back to the area and initiated a search. About eight hours later, the dogs and I hit paydirt.

"Wolves had chewn away most of the man's upper torso, but you could still tell what had happened. Malvin was dead, about ten yards off the roadside. There was a .357 Magnum in his hand. His wallet was intact, filled with cash. I ran back to my cruiser and radioed for an ambulance, then I started thinking."

Trooper Anderson's ultimate theory—that the late Saul Malvin was the Wisconsin Whipsaw, and that he committed suicide in a moment of guilt over his crimes, has created a furor among his W.S.P. colleagues, and opinions are divided on the subject of the former insurance executive's culpability. Lieutenant W. S. Havermeyer, the commander of the Huyserville Substation, summed up the pros and cons at a press conference last week. "As of now, we're assuming that if the Whipsaw isn't Mr. Malvin, he's in jail or the loony bin, or he's moved on. The shrink boys in Madison say that sometimes these repeating psychos have a moment of clarity and kill themselves, especially right after an especially brutal job, so that fits circumstantially, and Malvin did have O positive blood. We've checked out his whereabouts at the times of the three killings. His car was found just a few miles from where the Kozol girl's body was discovered, and on the dates of the two previous murders, December 16 and Christmas, he was allegedly working at home alone and waiting at home for his wife to return from celebrating the holiday with her invalid sister.

"So, circumstantially, Malvin could have been the perpetrator, although he does not 'play' as one. He had no criminal record, was happily married with grown children, was successful and well-liked by friends and family. That is in his favor.

"But he did commit suicide with a gun that to this day cannot be traced, and relatives and friends have told us that he had no logical reason to take his own life. Unfortunately, wolves had attacked Malvin's body just before Sergeant Anderson discovered it, and if there was any physical evidence on his person linking him to Claire Kozol, the animals probably destroyed it. All in all, I'm grateful there have been no more killings."

Sergeant Anderson, believed by many of his colleagues to have "cracked" the case, will be moving on to different duties—carrying extradition warrants to midwestern and eastern cities and returning with felons wanted by the Wisconsin State authorities. He is grateful for the change of pace, and told reporters: "The Whipsaw case took a lot out of me. It's going to be nice to get a change of scenery, to ply my trade in new places."

From the Louisville, Kentucky, Herald, April 18, 1979:

WOMAN FOUND MURDERED IN PORN DISTRICT

The body of a 20-year-old woman who worked as a nude dancer was discovered this morning by her boyfriend, who wept when he saw her butchered remains and immediately called police. The victim, Kristine Pasquale, who worked at the nearby Swinger's Rendezvous Bar, had been slashed to death and dismembered, and police who viewed the remains of the attractive blonde were shocked and stunned. Sergeant James Ruley, one of the first officers to arrive at Miss Pasquale's bloodsoaked apartment, told reporters: "Bar none, the worst crime upon a woman I've ever seen, and you can quote me on that. It's either going to be an open-and-shut case, or a toughie, because Miss Pasquale was, if you follow my drift, not exactly a blushing flower. I busted her for prostitution myself when I worked Vice, and the Swinger's Rendezvous, the joint where she worked, is a notorious criminal gathering place. My guess right off the top of my head is that her killer was a longtime known associate, or she wouldn't have buzzed him up to her pad. She was a street-smart girl, and choosy about her tricks."

Miss Pasquale's body was removed, and her apartment was sealed off. Forensic technicians went to work, and Miss Pasquale's boyfriend, David Komondy, 27, the bouncer at Swinger's Rendezvous, was questioned and released. No clues were discovered at the apartment, and eight hours later, Dr. Winton Walker, Assistant Medical Examiner for the City of Louisville, announced his findings:

"Miss Pasquale was raped, then murdered. The cause of death was massive trauma and loss of blood, caused by a severed throat. More details will be released later."

Meanwhile, Louisville police are swarming over the porn district, looking for what Sergeant Ruley called "a very angry man."

Follow-up report on Louisville Homicide # 116–79, 4–18–79, filed on 4–27–79 by Det. Sergeant J. M. Ruley, Badge 212, Louisville Police Department, Homicide Division. Titled "Progress Report, Rape/Murder—Pasquale, Kristine Michelle," it was distributed to all Louisville detective units on 4–28–79.

PROGRESS REPORT:

Rape/Murder—Pasquale, Kristine Michelle, D.O.D. 4–18–79.

Note: This report updates previously filed Crime Scene reports, M.E.'s reports, Canvassing and Interview reports, Sex Offender reports, Property reports and Detective's log sheets. (See case file # 116–79 under those designations.) This is my first summary report, filed as the catching officer.

Gentlemen:

Updating # 116–79, now ten days old. The victim was

raped, the victim's throat was slashed while the perpetrator held a pillow over her head. He cut off her arms and legs with a different instrument than the knife the throat wound was made with (see Cr. Sc. Rpt. #116–79 for det.). No weapons found at scene or in surrounding area. We are looking for: 1—Sharp-bladed hunting knife, blade 7″ long, possibly "Buck" brand (all knives of this type confiscated from arrestees or found on male suspects during field interrogations should be given chemical tests to determine presence of blood, & detain all suspects). 2—Hacksaw, with teeth approx. 1/32″, also sharp. Force of incisions indicates strong man. Recent sales of above being checked out. Also on suspect—he *may* have O+ blood (I say *may* because semen found in victim's vagina secretor O+ and abrasions indicate forced entry. However—victim was known prostitute & given killer's caution in other matters, he may have had smarts to wear a condom). (Note: Victim's pimp-lover said deceased was on pill, but sometimes asked tricks to use condom. No other semen found in vag. vault, so this may not be conclusive.)

Known associates—nothing so far (see # 116–79 Interviews, # 116–79 Log Sheets).

Canvassing—ditto—see # 116–79 Canvassing.

Property—inventory with boyfriend indicates nothing stolen, narcotic substances (cocaine, hashish) confiscated.

Physical evidence—interesting, pointing to smart killer. Prints eliminated by cross checks with K.A.'s—none unexplained. No blood tracks leading down to street floor, no prints on buzzer killer probably used to gain entrance to apt: Lack of above point out my personal reconstruction:

The victim, with *nine* prev. arrests for prostitution and known to be very cautious, would have buzzed up only three types of men—policemen, pimps & boyfriends or customers. Eliminating the first two (pimp & old boyfriends cleared—see # 116–79 Interviews), that leaves *customers*. I reconstruct the killing as being perpetrated by a former John harboring a long-term grudge, who carried a spare set of clothes up to the apartment, wearing gloves. Since most Louisville-area deviates have been or are now being questioned, and there are no similar killings on the books, I am directing my efforts toward questioning local prostitutes and men convicted of and arrested for soliciting indecent acts. Patrol & other officers with knowledge of possible suspects should contact me at H.Q. Div. Ext. 409.

Let's get him!

Sgt. J. M. Ruley.

From the Evanston, Illinois, Eagle, May 8, 1979:

BODY OF UNIDENTIFIED MAN FOUND IN GARBAGE DUMP

A group of rubbish dumpers made a ghastly discovery this morning when they hauled their trash over to an empty stretch of the city dump site on Kingsbury Road. It was a dead man, spread-eagled on the ground. Congealed blood was staining the dirt by his head. Mrs. Katherine Daniel, the only woman in the group, fainted, and her husband, Mr. Daniel Daniel, of Muirfield Road in Evanston, revived her while their neighbor, Mr. Jason Granger, ran to summon police.

They arrived soon after, and determined that the dead man had been shot in the head. His pockets had been turned out, and at this early point in their investigation they think robbery may be the motive for the killing.

But right now their most pressing problem is identifying the deceased. The man is described as Caucasian, approximately thirty years old, six feet two and one hundred and ninety pounds, dark brown hair and hazel eyes. Anyone having information on missing men who match that description should contact the Evanston Police Department.

Memorandum submitted on 5/11/79 by Captain William Silbersack, Chief of Detectives of the Evanston Police Department, to Thomas Thyssen, Chief of Police.

Memo:

Sir—

Here's the update on the Kingsbury Road homicide you requested. First, we got an ID on the decedent. He's Robert Willard Borgie, W.M., D.O.B. 6/30/51, 6'2", 193, brown & hazel. Address: The board and care home at 814 Kingsbury. (Four blocks from the dump.)

Borgie was mentally retarded. He'd go anywhere with anybody, and he used to wander off for days at a time, which accounts for the delay in making the ID (the supervisor at the home came forward when she saw a T.V. spot on the homicide). She told Sgts. Lane and Vecchio that Borgie used to hook up with homosexuals, and had oral sex with them for money. He would allegedly trust *anyone*.

As per the coroner's report: Borgie was shot *in the mouth* with a .38. The one shot caused his death. We got a break on the spent shell the M.E. took out of his skull—the striations were extreme, and the shot could only have been fired by a .38 snub-nose with a badly aligned barrel and cylinder housing. Naturally, I'll run a Ballistics Bulletin statewide.

On motive—robbery seems farfetched, although Borgie's pockets were turned out. Subterfuge? Possibly, because Borgie never had more than a few dollars. It's the shot *in the mouth* that bothers me. Borgie was shot *at* the dump (two sets of footprints leading to, one returning from the place where the body was found indicate the killer was a man wearing a size 11½ work boot), and the killer obviously ordered him to open his mouth before he stuck the gun in. All these factors (Borgie's low intelligence, trusting nature, history of homosexual trafficking), and the obviously perverse nature of the shooting, point to a homosexual killer.

So far, Sgts. Lane and Vecchio have conducted their investigation along standard lines (see case file # 79–008–H for details). There have been no leads, and I am now instructing the officers to strongly follow up on the homosexual angle.

Respectfully, Bill Silbersack.

*   *   *

From the Des Moines, Iowa, Register, October 2, 1979:

SEX SLAYING SHOCKS CITY

A teenaged girl was found raped and brutally knife-hacked in an abandoned grain-storage bin outside Des Moines last night.

The victim was discovered by two teenage boys who broke in to vandalize the bin. Realizing their civic duty, the boys called police and confessed their own crime while reporting the grisly scene. Des Moines police arrived, and forgot about misdemeanor Breaking and Entering the very second they saw the remains of Wilma Grace Thurmann, 19, of Brewster Street in Des Moines.

"The girl's throat was slashed from ear to ear, and her arms and legs were amputated and strewn about the floor of the bin," Officer John Belton told the press. "An ID was easy, because I knew Wilma myself, not personally, but by sight."

When pressed as to how he knew the late Miss Thurmann, Officer Belton refused to comment. Later our reporters learned that the deceased was a "hustler" who used to solicit truck drivers at the diner two miles south of the bin. She was known to have a key to the abandoned structure, and known also to take her "tricks" there.

"The victim's occupation might make for a difficult investigation," an unnamed police spokesman wrote in a general press handout distributed this morning. "But rest assured that Miss Thurmann's killer will be pursued with vigor."

Summary Homicide Investigation Fact Sheet, distributed to all personnel points within the Des Moines Police Department on 10/4/79.

Crime(s)—Murder (1st Degree), Aggrav. Sex Asslt.

Place of Occurrence—R.F.D. # 71-A (near Sagamore Truck Stop-Exit) East Des Moines

Victim—Thurmann, Wilma Grace, W.F., blond, blue, 5'1", 105 lbs., D.O.B. 7/3/60

Time of occurrence—approx. 2100 hours, 10/1/79

Disposition of victim at time of occurrence—victim found by youths B&Eing. Catching officer stated in crime scene rep. # 79–14–H: "I entered the bin carrying a five-cell from my patrol unit and saw a young white female with her arms and legs chopped off and her throat cut. I examined the body up close and determined it to be Wilma Thurmann, a local hooker. I checked out the rest of the bin and found her arms and legs lying on top of mounds of hay."

Forensic disposition—raped before death. Blade marks behind right ear indicate rapist/killer held knife there while performing intercourse. Semen found in victim's vagina at time of autopsy (O+ secretor) differs from semen traces found in victim's stomach (AB+ & O-). Victim's police record shows five convictions for soliciting sex acts, and she was known to use bin for performing oral sex acts on customers, hence O+ secretor is probably rapist/killer's blood type.

Exact cause of death—asphyxiation caused by choking on blood from throat wound.

Evidence found at crime scene—none. Dirt leading to, from & inside bin brushed free of footprints. Latent fingerprints at scene—none (absence of viable print-sustaining surfaces accts. for this).

Eyewitnesses—none

Prev. area crimes with corresponding M.O.—none since 1947, connection implausible

Disposition of weapon—not found during search of area, canvassing of local retailers being conducted. *All units watch for:* single-edged knife, 7" long, cadmium steel hacksaw, blade teeth 1/32". Detain all male suspects harboring or known to harbor.

Current status of investigation—unsolved, no hard suspects, eight detectives assigned full-time. All officers who have arrested or otherwise interrogated Wilma Grace Thurmann or any of her known associates are instructed to phone in salient information to Det. Lt. H. V. Miller, Squad Commander, East Des Moines Precinct.

For further information regarding the progress of this investigation, see case file # 79–14–H. All reports under that designation are available to all D.M.P.D. personnel wishing to acquaint themselves with this assault/homicide.

From the Lincoln, Nebraska, Plains-Advocate, *December 10, 1979:*

WHEAT FIELD SHOOTING TROUBLES POLICE

It is now a week since Russell Luxxlor was found shot through the head in a wheat field outside Lincoln. Leads are few, and police are baffled.

At first, the authorities thought the killing was part of a bungled robbery attempt. Luxxlor's wallet was in his pants pocket, picked clean of identification and credit cards, while three hundred dollars in cash remained untouched in a "secret compartment" in the victim's windbreaker. That theory was then abandoned when it was learned that Luxxlor was a homosexual and a long-term denizen of Lincoln's "gay" scene.

Lincoln Police Department spokesman Lt. Mills Putnam told *Plains-Advocate* reporters: "We base the homosexual theory on a fact pertaining to the way Mr. Luxxlor was shot. We are not disclosing the fact in order that we may save it for interrogation purposes."

In a later press release, Lt. Putnam stated: "We have now slightly amended our homosexual hypothesis. We think Mr. Luxxlor was killed for the identification he was carrying. We base this on the fact that all his ID was gone when his body was found, and he was last seen in a bar in Lincoln with a man who matched his own physical description. We are now looking for a white man in his early thirties, 6'2"–6'4", 190–210 lbs., dark hair and eyes and large build."

Mr. Luxxlor was buried in a Methodist service yesterday, and the victim's father, the Reverend Maddox Luxxlor of Cheyenne, Wyoming, told a group of reporters and police gathered at the funeral home: "You people have no right to defame my son! Your job is to catch his killer, not judge him!"

The effort to apprehend the killer continues.

* * *

Addendum Report, submitted by Detective Sergeant Joseph Stinson to Detective Lieutenant Mills Putnam, both officers attached to Homicide Sector Three, Lincoln Police Department.

10/18/79

Lt.—

Here's another wrap-up on the Luxxlor job. 1.—Mugs have been shown to gay-bar people—no ID on the guy Luxxlor was seen with.

2.—Friends, relatives, K.A.'s—goose egg. Statewide query on the weirdly striated .38 slug—ditto, but if this thing doesn't crack soon I'll run a nationwide bulletin. Gun in mouth M.O. the same, I'll draft an "urgent" on that one soon and hit the surrounding states and the feds with it.

******!!!!!!—Man matching description of Luxxlor & suspect seen last night—trying to sell "cold" credit cards at Henderson's Hot Spot Bar (11819 Cornhusker Road). Informer phoned in tip anonymously, said suspect was 6'3", 200, brown eyes, dark hair—"big and intense-looking." The suspect got hinky and left when the tip man asked the name on the cards. Tip man said suspect may be driving a metallic blue van. I've issued an A.P.B. & vehicle detain order county-wide, and I've told the men on the squad to shake down their informants.

That's it for now—Joe

From the Charleston, South Carolina, Clarion, *June 2, 1980:*

NO LEADS IN SAVAGE MURDER OF HOSTESS: CONNECTION TO SIMILAR KILLINGS BEING EXPLORED

With no leads in the investigation into the heinous murder of Candice Tucker, 18, the lovely blond bar hostess found raped and butchered in her Magnolia Street apartment last week, Charleston Police are turning their attention to two identical killings committed in different states throughout the past fourteen months.

On April 18 of last year, Kristine Pasquale, a go-go dancer, was found raped and dismembered in her Louisville, Kentucky, apartment. Wilma Thurmann, a Des Moines, Iowa, prostitute, was found identically devastated in a feed bin outside Des Moines on October 1, 1979. Physical evidence, Charleston Police told newsmen, is identical in all three cases. At a press conference held yesterday, Charleston District Attorney Timothy Kleist said, "In the interest of public safety and crime-fighting efficacy, we're keeping our liaison investigation with the Louisville and Des Moines P.D.'s under wraps, but I will tell the media this: It's a biggie. All three killings are most certainly the work of one man, and we intend to apprehend this fiend!"

In a related note, City Councilman Michael Cleary accused D.A. Kleist of using the Tucker case as a political football. "We all know Tim is getting ready to run for the Senate, and a nice juicy murder conviction would sure look good on his record. Let's hope he doesn't pull any railroad jobs in his haste to get to Washington. His party is famous for them, and I sure would hate to see innocent men get rousted."

Supplemental Memorandum, filed on 6/6/80 as part of Charleston Police Department Case File # 80–64–Rape/ Homicide, *Canvassing* and *Physical Evidence* sub-files.

To: All Investigating Officers

From: Det. Sgt. W. W. Brown, 19th Precinct

While re-canvassing Magnolia Street area, I questioned a male negro named Steven "Sterno Steve" Washington, a transient with no visible means of support. He told me that on the night of the Tucker killing he was drinking wine under the stoop directly across the street, and that "about midnight" he saw "a white man with a cop vibe" enter the vestibule *wearing gloves* & carrying a *wadded-up plastic trash bag*. Washington left the stoop then, as *the man pressed a buzzer and went upstairs*. (Washington said he was afraid the man would take away his wine when he returned downstairs.)

Since shredded plastic was mentioned among trace elements found at crime scene, I think this is a major lead.

(Washington being held at 19th Pct. drunk tank in case further questioning deemed necessary.)

W. W. Brown, Sgt., 19th Squad.

From the Kalamazoo, Michigan, Standard-Leader, *September 10, 1980:*

REMAINS OF KALAMAZOO MAN FOUND IN LAKE MICHIGAN; "NEPHEW" SOUGHT

The body of a Kalamazoo resident known for his eccentricities was found in the shallow water of Lake Michigan near the Benton Heights Pier three days ago. Although decomposition was close to complete, bullets embedded in the skull pointed to shooting as the cause of the man's death, and a teletyping of his unique dental bridgework to local dental labs yielded a rapid identification. The victim was Rheinhardt Wildebrand, 72, of Kalamazoo.

Wildebrand, a lifelong Kalamazoo resident, was an inventor who lived off of royalties from tool and die devices he developed back in the 1930's. He was a local "character" who lived in a big gingerbread house at 8493 S. Kenilworth, flew the flag of his ancestral Austria on American holidays, seldom left his block and kept a 1953 Packard in his driveway—but never drove it. He was assumed to have no living family (his parents and one sister having died in the '40's), but recently a man who he told neighbors was his "nephew" was staying with him—and Benton Heights and Kalamazoo Police are now searching for that man as Wildebrand's presumed killer.

The retired inventor's neighbors told police that the nephew arrived sometime in early August, and that they often saw him with Wildebrand on the latter's front porch, but that the man, like his alleged uncle, kept to himself. Neighbors described him as being "tall and strongly built, early thirties, dark hair and eyes and full beard."

Lieutenant Loren Kelleher of the Kalamazoo Police Department, which is aiding the Benton Heights P.D. in its investigation, told *Standard-Leader* reporter Bob Shaeffer: "We've checked out the records on the Wildebrand family. The old man had one sister, a spinster, who died in 1941, which in all likelihood is before our suspect was born. So we know the 'nephew' stuff is baloney. We think robbery is the motive. The so-called nephew in all likelihood gained Wildebrand's confidence, then stole his money and killed him. The old man was rumored to have large sums of cash hidden in the cellar. Right now we are going over the house for physical evidence and showing mug shots of Michigan, Illinois and Ohio criminals to neighbors in an attempt to identify the 'nephew.'"

As for the neighbors themselves, they mourn the fact that there seems to be no one mourning the late inventor. "Rheinhardt was a strange old bird," a Kenilworth Avenue resident told our newsmen. "But nobody—not even a weirdo like that—should have to get shot and dumped in the drink."

Details on the investigation will be forthcoming.

Liaison Memorandum, sent to the Homicide Squad, Benton Heights Police Department by Lt. Loren Kelleher of the Kalamazoo Police Department.
9/15/80
Officers—
On the Kalamazoo end of Wildebrand, Rheinhardt J.— a big zero along with some interesting stuff.

A.—Victim's bank accounts not hit—savings balance $41,000, checking balance $12,000 (R. W. Sent out large checks to credit-card companies before he disappeared).

B.—No turn-up on stolen or sold .38 with defective parts & no matchup on the shells (I ran statewide).

No ID on the "nephew," & no one saw suspect with a vehicle.

C.—Canvassing of local res.—zero.

D.—Victim's house searched, no wallet or ID found (probably floating in Lake Mich.). No money found, which confirms robbery as motive.

E.—The clincher on "nephew" as our man—all 3 stories, 12 rooms of house completely wiped clean of latents—washcloth marks everywhere. Nephew knows his stuff.

F.—Will you call me with feedback from your end soon?— Lt. L. Kelleher.

From the Baltimore, Maryland, Sun, May 19, 1981:

PROSTITUTE'S MURDER LINKED TO THREE OTHER SEX-SLAYINGS

The shocking murder of Carol Neilton, found raped and brutally hatcheted in her apartment last week, appears to be the fourth in a series of slayings that began in Louisville, Kentucky, over two years ago.

In April of 1979, Kristine Pasquale, a nude dancer, was discovered in her Louisville apartment, butchered exactly like Ms. Neilton; Wilma Thurmann was killed in Des Moines, Iowa, similarly, on October 1 of that year; and last May 27, Candice Tucker of Charleston, South Carolina, met an equally gruesome end in that city. The physical evidence is identical in all four homicides—and there is an identical absence of clues. Baffled, the four police agencies involved in the investigations are discussing pooling their information in the hopes of avoiding a fifth death.

Time is working against them, however. Captain Reynolds Conklin, second in command of the Baltimore P.D. Homicide Division, told a media assembly last night: "These four homicides have spanned two years, and the official investigations on the first three are, in police parlance, cold. No suspect names have turned up in more than one city in the mass of paperwork thus far collected. No airplane, bus or train reservation lists have the same men visiting the four cities on the applicable dates, and right now we are simply doing paperwork and running with hypothetical footballs. That is how this case will be solved."

But after how many more victims, Captain?

Inter-Office Memorandum, found under "Miscellaneous Reports" in Baltimore Police Department Case File # 199–5/81.

Skipper—

You said I should be candid, so here it is—nothing, except some decent theorizing from reading through Xeroxes of the Louisville/Des Moines/Charleston case files and talking on phone to two officers previously involved (Sgt. Ruley, Louisville—Sgt. Brown, Charleston).

Both these (smart) officers feature a cop impersonator who got access to the victims by threatening shakedowns or arrest if they didn't come across sexually. This would explain how killer entered pads of vict's 1, 3, 4. Also, impersonating cops seems to be popular among psychos these days—witness that Hillside Strangler scumbag out in L.A.

I'll take the reconstruction one step further—suppose the killer actually is a cop? Since the killings originated in Louisville, a check of airline/train/bus records for applicable dates of last 3 killings cross-checked against L.P.D. officers roster (unexplained or unusual officer absences too) might be in order. Needle-haystack stuff, but something to do.

Off the record—I think we should keep going through the standard motions, then bury this thing. Neilton was a hooker, this guy will never kill in our jurisdiction again, and Homicide has got eight major gang/killings & robbery/killings running hot—they should be our priority. I've heard the feds are setting up something big called the Serial Killer Task Force (they're going to be soliciting data from Municipal & State P.D.'s on old unsolveds, computer-checking them, etc.). Maybe that's our best bet.

See you for the Orioles next Tuesday—Jack.

From the Columbus, Ohio, Telegram, May 30, 1981:

DRIFTER'S BODY EXCAVATED AT BUILDING SITE

Sunbury, Ohio, May 29:

Workmen digging up a stretch of land with high-powered earth movers uncovered the buried body of a transient ex-convict yesterday morning. The man had been dead for over a month, Columbus County Coroner Roger Diskant told reporters, and although "90% decomposed," an identification was made from his fingerprints. The man was William Rohrsfield, age 33, a vagrant with convictions for burglary and soliciting homosexual acts. The death was listed as a "gunshot homicide," and the Ohio State Police are now investigating.

Summary Homicide Report filed by Lieutenant D. D. Bucklin of the Sunbury, Ohio, Sheriff's Department on June 1, 1981:

Chief—

Here's the rundown on the stiff found near that 7–11 site out by Route 3:

Name—Rohrsfield, William Walter

Race—Cauc.

D.O.B.—5–4–48

Phys Stats—6'3", 210, brown & brown, build large

Cause of death—shot in head, .38 spents found in dirt by body (unusual lands & grooves) (see attached ballistic workup done by State Officers). Body buried 12 feet deep (strange).

Preliminary investigation—*State Detectives*. Although this is technically our case, Dead Body Report was filed by State unit that caught the squeal, and since Rohrsfield was an ex-con and not a Sunbury resident, I say let them do the work. Here's Rohrsfield's record:

Juvie—B&E—12–12–65—(received counseling). Poss. of Marijuana—1–8–66—(6 mos Chillicothe Youth Fac.).

Adult—House Burg. & Rec. Stolen Goods—8–2–67 (1 yr. Chillicothe Adult Fac. 3 yrs. prob.). 1st Deg. Burg.— Convictions (2) on 4/20/69, (3 yrs.—Ohio State Pen.); also on 7/2/74 with added charges of Soliciting for Purposes of Male Prostitution, Loitering in the Vicinity of Public Restrooms and Indecent Exposure (5 yrs. State time—refused parole, topped out sentence). Released 7/14/79, a dozen drunk arrests since.

The State dicks can have him—I say good riddance to bad rubbish—D. D. Bucklin, Lieutenant, Watch Commander.

VI

AS A FUGITIVE: FILLING IN THE MAP (JANUARY 1979– SEPTEMBER 1981)

17.

And so the kiss made me a fugitive, and set the man who gave it free to kill with the stylish ease that I used to own.

At the time, of course, I had no idea what Ross was doing. Panic and unnamed desires kept him shut out but close—like a hot wind at my back, one that would turn me blind if I stared into it. Today, with manuscript pages and police documents accumulating on my desk and pins marking my journey on the map covering my cell wall, the lines connecting our respective murders make the dichotomy stand out in boldface: Ross discreetly choosing his victims, cloaked with a badge and extradition warrants, always returning safely to rural Wisconsin; Martin tearing cross-country in flight from real sex, seeking the perfect non-Martin to become, burning like an ant caught in sunlight through a magnifying glass held by a sadistic child.

Burning my way back to my own childhood;

Feeding sacrificial fires with a grandfather and three brothers;

Sabotaging my old caution by skipping at the edge of the flames...

Blasted out of Huyserville, I drove due east on sludgy two-lanes to Lake Geneva. The resort was thronged with athletic youths in brightly colored sportswear, and in the wake of Ross I felt inadequate to the task of working among them. The snub-nose .38, loaded in an undercarriage compartment, seemed like a poor substitute for my magnum; and I knew that if I put my hands on a victim—man, woman, young, old, ugly or attractive—they would feel like Ross, and I wouldn't be able to finish the job. My only recourse was to force myself to forget the man—his looks, his feel, his style.

That night I did something extraordinarily out of character.

I booked a suite at the Lake Geneva Playboy Club and spent an evening celebrating an auspicious unnamed occasion, forcing myself to act like a reveler blowing off steam. I ate an overpriced meal at the "Sultan's Steakhouse," tipped lavishly and watched the floor show at the "Jet Setter's Lounge." Young hostesses in low-cut rabbit costumes looked disapprovingly at my out-of-style clothing there, but changed their tunes when I showed them my rabbit-ear room key with "Potentate's Pad" embossed on the back. *Then* they accepted my stylishly handed-out twenty-dollar bills with proper humility and led me to a front-row table in the "VIP" section. I ordered Dom Perignon champagne for myself and my fellow VIP's, and was roundly applauded. Soon the man next to me was offering cocaine, and in the spirit of the unnamed occasion I snorted it and drank greedily from the bottle at my table.

The floor show featured a vulgar buffoon named Professor Irwin Corey. His act consisted of ad-libbed double entendres and malapropisms aimed at the people sitting at the ringside tables; and although at first I found him tedious, as I snorted and drank on he became the funniest thing I had ever seen. Old notions of control kept my laughter internal until Corey pointed to a fat drunk who was snoring with his head on the table. In the voice of an oriental sage, the Professor said, "You drink to forget, Papa San?" and reflexively I thought of Ross, dug through my mind for a portrait and came up instead with the face of a pretty boy from a Calvin Klein ad. Then I did laugh out loud, spewing spittle and tears across my table until Corey noticed me, walked over and slapped my back and said, "There, there, big guy. Take a shot of meth, two bunnies, four Excedrin and call your broker in the morning. There, there."

I don't know how I made it back to my suite; my last
waking image was of rabbit girls solicitously opening a door
into ice-cold air. When I did awaken, my head was throbbing
and I was sprawled fully clothed across a red satin heart-
shaped bed. I thought of Ross and got another vacuously
handsome model, then a flashback of the evening hit, ringed
with question marks and dollar signs. This led to a series
of four-figure speculations followed by ???, and I comforted
myself with the thought that the night was a one-time-only
blowout. Then I ran a mental litany of my safe-deposit box
balances and key hiding places—and came up three short.

Now Ross appeared in detail, smoothing his mustache
with utter cool, murmuring, "Martin, you dumb shit."

I lashed out at the bed with my fists and knees; Ross
was saying, "Thought I let you off easy, huh? Sweetie, who
could ever forget a face like mine? Ross the Boss, what a
guy."

I jumped up and tore through the suite until I found
stationery and pens on a table by the telephone. With shaking hands I wrote down bank names, figures and hiding
places, ending with a total of five boxes and $6,214.00.
Simple subtraction gave me the cost of my evening of prosaic debauchery: $11,470.00 minus $6,214.00 equaled
$5,256.00.

Ross said, "You'll never make it as a swinger, Martin.
Splitting on the tab'll save you a few bucks, though. They
didn't see your van when you registered, so all they've got
is your name... *WHICH YOU CAN CHANGE.*

I was back on the road inside of ten minutes, and Ross,
faceless but huge, was like a Santa Ana wind behind me.

I never mentally regained the lost money, and I spent a
month traveling throughout the West picking my remaining safety boxes clean. I can only describe that month as
savage. Driving into cities where I had previously killed
felt savagely stupid; keeping the money in the Deathmobile's glove compartment felt necessary, but savagely
risky. Ross loomed all around me—faceless as an advisor,

but savagely beautiful and dangerous when I didn't listen
to him.

Other faces were there, always on roadsides. Men, women,
old, young, pretty, ugly—they all had big open mouths that
shouted, "Love me, fuck me, kill me." Ross, faceless, only
a voice, kept me from wasting them, kept the idea of a new
identity in my mind. In the counselor role that Shroud
Shifter used to play, he told me to take my time and eschew
murder until I found a perfectly expendable man to become,
a man who looked exactly like me and who would never be
missed. Knowing that Ross would remain sexless only if I
obeyed him, I waited.

Reversing directions after picking up my last cache of
money, I headed East again, driving all day, sleeping in
cheap motels. Ross's presence was always with me, and *his*
obsession of making me kill for a non–Martin Plunkett
persona grew in *my* brain, buttressed by savage questions:

What if the dead man and his car are discovered in Wisconsin?

What if the troopers remember that you were detained
at the same time that he disappeared?

What if the two facts are connected?

What if the spent shells that you discarded by the roadblock are found?

What if the Playboy Club management files on you for
Defrauding an Innkeeper, and that fact gets connected to
the others, resulting in a fugitive warrant?

Those questions gave me the courage to act independ-
ently of Ross the faceless counselor, and surprisingly, the
beauty that I thought would descend on me didn't.

But on my own, I failed.

I spent a week in Chicago, prowling lowlife dives, trying
to buy a set of fake ID. No one would sell to me, and after
a half-dozen attempts I knew my old criminal touch was
fear-riddled—that I came across as a snitch and a fool. I
drove out of the Windy City chased by Ross's derisive
laughter and "I told you so's."

I was skirting Lake Michigan when I snapped to a com-
promise plan: settle down for a month or so, alter the ap-

pearance of the Deathmobile, re-register it and get Illinois
plates to replace my old Colorado ones. I searched out flaws
to the plan, saw a huge major risk, and decided to go through
with it anyway. The boldness of the measure seemed to
please Ross; he said, "Do your own thing" and went faceless
as I set to work.

First I pulled into Evanston, found a furnished room and
paid two months' rent in advance; then I drove to the local
Department of Motor Vehicles office, boldly displayed my
Colorado license and registration and told them I wanted
Illinois license plates for my van. After filling out forms,
the clerk did exactly what I knew he would—he went
straight to a teletype machine and ran my name and vehicle
nationwide for wants and warrants. While the man waited
for the computer kick-out, I gripped the .38 snubnose in my
pocket and watched his face. If I came up Wanted in Wisconsin or elsewhere, he would react, and I would shoot him
and the other two clerks by the coffee machine, steal one
of their cars and *GO*.

I did not have to revert to such melodrama; the man
returned smiling, and I paid my fee and listened to him tell
me my temporary license sticker would arrive in one week,
my plates in six. I thanked him and went looking for an
automobile paint shop.

I found one near the town dump on Kingsbury Road, and
waited reading magazines while Deathmobile II was face-
lifted from silver to metallic blue. When it rolled out of the
paint barn looking brand-spanking different, a Latin youth
sitting next to me said, "Sharp fucking sled, man. What
you call it?"

"What?"

"You know, man. Its name. Like Dragon Wagon or Pussy
Pit or Fuck Truck. A sled that cool's gotta have a name."

Still feeling bold from my DMV office showdown, I said,
"I call it the Killer's Kayak."

The kid slapped his thighs. "Right on O-matic!"

I settled into Evanston. It was a wealthy town, a Chicago
suburb more or less—and there was a profusion of small

colleges to give me the protective coloration of the perpetual
graduate student. With temporary roots laid down I thought
of Ross less and less, and began to realize that his audial
and physical presences were no more than mirror forms of
self-love—I was infatuated with the man because we both
excelled at the same profession and were Spartan in other
aspects of our lives—me always moving, him pursuing a
career that obviously entailed long hours of boredom. He
came to my aid in times of panic as Shroud Shifter used to,
when my own reservoir of self-love was depleted by the
exigencies of living on the road. If, symbiotically, I was
serving him in the same capacity, fine; if not, I didn't care.
Also, there were other faces to look at; the Evanston campuses were crawling with them. With the Ross face/voice
symbolism tagged, I slowly became convinced that giving
up Martin Plunkett, transient convicted burglar, in favor
of another identity was imperative—and I started looking
for a twin brother to kill.

The quiet lucidity of the idea, conceived in terror but
time-tested through various emotional states, allowed me
to move methodically toward my first fratricide. I fashioned
a silencer out of metal tubing and wire and test-fired the
.38 at buoys on Lake Michigan; I prowled campuses after
dark, the snubnose in my pocket, my game plan to shoot
my quarry on a quiet walkway, steal his wallet and quietly
walk away. I had four look-alikes spotted and was in the
process of weeding them out when I first noticed the idiot.

I knew two things about him immediately: that he was
mentally deficient and that his physical resemblance to me,
although substantial, went deeper. I knew we were bonded
hypothetically; that if I had grown up innocent instead of
irredeemably jaded, this is what I would be.

With no intention of ever hurting the man, I watched
him play in the garbage dump every day for a week running. The boardinghouse I lived in was on a hill three blocks
from the dump, and with binoculars I could see my hybrid
brother toss rocks at abandoned cars and rummage around
for rusted auto parts to put to use as toys. Toward dusk, an

attendant from the "Home" would lead him away from his playground, and it was she that I wanted to hurt.

I had narrowed down my hit list to two, and was heading toward the Evanston Junior College campus to make my final decision when I met the could-have-been Martin face-to-face. It was early evening, and only an hour earlier I had watched with amusement as the man hid in the weeds, foiling the nasty-looking spinster type who came to drag him away from his fun. Now, as I slowly cruised past the dump, he emerged from the shadows and flagged down the van.

I stopped, and flicked on the cab light. The man walked over and stuck his head in the passenger window; in extreme close-up I saw that his features were a hideously slack version of my own. "I'm Bobby," he said in a squeaky tenor voice. "Wanna see my playhouse?"

I could not refuse; it would have been like denying my childhood. Nodding, I got out of the van and walked with Bobby through the dump site. His shoulder brushed mine, and it felt soft, weak. I found myself wishing that someone would make him build up his body, and was about to offer brotherly words of advice on the subject when Bobby pointed to a light flickering up ahead. "My house," he said. "See?"

The house was two rotted car seats arranged facing each other, with a Coleman lamp in the middle. The light from it shot straight up, forming a tunnel that illuminated Bobby's head hanging loosely out from his shoulders as if he couldn't hold himself erect without help. "My house," he said.

I put my hands on Bobby's shoulders; he jerked into a military posture and said, "Yes, sir," but his head still lolled off at an angle. I looked at the ground, then back at the askew idiot face bobbing now like a toy animal in a hot-rod backseat. Tightening my grip, I said, "You don't have to call me that. You don't have to call anybody that."

Bobby grinned, and I felt his spongy body quiver under my hands. His grin got bigger and more contorted, and I saw that he was in some kind of idiot ecstasy. Finally his

tongue and palate and lips connected, and he got out, "You
wann be my friend?"

Now I started to quiver, and my hands on Bobby quiv-
ered, and the glow from the lantern burned the tears that
were running down my cheeks. I turned my head away so
my idiot brother wouldn't think me weak, and I heard him
making wet noises as though he was crying. I looked at
him then, and saw that the sounds were coming from the
obscenity of the big round O he was making with his mouth,
and that he was waving a dollar bill, flaglike, in front of
my chest.

I took my hands from his shoulders and started to walk
away. Hearing contorted sobs and "Pl-pl-pl," I turned back
to see Bobby holding out the dollar, trying to beg for my
friendship and make his hideous overture at the same time.
I put my left hand back on his shoulder; I took the .38 from
my windbreaker pocket. Bobby tried to smile as he wrapped
his lips around the silencer. I pulled the trigger and my
hybrid brother flew into the dirt, and I stole his wallet only
to have it as a memento of my first mercy killing.

Robert Willard Borgie ruined Evanston for me, and I got
out a month after my one-and-only routine police questioning. I drove West then, Illinois plates on the blue Deathmobile, no Ross or Shroud Shifter advising me, only an
awful sickly-sweet smell clinging to my person. I felt per-
ilously close to self-annihilating revelations, and as I sped
across brutally long and flat and hot stretches of farmland,
I schemed and daydreamed and even ran old brain-movies
to keep them pushed down. Troubling thoughts broke out
anyway:

Borgie was subhumanly intelligent, and he wanted you
that way—

You fixed on him as your brother, and didn't plan to kill
him, even though he looked just like you—

He made you cry—

If he made you cry out of empathy, then your will is
slipping—

If he made you cry for yourself, you're finished.

I ended that long and hot and flat leg of my journey in Lincoln, Nebraska, renting a boxlike, cramped and hot bachelor apartment on the city's north side. I found a night watchman job, and was assigned to sit in the foyer of a downtown office building from midnight to eight each morning, wearing a gold-braided uniform and a mace gun and handcuffs in a plastic scabbard. Aside from rounds of the hallways once an hour, my time was my own. The former night man had left a dozen cartons of magazines behind, and rather than go stir-crazy brooding over dead retards and what they boded, I devoured copies of *Time* and *People* and *Us*.

It was a complete new education at age thirty-one. Years had passed since I last explored the written word, and the culture I had moved through had changed dramatically—changes lost on me as I maneuvered with tunnel vision. Between June and late November of '79 I read hundreds of magazines cover-to-cover. Although the snippets of information I sucked in detailed disparate events, one theme dominated.

Family.

It was back, it was strong, it was "in," it had never gone away. It was the antidote to new strains of sexually transmitted virus, to Communism, to booze and dope addiction, to boredom and malaise and loneliness. Androgynous musicians and Fascist preachers and muscle-bound black buffoons with Mohawk haircuts and gold chains proclaimed that you were fucked without it. Pop philosophers said that the years of rootlessness were over in America, and the nuclear family was the new-old constituency, period. Family was what you yearned for, worked for, bled for and sacrificed for. Family was what you came home for. Family was what you had while certain scum roamed around the country having nightmares and killing people and weeping when mirror-image idiots offered them blow-jobs for a dollar. Lack of family was the root of all hurt, all evil, all death.

My anger simmered, sizzled, bubbled and stewed all those

reading months, and Ross popped up periodically, offering comments like a Greek chorus:

"Martin, if I thought it'd help you out, I'd be your family ... but you know ... blood *is* thicker than water."

"The thing about family is, you can't choose your own."

"The thing about being alone like you is that you can take anything you want from anybody."

"Awww, poor Marty's mommy was a doper and his daddy took off and the nasty retardo made Marty cry. Awwww."

"Didn't I tell you back in January to get yourself a new ID?"

I started looking for a genealogy to usurp. *People* magazine said that bars were "The new meeting places for singles seeking to become duos," and since I wanted to connect with a man to kill, it was only fitting to go to bars where single men were seeking to become duos with other men. *Christian Times* magazine called such places "dens of sexual depravity that should be banned by a constitutional amendment," and somewhere between the two statements the truth probably hid. I didn't care either way, and the idea of gay-bar-hopping for a new ID was my antidote for a slipping will to murder. So I read men's fashion magazines, bought myself a slick new wardrobe and jumped will-first into the scene.

Which in Bible Belt Lincoln consisted of two bars, side by side on the east edge of the industrial district. I gave myself a strict timetable: four nights of searching only, out of the bars by 11:30 and at my job by 12:00 the first three nights, after-hours prowling only allowed on the fourth night—Friday, my work night off. If no one suitable materialized during the four nights, I would abandon the plan. A newspaper article I had read mentioned that college boys sometimes cruised "Fag Row" looking for bar patrons' cars to deface, so I would park Deathmobile II a half-mile away and walk over. No leaving fingerprints on bar tops or glasses, my face to be kept averted from everyone but possible hits.

I was well programmed for caution and control, but I wasn't prepared for the distractions I met, the variations on Ross and blondness. "Tommy's" and "The Place" were

simply dingy rooms with long oak bars, tiny wrought-iron
tables and jukeboxes: disco-blaring dives where conversation was next to impossible. But they were packed with
blonds cloned from the Ross Anderson style: compact muscles that only hard work could have developed, short hair,
toothbrush mustaches and tight-fitting "he-man" clothes—
Pendleton shirts, faded Levi's and work boots. It took me
two nights of drinking club soda at the bar, eyeballing for
tall, dark-haired men like me, to figure it out: I was in the
middle of blue-collar homosexuals at play—hod-carrying,
meat-packing, truck-driving men, the blonds among them
most often Eastern European types with high cheekbones
and ice-blue eyes. It was a subculture that neither my trav-
els nor my recent reading spurt had prepared me for, and
as a dark-haired WASP in a polo shirt and crewneck sweater,
I felt completely anomalous. Expecting swishy types who
would be drawn to me like moths to a flame and just as
easily snuffed out, I found shit-kickers who would be ex-
ceedingly tough *mano a mano*.

So for two nights I drank club soda, the nonsexual wall-
flower at the homosexual prom. The tall, dark-haired men
I spotted tended to run too lean or too young to be me; my
constantly trawling eyes were rebuffed when I made contact
with others; the Ross and blondness clones kept me nervous,
fingering my glass for something to do with my hands. I
had been prepared to be frightened and angry and possibly
tempted, but now something else was settling on me, like
an undercurrent in the constantly throbbing music. It was
a weight that felt like regret. The men surrounding me,
frivolous but masculine, made me feel old and numbed by
my history of brutal experience.

Early on the third night of my mission I found out why
I was being avoided. I was washing my hands in the rest-
room at Tommy's when I heard voices just outside the door.

"...I tell you, he's a cop. He's been hanging out here and
next door for the past couple of nights trying to look oh so
cool, and you can just tell."

"You're just being paranoid because you're on probation."

"No, I'm not! God, slacks and a sweater, how tacky! He's L.P.D. Vice, baby, so hit on him at your own risk."

There was a giggle. "You think he's got handcuffs and a big gun?"

"Yes, baby, I do. And a wife and three kids and an entrapment quota."

The two voices joined in laughter, then trailed off. Thinking of Ross and how he would have reacted to the conversation, I walked back to my seat at the bar. I was wondering about the feasibility of continuing my mission when I felt a tentative hand on my elbow. I turned around, and there I was.

"Hi."

It was the voice of my admirer. I stepped off the stool, saw that he was within an inch of my height, ten pounds of my weight and two years of my age. By squinting, I picked up brown eyes. Turning away from him, I wiped the bar top and my glass with my sleeve, then pivoted back with male-model grace. "Hi," I said.

"You move real nicely," the man shouted above the music. Ross zipped through my mind and said, "Kill him for me," and I cupped my ear and pointed to the door. The man caught my drift and walked ahead of me, and when we hit the sidewalk, I looked around for witnesses. Seeing nothing but a cold, deserted street, I mentally affixed myself as L.P.D. Sergeant Anderson and said, "I'm a police officer. You can take a ride with me out to the wheat flats, or a ride to the station. Take your pick."

The almost-Martin laughed. "Is this entrapment or a proposition?"

I laughed à la Ross. "Both, sweetie."

The man poked my arm. "Hard. I'm Russ."

"Ross."

"Russ and Ross, that's cute. Your car or mine?"

I pointed down the street to where Deathmobile II waited. "Mine."

Russ leaned into me coyly, then pulled himself back and started walking. I kept pace with him, staying up against the sides of buildings, thinking of late-night burials and

whether my old shovel was capable of cracking wheat-rooted
frozen earth. Russ kept quiet, and I imagined him imagining me naked. At Deathmobile II I opened the door and
squeezed his arm as I motioned him into the cab, and he
let out a little grunt of pleasure. Anticipation and exhilaration hit me, and when I got in behind the wheel I exploded
with an urge to know Russ/Martin's history.

"Tell me about your family," I said.

This time his laugh came out crude, his voice a midwestern bray. "Very romantic there, gay officer."

The "gay" angered me; I hit the ignition, gunned the gas
and said, "I'm a sergeant."

"Is that part of your typical gay sergeant's foreplay?"

The second "gay" accentuated the feel of the .38 tucked
into my waistband and kept me from lashing out. "That's
right, sweetie."

"Any man who calls me 'sweetie' can hear my tale of
woe." Russ tooted a fanfare on an imaginary horn, then
laughed and proclaimed, "This is your life! Russell Maddox
Luxxlor!"

The full name settled on me like a declaration of freedom.
The industrial district disappeared, prairie flats and a huge
starry sky loomed ahead, and I started to buzz all over. "Tell
me, sweetie."

The midwestern twang came out archly, theatrically.
"Welll, I'm from Cheyenne, Wyoming, and I've known I
was gay since about age zero, and I've got three lovely
sisters who buffered me through the tough parts. You know,
being picked on, that kind of thing. And Daddy's a Con-
gregational minister, and he's uptight about it, but not crazy
on the subject like the born-agains, and Momma's like a
big sister, she accepted me real—"

The monologue's sex drift was turning my buzzing ugly,
itchy. "Tell me other things," I said, holding my voice down.
"Cheyenne. Your sisters. What it's like to have a minister
for a father."

Russ pouted. "I guess you know all about that other stuff
already. Okay, Cheyenne was a bore, Molly's my favorite
sister. She's thirty-four now, three years older than me.

Laurie's my next favorite, she's twenty-nine and married to this awful farmer man who hits her; and Susan's the youngest, twenty-seven. She had a drinking problem, then she joined A.A. Daddy's a good guy, he doesn't judge me, and Momma quit smoking a few months ago. And oh God, this is so boring."

I tightened my grip on the wheel until I thought my knuckles would pop. "Tell me more, sweetie."

The dead man's effete bray rattled through the cab. "It's your funeral; my family would bore Jesus to death. Okay, Susan's the prettiest, and she's a dental tech; Laurie's fat, and she's got three rug rats with her awful husband, and I'm the smartest and the most sophisticated and the most sensit—"

I said the words the very instant the idea took hold. "Let me see the pictures in your wallet."

Martin/Russ said, "Sweetie, don't you think this is getting a little far afield? I'm up to party, but this is getting weird."

I looked in my rearview, saw nothing but dark prairie, decelerated and pulled over to the side of the road. The dead man gave me a spooked look, and I took the .38 from my waistband and leveled it at him. "Give me your wallet or I'll kill you."

With jerky hands he plucked it from his back pocket and put it on the dashboard. With calm hands worthy of Ross Anderson, I lowered the gun to my lap and fingered my way through the photo and credit-card compartments. Seeing three young women in graduation gowns and a couple in '40's wedding attire, I winced; seeing a pictureless Nebraska driver's license, valid draft card and Visa, American Express, and Diner's Club, I smiled and said, "Get out of the van."

Martin got out and stood by the door, shaking and murmuring prayers. I put the wallet in my pocket and joined him on the roadside, savoring mental images of my three new sisters until their about-to-be-excommunicated brother started to weep. Then, jarred, I poked the silencered snout of my weapon into his back and said, "Walk."

I marched him exactly sixty-two paces, one step for each year of our lives, then said, "Turn around and open your mouth." With chattering teeth he did, and I stuck the barrel in and pulled the trigger. His pitch backward almost wrenched the gun from my hand, but I managed to hold on.

The cold prairie air singed my lungs as I mentally regrouped. I thought of making a search for the expended round, then rejected the idea—my only other hit with Ross's piece had been in Illinois seven months before; there was no way the killings would be connected.

I was walking back to Deathmobile II and my shovel when I saw headlights approaching from the direction of Lincoln. The abruptness of it spooked me, and I got in, hung a U-turn and headed to work. I was on the job early, and I spent the entire shift memorizing the photographs of my new family. In the morning I burned them to ash in the ground-floor men's room, and when I flushed the sooty remains I knew the faces were imprinted in my memory bank forever.

18.

Forever lasted eleven days.

Those days were happy, peaceful. I had earned a family to fill up empty spaces in my past, and although Russell Luxxlor's body was discovered, nullifying my attempt to steal his identity, I still had Dad and Mom and Molly and Laurie and Susan as consolation prizes. Salable credit cards were a bonus on top of that, and I decided to unload them when I left Lincoln for good—a prescheduled two weeks after the killing.

Luxxlor's death made the local media, and one newspaper account had police accurately speculating that he was killed for his ID; I was even mentioned as having been seen with him at Tommy's. Still, I wasn't questioned, nor was I worried—it was the homosexual community that would bear the brunt of the heat.

So, for eleven days I existed in a realistic fantasy world devoid of violence and sexual urges. I laughed with favorite sister Molly and comforted sister Laurie when her husband gave her grief; I encouraged sister Susan to stay sober and teased Mom and Dad about their religious fervor. I was running on a fuel mixture that was 80% fantasy, 20% a detachment that knew the game the rest of me was playing. The point spread existed harmoniously within me, and my new family drifted through my sleeping dreams in a jumble that made them seem old and well thumbed.

On my twelfth post-killing morning I woke up and couldn't remember Molly's face. Wracking my memory wouldn't bring it back; small chores to ease my mind were

no help. Fantasizing with other family members made my
20% detachment zoom to 90% plus, and toward evening
every time I memory-searched for Molly I came up with the
bloodied faces of old women victims.

That night I panicked.

Sister Laurie was starting to slip into blankness, and I
loaded all my belongings into Deathmobile II and headed
out of Lincoln on the Cornhusker Highway. Recalling a
newspaper article on the local crime scene and its meeting
places, I stopped at a roadhouse called Henderson's Hot Spot
and tried to sell Russell Luxxlor's credit cards to two men
playing pool. Nervous and twitchy, I said all the wrong
things and spooked them. When their hardboiled fish eyes
zoomed in on me, I ran to the Deathmobile and sped out of
Nebraska at ten miles over the speed limit.

The incident sent me into a tailspin, and where before
I would have killed boldly to counteract my feelings of powerlessness, now I sought solace, creature comforts, the
quenching of an extraordinary curiosity as to how other
people lived.

For eight months I traveled slowly northeast, staying
for weeks at a time at expensive motor inns, exploring the
local terrain. I slept in big soft beds and watched cable T.V.;
I ate expensive meals that devoured my bankroll. The remaining members of my adopted family dropped from my
mind, one at a time, as I notched eastbound miles; to replace
them I picked up hitchhikers, plied them with marijuana
and got them to talk about themselves and their families.
Letting them out unharmed, their past mine in 80%/20%
fashion, I always felt just a little bit more secure, more safe.
Ross began to seem like a distant apparition.

Then 80/20 revolted against me, becoming 100% nightmare.

It happened suddenly. I was asleep in a big, soft Howard
Johnson's bed in Clear Lake, Iowa. Recent hitchhikers were
walking through my slumber, their faces getting more and
more distinct. My anticipation grew as I sensed all of them
were blond; I moved in their direction. Then I saw that they

were wearing powder-white wigs; then I saw that they were all child versions of people I had killed; then they all bared long, sharp fangs and went for my genitals.

I woke up screaming, and was on the road inside of two minutes.

Frightened out of another city, again I fought the fear out of character.

I stayed awake for 106 straight hours; I let my beard grow; I changed my hairstyle. I smoked big pipefuls of my own marijuana, experiencing its effects for the second time; I laughed giddily and ate like a pig under its spell. When I finally knew I could no longer remain conscious, I pulled off the roadside, only to have Ross Anderson snuggle up next to me in my dreams.

"You're getting soft, soft, softer";

"You're getting soft on people";

"You're getting soft on people so you won't have to kill them";

"If you quit killing you'll die."

"KILL SOMEONE *NICE* FOR ME";

"KILL SOMEONE *NICE* FOR ME";

"KILL SOMEONE *NICE* FOR ME";

"KILL SOMEONE *NICE* FOR ME";

"KILL SOMEONE *NICE* FOR ME";

"KILL SOMEONE *NICE* FOR ME."

19.

A nightmarish week later I met Rheinhardt Wildebrand, and in the end, superbly refortified, I killed him without hesitation—despite admiring his superb lack of niceness.

The prologue to my symbolic grandfather was seven days of fitful sleep filled with victim-faced animals snapping at me and constant kill-urgings from Ross. My tailspin was moving into its nadir—I was running out of money; my beard was growing out patchy and incongruously light; and Deathmobile II was coming down with engine trouble, pings and rattles that reflected my own inside/outside deluge. Pulling into Benton Heights, Michigan, it threw a piston, and I pushed it to a nearby repair shop and placed half of my remaining cash down as a deposit on a ring job and a complete engine overhaul. Handing me an itemized list of the van's maladies, the head mechanic said, "You been drivin' mean, boyo. You ever hear about oil changes and transmission fluid? You're lucky the fucker didn't blow up on you."

If only he knew.

It was now a question of finding a place to stay and a job for money to restore the Deathmobile. With my .38 in my pocket, I walked around Benton Heights. It stood on a bluff overlooking Lake Michigan, and the constant view of sludgy dark water reminded me of Bobby Borgie, dead in Evanston some hundreds of miles across it. Knowing his presence would haunt me in the place, I hopped a bus to the nearest large city—Kalamazoo.

Where, walking aimlessly through its environs, I met

Rheinhardt. I was coming out of a convenience store with a container of milk when he spotted me and dropped the first of his many memorable one-liners: "What's a subversive like you doing in a dull neighborhood like mine?"

Warming to the flattery and the geezer's crusty style, I said, "Looking for victims."

Laughing, the old man said, "You'll find them. Is that a Colt or a Smith and Wesson in your pants?"

I looked at my waistband and saw that the grip of my .38 was exposed. Correcting the matter, I said, "S. and W. Detective's Special."

"With a long barrel like that?"

I hesitated, then said, "Silencer."

"You make it yourself?"

"Yes."

"You a tool and die man?"

"No."

"Traveling man?"

"Yes."

"I'm a tool and die man. Come to my house, we'll drink and talk."

I hesitated again. But when the old man said, "I'm not afraid of you, so don't be afraid of me," I followed him down the block to his musty old house of memories.

And I stayed.

Years before, "Uncle" Walt Borchard had bored me with his stories. Now, "Grandpa" Rheinhardt Wildebrand enthralled me with his, and the telling/listening hinged on a simple dynamic: Borchard's need for an audience was indiscriminate, Rheinhardt's specific—he was slowly dying of congestive heart disease, and he wanted someone as solitary and idiosyncratic as himself to know what he had done.

So I became his nephew, allegedly motivated by Rheinhardt's oblique references to leaving me his wealth. In reality, that dynamic was shelter. As long as I slept in the gingerbread house and listened, I endured no nightmares.

Rheinhardt Wildebrand had been a Prohibition bootlegger, hauling whiskey down the Great Lakes on a barge; he had sold die-making devices to Canada-based agents of Hitler's regime, pocketing the payment, then selling the same equipment to the U.S. Army. He had harbored Dillinger in the gingerbread house after the public enemy's shoot-out at the Little Bohemia Lodge in Minnesota, and the mint-condition 1953 Packard Caribbean sitting chaste in his driveway was a present from the late Cuban dictator Fulgencio Batista, given in appreciation of Rheinhardt's blueprints for jail-bar construction and placement, the car driven up from Miami by Meyer Lansky himself.

I believed the stories absolutely, and Rheinhardt believed mine—that I was an armed robber on the run from a parole violation and a botched payroll job in Wisconsin. That was why I shared his hermit life-style so willingly; that was why I endured my patchy beard and kept my face averted from prying neighbor eyes when we talked on the front porch. My only other lie was in response to a direct question, Rheinhardt knocking back a shot of Canadian Club and asking, "Have you ever killed a man?"

"No," I answered.

After two weeks in the gingerbread house, I knew the old man's habits and that I was going to murder him for the advantage I could gain by exploiting them. He kept a cache of several thousand dollars in his basement—I would steal it. He purchased all his clothing, household utensils and books from mail-order catalogs, paying for them with high-limit Visa, American Express Gold and Diner's Club cards, sending in one check a year, with the 19.80% annual interest the credit-card companies loved. Since those companies were used to his eccentricities, I would destroy his checking account by sending in big forged checks for a year of *future* card transactions, accompanied by forged notes stating in Rheinhardt's inimitable style that he was "Taking my act on the road until I kick the bucket, and this check is to cover all my possible charges, so you won't have to dun me." I would wipe the house free of my fingerprints, slip Rheinhardt a sedative, drive him out to Lake Michigan, shoot him and dump him in the water, appropriately weighted down. He would not be missed for weeks, and by then I would be long gone.

The plan was brilliant, but formulating it destroyed my love of Rheinhardt's stories, and the nightmares came back.

Now it was the old man's neighbors who attacked me, wig-wearing monsters informed with telepathic powers. They knew I was going to murder Rheinhardt, and they told me they would let me escape from the deed only if I gave them the old pirate's money. When I refused, they took on the faces of my Aspen victims, taunting me with the refrain from an old big band tune—"I've Got a Kraut in Kalamazoo! Kalamazoo! Kalamazoo! Kala-ma-zoo-zoo-zoo!"

Nine straight mornings I woke up shrieking and kicking and flailing. On my feet but still in my dreams, I lashed out at the furniture in my bedroom, knocking over night-stands and chairs. The first time, Rheinhardt rushed in, concerned. Then, day by day, he grew more and more worried. As the nightmare mornings continued, they eclipsed our storytelling hours, and I saw the old man's worry turn to disgust. I was not the hard case he had thought; Lansky and Dillinger would have considered me a sissy; he was a sissy himself for sharing his secrets with someone so weak.

Now Rheinhardt's tales were told in a desultory tone, and Ross took over the many faces of his characters. I knew it was time to kill the old man or get out.

Knowing that one more screaming/stumbling/lashing episode would push Rheinhardt into ordering me to leave, I foiled potential nightmares by staying awake to scheme. After one sleepless night I had the old man's handwriting down pat; after two I had notes written to Visa, Diner's Club and American Express. My third night was a trip to Kalamazoo's South Side, where I scored a half-dozen 1½-grain Seconal. Night four—dingy, zorched, whacked-out and fried from 108 hours of continuous consciousness—was when I struck.

First I emptied the Seconals into Rheinhardt's nightcap of Canadian Club and milk. He chugged the drink down as he usually did, and half an hour later I saw him asleep on his bedroom floor, half in and half out of his pajamas. Leaving him there, I tore through the house with a wet wash-cloth, wiping every wall and furniture surface in every room I had been in. With that elementary track-covering accomplished, I raided Rheinhardt's basement money cache, stuffed huge wads of bills into my pockets and ran the uphill mile to the Kalamazoo Bus Depot, catching the late bus to Benton Heights with only seconds to spare. An hour later and eight hundred Wildebrand dollars poorer, I was behind the wheel of the now velvet-running Deathmobile II, heading back to the gingerbread house.

Reentering it, my nerve ends felt as though they were being ground with sandpaper, and my heart beat so hard that I knew it would have to burst before I completed the kill. My throat was constricted and my hands shook, and sweat buzzed on my skin as if I were a live wire. Only concentrating on not touching anything extraneous kept me from imploding, and I bolted the stairs up to Rheinhardt's bedroom.

He was still on the floor, and a small pulsing vein in his neck told me he was still alive. Again leaving him there, I ran to my bedroom and picked up the three credit-card letters, then ran back to search the desk and dresser for checkbooks. My hands were closing on a pile of them when I heard "Imposter!" and turned around to see Rheinhardt leveling a double-barreled shotgun at me.

"IMPOSTER!"

We drew down on each other. I snagged the muzzle of my .38 as I pulled it out of my pants; Rheinhardt jerked both triggers. They hit empty chambers, and the old man smiled at me, then fell dead at my feet. Another hour later, on a shelf of rock overlooking Lake Michigan, I gave him a formal execution befitting his dignity—two shots in the head and an overhand hurl into the deep six. With his grandfatherly bequests in my glove compartment, I then took off at a law-abiding 35, all my exhaustion evaporated. Thinking of Ross, I said, "Look, Dad, no fear," and went cruising for someone with appropriate ID to kill.

20.

The following maxims form a summation of my next several months and epigrammatically describe certain perils inherent in roaming around America killing people:

Seek and ye shall find;
The journey, not the destination;
Beware of what ye seek;
You can run, but you can't hide.

Mr. Perfect staggered in front of my windshield on a deserted stretch of U.S. 6 east of Columbus, Ohio, one early evening in April of '81, and within ten miles I had heard his entire life story—family misunderstandings, shoplifting, burglary, reformatories, prison, parole and the search for the "Big Break." At dusk we turned off the road to share a bottle I allegedly had, and moments later I shot the man twice in the head. His pockets yielded identification belonging to William Robert Rohrsfield, born within a month of my own birthday, an extra seven pounds the only physical point distinguishing him from me. I buried Martin Plunkett deep under the hard soil by the Interstate and became Billy Rohrsfield. The irony of transmogrifying myself into a fellow burglar combined with Grandpa Rheinhardt's foolproof credit made me feel loose, cocky, stylish. From there I moved into a wordless, sleepless euphoria that felt like a permanent one-way ticket to Panaceaville, Fat City, the Big Contentment. Had I been able to verbalize in my trance, I would have told myself that at thirty-three all my needs were met,

all my destinations had been reached, all my curiosities
and desires had been sated. Instead of putting forth the sly
spiritual epigrams that begin this chapter, I would have
advanced the ethos of a Vegas hustler on a roll—I've got it
made.

But something happened.

I had just crossed the Ohio-Pennsylvania border when I
was tossed by hand out of the Deathmobile's cab. Flying
head over heels, I had a view of blue sky, U.S. 6 and my
van continuing without me. Then I was back in the cab and
shimmying across the dotted yellow line; then I was side-
swiping a chain-link fence on the right shoulder; then I
braked and banged my head on the dashboard.

When the shock was over I began crying. Too many days
of too little sleep, I told myself through my tears. Be good
to yourself, another voice added. I agreed in the German
accent I affected when using Rheinhardt Wildebrand's credit
cards, drove very slowly to a motel and slept.

The next morning, the first thing I encountered upon
rising was a perfect mental image of my "sister" Molly
Luxxlor, lost since December of '79. I wept in gratitude,
then remembered that I was Billy Rohrsfield, not Russ
Luxxlor, and that Billy's sister Janet was a child-beating
shrew. Molly vanished, and a facsimile of Janet took her
place, curlers in her hair, a rolling pin in her hand. I laughed
my tears away, shaved, showered and walked out to the
motel office to return my key. The clerk greeted me with,
"Auf Wiedersehn, Herr Wildebrand!" and I ran from the
salutation straight to Deathmobile II, straight to another
head-over-heels toss into the sky.

Airborne, I saw travel posters and billboards for the Jook
Savages and Marmalade; hitting the driver's seat, I saw
L.A. County Sheriffs spread-searching a scared young man.
At first he looked like Billy Rohrsfield, then he looked like
Russ Luxxlor. Then I automatically moved into my old 80%/
20% fantasy-detachment game and saw what was happen-
ing.

You can run, but you can't hide.

My first lucid impulse was to destroy the Wildebrand

credit cards and Rohrsfield ID. A second, more lucid thought stopped me: discarding such valuable tools would be an implicit admission that I couldn't control my own selfhood. A third, most cogent thought took over from there: You are Martin Plunkett. Driving away, colors stacked up behind the litany that allowed me to hold the wheel steady and Deathmobile II at an even 55. The words were *I am Martin Plunkett,* and the colors were telling me exactly what they did in San Francisco back in '74.

Landing in Sharon, Pennsylvania, I went verbal beyond my litany and took tight hold of my destiny. The color days had cleared my mind and had given me the courage to make certain admissions and arrive at conclusions as to how to restore order to my life. Wanting the prosaics of resettling out of the way before I formally stated the words to the summer air, I bought three rooms full of medium-priced furniture with Rheinhardt Wildebrand's Visa card and rented a three-room apartment on the town's west side, using the name William Rohrsfield. Juggling the two fake identities produced no moments of schizophrenia or disturbing euphoria, and when I was alone in my new home, I made my declaration:

Since Wisconsin you have been in flight from your own unique strain of sexuality, warrior in nature; you have been running from old fears and old indignities, experiencing near-psychotic hallucinations as a result; you have lost your will to kill coldly, brutally and with your hands; killing simply and anonymously has rendered you a nonentity, devoid of pride, slothful in your habits. You have become a comfort seeker of the most despicable sort, and the only way to reverse the above is to plan and carry out a perfect, methodical, symbolically exact set of sex murders.

You can run, but you can't hide.

Tears of joy were streaming down my face when I finished my self-confrontation, and I wept against the nearest object available to hold—a cardboard box filled with dishes and cooking utensils.

*   *   *

Over the next four months I secured the symbolic ac-
coutrements: airline posters and rock posters identical to
the ones adorning the walls of Charlie Manson's fuck pad
back in '69, a set of burglar's tools and a theatrical makeup
kit. Locksmith technology had improved since my burglary
days, so I bought do-it-yourself door locks representing the
new technological spectrum and practiced neutralizing them
at home. Hours of makeup practice in front of my bathroom
mirror got me adept at working pancake and fake noses
into non–Martin Plunkett visages, and as my steel-town
summer wound down, all that remained was to find the
perfect victims.

Easier said than done.

Sharon was a rough-hewn industrial city, Polish/Rus-
sian in its basic ethnic thrust, honky-tonk in its life-style.
There were plenty of blonds out on the street projecting
"kill me" auras, but an entire summer of cruising for an
attractive blond-blonde couple brought me nothing but
eyestrain. To combat the frustration and stay in reality
while doing it, I went on another pop-culture jaunt, courtesy
of *People* and *Cosmopolitan*.

"Family" was still big, as were religion, drugs and right-
wing politics, but physical fitness seemed to be moving into
first place among America's fads. Health clubs were the
newer "new meeting grounds" for singles; body awareness
had spawned the "new narcissism"; and bodybuilding
equipment and techniques had progressed to the point where
one "new fitness" guru flatly stated that weight workouts
were the "new religious service," while muscle-toning machines themselves were "the new totems of worship, because
they unleash the godhead physical perfection in all of us."
The entire craze reeked of a bottom line of people wanting
to look good so that they could fuck with a higher class of
partner, but if that was where the attractive ones were
congregating...

Sharon had three health clubs—"Now & Wow Fitness,"
"The Co-Ed Connection" and the "Jack La Lanne European
Health Spa." A battery of phone calls got me the rundown
on their respective merits: Jack "La Strain" was for the

serious iron pumpers, the Co-Ed Connection and Now &
Wow were pick-up joints where men and women worked
out on Nautilus equipment and took saunas together. All
three bright-voiced phone people invited me to come down
for a "free introduction workout," and I took the latter two
up on their offer.

Now & Wow Fitness was, in the words of the bored black
man who handed me a towel and "gym kit" upon entering,
"A fat farm. All Polack chicks lookin' to get skinny so they
can glom themselves a steelworker, then eat themselves fat
again when they get married." The two rooms full of chubby
women in pastel Danskins confirmed his appraisal, and I
walked back out immediately, returning my towel and gym
kit still fresh. "I told you so," the man said.

The Co-Ed Connection, a block away, had the feel of
instant paydirt. The cars in the parking lot were all sleek
late models, as were the instructors of both genders who
waited in the foyer to greet prospective members. Again
handed a towel and "workout kit," I was led into a football-
field-size room filled with gleaming metal equipment. Only
a few men and women were straining under bars and pulleys, and the instructor noticed my look and said, "The
after-work rush starts in about an hour. It's wild."

I nodded, and the sleek young woman smiled and left
me at the entrance to the men's locker room. The sleek
young male attendant inside assigned me a locker, and I
changed into gym shorts and a tank top emblazoned with
the Co-Ed Connection logo—a sleek masculine silhouette
and a sleek feminine silhouette holding hands. Checking
my appearance in one of the locker room's many full-length
mirrors, I saw that I was more large than sleek, more blunt
than stylish. Satisfied, I pushed through the door and started
pumping iron.

It felt good, and I was pleased to know that I could still
bench-press two hundred and fifty pounds twenty times. I
moved from machine to machine, experiencing pleasant
aches, getting in sync with the jar of metal, the hiss of
pulleys, the smell of my own sweat. The room started filling
up, and soon there were lines forming in front of the various

contraptions. Bluff-hearty macho men were offering encouragement to pushing, pulling, squatting and lifting macho women all around me, and I felt like a visitor from another planet observing quaint earthling mating rituals. Then I saw *THEM*, eased my shoulder-press load down and said to myself, "Dead."

They were obviously brother and sister. Both clad in purple satin instructor's uniforms, both blond and superbly shapely in classic male/female modes, both slightly more than vacuously pretty, they breathed a long history of familial intimacy. Watching them explain the benching machine to a skinny teenage boy, I saw how their gestures accommodated each other. When he used a chopped hand for emphasis, she repeated the motion, only gently. When he brought flat palms up to show how the pulleys worked, she did it just a little bit slower. Staring hard at them, I knew that they had performed incest early on, and that it was the one thing they never talked about.

I dismounted from the shoulder-press machine and walked to the locker room. Sweating from exhilaration now, I discarded my gym outfit and put on my street clothes, then strode back through the workout area. The siblings were explaining muscle development to a group by the jogging treadmill, pointing out laterals and pectorals on each other, letting their fingers touch the places. Touching the same parts of myself, I felt my sore muscles throb, then beat to the word "Dead." At the front of the area I noticed a picture roster of the club's instructors. George Kurzinski and Paula Kurzinski smiled side by side at the top. I dated their death warrant nine months in the future—June 5, 1982, fourteen years to the day since I saw my first couple make love. Leaving the Co-Ed Connection, I turned on my mental stopwatch. Pleased with the sound of its spring-loaded movement, I let it run continually while I activated my plan one step at a time.

Tick tick tick tick tick tick tick tick tick.

September, 1981:

Learning that the Kurzinskis live together, sleep in sep-

arate bedrooms and visit their widowed mother at the san-
itarium every Sunday. Tick tick tick tick.

November, 1981:

Surveillance reveals that Paula Kurzinski sleeps over
at her boyfriend's house on Wednesday and Saturday nights;
George Kurzinski's girl friend sleeps with him, at the siblings' apartment, on those nights. Tick tick tick tick tick.

January, 1982:

Securing the floor plan of the Kurzinskis' apartment
from the Sharon Office of City Planning. Tick tick tick tick
tick tick.

February, 1982:

Becoming expert at picking locks identical to the lackluster "Security King" on the Kurzinskis' front door. Tick
tick tick tick.

April, 1982:

Disguise, drugs and weaponry procured; escape route
and four alternates mapped out. Tick tick tick tick tick tick
tick tick.

May 15, 1982:

Run-through of the Kurzinskis' apartment sucessfully
executed; auxiliary blades stashed under bedroom and
living-room carpets; loaded .25-caliber Beretta found in
Paula's top dresser drawer; loaded .32 S. & W. revolver
found under George's mattress. Tick tick tick tick tick.

May 28, 1982:

Second run-through of Kurzinskis' apartment; blank
cartridges placed in both weapons; as added precaution both
hammers bent ⅛"-to the side to ensure misfire.

Tick

Tick

Tick

Tick

Tick

Tick

-Tick

Tick

Tick........

From Law Enforcement Journal, *May 30, 1982, issue:*

FEDERAL TASK FORCE "ATTACKING" SERIAL KILLERS WITH DIVERSIFIED APPROACH STRATEGY

Quantico, Virginia, May 15:

Criminal phenomena, however long-standing, are not really certified until they are given a title. "Mass Murderer" and "Thrill Killer" are old staples of public and law-enforcement jargon, used to designate, respectively, people who murder more than one person in a one-time-only fit of rage, and people (almost always men) who kill for no apparent reason. Recent revelations, primarily the Ted Bundy case (See *LEJ* 10/9/81), have spawned a new title, a "buzz-word" that seems certain to capture the public's imagination. The F.B.I., cognizant of the phenomenon for some time, will be the likely instrument of popularizing the title, for they are the first American law enforcement agency to concertedly "attack" the type of criminal the title designates—the Serial Killer.

According to F.B.I. Inspector Thomas Dusenberry, the serial killer is defined as: "A perpetrator who kills repeatedly, one victim or set of victims at a time. Our statistical prototype serial killer is a white male of above average to high intelligence, twenty-five to forty-five years old. That is a constant, while everything else regarding this type of perpetrator isn't, which is what makes them so difficult to apprehend.

"For one thing, serial killers often alter their M.O. to suit their victim of the moment. They may kill one person for sexual gratification, one for money. They may strangle one person, shoot another. Serial killers have been known to rape a half-dozen women victims, then sexually ignore a half-dozen others.

"Also, these men tend to travel and tend to dispose of their victims so that their bodies cannot be found. Aside from the complex serial-killer psyche and M.O. patterns, it is their often transient life-style that adds to their elusiveness—they play on the inadequacy of American police communication systems.

"There are fifty states in this country, served by untold thousands of police agencies. Agency-to-agency communication within individual states has been adequate at the identification level for years, but state-to-state communication of information is a joke, and is the number-one impeding factor in the investigation of possibly related homicides and disappearances."

How, then, does the F.B.I.'s Serial Killer Task Force intend to address this problem?

Inspector Dusenberry: "Once a killer crosses a state line after committing a murder, he's a federal offender. So what we'll be doing is cross-checking computer statistics on unsolved homicides and disappearances from all fifty states, going back ten years. If state-to-state links are made, we will be requesting the complete case files from the applicable agencies, and we will be communicating by telephone with the investigating officers. We will have M.O. cross-checking logs, and logs for physical evidence, circumstantial probability and a half-dozen logs compiled from reports made by the forensic psychologists attached to the Task Force. Patterns are likely to emerge from all this information, and we will hypothesize from that information, then initiate follow-up investigations staffed with experienced Criminal Division agents."

An entire wing of a building on the grounds of the F.B.I. Academy at Quantico has been taken over by the Task Force. The offices are packed with reams of blank paper, desks and computer terminals, along with a giant computer with fifty-state police feed-in. Known to Task Force agents as "Serial Sally," this brain device will be the starting point of all possible investigations. Already programmed with data on twenty-seven resolved serial killer cases, "Serial Sally" will be assisted by a half-dozen crack forensic psychologists with extensive field experience, three forensic pathologists specializing in homicide evidence, and four criminal division agents, men with fifteen years and up with the Bureau—the "Paperwork Jockeys" who will be trawling for links, connections and clues.

"I'm anxious to get started," Inspector Dusenberry, 47, the Task Force's Agent in Charge, told *L.E.J.* "I've already read up a storm on the subject. It's depressing stuff, and the numbers are staggering. A man in Alabama killed twenty-nine women in two years; Gacy in Chicago killed thirty-three. There's our friend Ted Bundy, of course, and then we've got the stats on missing and presumed-murdered children. They're more than staggering. The police in Anchorage, Alaska, have a suspect that they make for sixty-one killings, perpetrated within eighteen months. The pain behind all of it is staggering, and I think the serial killer problem is America's number-one law-enforcement priority."

Inspector Dusenberry, who joined the Bureau in 1961, is a graduate of Notre Dame Law School and has sixteen years of Criminal Division experience, mostly in supervising bank robbery investigations. Married and with a college-age son and daughter, he is grateful that the Task Force assignment came at a time when his children are grown and his wife is back in college getting an advanced degree in Art History. "It's going to be a long load of long hours," he told *L.E.J.* "My kids and wife in school, and the desk nature of the job will make it a whole lot easier to apply myself. If I was spending this kind of time on the street doing robbery investigations, I'd be worried about them worrying about me."

VII

IMPLOSION

21.

Tick
Tick
Tick
Tick
Tick
Tick
Tick
Tick
Stop-time.
12:16 A.M., June 5, 1982.

I stuck my breaker pick in the keyhole of the Kurzinskis' apartment door. There was a slight give, and I pushed the door inward, to a point just short of where I knew the inside chain would stop it. There was a snap/clink noise as the chain rattled, and I pulled the door toward me for slack, then popped the chain off with the handle of my pick gouger. The loose end hit the doorjamb, and I heard an unmistakable sound register in George Kurzinski's bedroom: the hammer of his .32 being pulled back.

I eased the door shut and padded through the dark living room, then flattened myself into the far wall, by the hallway and the light switch. Unclipping the ax that hung from my web belt, I waited for footsteps to creak in my direction. When the first one hit my ears, I tingled. It was exactly nine paces from George Kurzinski's bedroom to here; his life would consist of that many more seconds.

The creaking drew nearer, and at the ninth footfall I flicked on the light switch and swung my ax blind into the

hallway. Impact and blood spray told me I had hit on-target
before I even saw the dead man. Stepping forward, I heard
liquid gurgles and felt a strong hand yank the blade free.
When I looked into the hall, George Kurzinski was up
against the wall, trying to form a one-hand tourniquet to
stop the gushing from his side-to-side neck wound. He was
trying to shout at the same time, but his severed larynx
made the task impossible.

Blood spattered off my black plastic jump suit; a little
jet hit my face, and I licked at the trickle that reached my
lips. George slid to the floor, raised his gun and shot me six
times. At the click of the last misfire, I heard a faint, "Georgie? Georgie?" from Paula's bedroom, then the sound of her
groping through the dresser for her Beretta. Leaving George
in the hallway to die, I walked toward the lovely metallic
echo of a blank round being slid into a chamber, never to
connect with a firing pin.

Paula greeted me from the bed, pride and fire in her eyes
as she spat out a T.V.-movie warning: "Freeze, sucker." Dis-
obeying, I walked slowly toward her, baring my fangs like
Shroud Shifter and Lucretia out for fuel. She pulled the
trigger; nothing happened; she worked the slide and fired
again, getting another click. Watching her throat muscles
for the scream that had to be coming, I said, "I'm invul-
nerable," and jumped on her.

She fought hard, all elbows and knees, but I got my
hands around her throat just as she finally expelled the
first syllable of "Mother." Squeezing full force, I saw colors;
biting full force at her neck, I came. When she went limp,
I picked her up by one ankle and twirled her around and
around and around the room in perfect circles, never letting
her limbs touch the four walls. Arranging her limp form
on the bed, I felt my indignities move to her body, one-two-
three, as businesslike as a handshake.

Setting my brain watch at 3:00, I took the airline and
rock posters from the inner compartment of my jump suit
and looked at myself in the wall mirror. Shroud Shifter's
stern, hawklike features stared back. My makeup artistry
was superb, and accomplished without "Cougarman Co-

mix" as a visual aid. Self-transformed, blood-validated, at last the only alter ego that counted, I found tacks in the kitchen and fixed the posters to the living room walls, then dipped my surgical-rubber hands in George Kurzinski's blood and wrote "Shroud Shifter Prevails" on the wall above his body. Entering the apartment ten minutes before, I had been a thirty-four-year-old boy-man hoping to resolve an identity crisis; leaving it, I was a terrorist.

HEADLINES:

From the Philadelphia Inquirer, *June 7, 1982:*

BROTHER AND SISTER BRUTALLY SLAIN IN SHARON APARTMENT

From the Sharon News-Register, *June 7, 1982:*

BRUTAL DUAL SLAYING ROCKS TOWN! FRIENDS AND FAMILY MOURN

From the Philadelphia Post, *June 10, 1982:*

NO LEADS IN BRUTAL SHARON KILLINGS: POLICE WITHHOLDING "BLOOD MESSAGE" AS "MYSTERY CLUE"

From the Sharon News-Register, *June 13, 1982:*

KURZINSKIS' FUNERAL DRAWS HUGE CROWD; LOCAL HEALTH CLUBS CLOSE

From the Philadelphia Inquirer, *June 17, 1982:*

STILL NO LEADS IN SHARON SLAYINGS; STEEL TOWN LIVES IN FEAR, OUTRAGE

From the Philadelphia Post, *June 19, 1982:*

MOTIVE FOR KURZINSKI SLAYINGS BAFFLES POLICE; FALSE CONFESSORS POURING IN

From the Sharon News-Register, *July 14, 1982:*

VIGILANTE GROUPS FORMING TO HUNT FOR KURZINSKI KILLER

From the Sharon News-Register, *August 1, 1982:*

KURZINSKI MURDERS TRIGGER PANIC BACK-LASH—WIFE SHOOTS HUSBAND BY MISTAKE

From the Sharon News-Register, *December 8, 1982:*

STILL NO CLUES IN KURZINSKI MURDERS

From the Sharon News-Register, *January 6, 1983:*

KURZINSKI CASE CONTINUES TO BAFFLE LOCAL POLICE

From the Sharon News-Register, *March 11, 1983:*

NINE MONTHS AFTER: KURZINSKI CASE STILL "OPEN," SHARON STILL MOURNS

From the Sharon News-Register, *May 14, 1983:*

TRAIL ON KURZINSKI CASE "DEAD COLD," CHIEF ADMITS

From the Sharon News-Register, *May 20, 1983:*

POLICE WILL NOT REVEAL "BLOOD CLUE" IN KURZINSKI CASE— STILL "HOPING AGAINST HOPE," CHIEF SAYS

From the diary of Inspector Thomas Dusenberry, F.B.I. Serial Killer Task Force:

5/22/83

True to form, I'm running about a year behind in starting this diary. If Carol weren't out studying those ornate Renaissance guys with college kids less than half her age, she'd be looking over my shoulder at what I'm writing. She'd note the statement that begins the diary, and she'd say, "As in all things in your *personal* life, dear." True to form, I wouldn't know if it was a dig or an expression of love, because Carol is a tad smarter than I am, and a big tad better than me at everything except chasing felony offenders and earning money. And if she'd ever get off her (still curvaceous at 44) ass and take the real estate brokers' board, she'd beat me at the latter. And if Mark and Susan decided to quit school and become felons, forget it.

Backtracking, about ten years ago, right after Hoover died, every agent in captivity started writing his memoirs. Some actually got published. All were self-serving, full of fantasy and hearsay anecdotes about the Big Man. I was envious of the guys who got published, but enraged that they portrayed themselves as such sensitive liberals, when in fact most of them were to the right of your typical banana republic dictator shouting anti-commie slogans and pushing cocaine on the side. I looked at them ($10,000–$20,000 publishers' advances, royalties, movie options and glory for doing something I always figured I'd be pretty good at), and I looked at me—living above my means as a sop to my family for always moving them around the country with my assignments, telling Carol "Don't get a job, baby, I'll teach another night-school class," and I thought, "Shit, I've been taking out bank robbers for years; I'll write a book, and I won't even mention J. Edgar."

But the truth is—bank robbery is a bore, unless you take personal satisfaction from removing bank robbers from the streets. I do, and that's the rub. Either the bastards get caught right off the bat by municipal P.D.'s and we take over the legal end after they plead, or, predictable creatures with well-established criminal patterns that they are, they go where we know they will, and we find them. Personally satisfying, occasionally exciting, but most of the time my job was to read reports in my office and figure out where the dummies would go if they were suddenly rich. So scratch one best-seller about a hotshot Fed robbery investigator. Joe Blow over in Fraud Division—you deal with a higher class of criminal—you write the book.

I thought that working the Task Force would make this diary (book later?) easy. It hasn't, and the Force is a year old already. I thought that Carol would be supportive and help me with editing, but she's engrossed in her studies, and every time I mention possible chains of missing children, she freezes up and we don't make love for a week.

When I try to get intellectual and relate some of the monsters that come out of Serial Sally to van Gogh (poor bastard) or Hieronymous Bosch, she freezes me out with gooey landscapes from her texts. The hidden truth: she regrets never having a career, and envies my dedication to mine. She's also pushed Susan and Mark in the direction of the arts, which should keep me on Broke Street and teaching classes until they're 30 and Ph.D.'s. And that's fine—although I suspect Mark would be happier as a carpenter or contractor and Susan happier as a wife and art-dabbler.

But I'm rambling from the point, which is that the Task Force is the *big* assignment of my life, the most satisfying and troubling, and it's still hard to write about it. To be honest, it's Carol's freeze that's allowed me to get this far. I come home late, still pumped up, still hot to work, and the snowy art woman (unfair, darling, but allow me temporary license) piles on a few more snowdrifts. The Task Force has got me thinking family, so I'll use Susan to switch from one subject to the other.

Susie called long-distance (requesting money) last night. We bat the breeze, and I ask her if she's dating anyone, what her general philosophy regarding marriage is. She says, "Well, Dad, I believe in serial monogamy, and I imagine I'll keep practicing it."

I hit the fucking ceiling and yelled at Susie, something I rarely do. It was the word "serial" and its connotations, of course. I wasn't too coherent while Susie and I were arguing, and we said good-bye a few minutes later, but this morning I put it all in place. It was her absence of romantic illusion. She's 22, she sleeps with her boyfriends, it doesn't particularly bother me. It's just that she knows that sooner or later it will end; she doesn't have that youthful feeling of "forever" that you lose soon enough anyway. I would rather wish her the way of Gretchen, the Force's exec. secretary, than the way of that awful word. Gretch is 31, two kids from a bum marriage that she thought would last forever, has affairs with the wrong guys, who ultimately split because the kids scare the shit out of them. She's smart, she's funny, she's a great mother, she's got some gay men friends who're funnier than Bob Hope, Jackie Gleason and Richard Pryor put together, and she's still got hope. We hug every once in a while, and if I weren't such a loyal dog, I'd go where Gretch seems to wish the hugs would go.

With "serial" you just go on to the next one. Lover or murder victim, you just go. This morning, getting up the guts to start this diary, I wanted to see my name in print, so I looked at a copy of *Law Enforcement Journal* from last year. There I was, Inspector Thomas Dusenberry, using my Bureau-learned verbal style, all "perpetrator," "apprehend" and "circumstantial." I also used "staggering" a lot, and with that I'll jump to the real purpose of this diary:

It's more than staggering. I'm a veteran criminal investigator, and for the sake of reality I wish there were adjectives to top "staggering," "mind-boggling," "incredible," etc. Sixteen months ago I would have told you that the only thing deserving of the above hype was my wife's hauteur at a Bureau cocktail party. Today I would beg Carol's pardon and say, "Sorry, baby, there are human beings out there, college-educated, with executive-level jobs, who beat people to death, steal their cufflinks as souvenirs, then go home and round up the kids, take them to Little League practice and foot the bill for the whole team at Haagen Dazs on the way back to the wife and tender sex." If Carol balked, I would point out one of the three serial killers our Task Force has thus far taken out in its year of existence: Federal case file 086-83—Whalen, William Edmund, aka the "Chappaqua Chopper."

Willy, an upper-level executive at a New York advertising agency, beat a total of fourteen people to death in suburban New York and New Jersey during the years 1976–1982. He used to prowl the park areas along the Hudson River, find solitary nature lovers (old, young, male, female, black, white—Willy was an Equal Opportunity killer), beat them to death with a rock, steal some kind of keepsake from them, then toss them in the river. I got him on a fluke. I found out all the side streets leading to the parks he used to prowl had one-side-of-the-street-only parking, so I ran computer checks on parking tickets issued near the days the coroner tagged the victims' D.O.D. Bingo! Old Willy was careless three times out of fourteen.

He had a nice three-story colonial in Chappaqua, and his gross income for the previous year was $275,000 and stock options. When I knocked on his door I wasn't 100% sure of his guilt, so I asked him flat out, "Mr. Whalen, are you the Chappaqua Chopper?"

His reply: "Yes, I am. I'll come along peacefully, Officer, but will you have a martini with me first? My wife and children are soon to leave for the theatre, and I wouldn't want to spoil their fun. I'll tell them you're with the agency."

Willy's in Lewisburg now, wearing federal denims instead of Paul Stuart suits. I got a lot of awed laughs when I told people about belting a few Beefeaters with him, and I actually sort of liked the crazy cocksucker. Then, pissed at myself for it, I dug up the coroner's photos of his victims. I don't like Willy anymore.

Nor do I understand him.

The other two take-outs belong to my colleague Jim Schwartzwalder, formerly a S.A.C. in Houston. He's a forensics whiz, and he *asked* to work the stats on missing children (no one else wanted the job). Jim got ahold of some figures on missing kids in Northern Louisiana, and two dead kids (raped and covered with bite marks) down near Baton Rouge. Hypothesizing a transient killer, possibly a car thief, Jim ran auto-theft reports from the Shreveport area, got one that felt "panicky," then ran the forensic dental report made from the teeth marks on the dead kids, along with queries on repeating felons popped for Grand Theft Auto. Double bingo from the Texas State Prison in Brownsville. The teeth marks exactly matched dentures fashioned for former inmate Leonard Carl Strohner there at the pen, back when he was serving 3–5 for G.T.A. in the late '70's. An A.P.B. bagged Strohner in New Mexico a few months later. He confessed biting, raping and killing twenty-two children throughout the South and Southwest, aided by his sometime sidekick Charles Sidney Hoyt. A routine roundup of vagrants got Hoyt in Tucson, Arizona, the following week. He laughed when he confessed his crimes, and when one of the arresting officers asked him why he liked to bite children, Hoyt said, "The closer the bone, the sweeter the meat."

I'm rambling again, so I'll give myself a little more slack, then get back to the point. Digression one—for a cop, I'm sort of a liberal. Poverty is your number-one cause of crime, period. All that stuff about moral breakdowns and the breakdown of the family unit is bullshit. Aside from poverty and its direct correlative of hard narcotics use, we have individual psychological motivation, which is pretty much unfathomable, although the forensic psychologists attached to the Force are pretty good at extrapolating from workups and physical evidence. As a cop, psychological motivation has always been my chief professional interest. Willie Roosevelt Washington, black heroin addict from Philly's South Side, became a bank robber. Willie's dad and mom were good people who never hit him. Willie's next-door neighbor growing up, Robert Dewey Brown, got the shit kicked out of him regularly by his sadistic boozehound parents, and he is now a brilliant young forensic chemist with the Bureau. What happened?

City cops often have a stock answer. Working liaison with them over the years, I've heard it often: Evil. Cause and effect and traumatic episodes mean zilch, what is *is*; look for the cause and effect, and what you'll get is what is *is* and good and evil mitigated by shades of gray. I'm a logical, methodical man with only a nominal belief in God, and that answer has always offended me.

Digression two—aside from marrying Carol against my parents' wishes, the chief act of rebellion in my life has been disavowing the faith I was reared in. I was seventeen when I ceased to believe in the tenets of the Dutch Reformed Church. The sanctity of Jesus Christ, shadeless good and evil, and God the puppet master in the sky doing his pre-destination number at the birth of members of his flock, was too ugly, mean-spirited and stupid for a logical, me-thodical kid who wanted to be either a lawyer or a cop. So I enrolled at a Jesuit college and went to Notre Dame Law and became both a cop and a lawyer, and I'm still logical and methodical and obsessed with knowing *why* at close to fifty. And, *punch line*—maybe what is *is*, and good and evil are the real stuff, with the serial killer stats I've been working on as unimpeachable proof of it.

Here are some choice tidbits of information to support that thesis:

In serial killings where robbery was (in forensic psych parlance) the "motive of the moment," the 1981 average take was less than twenty dollars per victim.

A man convicted of nine murders, perpetrated in three states over a five-year period, was a conscientious objector during the Vietnam War and went to jail for holding draft-resistance seminars in violation of federal law. In light of that, he was asked how he could murder nine people in cold blood. "I adapted my philosophy to accommodate my desire to kill," he said.

A man caught in the act of raping an elderly woman he had murdered a few moments before was revealed to have been a released suspect in several other killings. The man passed polygraph testing before he was let go. When asked how he accomplished it, he said, "Listen, I groove on killing. I feel no guilt over it, so how can a machine programmed to detect guilt snitch me off?"

None of the six serial murderers of children successfully prosecuted in the United States during the year 1981 had been molested when they were children.

Serial killers are more often than not capable of sustaining normal, monogamous sexual relationships.

A final shocker supplied by Doc Seidman, the head shrink with the Task Force: Hardcore sociopathic career criminals with records of violence that stop short of murder outscore convicted serial killers on psychological tests aimed at detecting lack of moral restraint and criminal lack of conscience. Doc Seidman says that where your typical sociopath will steal you blind and exploit you in all matters from the most picayune on up—pathologically compelled to act with absolute selfishness—serial killers will not. They are, he says, sometimes capable of genuine love and passion. That "fact" heartened me, and it felt like it might be both a good hunting tool and a buffer against depression. Reading reports of sodomy, dismembering and murder, murder, murder can creep up on you. Passion is logical sometimes; I can almost logically harpoon why I love Carol so much, despite the fact a lot of people consider her a bitch. Then I blew it seeking more logical reinforcement. "How are they capable, Doc?"

"They have an exalted sense of style," he answered.

So I'm back with good vs evil, the elation of the hunt vs the depression of the territory, cause and effect and Doc's passion and style. It's getting late, Carol should be back soon, and I want to be able to talk about her stuff, so I'll put down the connecting links I credit so far, along with some pure cop observations:

1.—Two different sets of rape-dismemberments. The first set (three teenaged girls, all brunette) occurred in Southern Wisconsin in late '78–early '79, and may be attributed to a Chicago man, Saul Malvin, who committed suicide directly after and near the scene of the third killing. Malvin had O+ blood, like the killer (semen-typed from his victims), but there is no other physical evidence linking him to the killings. Circumstantially, he fits: he was near the scene of the third killing, and he was allegedly at home alone during the time spread on the first two. Malvin had no criminal record and no history of psychiatric counseling, which is a moot factor as far as serials go. The shrinks on the Force say suicide after a particularly brutal killing is not unusual—it results from moments of clarity. (Nice they can feel it, but too bad it's too late to do their last victim any good.)

2.—Four teenaged–early 20's girls, raped and similarly dismembered, D.O.D.'s 4/18/79, Louisville, Kentucky; 10/1/79, Des Moines, Iowa; 5/27/80, Charleston, South Carolina; 5/19/81, Baltimore, Maryland. All four girls were blondes, all were hookers with multiple prostitution convictions. The killer/rapist was again an O+ secretor (very common type), and the physical evidence (knife marks and hacksaw-blade dimensions) was identical in all four cases. Interdepartmental notations included in the four case files and the master case file the four P.D.'s worked up when they formed their own short-lived "Task Force" speculate on either a legitimate policeman killer or a cop impersonator. So far that's just theory, based on the observation of an old wino who said that he saw a man with a "cop vibe" enter the vestibule of the Charleston victim's apartment building on the night of her death. Iffy stuff. Right now I want to see if Malvin can be made or dismissed as the Wisconsin killer, and if dismissed, I want to check the physical evidence from the Wisconsin jobs against the other four. I requested the files from the Wisconsin State Police two weeks ago, no reply as yet. The blonde-brunette point is interesting. S.K.'s are tricky, and if one perpetrator is responsible for all seven deaths, maybe he just got the urge to change his "style."

3.—Jim Schwartzwalder has five linkups of missing children, all in western, southwestern and southern states. Some of the links cross, and he's having trouble determining how many perpetrators he's dealing with. But... he's got a vehicle description on one of his links, and so now he's got the real shitwork that solves cases on his hands—cross-checking automobile registration against opportunity and the registerees' criminal and/or psychiatric records. Thanks for taking the kids, Jim. I owe you one.

4.—I've got several transient killing links going back nine years. Different M.O.'s, but they run west to east chronologically, and I've connected two of them. Backtracking: thirteen roadside disappearance/killings in Nevada and Utah, spanning late 1974 to late 1975. Some were shot, some were bludgeoned; most of the bodies found had been robbed of valuables. The first two in the chain, a young man and woman discovered by campers in rural Nevada in December of '74, had been shot with a .357 Magnum and arranged nude in a sexual posture. Following that, four affluent young hitchhikers, all male, were found variously beaten, shot (no expended rounds uncovered) and strangled in Nevada and Utah in January of 1975. All were robbed, and credit cards belonging to one victim were uncovered in Salt Lake City. The suspect harboring them, who was cleared as a suspect, said that the cards were sold to him by a tall, nondescript man in his early twenties named "Shifter."

Jump to: five people, male and female, ages ranging from 14 to 71, disappeared from Utah and Nevada roadways in the spring of 1975. *No leads—vanished.*

Jump to: Ogden, Utah, 10/30/75: two solid-citizen motorists are last seen talking to a "tall young white man" outside Ogden, then—poof!—vanish.

That's thirteen dead and presumed dead so far. Now, big jump, geographically and life-style—wise: eight young people disappear from Aspen, Colorado, during the months of January to June 1976. Four are husband-and-wife couples, all are affluent. The disappearances are never really connected, even when three of the missing people turn up in the snow, preserved, during the spring '76 thaw—*mutilated,* the husband and wife arranged nude in an intercourse posture, a third missing man (last seen eight days after the first two!) positioned nude a few feet from them.

Add eight to thirteen, you get twenty-one. Now, another big jump. The letters "S.S." are carved on the victims' legs. At first the local police think it's Nazi stuff, then some comic-book freak says it may be a reference to the "Shroud Shifter," a comic-book bad guy from years ago. Connection: "Shifter" the credit-card pusher; "Shroud Shifter" the inspiration for the S.S. markings? I've run both names nationwide, and am awaiting results from municipal P.D. monicker files. Very, very tenuous stuff, but something to work on.

Jump to: nine Caucasian college students go poof! and disappear from various parts of Kansas and Missouri— April '77 to October '78. One young man was last seen talking to a "large white man, possibly the owner of a van," and his credit cards were recovered from a card-frauder in St. Louis. The frauder stated in a polygraph exam: "The guy I bought them from said he got them from another guy with a weird name like Stick Shifter."

That makes thirty, and it's now getting a little less tenuous. The sometime sex killings, the recurring "tall," "large," white man and the "Shifter" card seller point to one perpetrator. The "Shroud Shifter" stuff is dubious, but I'm going to query the Aspen cops on the comic-book freak who called in the info—maybe the guy has more salient stuff. All this data is going into Serial Sally, and the shrinks are reading my reports on the chain. They'll be doing their own studies, going over prison and mental hospital records that immediately predate the first killings—"Shifter" may well have been just paroled or released. The pisser is that all of this is going to take time. Happily though, Shifter has been a good boy since late '78. Jack Mulhearn has a chain of four killings that he thinks are transient-perpetrated, but chronologically and geographically they're slightly out of Shifter's kilter (Illinois 5/8/79; Nebraska 12/3/79; Michigan 9/80; Ohio 5/81). All four men were shot in the mouth with the same cheapo handgun, and Doc Seidman hypothesizes a homosexual killer, which doesn't sound like my boy. Where are you, Shifter?

There's Carol! I'm going to tell her I wrote fourteen pages today, and mentioned her at least that many times.

22.

On June 5, 1983, a year to the day from my finest moment as a killer, I left Sharon and drove nonstop to Westchester County, New York. Crossing the Tappan Zee Bridge, I hurled my overused and now dangerous Rheinhardt Wildebrand credit cards into the Hudson River below me; driving South on Route 22 to look for country clubs and boat clubs offering summer jobs, I felt like a teenager who left the party early to look cool, without realizing he had no place to go.

The "party" was my status as the biggest thing ever to hit Sharon, Pennsylvania, and the reason I had to leave it behind was a slow, steady ticking in my head. On the road or in my projected safe harbor of suburban New York the sound would have been just my old brain-clock; back in Sharon it was a fuse. Sooner or later I would have had to duplicate my transformation into Shroud Shifter there, not out of blood lust, but to hear the thunderclaps of the town's awe go huge once more. And, given the vigilance I had created, the attempt might have been suicidal.

As in San Francisco after Eversall/Sifakis, I had listened. But in Sharon, one-tenth the size and one-fiftieth as sophisticated, the echoes had resounded ten thousand times as loud. The Kurzinskis were known, liked, envied and admired by the entire town; I had destroyed a part of the town along with them. My presence *was* the town, in much the manner that a powerful lover becomes every piece of space surrounding the one who loves him. I was everything

Sharon, Pennsylvania, saw; for my post-killing year there,
I was the regulator of its heartbeat.

I had been Billy Rohrsfield, library clerk and Co-ed Connection iron pumper by day, Shroud Shifter by night. For
365 straight dusks I performed ritual identity changes:
slacks, shirt and jacket into the hamper; black jump suit
on, hawk nose formed and applied out of putty. Cheekbones
and eyebrows shaded, so that my whole face came to points.
A police-band radio and my party-line hookup for listening
to THEM talk about ME; wondering when they would drop
their "mystery clue" pretense and speak my night name to
the world. Getting hard when old biddies worshipped me
with fearful voices; climaxing when men spoke of me in
rage. It was paradise until something began going ssss/tick,
ssss/tick, ssss/tick in my ears, and I started thinking about
voiding the security patrols I had inspired, slipping through
their neighborly nets to waste an entire family. Underneath
ssss/tick ssss/tick, ssss/tick, I knew it was foolhardy, so discreetly I left the town, with regret and some gratitude for
the return of plain old ticking.

I picked up a young man hitching just south of White
Plains, and he told me I could caddy the season at any one
of a half-dozen Westchester country clubs—all I had to do
was look hearty and presentable. He also mentioned a rental
bureau in Yonkers that matched up summer passers-through
with the apartments of Sarah Lawrence College students
on vacation. I took the kid's advice on both counts, and by
the end of the day Billy Rohrsfield was ensconsed in a small
bachelor pad on the Yonkers edge of Bronxville and had
caddied nine holes at Siwanoy Country Club.

And that night Billy became Shroud Shifter for the first
time in New York.

With no local celebrity, no radio band or primitive party
line, there was nothing to do but listen to the tick tick tick
tick ticks grow louder and wonder who and when and where.
So I did—Billy at the golf course days, my special self of
hard facial edges at night. The ticking continued, and on
a hot day in mid-July I stopped the clock right in the heart

of midtown Manhattan, strangling a drunk passed out in
a pew at Saint Patrick's Cathedral.

Post and Daily News headlines turned the ticking to a
whimper, and I went Billy/Shifter, Billy/Shifter, Billy/Shif-
ter into the heat of August and another excursion into the
Big Apple. This time the alarm went BLAAAAAAAR when
I was strolling through Central Park and a bum asked me
for change. Surrounded by other strollers, I motioned him
behind a mound of bushes and slit his throat. The artist's
sketch of me that adorned page two of the Post the following
day was a poor likeness, and as Shroud Shifter that night,
I put my mind to the task of creating a prolonged reign of
terror.

From Thomas Dusenberry's Diary:

8/17/83

I'm back again, coming up for air after three straight
months of paper prowling, helping Jim Schwartzwalder
conduct field interviews in Minneapolis, conferences with
the shrinks and what amount to conferences with Carol—
she's gotten that formal and severe. I come home late, exhausted and edgy from too much coffee, and she's studying.
I put on reruns of the Honeymooners or Sergeant Bilko—
nice frivolous antidotes to coroners' reports filled with dis-
emboweling and severed penises—and she tells me that
the frantic nature of '50's comedies created a whole gen-
eration of kids prone to quick laughs, quick gratification
and violence. Since her diatribes sound preprogrammed, I
figure she's picked them up from one of her professors. It
is getting undeniably bad with her; we will have to talk
seriously soon. I hope the cause of all Carol's anger at me
is clinical—menopause sounds like a logical, methodical
way to wrap it all up. I miss the old her.

Speaking of wrapping up, Jim Schwartzwalder's vehicle
cross-checks got him the name of a suspect he makes for

thirteen child abduction/murders in the Midwest. Anthony Joseph Anzerhaus of Minneapolis, a traveling salesman for a stationery-supply company. I went with Jim to Minneapolis. We found out from Anzerhaus's boss that he was on the road and probably hitting Sioux Falls, South Dakota, that night. We called the S.A.C. in Sioux Falls, gave him the name of the motel Anzerhaus usually stays at and told him to wait for him there. Then we checked out Anzerhaus's apartment. We found the scalps of six children in an ice cooler. Jim completely blew it and trashed the place, throwing furniture, breaking bottles. I finally got him calmed down, but then the Sioux Falls S.A.C. called and said that Anzerhaus never showed up. I figured that his boss tipped him off, so I left Jim at a bar to chill out and confronted the guy. He admitted it, and then *I* completely blew it—busting the asshole for Impeding the Progress of a Federal Investigation and Aiding and Abetting the Escape of an Interstate Fugitive. I would have hit him with an Accessory charge if I thought I could make it stick.

When I got back to the bar, Jim was fried. He told me that if Anzerhaus killed another child before we got him, he was going to kill his boss. I'm 40% sure he means it. Jim's sticking in Minneapolis to supervise the investigation, and Anthony Joseph Anzerhaus, my professional advice is for you to commit suicide, because you will be caught, and between Jim Schwartzwalder and the moralistic organized-crime boys who rule the federal pens, you will be thrown into deep, deep shit.

Enough on that—Anzerhaus is no pro fugitive, he won't last another week. The big news—the big jump—is that my "Shifter" and "Shroud Shifter" queries just got red-hot. Last June 5, a brother and sister were killed in their Sharon, Pa., apartment. He died from a neck wound caused by an ax blow, she was strangled. The killer wrote "Shroud Shifter Prevails" on the wall in the male victim's blood, and the Sharon cops kept it under wraps to eliminate phony confessors. No confessors (611 came forth) admitted writing the words, and the cops did a super job of stonewalling the clue. I've got the entire Sharon P.D. case file—1,100 pages,

784 F.I. cards alone, and am going over it with the shrinks and Jack Mulhearn. No F.I. names match to any of the names from the case files of the previous disappearance/killings we make Shifter for, and I've called the Aspen cops and browbeat them for info on the guy who called in the initial Shroud Shifter notation. No one there remembers the guy, it's not in any of the Aspen files, and they've had a big turnover in personnel since '76. Heavily extrapolating on that, Doc Seidman thinks the guy who called in the information *is* Shifter, that he's got genius-level intelligence and a huge ego, and is probably bisexual with a slight preference for men. Doc got ahold of some old issues of "Cougarman Comics"—the comic book that featured Shroud Shifter. He says it's sick shit—sadomasochistic and necrophiliac in tone. Beyond all that, he thinks Shifter is between 32 and 37, and that he comes from a "Car Culture Milieu"—the Southwest or California. Doc leans toward Southern California because "Cougarman Comics" was most heavily distributed there, and because he makes Shifter as coming from an environment that worships good looks and physical fitness. Whoever chopped the male victim in Sharon was tremendously strong, and the victim and his sister were bodybuilders, so his theory does jibe with our existing hard evidence.

Where are you, Shifter?

I've directed a team of Denver agents to go to Aspen and turn the place upside down until they find out who called in the Shifter info, and a team out of the Philly office is going to Sharon tomorrow to do backup interviews. On Doc's advice, I've requested information on unsolved homicides in California immediately before the first Shifter probable in 12/74. If Aspen doesn't yield a name within a week or so, I'll go there myself. You want your huge ego rubbed, Shifter? Turn yourself in to Uncle Tom, he'll make you a star.

Doc's been doing the bulk of the theorizing on Shifter, but I've been doing my own share on the link-links I now call "Blond-Brunette." It's heavily suppositional, theoretical and circumstantial, but I trust the overall feel.

One, I now buy a policeman killer for all seven victims. Checking through the case files, I saw that all of the blond four had been recently arrested for prostitution, making them particularly easy marks for police or pseudo-police intimidation, which would account for why such streetwise ladies let strange men into their apartments. Two, I don't buy Saul Malvin as the Brunette Killer. I buy him as a suicide (the report filed by the officer who found his car and later his body was a model of cop smarts and clarity, if a little overboard on his own theorizing)—but O+ blood is very common, and I made some discreet calls to the Chicago S.A.C., who learned that Malvin had a thing going with a friend of his wife, and the friend was demanding a commitment. Suicide territory for a certain kind of man.

Three, a big jump, and a mind-boggling one that really feels right: the Wisconsin State Police and the two municipal P.D.'s aiding them in the brunette-killing investigations cannot find their files on the three homicides, which is one of the most incredible things I have heard in my twenty-two years as an investigator. Nine recent case files—vanished.

I think we've got a Wisconsin-based policeman-killer as the perpetrator of all seven blond-brunette homicides, and I think he destroyed the three brunette files to avoid a connection being made, most likely one based on identical physical evidence. And with physical evidence links destroyed from a legal standpoint (some Wisconsin M.E. or pathologist probably remembers blade specifications, etc., which wouldn't hold up in court), all I've got left is opportunity.

So, any Southern Wisconsin cop missing from his assignment solely on the dates of the four blond homicides is my killer. I've already put in sub rosa queries with the Internal Affairs Department of the Wisconsin State Police, and the Milwaukee S.A.C. is doing the same with the personnel directors of the Janesville and Beloit P.D.'s. All I can do now is wait. Jack Mulhearn thinks my theory sucks—he thinks some cop sold the files to the media or a crime writer. We've got a hundred-dollar bet riding on the outcome of my queries. I can't afford to lose—Mark and Susan's fall tuition kick-out is coming up, but I feel solid on this one. It's 11:23. Where are you, Carol?

23.

Tick
Tick
Tick
Tick
Tick
Tick
Tick
Tick

Dusk, September 7, 1983. Clock noise was in my head, and a bag holding #9 pancake and theatrical putty was in my hands when I returned home from the golf course and shopping in Bronxville. Opening the door, I was anxious to begin my nightly transformation and almost missed the scrapbook pages spread out on my bed.

Feeling what must have happened, I gasped and looked at my bathroom and closet doors—the only places where he could be waiting. With tick tick tick tick tick tick tick tick out-decibeled by adrenaline hitting my heart, I somehow managed not to run to either of them, knowing that betraying my eagerness would be an affront to the Shroud Shifter me. About to burst on all sensory levels, I forced myself to read the reunion message.

It was a newspaper article dated February 19, 1979, and it detailed the brilliant machinations that Ross Anderson had undertaken to safeguard the two of us from exposure of our latest murders. Reading and rereading the account in rapid succession, a Technicolor vision of the key points swallowed me whole, and I grabbed the bed for support.

Ross locating the dead man's car, seeing the O+ donor card and going "Eureka!";

Ross driving back to Huyserville for a K-9 team, even though he already knew where the body was;

Ross putting his own money in the dead man's wallet and my old .357, sans silencer, in his hand;

Ross desecrating the man's chest so that pathologists couldn't tell that two shots had been the cause of his death.

My burst level decelerating, I reran the mental film; reversed the action; ran it in slow motion. In all versions, it played as pure genius—and something else.

"And you thought I was just another pretty face. Ross the Boss, what a guy."

I warmed all over, and the spreading heat gave me poise. I got up from the bed, turned around and smiled. "Bravo, Sergeant."

Ross smoothed his mustache and stroked the alligator emblem on his blue polo shirt. Civilian clothes, four and a half years and a thousand miles had not changed him at all; every bit of the man had stepped intact out of the time warp. "It's Lieutenant," he said, "but thanks."

Made cool by his cool, I held back my barrage of questions and said, "Congratulations."

Ross shut the bathroom door and said, "Thanks. I'm the youngest lieutenant in the history of the Wisconsin State Police, by the way. Turn those scrapbook pages over: there's some stuff you'll like on the back."

I did it. More newspaper accounts were taped to the reverse sides, accompanied by faded Polaroid snapshots of butchered blond girls. While my eyes scanned the type and my brain played a film of Ross traveling and risking and killing for me, the man himself spoke slowly, his words wafting as background music.

"You were easy to track, sweetie. I am a world-class abuser of police power and an even better skip-tracer. The .38 I gave you was my tracker. I gouged the inside of the barrel, test-fired it into a ballistics tank, then kept the spents. Very distinctive lands and grooves, not even the silencer I figured you'd get could alter the striations. Soooo,

all I had to do was make statewide queries on Dead Body
Reports filed under 'Gunshot,' check the ballistics bulletins
and see where my old buddy Martin was hanging out. It
took a lot of phoning, but I'm the persistent type. I made
you for the retard in Illinois and the fag in Nebraska—you
come out of the closet yet, sweetie? They were both big dark-
haired guys about your age, and I thought, 'Uh, oh, Martin
wants some new ID because he knows Ross the Boss has
got his number.' Then you offed the old kraut in Michigan,
almost two years had passed; I figured if you snuffed an old
guy like that, maybe you already got your ID from a stiff
you didn't shoot or the cops never found. I also had a hunch
you were getting hinky and cautious, that you must have
snuffed Pops for a reason. So I wangled a Xerox of the case
file from the Kalamazoo cops.

"And damned if I don't make you for a pretty good forger.
Twelve K in checks to credit-card companies? The dumbfuck
Kalamazoo cops don't even bother to check with the companies, but I do. *Future* credit-card transactions? Sweetie,
you have got a pair of platinum balls, and I've been following those balls cross-country, courtesy of Telecredit. There's
Martin in Ohio, maybe doing some cutting in Sharon, P.A.
Follow up on that Rohrsfield dead-body report, call the
rental-listing hotline the cops have access to to keep track
of parole absconders, damned if I don't get a William Rohrsfield right down the road from this family reunion that I
thought would be too boring to attend. Good work on Rohrsfield, Martin, but you shouldn't have buried him under the
site of a future 7–11. Sweetie, you want to put those pictures down and look at me?"

The request took my eyes away from the death portraits.
Feeling only awe for the way Ross had set me up, I said,
"How did you manage *this?* Different cities? Spacing them
like that?"

Petting the alligator on his chest, Ross said, "Extradition
assignments. I'd hit the municipal P.D.'s, file my papers,
shoot the shit with the investigating officers, then mosey
by the Vice files and look for some nice blond meat with
recent hooking convictions. Easy. Get the information, buzz

their door, say it's Sergeant Plunkett or whoever, do the deed, take the pictures and split. Space the jobs, different cities. It took four jobs for the connection to get made, and I just stopped. New-breed killer, capable of control. I also booked my flights to and from the extradition cities under assumed names, then turned in forged vouchers for myself and my returnee, so that I'm not listed on any passenger manifests. Saul Malvin was the fall guy on the brunettes, and I destroyed the files on them in case somebody connects the 'Wisconsin Whipsaw' and the 'Four-State Hooker Hacker' and decides to start comparing forensic specs. I've just figured out something about the two of us, Martin. We equal out in the end, but you excel in quantity while I excel in quality."

Despite all my awe and that something else, the condescension rankled, and I said, "What about one-on-one?"

Ross smiled, and I caught a flash of his awe. "I don't know, sweetie. I truly, honestly don't. You feel like taking a ride? Maybe meeting some family of mine?"

Ross had taken a cab, so we took Deathmobile II to the summer house where the younger reunion people were staying. Having him in the passenger seat beside me was softly warming, and he spoke softly while we drove north on the Saw Mill Parkway.

"I used to spend summers here as a kid. This bash is being thrown by the Liggetts, my mother's people. Big bucks. They all thought Mom married beneath herself—Lars Anderson, big dumb handsome squarehead, cabinetmaker from the Wisconsin boonies, no future. They used to let me know in subtle ways, kill me with kindness while they were doing it. Every September around this time, right before they sent me back to Beloit, they bought me a humongous load of fall school clothes, marched me into Brooks Brothers like I was Little Lord Fauntleroy. The salesmen hated me because they thought I was a rich kid with a silver spoon up his ass; the Liggetts blew the wad so they could make my dad look low; and I always ordered everything too big or too small so I could sell it or ditch it when I got home. You

remember that buddy of mine? The late Billy Gretzler? You
should have seen him wearing this five-hundred-dollar
cashmere Chesterfield when he worked on his truck. It finally got so black and greasy that I told him, A joke's a
joke, throw it away. He wouldn't, though. He chopped the
coat up and used the pieces as gun-cleaning rags. We're
almost to Croton, so turn off at the next exit and hang a
left."

Easing over toward the off-ramp lane, I asked, "What
was having a family like?"

Ross stroked his alligator. "You didn't have one, sweetie?"

"Orphaned early," I said.

"Well, I'll tell you. I've got Andersons and Liggetts and
Caffertys up the ying-yang, and mostly they're just people
you see through as being what they are. My mom and sis
are weak; my dad's stupid and proud; Richie Liggett—my
cousin who you'll probably meet—he's smart, but so lost in
this grad-school vision of what he thinks life is that you'd
never know it. Another cousin, Rosie Cafferty, she's your
prototypical hot-pants teenybopper with a yen for Italian
guys and muscle cars. Good she's got bucks—she'd be a
whore otherwise. She's—"

Pulling off the parkway, I interrupted: "But what's it
like?"

Ross considered the question as I drove past huge white
homes for over a mile. Station wagons crowded with people
and luggage were pulling out of driveways, and renters
were handing over keys on a score of front lawns. The lights
in the houses reminded me of burglary, and I blurted, "Tell
me, goddamnit."

Ross laughed. "You want a definition of family, I'll give
you one. Family is feeling sort of close to people because
you know they're connected to you by blood, and you have
to tolerate them, regardless of what you think of them. So
over the years they grow on you, in one way or the other,
and it's interesting to observe them and know you're smarter
than they are. Also, they're beholden to you and can do you
solids. Turn left on the corner and park."

I slowed, accomplished the turn and pulled to the curb

in front of a large white house that must have dated back
to the Revolutionary War. Ross said, "Nice pad, huh?" and
pointed to mounds of toys strewn across the immaculate
front lawn. "There's family and money for you in a nutshell.
Lots of bucks in this area, and the kids still carry on like
niggers. Come on."

We walked across the grass and veranda and through
the open front door. Inside, the house was expensive furniture and carpeting in need of dusting, with sports clothes,
tennis rackets and odd golf clubs scattered around the living
room and foyer. Ross put his fingers in his mouth and whistled, then said, "What a bunch of slobs. Richie and Rosie
are shacked up here with their paramours, and I've been
staying in a room about the size of a broom closet. The
reunion starts tomorrow night at this yacht club in Ma-
maroneck, and the unmarried cousins have got this place
so they won't embarrass Big Daddy Liggett by porking in
the cabanas. Hey! Achtung! Ross the Boss is here!"

I heard footsteps upstairs, and moments later two couples in tennis whites bounded down the staircase. The young
men were wholesome fitness personified, one WASP style,
one Italian; the young women were brunette and redheaded
outtakes from the Ralph Lauren ads I had seen during my
reading spurts. All four started babbling "Hi!" and "Hi,
Ross," at once, looking at me sidelong, like an afterthought.
Ross pumped the male hands and hugged the girls, then
put his fingers in his mouth and whistled. The shrill report
froze all the jabbering, and Ross said, "Hey kids, let's mind
our manners. Cousins, this is my friend Billy Rohrsfield.
Billy, we have, left to right, Richie Liggett, Mady Behrens,
Rosie Cafferty and Dom De Nunzio."

Thinking *style*, I shook the male hands and kissed the
female ones. The boys guffawed and the girls giggled, and
catching a glimpse of Ross petting his shirt, I went warm
again. Winking, Ross said, "Mixed doubles indoors and out?"
and the kids all laughed at the wit of the man they obviously
adored, then dispersed, picking up gym bags and tennis
rackets from the floor. They flew out the door in a cacophony
of "See you's!" and "Bye's!" and "Nice meeting you's!"; and

the entire scene ended so abruptly that I had to blink my
eyes and dig my feet into the carpet to get my bearings.

Ross noticed my look and said, "Culture shock. Come on,
I'll show you around the house. We've got it to ourselves
now." He stroked the emblem on his chest, and suddenly I
knew he kept doing that to keep from touching me. "Show
me your room first," I said.

We both knew what I meant.

Ross touched his chest. "Alice the alligator. The only
woman who never let me down, so I keep her close to my
heart." Pointing up the stairs, he winked. Bowing at the
waist, I said, "Walk, sweetie," and Ross unwittingly ac-
knowledged match point by laughing out loud and exposing
a tiny flaw in his almost-perfection—poorly capped teeth
that were usually subterfuged by tight smiles and mustache
bristles. He walked ahead then, and I winced at the lover's
epiphany.

I couldn't feel my footsteps as I followed him to the bedroom, and when he reached for the inside light switch I
could hardly hear myself say, "No." Ross's "Bye, Alice,"
boomed in the darkness, and then zippers rasped and belt
buckles and shoes hit the floor. Bedsprings squeaked, and
then we were together.

We held; we rubbed; we kissed. We felt the weight of
each other and made friction with our hands. We were impact rather than melding, force rather than softness. Our
fever escalated commensurate with the pressure of our muscles. We strained in embraces, each trying to be stronger,
and when we both sensed we were equal combatants, all of
us went into our groins and we pushed ourselves there until
we were done, over, past it and dead—together.

We lay there, gasping and sweating. My lips were brushing Ross's chest, and he shifted himself so that the contact
was broken. I wanted to fuse the bond again, but inside
Ross's fits of breath I could feel him regrouping, rationalizing, running from what it made us, made *him*. I knew
that soon he'd say something quintessentially cool to dilute
the power of *us,* and I knew I couldn't let myself hear it.
Drawing myself into a child's sleep ball, I cupped my ears

and squeezed my eyes shut until I was numb. Dimly I could hear Ross's heart beating; very dimly I could hear him muttering stylish denials of what we had just done. Though not audible, the words raked my body, and I shut them out with all *my* power, *my* muscle, my will—wrapping myself tighter and tighter, until I lost control of my senses—and my control.

Tick/beat, tick/beat, tick/beat, the strange music lilting, its cadence telling me "This is a dream." Tight in my ball, I know I'm a child, four or five, it's about 1953 and a different world. I'm in bed, and pressure in what my mother calls "that place" forces me to the bathroom and relief. Footsteps coming upstairs divert me from returning to my ball, and I stand in hallway shadows, hoping to see my mother and father's secret places. When the footsteps reach the landing it's a man and woman wearing powder-white wigs and costumes out of my kindergarten picture books— clothes like George Washington and the European royalty used to wear in their different world. I smell liquor, and know the man is my father; but the woman is too pretty to be my mother.

They go to the big bedroom and turn on the light. My father says, "She's at her aunt's in San Berdoo and the kid is asleep"; the woman says, "Let's leave the wigs on for kicks, I've always wanted to be a blonde." My father reaches for the light switch, and the woman says, *"No."*

Heavy corsets and shoes and belt buckles go "thud" on the floor, and my father and the woman are naked, both with dark hair at their secret places. He has what I do, only bigger; she has just the hair. The light wigs and the dark hair there are *wrong,* and what *I* feel there is wrong, but I tiptoe to the door and watch anyway.

It looks ugly and good. My father is fit and strong, with broad shoulders and chest and a trim waist. He's good, but the woman has fat legs and thick ankles and big horse teeth and a scar on her stomach and chipped nail polish. They get on the bed and roll around, and the mattress goes tick tick tick. She says, "Put it in," my father does and it looks ugly, so I close my eyes and listen to the tick tick. They both *sound* good, and I feel good there, better and better as my father grunts along with the TICK TICK TICK. He grunts harder and harder, TICK TICK TICK TICK TICK TICK TICK—and I'm touching myself there too. It feels better and better, and I run to the bathroom because I know something has to come out. Nothing does, but *I'm* big.

I listen for more ticking to make me bigger, but there isn't any. I walk to the bedroom door and see my father asleep, snoring. The woman sees me and crooks her finger. Proud of what I have, I go to show her.

She's ugly and her breath stinks, but her wig is pretty and her hand there feels good. I want my father to see it, and I try to reach across the woman. She stops me by putting her mouth there.

Tick tick tick tick tick as she moves on the bed, straining with her lips around me; tick tick tick tick I shut my eyes; tick tick tick tick she's biting me and I open my eyes, and my mother is there swinging a brushed-steel spatula and frying pan, and I pull away, and the woman is bleeding at the lips. She pushes my mother and runs, losing her wig; my father snores and my mother holds the wig over my face, and I fall asleep pushed into suffocating liquor breath that goes tick tick tick tick.

Then it's still about 1953, but later. My mother is giving me pills so I won't remember. The pills come from a bottle labeled Sodium Phenobarbital, and every time she gives me one she puts a note in another bottle. The notes ask God to forgive me for what I did with the wig woman.

Rough hands pulled at my sleep ball, and a once perfectly stylish voice was oozing agitation. "Hey! Hey man! You going cuntish on me?"

I came out of my self-made womb weeping and swinging, and a backhand caught Ross on the jaw and knocked him off the bed. He got to his feet, and I saw that he had already put on his clothes. Naked, I felt at an advantage. Ross stroked his mustache and said, "Better. You had me worried for a while."

We just stood there. Ross did his number with the alligator, and I confronted what had happened to me thirty years in the past. The heat in the tiny room dried my tears, and the only thing in the world that I knew was that the next perfect human being who crossed my path was either going to die horribly beyond words or walk away unharmed, their death sentence commuted by my mother in her grave and the killer standing in front of me. Putting on my clothes under Ross's stare, I thought that the only awful thing about the choice of resolutions would be waiting to know. Staring back at Ross, I said, "Thanks."

Ross gave me his patented hand-in-the-cookie-jar smirk. "You're welcome. Spartan revelry's good sport every once in a while. Bad dreams you had?"

"Old stuff. Nothing earthshaking."

"I never dream, probably because I lead such an adventurous life. If any other man had hit me, I would have killed him."

"You could have killed me, Lieutenant. You could have killed me and made it look like anything you wanted to, and you could have profited from the act."

Ross smiled broadly and showed his bad teeth, and in that moment I loved him. "It's because you know that that I'd never hurt you, sweetie."

A merciful shortcut out of my dilemma ticked across my mind, and I passed it to Ross immediately, knowing the plan's full implications only too well. "You know this area intimately, don't you?"

"The back of my hand, sweetie."

"Let's do a job together. Blonds, brunettes, I don't care— as long as they're perfect."

Stroking Alice, Ross said, "Pick me up tomorrow around noon. We'll cruise the summer sessions at Vassar and Sarah Lawrence. Wear a jacket and tie so you'll look like a cop, and I'll guarantee you some great sport."

I walked to Ross and kissed him on the lips, knowing that if I couldn't kill our perfect one, I would have to close out my blood journey by killing the man himself—my liberator and only eyewitness. Calmed by that, I broke the hands-to-shoulders embrace and walked out of the bedroom. The house was alive with chatter as I moved downstairs, and the last thing I heard as I opened the front door was a titillated soprano trill: "Richie, do you think maybe Ross is gay?"

From Thomas Dusenberry's diary:

9/8/83
1:10 A.M.
Aboard Eastern Flight
228, D.C. to N.Y.C.

Got one!

I'm now en route to Croton, New York. A team of agents out of the Westchester Office are meeting me at La Guardia, then we're driving to a summer house in Croton to arrest a Wisconsin State Police lieutenant for all seven blond-brunette homicides plus, incredibly, the murder of Saul Malvin.

It went down this way: the exec at W.S.P. Internal Affairs called me at Quantico three hours ago. He told me that his only possible was Lieutenant Ross Anderson, Daywatch Commander of the Huyserville Substation. As a sergeant working Extraditions and Warrants, Anderson was in the four blond-killing cities on the nights of the homicides, having flown there 1–3 days before each murder. In each case, he returned with his prisoner 24–48 hours after the coroner's estimated time of the victim's death. On top of that:

1.—Anderson has O+ blood.

2.—As a patrol sergeant in late '78–early '79, Anderson worked the sector where the three brunette bodies were found.

3.—Anderson supervised the surveillance deployment to catch the brunette killer.

4.—On 3/11/76, Anderson shot and killed an armed marijuana trafficker in the line of duty. The man, William Gretzler, was a boyhood friend of his.

5.—The W.S.P. case file on the brunette killings was stored in the Detective's Squadroom at the Huyserville Substation, where Anderson has served in various capacities over the past six years, the last eight months as Daywatch Commander.

6.—Since his promotion to Lieutenant eight months ago, Anderson has often been seen in the squadrooms of the Janesville and Beloit P.D.'s, where the other brunette files are missing from.

7.—Anderson was seen perusing the Vice files of the Louisville and Des Moines P.D.'s twenty-four hours before the homicides in those cities.

8.—The kicker of all kickers: Anderson was the officer who discovered the car, donor card and later the body of Saul Malvin, who the W.S.P. unofficially made as the brunette killer.

Fucking astonishing. On an earlier page of this diary I called Anderson's report on his discovery of Malvin's body "a model of cop smarts." The fucking audacity of it!

Here's my reconstruction of the Malvin killing. Anderson has just killed Claire Kozol, his third brunette victim. He resumes patrol, sees Malvin's Caddy on the shoulder of I–5 and investigates. Malvin is in the car, and while checking the glove compartment for his registration Anderson spots the O+ donor card. He thinks "patsy," and tells Malvin he'll drive him to the next town. He tells Malvin to walk to his cruiser, then somehow, making it look accidental, he pushes the Caddy off the road.

It's snowing hard, few cars are on the road. Maybe Anderson gently questions Malvin on his whereabouts at the times of the first two killings, maybe he doesn't, and just decides to play the factor open and hope for the best. In any event he has the .357 in the cruiser (this is probably the way he implemented the now presumably premeditated killing of William Gretzler), and on some pretext he stops the car and forces Malvin to walk into the woods. He shoots him in the chest, then puts the gun in his hand, knowing full well the blizzard will cover up the two sets of footprints and keep Malvin's body from being discovered—at least overnight.

The following day, with the snow ended, Anderson makes his phony discovery of Malvin's car and donor card, does his brilliant impromptu theorizing, makes a charade of going to Huyserville for a K-9 team, "finds" Malvin's body and ham-acts the smart young cop to the hilt from there on in. He lucks out on Malvin's whereabouts at the times of the first two homicides, and he's home free.

Fucking astonishing.

As I write, Milwaukee agents are securing warrants to search Anderson's apartment in Huyserville. If he confesses tonight or the Milwaukee guys find weaponry matching the stats on the blond killings, he's dead and buried. I've got only one real question. What has the bastard been doing during the two years since his last killing? That's scary.

To top things off, I've got a list of six names from the Denver S.A.C., phoned in less than an hour ago. An Aspen cop located some old notes of his old partner's, who was the officer who caught the phone call volunteering the Shroud Shifter info. The officer himself died last year, and the notes he left are in some weird shorthand, but six names are discernible in one column, with S.S.—Com. bk.? written directly across from them. The names—George Magdaleno, Aaron BeauJean, Martin Plunkett, Henry Hernandez, Steven Hartov, and Gary Mazmanian—are being run over the nationwide computer right now, and Jack Mulhearn is going to call the Westchester Office later with the results.

I'm getting tingly. The Anderson bust is going to be all Bureau, just us four agents with shotguns. He's the youngest lieutenant in Wisconsin State Police history. What happened?

And Shifter is narrowing down. Two of the names are Latin, and the other four are uncommon enough so that a nationwide kick-out should run no more than twenty possibles per man. Run big, tall, dark-haired and mid to late 30's against the kick-out, and the list will narrow; shoot the hard probables' mug shots or D.M.V. photos to agents in the cities where the credit-card frauder eyewitnesses are, and I'd lay 3 to 1 that they confirm rather than deny. I won a C-note on Anderson, and I'm still feeling lucky. Who are you, Shifter? Where are you? Come to Uncle Tom. He'll arrest you and get you indicted and prosecuted, and when you're convicted he'll get you a nice cell at a nice federal prison. If you're really lucky, maybe you could bunk with former Lieutenant Ross Anderson. I'm sure the two of you would have a lot to talk about.

24.

Edgy like the movie sheriff awaiting High Noon, I spent my morning preparing for the big moment.

First I drove to Brooks Brothers in Scarsdale. Ross wanted me to look like a cop, and since I didn't own any suits or sports jacket–slacks combinations, I decided to purchase a suitably elegant outfit for my debut as a policeman. Walking into the store, I realized I hadn't worn a coat and tie since I was a child, and I felt every bit of Ross's boyhood humiliation when I asked a salesman to show me the extra-large summer blazers. Condescendingly, he said that blazers came in numbered sizes, and suggested I try on a selection of 44 longs. Angry now, I complied, opting for a navy blue linen jacket that looked as though it had the class to disarm a Vassar coed. The salesman did a slow burn at my manner, and when I said, "Slacks, thirty-four, thirty-four," he pointed to rows of them arrayed on metal rods and walked away. I found a pair of light blue trousers that complemented the blazer and grabbed them; on my way to the cashier I picked up a white shirt and the first necktie I saw—a maroon print with crossed golf clubs. The total price of my showdown costume was $311.00, and leaving the store felt like getting out of jail.

I changed in the back of Deathmobile II, cursing when I found that I'd forgotten how to knot a necktie. Stringing it through my open collar, I drove to a gun shop in Yonkers and spent ninety dollars on something useful—a black leather hip holster for my snubnose .38. Transferring the gun from the Deathmobile's safety compartment to the beautiful new rig and snapping it onto my belt, cross-draw style, turned the morning around, and I drove to Croton.

The big summer house looked different in daylight, and knocking on the door I sensed the reason—everything about me, from my clothes to my past to my future, was changing at a breakneck speed that subtly altered whatever I saw.

Mady Behrens opened the door, altered almost past recognition—yesterday's bubbly blonde in tennis whites now looked haggard and suspicious, a shrew-in-waiting dressed in a soggy bathrobe. "Ross was arrested last night," she said. "Police with shotguns took him away. Richie's dad says it's real serious."

The veranda turned to quicksand under my feet, and the shrew's open mouth looked like an invitation to the easiest resolution in the world. I went for my holster, but she spoiled my target by bawling, "I knew Ross had a mean streak, but I just can't believe that he'd—"

I ran to the Deathmobile. Monsters danced on my windshield as I drove away into hiding.

Transcript of the initial interrogation of Ross Anderson. Conducted at Westchester County F.B.I. Headquarters, New Rochelle, New York, 1400 hours, 9/8/83. Present: Ross Anderson; John Bigelow, his attorney, retained by Richard Liggett Sr., Lt. Anderson's uncle; Inspector Thomas Dusenberry and Special Agent John Mulhearn, of the Federal Serial Killer Task Force; S.A. Sidney Peak, Agent in Charge, New Rochelle Office.

Suspect held in custody since 0340 hours, 9/8/83; informed of his rights in the presence of his attorney, 12:00 hours, 9/8/83; agreed to questioning after consulting with Mr. Bigelow—1330 hours. This interrogation was both tape-recorded and transcribed in shorthand by Margaret Wysoski, Stenographer, Division 104, Westchester County Superior Court.

Inspector Dusenberry: Mr. Anderson, let's start—

Ross Anderson: Call me Lieutenant.

Dusenberry: Very well, Lieutenant. Let's start by having you clarify something, if you will. Have you volunteered any statements since you were arrested early this morning?

Anderson: No. Just my name, rank and serial number.

Dusenberry: Have you been physically abused at any time—either in the course of your arrest or during your detention?

Anderson: You served me instant coffee at the holding tank. Tacky. Make it fresh ground next time, or I'll check into another hotel.

John Bigelow: Be serious, Ross.

Anderson: I am serious. You didn't taste it, Counselor. Evil shit.

Bigelow: This is very serious, Ross.

Anderson: You're telling me? I'm a French roast junkie. I'll be going into withdrawals soon. Then you'll be sorry.

Bigelow: Ross—

Dusenberry: Lieutenant, did Mr. Bigelow tell you about the charges you face?

Anderson: Yeah. Murder.

Dusenberry: That's correct. Do you have any idea whose murder or murders?

Anderson: How's Billy Gretzler sound? I blew him away in the line of duty back in '76. He's the only person I ever killed.

Dusenberry: Come on, Lieutenant. You've been a police officer how long?

Anderson: Ten and a half years.

Dusenberry: Then you know that homicides within individual municipal police jurisdictions are not federal crimes.

Anderson: I know that.

Dusenberry: Then I'm sure you also know that as far as federal statutes go, you'd either have to kill an employee of the federal government or engage in interstate flight after killing an ordinary citizen to interest us.

Anderson: I'm an interesting guy in general.

Dusenberry: You certainly are. Do you know what my job is with the Bureau?

Anderson: What, pray tell?

Dusenberry: I'm the Agent in Charge at the Serial Killer Task Force in Quantico, Virginia. Do you know what serial killers are?

Anderson: Psychopaths who commit murder under the influence of Rice Krispies?

Bigelow: Ross, goddamnit.

Dusenberry: That's all right, Mr. Bigelow. Lieutenant, are these names familiar to you? Gretchen Weymouth, Mary Coontz, Claire Kozol?

Anderson: Those are the names of murder victims in Wisconsin back in late '78 and early '79.

Dusenberry: That's correct. Who do you think killed them?

Anderson: I think it was a man named Saul Malvin. I discovered his abandoned car and later his body. He was a suicide.

Dusenberry: I see. Are these names familiar? Kristine Pasquale, Wilma Thurmann, Candice Tucker, Carol Neilton?

Anderson: No, who are they?

Dusenberry: Young women murdered in a manner identical to the ones in Wisconsin.

Anderson: That's too bad. Where were they killed?

Dusenberry: In Louisville, Kentucky; Des Moines, Iowa; Charleston, South Carolina and Baltimore, Maryland. Have you ever been in those cities?

Anderson: Yes, I have.

Dusenberry: Under what circumstances?

Anderson: Serving extradition warrants and returning prisoners from there to various cities in Wisconsin.

Dusenberry: I see. Can you recall the exact dates you were there?

Anderson: Not offhand. Sometime during early '79 to late '81, though. That's when I worked the extradition assignment. If you want the exact dates, check the W.S.P. records.

Dusenberry: I have. You were in those cities at the time the four women were killed.

Anderson: Wow. What a coincidence.

Dusenberry: You were also on patrol at the time and near the area where Claire Kozol met her death.

Anderson: Wow.

Dusenberry: And you patrolled the general area where the first two Wisconsin victims were found, and you found the body of their alleged killer.

Anderson: Inspector, I pride myself on my good humor, but this shit is getting old. We're both college men and ranking officers, so I'll give you my informed opinion on what you've got. Ready?

Dusenberry: Go ahead, Lieutenant.

Anderson: You've been cross-referencing chronological factors against the two sets of homicides and compiling lists based on suspect opportunity. I was involved in the Wisconsin Whipsaw investigation, and apparently I was in the other cities when those other girls were killed. So I fit into your pattern circumstantially. But you'll have to do a lot better if you want an indictment. You'll get laughed out of court with what you have.

Dusenberry: You or me, Jack?

Agent Mulhearn: You, Tom. He's your boy.

Dusenberry: Lieutenant, since last night a team of ten agents have been turning Huyserville upside down. They've searched your apartment—

Anderson: And found nothing incriminating, because I've done nothing criminal.

Dusenberry: Do you know a man named Thornton Blanchard?

Anderson: Sure, old Thorny. He's a retired switchman for the Great Lakes Line.

Dusenberry: That's correct. He also likes to take walks through the nature-study woods adjoining Orchard Park. You know the area?

Anderson: Sure.

Dusenberry: Last night Mr. Blanchard told one of the Milwaukee agents that he's seen you digging in the woods

on three or four occasions. He pointed out the approximate
area to the team at about three this morning, and they
brought in arc lights and started digging. At about eleven
A.M. they found two triple-wrapped plastic baggies. One
baggie had a Buck knife and a hacksaw in it. We found a
latent thumbprint on the knife handle. It was yours. There
was brownish matter and gristle on the saw teeth. It's being
tested now. It's obviously blood and hardened tissue, and
we're going to try to type the blood and compare it to the
blood types of the seven girls. The dimensions of the knife
blade and saw teeth exactly match the dimensions of the
knife and saw marks on the last four victims. The other
baggie was filled with photographs of those four girls, naked
and chopped up. We found dried semen on three of the photographs, and it's being typed now. We got a total of five
viable latents off the photographs. They were all yours.

Bigelow: Ross? Ross? Goddamnit, somebody get a doctor.

Dusenberry: Get one, Jack. Let the transcript show that
at 14:24 hours Lieutenant Anderson experienced an attack
of nausea and fainted. We'll break for now. Talk to your
client, Mr. Bigelow. We're booking him on Interstate Flight
to Avoid Prosecution for Murder. He'll be arraigned tomorrow morning. Representatives of the Louisville, Des Moines,
Charleston and Baltimore D.A.'s Offices are flying up to
confer with me on the murder indictments and extradition
proceedings, so if Anderson wants to talk, I want his statement by this evening. Do you understand?

Bigelow: Yes, goddamnit. Where's the doctor? This man
is ill.

Dusenberry: Sid, stay with Anderson. Don't let the doctor give him any drugs, and when you take him back to the
tank, put him in handcuffs and leg manacles. Miss Wysoski,
sign out your transcription at 14:26 hours.

Transcript of the second interrogation and formal statement of Ross Anderson. Conducted at Westchester County
F.B.I. Headquarters, New Rochelle, New York. 21:30 hours,
9/8/83. Present: Ross Anderson; John Bigelow, Lt. Anderson's legal counsel; Stanton J. Buckford, Chief Federal Pros-

ecuting Attorney, Metropolitan New York District Office;
Inspector Thomas Dusenberry, S.A., John Mulhearn, S.A.,
Sidney Peak. This interrogation-statement was both tape-
recorded and transcribed in shorthand by Kathryn Giles,
Stenographer, Division 104, Westchester County Superior
Court.

Inspector Dusenberry: Lieutenant Anderson, did the doctor who treated you for your fainting spell give you any
mind-altering drugs?

Anderson: No.

Dusenberry: Have you been physically abused or threat-
ened since our first session this afternoon?

Anderson: No.

Dusenberry: Have you conferred with your attorney during that time?

Anderson: Yes.

Dusenberry: Are you ready to make a statement?

Anderson: Yes.

Dusenberry: Mr. Bigelow, have you discussed the matter
of Lieutenant Anderson's statement with Mr. Buckford?

John Bigelow: Yes, I have.

Dusenberry: Toward what end?

Bigelow: Toward the end of securing my client's immu-
nity from Kentucky, Iowa, South Carolina and Maryland
murder indictments.

Dusenberry: But not potential Wisconsin indictments?

Bigelow: Wisconsin has no death penalty, Inspector. Two
of the other states do.

Dusenberry: Mr. Buckford, do you have a statement to
make?

Stanton J. Buckford: Yes, I do. I wanted a transcription
of this plea-bargaining process, with federal agents as witnesses, in case controversy arises later on. I know only the
barest outline of what Lieutenant Anderson has to say, but
if his evidence is as powerful as Mr. Bigelow asserts, and
if it results in other indictments, I would be willing to file
on Lieutenant Anderson only with the Wisconsin and Federal Interstate Flight charges. As proof of your good faith,
Mr. Bigelow, I will require a confession from Lieutenant

Anderson beforehand, and should he confess, and should
the Wisconsin judiciary hand down any sentence less severe
than three consecutive life terms without possibility of parole, I will ask the judge presiding at the Flight trial to
hand down that sentence. Do you understand, Mr. Bigelow?

Bigelow: Yes, Mr. Buckford. I do.

Buckford: Lieutenant Anderson, do you understand?

Anderson: Yes.

Bigelow: Make your statement, Ross.

Anderson: On December 16, 1978, I raped and murdered
Gretchen Weymouth. On December 24, 1978, I raped and
murdered Mary Coontz. On January 4, 1979, I raped
and murdered Claire Kozol. On April 18, 1979, I raped and
murdered Kristine Pasquale. On October 1, 1979, I raped
and murdered Wilma Thurmann. On May 27, 1980, I
raped and murdered Candice Tucker. On May 19, 1981, I
raped and murdered Carol Neilton. This statement is made
of my own free will.

Dusenberry: Jack, get him some water.

Bigelow: I want you to take your time with the rest of
it, Ross.

Buckford: Are you ready to continue, Mr. Anderson?

Anderson: (Long pause) Yes.

Buckford: Then proceed.

Anderson: I didn't kill Saul Malvin, and he didn't commit
suicide. Right after I killed Claire Kozol, I drove up the
two-lane that parallels I-5. I saw a man check out Malvin's
abandoned Cadillac, then get into a van and slowly drive
north. I tracked the vehicle by radar, and I got the feeling
the man was looking for the driver of the Caddy, to rob him.
I stayed six hundred yards in back, and when the van
stopped, I stopped too, then found a perch on some rocks
and looked at the van through my binoculars. After about
five minutes I saw the man walk back out of the woods,
carrying a revolver. He put the gun somewhere underneath
the body of the van and kept driving north. I—

Dusenberry: Tell me the man's name, Anderson.

Buckford: Let him tell it his way, Inspector.

Anderson: Just then I got word on my radio that the

girl's body was discovered, and that roadblocks were being set up on I-5. I stayed on the two-lane, and I saw the van approach the first roadblock on a curve. When the man was about two hundred yards from it, he pulled over and tossed something into the snow by the roadside. I waited while he went through the detaining procedure—you know, search of the van, warrant checks, escort to the Huyserville Station for a blood test and more questioning if he turned up the right type. When things quieted down at the roadblock, I cruised over to I-5 and looked for what the man had thrown out. It was (pause) torn-up pictures of a dead man lying in the snow. Look, I knew I wanted to meet this guy. I drove into Huyserville, found his van parked in the station lot and found a .357 mag in a hidey-hole attached to the undercarraige. I ended up confronting him, and we talked, and he told me he'd killed lots and lots of people, just to do it, and for money and credit cards, and—

Dusenberry: Tell me his name, Anderson. Please, Mr. Buckford, there's a reason for this.

Buckford: Very well. The man's name, Mr. Anderson?

Anderson: Martin Plunkett. He's—

Dusenberry: Motherfucking God. Plunkett's the Shifter, Jack. He's on the Aspen suspect list. Put him on the wire, now.

Agent Mulhearn: Jesus Fuck.

Buckford: Maintain yourselves, gentlemen. This is a federal document, and what in God's name are you talking about?

Dusenberry: I don't fuck—I don't believe this. Plunkett is a long-term serial we've been tracking on paper for months. It's too involved to go into, and I want more confirmation. Describe him, Anderson.

Anderson: Caucasian, 6'3", 210, dark brown hair, brown eyes.

Dusenberry: It's him. Vehicle?

Anderson: He had a silver Dodge van back in '79.

Dusenberry: When did you see him last?

Buckford: Let him finish his way.

Dusenberry: I'll finish. You faked finding Malvin's body

and put Plunkett's magnum in his hand so you'd have a
fall guy for the girls and so your buddy wouldn't be remembered as a transient and get tagged for the Malvin job,
right?

Anderson: Right.

Buckford: Sit down, Inspector.

Dusenberry: Why, Anderson?

Anderson: What do you mean, 'Why'?

Buckford: Sit down and be quiet. This is a federal document.

Dusenberry: Where is he, Anderson?

Anderson: I don't know. It was a long time ago.

Dusenberry: You just beat the electric chair. Tell me, you
fuck.

Buckford: Sit down, Dusenberry, now, or I'll suspend you
from this case. (Pause) There. That's better. I don't follow
this offshoot, Mr. Anderson. Is the Inspector correct? Did
you fake a suicide on this man Malvin so that Plunkett
could escape?

Anderson: So we both could.

Buckford: Why? Plunkett, I mean.

Anderson: Because I liked his style.

Buckford: Have you seen him since then? Since 1979?

Anderson: No, he rode off into the sunset, like the Lone
Ranger.

Buckford: Do you have any idea where he is now?

Anderson: I'm tired. I want to go to sleep. Plunkett and
I were a one-night stand. I don't know where he is, so leave
me alone.

Buckford: Let's wrap it up, then. Inspector, I'll need to
talk to you about this. I'm marking the end of this transcript
at nine-fifteen P.M., September 8, 1983.

25.

I spent the night parked in a campground in Upper West-chester. Curled tight in a ball, I slept and dreamed of Ross; every time the hard metal floorboard jarred me awake, I thought of him in my first moments of consciousness and felt his body. At dawn, my muscles aching from long hours of holding myself womblike, I stood up on tenuous infant's legs. Shivering despite the blast-oven heat in the van, I wondered how it had ended all around me—without my even being there.

Still muscle-cramped, I inched up to the cab and turned the ignition key to Accessory, then flipped on the radio. Moving the tuner to an all-news station, I heard, "... and on the Wisconsin end of the investigation, authorities have discovered a Buck knife and hacksaw with Anderson's fingerprints on them buried in plastic bags in the woods near his apartment. Federal agents believe they are the weapons he used to murder and dismember his seven victims. Here on the New York end, we have a recorded statement made by Anderson's cousin, seventeen-year-old Rosemary Cafferty:

"I'm ... I'm just glad Ross is in jail where he can't hurt anybody else except other criminals. He ... he must be evil. I can't believe he's a member of my family. He ... he might have hurt one of us. All—"

I turned the radio off, stifling the soprano trill that had tried to relegate Ross and me to a cheap stereotype with the words, "Richie, do you think maybe Ross is gay?" I knew then that she and her tennis-clad chums had been my friend's betrayers. FAMILY typefaced itself across my vision, and I set out to become Shroud Shifter in broad daylight.

At a sporting goods store in Mt. Kisco, I bought a big Buck knife and a leather scabbard. From there I drove to a hardware store nearby and purchased a hacksaw with razor-sharp teeth. A trip to a punk-rock boutique in Yonkers netted me a black vinyl jump suit, and the green-haired salesgirl who sold it to me looked at my Brooks Brothers outfit and said, "You're really changing styles." From Yonkers it was only a hop, skip and jump to the Lord & Taylor in Scarsdale and the purchase of a woman's black silk opera cape and a makeup kit. With a ball of theatrical putty already in my glove compartment, I had everything I needed.

Walking out of Lord & Taylor, I saw a Scarsdale Police cruiser parked at the curb. The cop by the passenger door was saying to the driver, "... youngest fucking lieutenant in his department's history." He tapped a stack of papers on the dashboard and added, "And now the feds have got a want on some buddy of his."

In the most audacious move of my life, I approached the car, looked the passenger cop dead in the eye and said, "Excuse me, Officer. Were you talking about Ross Anderson, the killer?"

The cop gave my Ivy League persona a cursory glance and said, "Yes, sir."

Seeing that the papers on the dashboard were Wanted flyers, still damp with printer's ink, I asked, "May I have one of those? My son collects them."

Chuckling, the policeman handed me the top piece of paper. I said, "Thank you," then walked over to the shade of Deathmobile II to savor the moment of my formal public emergence.

The big black banner print read, "Wanted: Interstate Flight—Murder." Below it was two mug shots from my 1969 burglary arrest. I looked callow and sensitive. Underneath my physical statistics, police buzzwords made me buzz: consider armed, extremely dangerous and an escape risk; may be driving pre-1980 silver Dodge van; suspected of multiple murders in numerous states.

Only the "Escape Risk" rang untrue. It was over now; there was no escape. Thinking of Ross, I added plastic bags to my shopping list, ran across the street to a supermarket and bought a pack of a dozen. Returning to the Death-mobile, I looked at the dashboard clock and saw that it was almost noon. I sang "Do not forsake me, O my darling, on this our wedding day!" over and over as I drove to Croton.

Beer parties were in rowdy progress on front lawns up and down the summer-house block, and I cruised by slowly, trawling for Ross's cousins and their consorts. Not seeing them, I drove to a shopping center, found a pay phone and called Information. The operator gave me a Croton listing for Richard Liggett Senior, and I dialed the summer-house number, letting the phone ring twenty times. The dial tone ticked rather than buzzed, and I hung up and headed back toward my target street.

Parking a block away, I stepped into the back of the van and stripped off my preppy garb. Nude, I held my shaving mirror with one hand and with the other applied my Shroud Shifter face, turning my pug nose hawk with putty, my blunt cheekbones sharp with rouge, my eyebrows dark and menacing with mascara. Slicking back my hair with spittle, I wrapped my knife and hacksaw up in a paper bag, then put on my black jump suit and affixed my cape. Remembering a pair of scuffed black loafers under my spare tire, I dug them out, dusted them and slipped them on. Then, dripping with sweat and smelling of vinyl and face powder, I stepped out of my Shroud Shifter closet for the world to see.

Children waved at me from passing cars; an old man sitting on his porch drinking beer yelled out, "Halloween ain't till next month, buddy!" I bowed and fluffed my cape for all my fans, and when I turned onto my target block, the keg partyers pointed to me and gifted me with little rounds of applause and bursts of laughter. Walking across the Liggetts' front lawn, a boy roasting hot dogs on the veranda next door yelled, "Hey, Alex! That you, man!"

"Yeah, man!" I shouted back.

"You pledging Delta, man?"

"Yeah!"

"Boogie down, man! Richie and Mady are at the club, but there's brew in the fridge!"

I shouted, "Yeah, man," and swirled my cape, then walked across the porch and through the open door. Inside, the house was cool and quiet, and I moved from room to room memorizing the disarray, recalling how it had offended Ross. Overflowing ashtrays, unmade beds, clothes on the floor and expensive computer games upended atop sofas and chairs fascinated and enraged me, and I kept circuiting, upstairs and down, looking for more evidence of the bankruptcy known as HAPPY FAMILY LIFE.

Razor stubble and shaving cream caked on disposable razors; a toothpaste tube crimped all the way up to the top; a diaphragm in its case. Still life after still life after still life kept me in a swirl for hours, with the lengthening of shadows through the windows providing a dim awareness of time passing. Then, as I was examining paperback novels spilling out of a bookcase, I heard, "Alex, are you here?"

It was the voice of Richie Liggett, issuing from downstairs. I looked around for the bag holding my knife and hacksaw, saw it on a dresser across the bedroom and called out, "I'm upstairs, Richie!" Footsteps thudded on the stairway, and by the time they reached the second floor hallway I had the knife held in my right hand behind my back.

Richie Liggett appeared in the doorway and laughed. "Jesus, Alex. Delta? Your family's always gone Sigma O. Your mascara's running, by the way."

Disguising my voice with a movie-monster growl, I said, "Where's Mady?"

"In the kitchen. You hear about Ross?"

I monster-growled "traitor," then grabbed Richie by the hair, brought my knife up and slit his throat, straight through to the windpipe in one motion. He reached for his neck and pitched forward in another single movement, and I stepped away to avoid being sprayed by his blood. Hitting the floor with a crash, he started gurgling, and I flipped him onto his back. He kept trying to speak, his mouth flapping in spastic counterpoint to his twitching legs, and

I took a pillow off the bed and dropped it on his face. Straddling the traitor's head, I stepped on the ends of the pillowcase and held the death mask firm with all my weight. When the flailing stopped and the white fabric was seeping with red, I wiped my knife and walked down to the kitchen.

Mady Behrens was frying hamburgers. When she saw me, she let out a ladylike yelp and managed to say, "You're not Alex." I said, "You're right," and stabbed her in the stomach, then the chest, then the neck. In her death throes she knocked the frying pan off the stove, and the last thing she felt before her eyes closed was hot grease spattering her tennis-tan legs.

TICK/BEAT TICK/BEAT TICK/BEAT TICK/BEAT TICK/BEAT TICK/BEAT.

I stumbled upstairs, breathing blood and vinyl. Richie Liggett was now a piece of inanimate disarray to match the rest of the HAPPY FAMILY LIFE detritus. I carved SS on both of his legs, then sheared them off with the hacksaw and tossed them onto a dusty chair covered with tennis balls. With the blood smell now dominating all others, I took my tools and walked down to Mady Behrens. When she was similarly marked and vivisected, I threw her legs in the sink along with the dirty dishes.

BEAT/TICK
BEAT/TICK
BEAT/TICK
BEAT/TICK
BEAT/TICK

Exhausted, I ran my eyes over the kitchen. The disarray I had created looked soft and pretty; the unevenly hung calendar and framed mottoes undercut my art and buzzed me like angry little bees. Straightening them made me think of Ross, and with his image came a new surge of energy. I began to set the house right.

For hours I straightened, tidied and rearranged, putting the HAPPY FAMILY DWELLING in an order that spotlighted the Shroud Shifter and his revenge. With all the room lights blazing, I worked, forcing my brain away from Ross only to look at my watch and remind myself that Dom

De Nunzio and Rosie Cafferty were due. The more I toiled, the more I saw that required fixing, and when I heard voices on the veranda just after midnight, I was nowhere near finished.

I cut them down in the entrance hall, all stab and shriek and my Buck knife darting past protective arms to tear into the traitors' faces. Rosie Cafferty was already dead and my weapon was raised to give her boyfriend's throat a final slice when I remembered that Ross introduced me to them as Billy Rohrsfield, meaning someone else had betrayed the two of us. I hesitated, and for a split second Dom De Nunzio, helplessly pinioned under my knees, looked absolutely perfect—and perfectly like Ross. Hoarsely whispering "I'm sorry," I held his eyes shut while I stabbed and stabbed and stabbed his life away.

There were no ticks or tick/beats as I carved SS on two more pairs of lovely legs in tennis whites, sawed them off, then walked to the living-room wall and rolled a set of my bloody fingerprints on it, circling the area in blood so that even the most stupid cop wouldn't miss the evidence. Gathering up my knife and hacksaw, I walked to the Death-mobile, my cape flowing in the summer night wind. Inside the van I changed back to Brooks Brothers, then scrubbed blood from my hands and Shroud Shifter from my face. With calm hands I pressed fingerprints to the handles of my knife and saw, then triple-wrapped them in plastic bags. Rummaging through the van's tool kit, I found an earth spade. I took it up to the cab with me, then went looking for places to plant the means to rapid justice.

I buried the hacksaw at the base of a tree adjoining the Bronxville Library, and the knife by the lake in Huguenot Park in New Rochelle. Remembering a rooming house that several caddies had mentioned, I drove to the 800 block of South Lockwood and knocked on the door underneath a sign that read: "Rooms by the week—usually vacancies."

The old black woman who answered my knock feigned anger at my late-night intrusion, but when I said, "I want a room, and I'll pay two months cash in advance," she fell all over herself letting me in and pointing me toward a desk holding a large guest register. Handing her a big wad of hundreds that were useless to me now, I said, "My name is Martin Plunkett. Remember that. Martin Plunkett."

26.

It took them three days to find me.

I slept throughout most of those seventy-two hours, sating a weariness caused by one of the longest road tours in history, and when I heard the helicopters hovering directly over my head, I was relieved that it was over. Looking out my window I saw the flashing lights of a dozen police cars, and within moments whispers, sleep-blurred grunts and scurrying footsteps told me the rooming house was being evacuated. Then heavy boots went thump/tick, thump/tick, thump/tick all around me, and the ritual bullhorn warning sounded: "We have you surrounded, Plunkett! Surrender, or we'll come in and get you!"

I walked to the door and shouted through it. "I'm unarmed. I want to talk to the head man before you take me in."

Backing away, ready to hit the floor, I got my answer—loud voices arguing. I was able to pick out "You're crazy, Inspector," and "He's mine," and then the door was kicked in and an ordinary-looking middle-aged man in a gray suit was pointing a .38 at my head.

He didn't say "Freeze, motherfucker," or "Up against the wall, asshole." He said, "My name's Tom Dusenberry," as if we had just met at a cocktail party. I said, "Martin Plunkett," and when he pulled back the hammer of his gun, I smiled.

He didn't look as though he was deciding whether to shoot me; he looked like a man living deep within himself, wondering how far to let me in. Still smiling, I said, "Are you with the New Rochelle police?"

"F.B.I.," he said.

"The exact charges?"

"Interstate Flight from the Malvin killing for me; the four kids in Croton for keeps."

Something in the man's statement hit me low and hard, but I couldn't place it. Trying to nail the blow, I stalled for time, sizing Dusenberry up in the process. He was beginning to grow on me as extraordinary—and I didn't know why.

We remained silent for close to a minute, me thinking, him staring. Finally he said, "Why, Plunkett?" and I knew. The man was simply moderation personified—voice, body, clothes, soul. It was something he could never have cultivated; he just was it. "Why what, Mr. Dusenberry?"

"Why all of it."

"You're being ambiguous."

"I'll be specific. Why have you killed so many people, caused so much fucking pain?"

Now I could sense he was straining, getting itchy for something to happen fast. Sweat was darkening his shirt collar and his bland blue eyes were narrowing. Soon his legs were quivering with tension, and the only thing calm about the man was his finger on the trigger. He was growing feverish in his desire for pat answers.

"I'll make a formal statement," I said. "Then you'll know. And I won't make that statement unless it's released for the public at large, verbatim. Do you understand?"

"You've made that very clear."

"I've made it very clear because I know you want to know, and unless you let me confess my own way, you never will."

Dusenberry lowered his gun. "You've been wanting to tell it for a long time," he said. "You've been dropping hints for years."

If he thought it was a trump card, he was wrong; I knew my desire for glory had grown cancerously self-destructive a long way back on the road. "And that's how you found me?"

Dusenberry said, "In part," and smiled; the blandness of his perfectly capped teeth froze me and clarified his puzzling statement. The Interstate Flight charge stemmed from the Saul Malvin killing—and only Ross knew about that. *"In whole,"* I whispered.

Now the teeth were sharp and pointed, and the bland federal agent was a shark. "Anderson plea-bargained you to beat the death penalty," he said. "He threw you to the hungriest, most ambitious fed prosecutor who ever breathed—to save his own worthless, sadistic faggot ass."

The shark became a monster; his jaws opened wide to eat me with words: "You loved him, didn't you, you fuck? You snuffed the kids because they knew what you and Anderson were, and you couldn't take it. You loved him! Admit it, goddamn you!"

I moved forward, and Dusenberry raised his gun. It was two inches from my face with the trigger at half pull when I knew that attacking meant he was the winner; retreating meant I was. Smiling like Ross at his most stylish, speaking like Martin Plunkett at his most resolute, I said, "I used him, and I'll use you, and in the end I'll prevail."

Dusenberry lowered his weapon, and I held out my hands to be cuffed.

From the New York Times, *February 4, 1984:*

PLUNKETT TRIAL TAKES ONLY ONE DAY; LEGAL AND INVESTIGATORY JOCKEYING CONTINUE

The trial of Martin Michael Plunkett, the admitted murderer of four Westchester County citizens, took only four hours yesterday, but the legal controversy surrounding him may be as complex and far-reaching as his trial was short—and a certain mystique regarding the man himself seems to be building.

Arrested in New Rochelle last September 13 for the knife slayings of Dominic De Nunzio, Madeleine Behrens, Rosemary Cafferty and Richard Liggett, Plunkett refused to speak to investigators, court-referred psychiatrists and the legal counsel appointed him. In fact, he spoke to no one and offered no written statement until two weeks before yesterday's trial, when he admitted the four killings in a notarized statement that directed investigators to the spots where he buried the murder weapons. Spurning legal aid, he repeated the statement to the presiding judge and jury yesterday, and was convicted on both his statement and the corresponding physical evidence. The jury convicted him after deliberating for only ten minutes, and Judge Felix Cansler handed down a sentence of four consecutive life terms without possibility of parole. Plunkett was then driven to Sing Sing Prison and placed in a protective custody cell, where he remains silent on the details of his four murders, and on everything else.

Plunkett was captured as the result of testimony given by another admitted killer, Ross Anderson, 33, formerly an officer with the Wisconsin State Police and the cousin of Mr. Liggett and Miss Cafferty. Facing trial in Wisconsin next week on three counts of rape and murder dating back to 1978 and 1979, Anderson was not called on to testify against Plunkett because federal authorities deemed it "logistically messy." Stanton J. Buckford, Chief Federal Prosecutor for the Metropolitan New York area, told reporters last week: "Had Plunkett not made his statement and backed it up with corroborative evidence, we would have needed Anderson's testimony. As it stands now, we won't need it. Anderson's testimony has to do with a murder he alleges Plunkett committed in Wisconsin back in '79, and since Plunkett will most certainly receive the maximum sentence in New York, I do not want him traveling to Wisconsin—a non–death penalty state—just to get slapped with more time. The man is highly intelligent and extremely dangerous, and, I deem, a major escape risk. I want him to remain in maximum security in New York."

The alleged Wisconsin murder brings up the Plunkett case's most pressing point—how many more people has Martin Plunkett killed? Since suspicion originally fell on him as the result of probes conducted by the F.B.I.'s Serial Killer Task Force, police officials all over America are asking themselves that question.

Inspector Thomas Dusenberry, the head of the Task Force and the officer credited with solving the Anderson and Plunkett string of homicides, thinks many more. "I would say that Plunkett has murdered at least forty people, and that his killings date back to San Francisco in 1974. I think he killed George and Paula Kurzinski in Sharon, Pennsylvania, in 1982, a famous unsolved case, and that when you count unreported disappearances, his killings may number as many as a hundred. You may think, with Plunkett in custody and legally buried, knowing exactly how many people he killed isn't important—but it is. For one thing, it would spare the loved ones of missing people untold anxiety to finally know their people are dead; and, most important, if homicides we make Plunkett for are still being actively investigated, we can close the investigations out and save many police man-hours. At the time I arrested him, Plunkett implied he would make all the facts regarding his killings known. I only hope he does it fast."

Municipal police departments in at least four states are building cases against Plunkett. The Aspen, Colorado, authorities suspect him of eight murder/disappearances in 1975 and 1976, and Utah, Nevada and Kansas police officials suspect him of another fifteen to twenty within their jurisdictions.

Inspector Dusenberry said last week: "I've shared my Plunkett data with every department that's requested it. They deserve to know what we have. But prosecutors are getting indictment-happy, and it's ridiculous. Without a confession from Plunkett, it's all just too cold. No witnesses. No evidence. I've talked to two men Plunkett sold murder victims' credit cards to years ago. They couldn't make a positive ID based on his current appearance. It's all too old and too vague, and, at bottom, it's motivated by outrage and personal ambition. Plunkett is going to be convicted in a non–death penalty state, and no New York judge is going to let him be extradited elsewhere and executed, as much as he deserves it, and as much as a lot of hungry D.A.'s would love to fix it up."

As for the Anderson case, the former policeman is set to go to trial next week in Wisconsin. He pleaded guilty at his arraignment, and is expected to receive the maximum sentence Wisconsin state law allows: three consecutive life terms. Anderson has admitted raping and killing women in four other states (two of them with the death penalty), and prosecutors in Kentucky, Iowa, South Carolina and Maryland are seeking legal loopholes to gain indictment warrants on.

Anderson himself has remained quiet about his crimes and his relationship with Plunkett, offering "no comment" through his attorney when queried by out-of-state police officials and district attorneys. "It's all in their hands," Inspector Dusenberry has said. "If one of them wants to talk, lots of people, including me, will be all ears."

From the Milwaukee Post, *February 12, 1984:*

ANDERSON CONVICTED; GETS LIFE

Ross Anderson, the former Wisconsin State Police lieutenant who was also the killer known as the "Wisconsin Whipsaw" was convicted of the 1978–1979 rape-murders of Gretchen Weymouth, Mary Coontz and Claire Kozol in a brief trial held yesterday in Beloit District Court. Judge Harold Hirsch sentenced Anderson, 33, to three consecutive life terms without possibility of parole, directing that he be placed in an institution offering "full protective custody"—a term used to denote maximum security prisons that have special facilities for "high visibility" offenders, i.e., former police officers, celebrities and organized-crime figures who might be subject to attack if housed among the general inmate population.

After the verdict was handed down, Beloit D.A. Roger Mizrahi told reporters: "It's a disgrace. Three Wisconsin girls dead, and their killer spends the rest of his life playing golf at a country-club slammer."

From the editorial page of the Milwaukee Journal, *March 3, 1984:*

THE WAGES OF MURDER?

Ross Anderson murdered seven people. His friend Martin Plunkett murdered at least four people, and some policemen familiar with his case say without hesitation that his number of victims ends at about fifty. Both "men" had the good fortune to be convicted in states that do not allow capital punishment, and both men are such heinous criminals that they cannot be allowed to live with other criminals—for even hardened robbers and drug dealers would be so outraged by their presence on the prison yard that their safety would be jeopardized.

So Ross Anderson, aka "Wisconsin Whipsaw" and "Four-State Hooker Hacker," languishes in a special protective custody facility, lifting weights, reading science-fiction novels and building expensive balsa-wood airplanes. The prisoner in the cell next to his is Salvatore DiStefano, the Cleveland Mafia underboss serving fifteen years on Racketeering charges. He and Anderson talk baseball through the bars for hours each day.

Martin Plunkett resides at Sing Sing Prison in Ossining, New York. He talks to no one, but is rumored to be considering writing his memoirs. He corresponds with various New York literary agents, all of whom are eager to peddle any book he writes. Offers from Hollywood—rumor has it that some studios have offered him as much as fifty thousand dollars for a twenty-page outline of his life—abound. Fifty thousand dollars divided by fifty victims comes down to a thousand dollars per head.

That's obscene.

Plunkett wouldn't be able to keep the money; New York State law prohibits convicted criminals from reaping the financial rewards of published or filmed accounts of their crimes, and Plunkett probably wouldn't care—since his arrest he has brilliantly manipulated the legal and media establishments into waiting for him to tell his story *his* way. It is all he seems to want, and both well-intentioned legal people and literary voyeurs are drooling with anticipation.

It's all obscene, and inimical to the American concepts of blind justice and punishment to fit the crime. It's all obscene and points out the perfidies of free speech carried to the extreme of license. It's all obscene and points to the need for a National Death Penalty Statute.

From Thomas Dusenberry's Diary.

6/13/84

It's now nine months since I took Anderson and Plunkett off the streets. I've been busy with work—new links and chains—and with trying to reconstruct the two of them. Nothing's coming together with the former, and with the latter it's all coming bad.

Updating: Buckford was the brains behind prosecuting Plunkett. He built up a backlog of witnesses that never had to be tapped because of Plunkett's statement, and he laid down attack strategies for the lackluster Westchester D.A. He's got a big ace in the hole in the event other states ever secure extradition warrants: a series of Interstate Flight charges waiting, guaranteed to keep him in the limelight and Plunkett out of the chair. I feel ambivalent about the man and his machinations. He knows, and I know, that capital punishment is not a deterrent to violent crime, and the Southhampton aristocrat in him considers it vulgar. Fine, but he's also a comer in the Democratic Party, with a high-visibility racketeering strike-force job in the works, and he's looking to keep his liberal credentials untarnished for a Senate shot somewhere down the line. He's told me, and a half-dozen other agents, "America runs hot-cold, yin-yang, right-left, and the next time it hangs a left turn, I'll be there to hop on and make hay."

So Bucky Buckford's an opportunist, and I would be too, if I weren't so depressed. After the Anderson/Plunkett busts, I got a congratulatory telegram from the Director himself. He called my work "magnificent," and ended the telegram with a question: "Are you staying on active duty until the maximum retirement age?" In my reply I was noncommittal, even though the question was a veiled offer of an Assistant Directorship and maybe command of the entire Criminal Division.

Here's what all this ambivalence and depression is about: I want to see Plunkett dead.

Anderson doesn't bother me like Plunkett does—he actually wept when we told him two of his cousins had been murdered. But Plunkett can't feel that, or feel anything past his own intransigence. I feel like justifying myself here, so I will. I'm not a vindictive man, I'm not a far-right ideologue, I can separate the need for justice from the lust for vengeance. And I'm not besieged by irrational guilt over not putting the Croton house under surveillance—I believed Anderson when he told me he hadn't seen Plunkett since '79. I still want Plunkett dead. I want him dead because he will never feel remorse or guilt or a moment's pain or ambivalence regarding the grief he has caused, and because he is now preparing to write his life story, bankrolled by a literary agent who will be the conduit for official police documents to help him tell it. I want him dead because he is exploiting what I most believe in in order to sate his own ego. I want him dead because now I don't wonder why anymore—I just *know*. Evil exists.

About a month before Plunkett's trial, Bucky Buckford and I had a confab with the Director. He told me I looked stressed out, and ordered me to take a vacation leave. Carol couldn't go because of her classes, so I went alone. Where did I go? Janesville, Wisconsin, and Los Angeles, where Anderson and Plunkett grew up. What did I learn? Nothing except what is *is*, and evil exists.

I talked to about forty people who knew them. Anderson coerced younger boys into homosexual acts and tortured animals when he was a teenager. Plunkett prowled around his neighborhood looking in windows. The marijuana trafficker Anderson shot and killed in the line of duty was an old friend turned enemy, and I'm certain it was premeditated. Plunkett's first killing almost certainly took place in San Francisco in '74—he was F.I. carded by the S.F.P.D. three days after a man and woman living across the street from him were ax-murdered. Checking over their school records, I found the all-American boy and a strange boy with a big brain, but no mention of anything like pivotal, life-forming trauma. Coming home, I got drunk on the plane and toasted the Dutch Reformed Church. Evil exists, prepackaged at birth, predestined in the womb. If Plunkett and Anderson are, as Doc Seidman suggests, sadistic homosexuals, then their passion is based not on love, but on evil recognizing fellow evil. Mom, Dad, Reverend Hilliker, John Calvin, you were right. Reluctantly I salute you.

Getting home, still half in the bag, I did something I've never done in twenty-four years of marriage. I prowled around in Carol's dresser. When I saw that her diaphragm wasn't in its case, I started throwing things. After I sobered up a bit, I picked them up, and Carol came home. She didn't say a word and I didn't ask a thing, and lately she's been so sweet and attentive that I still can't say a thing. Something has to happen with her soon, but I'm afraid that if I make the first move, I'll blow us out of the water.

Some final thoughts on Plunkett:

Sometimes I think the only thing good to come out of what he has taught me is a resolve to continue seeing evil as what it is. If my destiny is to become a prototypical hardball homicide cop, so be it. If the cost to my personal life is great, so be it. If Plunkett was a directional pointer from God, a prepackaged villain to keep me taking out killers, so be it. If the above is true, then I can reconcile the logical and methodical part of me with the new mystical and disillusioned part and move on.

The only thing about it that doesn't float is me. I'm almost fifty years old, and I doubt if I've got the energy to make myself cold and hard and driven. That's a young man's game—and Plunkett's.

27.

June 15, 1984.

I was lying on my bunk when I heard movement on the catwalk in front of my cell. Thinking it was just another guard or administrator curious to see the silent killer in the flesh, I kept my eyes on the ceiling. Then I smelled alcohol, looked over and saw Dusenberry gripping the bars. "Talk to me," he said.

I decided not to. I had broken my silence in the course of retaining my literary agent, and had spoken to key Sing Sing administrators along with him, but my F.B.I. pursuer drunk at two in the afternoon wasn't worthy of repartee. I looked back at the ceiling and began brain-screening colors.

"Did you pork Anderson or did he pork you?"

The swirls I was seeing were soft pink and beige.

"Probably the latter. They're out to get you, boy. Ronnie's got the Supreme Court packed with hardballs. Colorado's got a whole team of legal hotshots looking into ways to fry your ass."

Dark tan and red now, blending softly.

"If you fry, you'll never get to write your book. You'll be forgotten."

Tan and red into blue, deepening.

"Look at me, you fuck!"

Still deepening, the colors slowly separating, returning to their original shades, only prettier.

"I'll never let you make me like you!"

Deeper, softer, prettier.

"Never, never, you fuck! Never be shit like you!"

Softer, prettier still as I heard the guards come and take Dusenberry away.

From Thomas Dusenberry's diary:

6/19/84

What happened with Plunkett got back to the Director. He sent a reprimand via Bucky Buckford—Don't let it or anything like it happen again. Bucky advises a very low profile and some quick, spectacular results at the Task Force, even if I have to steal the credit from another agent. I can't do that, of course; it's too Plunkett-pragmatic.

I had it out with Carol last night. She admitted having an affair with one of her professors. I was calm until she started rationalizing why it happened. She had logical reasons for all of it, and when she started ticking them off, I hit her. She cried and I cried, and ten minutes later she's logical and rational again, telling me, "Tom, we can't go on like this."

I knew it before she did.

Some good news, if you can call it that: Anthony Joseph Anzerhaus, the Minneapolis child scalper, was shot and killed crossing the Mexican border into Texas yesterday. A border patrolman recognized him and went for his gun, and Anzerhaus reached for something under the seat. Thinking it was a weapon, the officer shot him. It wasn't a gun. It was a stuffed panda bear. Anzerhaus died cradling it like a baby.

I called Jim Schwartzwalder and gave him the news. He broke down, then his wife came to the phone and I repeated the story, asking her why Jim took it so hard. She said, "You don't want to know."

She's right, I don't.

What I do want to know is that someone decent can profit from my stalemate with Plunkett. Once I figure it out, and *know* it, I'll cut the evil bastard loose forever.

From the New York Times, *June 24, 1984:*

HEAD OF PLUNKETT-ANDERSON INVESTIGATION FOUND DEAD NEAR HOME; SUICIDE RULED

Quantico, Virginia, June 23:

Thomas D. Dusenberry, 49, the F.B.I. Inspector who served as head of the Bureau's Serial Killer Task Force and the agent responsible for the captures of multiple murderers Martin Plunkett and Ross Anderson, was found dead in the woods near his Quantico home yesterday. A .38-caliber revolver with a crudely made silencer attached was in his right hand, and there was a single bullet wound in his head. Investigating officers found a suicide note in Dusenberry's handwriting on his dining room table, and the death has been officially certified as "self-inflicted homicide."

F.B.I. officials expressed shock at Dusenberry's death, but offered no speculation as to why he took his own life. Quantico police revealed that along with the suicide note there were two checks for twenty-five thousand dollars each, made out by Dusenberry to his son and daughter. Dusenberry had told a colleague, Special Agent James Schwartzwalder, that he had sold a diary he had kept on the Plunkett case to a literary agent representing Martin Plunkett in the sale of his autobiography—for the amount of money he left his children.

"Tom told me about the deal three days ago," Agent Schwartzwalder told the *Times.* "He seemed happy about it. I had no idea what he was planning."

Dusenberry will be buried in a Dutch Reformed Church service next week. He is survived by his wife, Carol, 45; his son, Mark, 22; and his daughter, Susan, 23.

28.

Save for this epilogue, my story is complete. I have been at Sing Sing for fourteen months; Dusenberry has been dead for nine. No extradition warrants have been filed on me, and there are sixty-two pins stuck in the map adorning my cell wall. I was thirty-seven yesterday.

Milton Alpert is reading the first pages of my manuscript in a cell directly across the catwalk from me. I have been observing him for an hour, and he looks frightened.

It's over now. I'm as dead and inanimate as the red-topped pins in my map. Looking back over these four-hundred-odd pages, I see that I was, by turns, frightened and enraged, bold and cowardly, vicious and possessed of a warrior's *noblesse oblige*. I fought and fled, and when I loved, my empathy was sparked by a will to power similar to my own. That he proved weak and traitorous is of no import; like all human beings, I cleaved to a comely lover who filled in my own blank spaces with grace, relinquishing parts of my will in sighs and embraces. Unlike most human beings, I did not let my desire destroy me. My last killings were for him, and I almost spared my final victim for him in a split-second's clarity, but in the end my will remained intact. I possessed the experience, but did not pay the ultimate price.

Others paid that price for me

Taking their lives, I knew them in their most exquisite moments of existence. Cutting them down young, ardent and healthy, I assimilated brashness and sex that would have gone timid had I not usurped it for my own use. Part of it was to kill my nightmares and staunch my awful rage, and part of it was for the sheer thrill and high-voltage sense of power that murder gave me. I cannot summarize my drives in any greater perspective than that.

So you look for cause and effect; you partake of my brilliant memory and absolute candor and conclude what you will. Build mountains out of ellipses and bastions of logic from interpretations of the truth I have given you. And if I have gained your credibility by portraying myself honestly, frailties and all, then believe me when I tell you this: I have been to points of power and lucidity that cannot be measured by anything logical or mystical or human. Such was the sanctity of my madness.

It's over now. I will not submit to the duration of my sentence. With this valediction in blood completed, my transit in human form has peaked, and to subsist past it is unacceptable. Scientists say that all matter disperses into unrecognizable but pervasive energy. I intend to find out, by turning myself inward and shutting down my senses until I implode into a space beyond all laws, all roadways, all speed limits. In some dark form, I will continue.